Nora Roberts is the number one *New York Times* bestseller of more than 200 novels. With over 400 million copies of her books in print, she is indisputably one of the most celebrated and popular writers in the world. She has achieved numerous top five bestsellers in the UK, including number one for *Savour the Moment*, and is a *Sunday Times* hardback bestseller writing as J. D. Robb.

Become a fan on Facebook at
www.facebook.com/norarobertsjdrobb
and be the first to hear all the latest from Piatkus
about Nora Roberts and J. D. Robb.

www.noraroberts.com
www.nora-roberts.co.uk
www.jd-robb.co.uk

By Nora Roberts

Many of Nora Roberts' other titles are now available in eBook and she is also the author of the In Death series using the pseudonym J.D. Robb. For more information please visit
www.noraroberts.com or www.nora-roberts.co.uk

Bed of Roses

nora
roberts

piatkus

PIATKUS

First published in the US in 2009 by The Berkley Publishing Group,
a member of Penguin Group (USA) Inc., New York
First published in Great Britain in 2009 by Piatkus

9 10 8

A CIP catalogue record for this book
is available from the British Library.

ISBN 978-0-7499-2888-9

Printed and bound by CPI Group (UK) Ltd, Croydon, CR0 4YY

Papers used by Piatkus are from well-managed forests
and other responsible sources.

MIX
Paper from
responsible sources
FSC
www.fsc.org FSC® C104740

Piatkus
An imprint of
Little, Brown Book Group
Carmelite House
50 Victoria Embankment
London EC4Y 0DZ

An Hachette UK Company
www.hachette.co.uk

www.piatkus.co.uk

For girlfriends

And 'tis my faith that every flower
Enjoys the air it breathes.

WORDSWORTH

Love is like a friendship caught on fire.

BRUCE LEE

PROLOGUE

$\mathcal{R}$OMANCE, IN EMMALINE'S OPINION, MADE BEING A WOMAN special. Romance made every woman beautiful, and every man a prince. A woman with romance in her life lived as grandly as a queen, because her heart was treasured.

Flowers, candlelight, long walks in the moonlight in a secluded garden . . . just the idea brought on a sigh. *Dancing* in the moonlight in a secluded garden, now that reached the height of romantic on her scale.

She could imagine it, the scent of summer roses, the music drifting out of the open windows of a ballroom, the way the light turned the edges of everything silver, like in the movies. The way her heart would beat (the way it beat now as she imagined it).

She longed to dance in the moonlight in a secluded garden.

She was eleven.

Because she could see so clearly how it should be—*would* be—she described the scene, every detail, to her best friends.

When they had sleepovers, they talked and talked for hours about everything, and listened to music or watched movies. They could stay up as long as they wanted, even *all* night. Though none of them had managed to. Yet.

When they had a sleepover at Parker's, they were allowed to sit or play on the terrace outside her bedroom until midnight if the weather was okay for it. In the spring, her favorite time there, she loved to stand on the bedroom terrace, smell the gardens of the Brown Estate and the green from the grass if the gardener had cut it that day.

Mrs. Grady, the housekeeper, would bring the cookies and milk. Or sometimes cupcakes. And Mrs. Brown would come in now and then to see what they were up to.

But mostly, it was just the four of them.

"When I'm a successful businesswoman living in New York, I won't have time for romance." Laurel, her own sunny blond hair streaked with green from a lime Kool-Aid treatment, worked her fashion sense on Mackensie's bright red.

"But you *have* to have romance," Emma insisted.

"Uh-uh." With her tongue caught in her teeth, Laurel tirelessly twined another section of Mac's hair into a long, thin braid. "I'm going to be like my aunt Jennifer. She tells my mother how she doesn't have time for marriage, and she doesn't need a man to be complete and stuff. She lives on the Upper East Side and goes to parties with Madonna. My dad says she's a ballbuster. So I'm going to be a ballbuster and go to parties with Madonna."

"As if." Mac snorted. The quick tug on the braid only made Mac giggle. "Dancing's fun, and I guess romance is okay as long as it doesn't make you stupid. Romance is all my mother thinks about. Except money. I guess it's both. It's like, how can she get romance and money at the same time."

"That's not really romance." But Emma rubbed her hand on

Mac's leg as she said it. "I think romance is when you just do things for each other because you're in love. I wish we were old enough to be in love." Emma sighed, hugely. "I think it must feel really good."

"We should kiss a boy and see what it's like."

Everyone stopped to stare at Parker. She lay belly-down on her bed, watching her friends play Hair Salon. "We should pick a boy and get him to kiss us. We're almost twelve. We need to try it and see if we like it."

Laurel narrowed her eyes. "Like an experiment?"

"But who would we kiss?" Emma wondered.

"We'll make a list." Parker rolled across the bed to grab her newest notebook from her nightstand. This one featured a pair of pink toe shoes on the cover. "We'll write down all the boys we know, then which ones we think might be okay to kiss. And why or why not."

"That doesn't really sound romantic."

Parker gave Emma a small smile. "We have to start somewhere, and lists always help. Now, I don't think we can use relatives. I mean like Del," she said, speaking of her brother, "or either of Emma's brothers. Besides, Emma's brothers are way too old."

She opened the book to a fresh page. "So—"

"Sometimes they stick their tongue in your mouth."

Mac's statement brought on squeals, gags, more giggles.

Parker slid off the bed to sit on the floor beside Emma. "Okay, after we make the master list, we can divide it. Yes and No. Then we pick from the Yes list. If we get the boy we pick to kiss us, we have to tell what it was like. And if he puts his tongue in your mouth, we have to know what that's like."

"What if we pick one and he doesn't want to kiss us?"

"Em?" Securing the last braid, Laurel shook her head. "A boy's going to want to kiss you for sure. You're really pretty, and

3

you talk to them like they're regular. Some of the girls get all stupid around boys, but you don't. Plus you're starting to get breasts."

"Boys like breasts," Mac said wisely. "Anyway, if he won't kiss you, you just kiss him. I don't think it's that big a deal anyway."

Emma thought it was, or should be.

But they wrote down the list, and just the act of it made them all laugh. Laurel and Mac acted out how one boy or another might approach the moment, and *that* had them rolling on the floor until Mr. Fish, the cat, stalked out of the bedroom to curl up in Parker's sitting room.

Parker tucked the notebook away when Mrs. Grady came in with cookies and milk. Then the idea of playing Girl Band had them all pawing through Parker's closet and dressers to find the right pieces for stage gear.

They fell asleep on the floor, across the bed. Curled up, sprawled out.

Emma woke before sunrise. The room was dark but for the glow of Parker's night-light, and the stream from the moon through her windows.

Someone had covered her with a light blanket and tucked a pillow under her head. Someone always did when they had sleepovers.

The moonlight drew her, and, half dreaming still, she walked to the terrace doors and out. Cool air, scented by roses, brushed her cheeks.

She looked out over the silver-edged gardens where spring lived in soft colors, sweet shapes. She could almost hear the music, almost see herself dancing among the roses and azaleas, the peonies that still held their petals and perfume in tight balls.

She could almost see the shape of her partner, the one who spun her in the dance. The waltz, she thought with a sigh. It should be a waltz, like in a storybook.

That was romance, she thought, and closed her eyes to breathe in the night air.

One day, she promised herself, she'd know what it was like.

CHAPTER ONE

$\mathcal{S}$INCE DETAILS CROWDED HER MIND, MANY OF THEM BLURRY, Emma checked her appointment book over her first cup of coffee. The back-to-back consults gave her nearly as much of a boost as the strong, sweet coffee. Basking in it, she leaned back in the chair in her cozy office to read over the side notes she'd added to each client.

In her experience, the personality of the couple—or often, more accurately, the bride—helped her determine the tone of the consult, the direction they'd pursue. To Emma's way of thinking, flowers were the heart of a wedding. Whether they were elegant or fun, elaborate or simple, the flowers were the romance.

It was her job to give the client all the heart and romance they desired.

She sighed, stretched, then smiled at the vase of petite roses on her desk. Spring, she thought, was the best. The wedding season kicked into high gear—which meant busy days and long nights designing, arranging, creating not only for *this* spring's weddings, but also next.

She loved the continuity as much as the work itself.

That's what Vows had given her and her three best friends. Continuity, rewarding work, and that sense of personal accomplishment. And she got to play with flowers, live with flowers, practically swim in flowers every day.

Thoughtfully, she examined her hands, and the little nicks and tiny cuts. Some days she thought of them as battle scars and others as medals of honor. This morning she just wished she'd remembered to fit in a manicure.

She glanced at the time, calculated. Boosted again, she sprang up. Detouring into her bedroom, she grabbed a scarlet hoodie to zip over her pjs. There was time to walk to the main house before she dressed and prepared for the day. At the main house Mrs. Grady would have breakfast, so Emma wouldn't have to forage or cook for herself.

Her life, she thought as she jogged downstairs, brimmed with lovely perks.

She passed through the living room she used as a reception and consult area, and took a quick scan around as she headed for the door. She'd freshen up the flowers on display before the first meeting, but oh, hadn't those stargazer lilies opened beautifully?

She stepped out of what had been a guest house on the Brown Estate and was now her home, and the base for Centerpiece—her part of Vows.

She took a deep breath of spring air. And shivered.

Damn it, why couldn't it be warmer? It was April, for God's sake. It was daffodil time. Look how cheerful the pansies she'd potted up looked. She refused to let a chilly morning—and okay, it was starting to drizzle on top of it—spoil her mood.

She hunched inside the hoodie, stuck the hand not holding

her coffee mug in her pocket, and began to walk to the main house.

Things were coming back to life all around her, she reminded herself. If you looked closely enough you could see the promise of green on the trees, the hint of what would be delicate blooms of dogwood and cherry blossoms. Those daffodils wanted to pop, and the crocus already had. Maybe there'd be another spring snow, but the worst was over.

Soon it would be time to dig in the dirt, to bring some of her beauties out of the greenhouse and put them on display. She added the bouquets, the swags and garlands, but nothing beat Mother Nature for providing the most poignant landscape for a wedding.

And nothing, in her opinion, beat the Brown Estate for showing it off.

The gardens, showpieces even now, would soon explode with color, bloom, scent, inviting people to stroll along the curving paths, or sit on a bench, relax in sun or shade. Parker put her in charge—as much as Parker could put anyone else in charge—of overseeing them, so every year she got to play, planting something new, or supervising the landscape team.

The terraces and patios created lovely outdoor living spaces, perfect for weddings and events. Poolside receptions, terrace receptions, ceremonies under the rose arbor or the pergola, or perhaps down by the pond under a willow.

We've got it all, she thought.

The house itself? Could anything be more graceful, more beautiful? The wonderful soft blue, those warm touches of yellow and cream. All the varied rooflines, the arching windows, the lacy balconies added up to elegant charm. And really, the entrance portico was made for crowding with lush greenery or elaborate colors and textures.

As a child she'd thought of it as a fairyland, complete with castle.

Now it was home.

She veered toward the pool house, where her partner Mac lived and kept her photography studio. Even as she aimed for it, the door opened. Emma beamed a smile, shot out a wave to the lanky man with shaggy hair and a tweed jacket who came out.

" 'Morning, Carter!"

"Hi, Emma."

Carter's family and hers had been friends almost as long as she could remember. Now, Carter Maguire, former Yale prof and current professor of English lit at their high school alma mater, was engaged to one of her best friends in the world.

Life wasn't just good, Emma thought. It was a freaking bed of roses.

Riding on that, she all but danced to Carter, tugged him down by his lapel as she angled up on her toes and kissed him noisily.

"Wow," he said, and blushed a little.

"Hey." Mackensie, her eyes sleepy, her cap of red hair bright in the gloom, leaned on the doorjamb. "Are you trying to make time with my guy?"

"If only. I'd steal him away but you've dazzled and vamped him."

"Damn right."

"Well." Carter offered them both a flustered smile. "This is a really nice start to my day. The staff meeting I'm headed to won't be half as enjoyable."

"Call in sick." Mac all but purred it. "I'll give you something enjoyable."

"Hah. Well. Anyway. Bye."

Emma grinned at his back as he hurried off to his car. "God, he is so *cute*."

"He really is."

"And look at you, Happy Girl."

10

"Happy Engaged Girl. Want to see my ring again?"

"Oooh," Emma said obligingly when Mac wiggled her fingers. "Ahhh."

"Are you going for breakfast?"

"That's the plan."

"Wait." Mac leaned in, grabbed a jacket, then pulled the door closed behind her. "I didn't have anything but coffee yet, so . . ." As they fell into step together, Mac frowned. "That's my mug."

"Do you want it back now?"

"I know why I'm cheerful this crappy morning, and it's the same reason I haven't had time for breakfast. It's called Let's Share the Shower."

"Happy Girl is also Bragging Bitch."

"And proud of it. Why are you so cheerful? Got a man in your house?"

"Sadly no. But I have five consults booked today. Which is a great start to the week, and comes on the tail of the lovely end to last week with yesterday's tea party wedding. It was really sweet, wasn't it?"

"Our sexagenarian couple exchanging vows and celebrating surrounded by his kids, her kids, grandchildren. Not just sweet, but also reassuring. Second time around for both of them, and there they are, ready to do it again, willing to share and blend. I got some really great shots. Anyway, I think those crazy kids are going to make it."

"Speaking of crazy kids, we really have to talk about your flowers. December may be far away—she says shivering—but it comes fast, as you well know."

"I haven't even decided on the look for the engagement shots yet. Or looked at dresses, or thought about colors."

"I look good in jewel tones," Emma said and fluttered her lashes.

"You look good in burlap. Talk about bragging bitches."

11

Mac opened the door to the mudroom, and since Mrs. Grady was back from her winter vacation, remembered to wipe her feet. "As soon as I find the dress, we'll brainstorm the rest."

"You're the first one of us to get married. To have your wedding here."

"Yeah. It's going to be interesting to see how we manage to run the wedding and be *in* the wedding."

"You know you can count on Parker to figure out the logistics. If anyone can make it run smooth, it's Parker."

They walked into the kitchen, and chaos.

While the equitable Maureen Grady worked at the stove, movements efficient, face placid, Parker and Laurel faced off across the room.

"It has to be done," Parker insisted.

"Bullshit, bullshit, bullshit."

"Laurel, this is business. In business you serve the client."

"Let me tell you what I'd like to serve the client."

"Just stop." Parker, her rich brown hair sleeked back in a tail, was already dressed in a meet-the-client suit of midnight blue. Eyes of nearly the same color flashed hot with impatience. "Look, I've already put together a list of her choices, the number of guests, her colors, her floral selections. You don't even have to speak to her. I'll liaise."

"Now let me tell you what you can do with your list."

"The bride—"

"The bride is an asshole. The bride is an idiot, a whiny baby bitch who made it very clear nearly one year ago that she neither needed nor wanted my particular services. The bride can bite me because she's not biting any of my cake now that she's realized her own stupidity."

In the cotton pajama pants and tank she'd slept in, her hair still in sleep tufts, Laurel dropped onto a chair in the breakfast nook.

"You need to calm down." Parker bent down to pick up a file. Probably tossed on the floor by Laurel, Emma mused. "Everything you need is in here." Parker laid the file on the table. "I've already assured the bride we'll accommodate her, so—"

"So you design and bake a four-layer wedding cake between now and Saturday, and a groom's cake, and a selection of desserts. To serve two hundred people. You do that with no previous preparation, and when you've got three other events over the weekend, and an evening event in three days."

Her face set in mutinous lines, Laurel picked up the file and deliberately dropped it on the floor.

"Now you're acting like a child."

"Fine. I'm a child."

"Girls, your little friends have come to play." Mrs. Grady sang it out, her tone overly sweet, her eyes laughing.

"Ah, I hear my mom calling me," Emma said and started to ease out of the room.

"No, you don't!" Laurel jumped up. "Just listen to this! The Folk-Harrigan wedding. Saturday, evening event. You'll remember, I'm sure, how the bride sniffed at the very idea of Icings at Vows providing the cake or any of the desserts. How she *sneered* at me and my suggestions and insisted her cousin, a pastry chef in New York, who studied in Paris and designed cakes for *important* affairs would be handling all the desserts.

"Do you remember what she said to me?"

"Ah." Emma shifted because Laurel's finger pointed at her heart. "Not in the exact words."

"Well, I do. She said she was sure—and said it with that sneer—she was sure I could handle *most* affairs well enough, but she wanted the *best* for her wedding. She said that to my face."

"Which was rude, no question," Parker began.

"I'm not finished," Laurel said between her teeth. "Now, at the eleventh hour, it seems her brilliant cousin has run off with one of her—the cousin's—clients. Scandal, scandal, as said client met brilliant cousin when he commissioned her to design a cake for *his* engagement party. Now they're MIA and the bride wants me to step in and save her day."

"Which is what we do here. Laurel—"

"I'm not asking you." She flicked her fingers at Parker, zeroed in on Mac and Emma. "I'm asking them."

"What? Did you say something?" Mac offered a toothy smile. "Sorry, I must've gotten water in my ears from the shower. Can't hear a thing."

"Coward. Em?"

"Ah . . ."

"Breakfast!" Mrs. Grady circled a finger in the air. "Everybody sit down. Egg-white omelettes on toasted brown bread. Sit, sit. Eat."

"I'm not eating until—"

"Let's just sit." Interrupting Laurel's next tirade, Emma tried a soothing tone. "Give me a minute to think. Let's just all sit down and . . . Oh, Mrs. G, that looks fabulous." She grabbed two plates, thinking of them as shields as she crossed to the breakfast nook and scooted in. "Let's remember we're a team," she began.

"You're not the one being insulted and overworked."

"Actually, I am. Or have been. Whitney Folk puts the *zilla* in Bridezilla. I could relay my personal nightmares with her, but that's a story for another day."

"I've got some of my own," Mac put in.

"So your hearing's back," Laurel muttered.

"She's rude, demanding, spoiled, difficult, and unpleasant," Emma continued. "Usually when we plan the event, even with the problems that can come up and the general weirdness of some couples, I like to think we're helping them showcase a day

14

that begins their happy ever after. With this one? I'd be surprised if they make it two years. She was rude to you, and I don't think it was a sneer, I think it was a smirk. I don't like her."

Obviously pleased with the support, Laurel sent her own smirk toward Parker, then began to eat.

"That being said, we're a team. And clients, even smirky bitch clients have to be served. Those are good reasons to do this," Emma said while Laurel scowled at her. "But there's a better one. You'll show her rude, smirky, flat, bony ass what a really brilliant pastry chef can do, and under pressure."

"Parker already tried that one on me."

"Oh." Emma sampled a skinny sliver of her omelette. "Well, it's true."

"I could bake her man-stealing cousin into the ground."

"No question. Personally, I think she should grovel, at least a little."

"I like groveling." Laurel considered it. "And begging."

"I might be able to arrange for some of each." Parker lifted her coffee. "I also informed her that in order to accommodate her on such short notice we would require an additional fee. I added twenty-five percent. She grabbed it like a lifeline, and actually wept in gratitude."

A new light beamed in Laurel's bluebell eyes. "She cried?"

Parker inclined her head, and cocked an eyebrow at Laurel. "So?"

"While the crying part warms me inside, she'll still have to take what I give her, and like it."

"Absolutely."

"You just let me know what you decide on when you decide on it," Emma told her. "I'll work in the flowers and decor for the table." She sent a sympathetic smile at Parker. "What time did she call you with all this?"

"Three twenty A.M."

Laurel reached over, gave Parker's hand a pat. "Sorry."

"That's my part of the deal. We'll get through it. We always do."

THEY ALWAYS DID, EMMA THOUGHT AS SHE REFRESHED HER LIVing room arrangements. She trusted they always would. She glanced at the photograph she kept in a simple white frame, one of three young girls playing Wedding Day in a summer garden. She'd been bride that day, and had held the bouquet of weeds and wildflowers, wore the lace veil. And had been just as charmed and delighted as her friends when the blue butterfly landed on the dandelion in her bouquet.

Mac had been there, too, of course. Behind the camera, capturing the moment. She considered it a not-so-small miracle that they'd turned what had been a favored childhood game of make believe into a thriving business.

No dandelions these days, she thought as she fluffed pillows. But how many times had she seen that same delighted, dazzled look on a bride's face when she'd offered her a bouquet she'd made for her? Just for her.

She hoped the meeting about to begin would end in a wedding next spring, with just that dazzled look on the bride's face.

She arranged her files, her albums, her books, then moved to the mirror to check her hair, her makeup, the line of the jacket and pants she'd changed into.

Presentation, she thought, was a priority of Vows.

She turned from the mirror to answer her phone with a cheerful, "Centerpiece of Vows. Yes, hello, Roseanne. Of course I remember you. October wedding, right? No, it's not too early to make those decisions."

As she spoke, Emma took a notebook out of her desk, flipped

16

it open. "We can set up a consultation next week if that works for you. Can you bring a photo of your dress? Great. And if you've selected the attendants' dresses, or their colors . . . ? Mmm-hmm. I'll help you with all of that. How about next Monday at two?"

She logged in the appointment, then glanced over her shoulder as she heard a car pull up.

A client on the phone, another coming to the door.

God, she *loved* spring!

$\mathcal{E}$MMA SHOWED HER LAST CLIENT OF THE DAY THROUGH THE DIS-play area where she kept silk arrangements and bouquets as well as various samples on tables and shelves.

"I made this up when you e-mailed me the photo of your dress, and gave me the basic idea of your colors and your favorite flowers. I know you'd talked about preferring a large cascade bouquet, but . . ."

Emma took the bouquet of lilies and roses, tied with white, pearl-studded ribbon off the shelf. "I just wanted you to see this before you made a firm decision."

"It's beautiful, plus my favorite flowers. But it doesn't seem, I don't know, big enough."

"With the lines of your dress, the column of the skirt, and the beautiful beadwork on the bodice, the more contemporary bouquet could be stunning. I want you to have exactly what you want, Miranda. This sample is closer to what you have in mind."

Emma took a cascade from the shelf.

"Oh, it's like a garden!"

"Yes, it is. Let me show you a couple of photos." She opened the folder on the counter, took out two.

"It's my dress! With the bouquets."

"My partner Mac is a whiz with Photoshop. These give you

17

a good idea how each style looks with your dress. There's no wrong choice. It's your day, and every detail should be exactly what you want."

"But you're right, aren't you?" Miranda studied both pictures. "The big one sort of, well, overwhelms the dress. But the other, it's like it was made for it. It's elegant, but it's still romantic. It is romantic, isn't it?"

"I think so. The lilies, with that blush of pink against the white roses, and the touches of pale green. The trail of the white ribbon, the glow of the pearls. I thought, if you liked it, we might do just the lilies for your attendants, maybe with a pink ribbon."

"I think . . ." Miranda carried the sample bouquet over to the old-fashioned cheval glass that stood in the corner. Her smile bloomed like the flowers as she studied herself. "I think it looks like some really creative fairies made it. And I love it."

Emma noted it down in her book. "I'm glad you do. We'll work around that, sort of spiraling out from the bouquets. I'll put clear vases on the head table, so the bouquets will not only stay fresh, but serve as part of the decor during the reception. Now, for your tossing bouquet, I was thinking just the white roses, smaller scale like this." Emma took down another sample. "Tied with pink and white ribbons."

"That would be perfect. This is turning out to be so much easier than I thought."

Pleased, Emma made another note. "The flowers are impor-tant, but they should also be fun. No wrong choices, remember. From everything you've told me, I see the feel of the wedding as modern romance."

"Yes, that's exactly what I'm after."

"Your niece, the flower girl, is five, right?"

"She just turned five last month. She's really excited about scattering rose petals down the aisle."

"I bet." Emma crossed the idea of a pomander off her mental

list. "We could use this style basket, covered with white satin, trimmed in baby roses, trailing the pink and white ribbons again. Pink and white rose petals. We could do a halo for her, pink and white baby roses again. Depending on her dress, and what you like, we can keep it simple, or we can trail ribbons down the back."

"The ribbons, absolutely. She's really girly. She'll be thrilled." Miranda took the sample halo Emma offered. "Oh, Emma. It's like a little crown! Princessy."

"Exactly." When Miranda lifted it onto her own head, Emma laughed. "A girly five-year-old will be in heaven. And you'll be her favorite aunt for life."

"She'll look so sweet. Yes, yes, to everything. Basket, halo, ribbons, roses, colors."

"Great. You're making it easy for me. Now you've got your mothers and your grandmothers. We could do corsages, wrist or pin-on, using the roses or the lilies or both. But—"

Smiling, Miranda set the halo down again. "Every time you say 'but' it turns out fantastic. So, but?"

"I thought we could update the classic tussy-mussy."

"I have no idea what that is."

"It's a small bouquet, like this, carried in a little holder to keep the flowers fresh. We'd put display stands on the tables by their places, which would also dress up their tables, just a little more than the others. We'd use the lilies and roses, in miniature, but maybe reverse the colors. Pink roses, white lilies, those touches of pale green. Or if that didn't go with their dresses, all white. Small, not quite delicate. I'd use something like this very simple silver one, nothing ornate. Then we could have them engraved with the wedding date, or your names, their names."

"It's like their own bouquets. Like a miniature of mine. Oh, my mother will . . ."

When Miranda's eyes filled, Emma reached over and picked up the box of tissue she kept handy.

"Thanks. I want them. I have to think about the monogramming. I'd like to talk that over with Brian."

"Plenty of time."

"But I want them. The reverse, I think, because it makes them more theirs. I'm going to sit down here a minute."

Emma went with her to the little seating area, put the tissue box where Miranda could reach. "It's going to be beautiful."

"I know. I can see it. I can already see it, and we haven't even started on the arrangements and centerpieces and, oh, everything else. But I can see it. I have to tell you something."

"Sure."

"My sister—my maid of honor? She really pushed for us to book Felfoot. It's been *the* place in Greenwich, you know, and it is beautiful."

"It's gorgeous, and they always do a fabulous job."

"But Brian and I just fell for this place. The look of it, the feel of it, the way the four of you work together. It felt right for us. Every time I come here, or meet with one of you, I know we were right. We're going to have the most amazing wedding. Sorry," she said, dabbing at her eyes again.

"Don't be." Emma took a tissue for herself. "I'm flattered, and nothing makes me happier than to have a bride sit here and cry happy tears. How about a glass of champagne to smooth things out before we start on the boutonnieres?"

"Seriously? Emmaline, if I wasn't madly in love with Brian, I'd ask *you* to marry me."

With a laugh, Emma rose. "I'll be right back."

$\mathcal{L}$ATER, EMMA SAW OFF HER EXCITED BRIDE AND, COMFORTably tired, settled down with a short pot of coffee in her office.

Miranda was right, she thought as she keyed in all the details. She was going to have the most amazing wedding. An abundance of flowers, a contemporary look with romantic touches. Candles and the sheen and shimmer of ribbons and gauze. Pinks and whites with pops of bold blues and greens for contrast and interest. Sleek silver and clear glass for accents. Long lines, and the whimsy of fairy lights.

As she drafted out the itemized contract, she congratulated herself on a very productive day. And since she'd spend most of the next working on the arrangements for their midweek evening event, she considered making it an early night.

She'd resist going over and seeing what Mrs. G had for dinner, make herself a salad, maybe some pasta. Curl up with a movie or her stack of magazines, call her mother. She could get everything done, have a relaxing evening, and be in bed by eleven.

As she proofed the contract, her phone let out the quick two rings that signaled her personal line. She glanced at the readout, smiled.

"Hi, Sam."

"Hello, Beautiful. What are you doing home when you should be out with me?"

"I'm working."

"It's after six. Pack it in, honey. Adam and Vicki are having a party. We can go grab some dinner first. I'll pick you up in an hour."

"Whoa, wait. I told Vicki tonight just wasn't good for me. I was booked solid today, and still have about another hour before—"

"You've got to eat, right? And if you've been working all day you deserve to play. Come play with me."

"That's sweet, but—"

"Don't make me go to the party by myself. We'll swing by,

have a drink, a couple laughs, leave whenever you want. Don't break my heart, Emma."

She cast her eyes up to the ceiling and saw her early night go up in smoke. "I can't make dinner, but I could meet you there around eight."

"I can pick you up at eight."

Then angle to come in when you bring me home, she thought. And that's not happening. "I'll meet you. That way if I need to go and you're having fun, you can stay."

"If that's the best I can get, I'll take it. I'll see you there."

CHAPTER TWO

$\mathscr{S}$HE LIKED PARTIES, EMMA REMINDED HERSELF. SHE LIKED
people and conversation. She enjoyed picking the right outfit,
doing her makeup, fussing with her hair.

She was a girl.

She liked Adam and Vicki—and had, in fact, introduced them
four years ago when it had become clear she and Adam made
better friends than lovers.

Vows had done their wedding.

She liked Sam, she thought with a sigh as she pulled up in
front of the contemporary two-story, then flipped down her vi-
sor mirror to check her makeup.

She enjoyed going out with Sam—to dinner, to a party, to a
concert. The problem was the spark-o-meter. When she'd met
him, he'd hit a solid seven, with upward potential. In addition,
she'd found him smart and funny, appreciated his smooth good
looks. But the first-date kiss had dropped to a measly two on the
spark-o-meter.

Not his fault, she admitted as she got out of the car. *It* just wasn't there. She'd given it a shot. A few more kisses—kissing was one of her favorite things. But they'd never risen over the two—and that was being generous.

It wasn't easy to tell a man you had no intention of sleeping with him. Feelings and egos were at stake. But she'd done it. The problem, as she saw it, was he didn't really believe her.

Maybe she'd find someone to introduce him to at the party.

She stepped inside, into the music, the voices, the lights—and felt an immediate lift of mood. She really did like parties.

After one quick scan, she saw a dozen people she knew.

She kissed cheeks, exchanged hugs, and kept moving in a search for her host and hostess. When she spotted a distant cousin by marriage she shot out a wave. Addison, she mused, and signaled that she'd be back around to say hi. Single, fun-loving, stunning. Yes, she could see Addison and Sam hitting it off.

She'd make sure she introduced them.

She found Vicki in the kitchen area of the generous great room, talking to friends while she refreshed a tray of party food.

"Emma! I didn't think you were going to make it."

"It's going to be practically a hit-and-run. You look great."

"So do you. Oh, thank you!" She took the bouquet of candy-striped tulips Emma offered. "They're beautiful."

"I'm in a 'Damn it, it's spring' frame of mind. These said I'm right. Can I give you a hand?"

"Absolutely not. Let me get you a glass of wine."

"Half a glass. I'm driving, and I really can't stay very long."

"Half a glass of cab." Vicki laid the flowers on the counter to free her hands. "Did you come alone?"

"Actually, I'm sort of meeting Sam."

"Oh," Vicki said, drawing out the syllable.

"Not really, no."

24

"Oh."

"Listen. Here, let me do that," she said when Vicki got out a vase for the flowers. Lowering her voice, Emma continued as she dealt with the flowers. "What do you think about Addison and Sam?"

"Are they an item? I didn't realize—"

"No. I was just speculating. I think they'd like each other."

"Sure. I suppose. You look so good together. You and Sam."

Emma made a noncommittal sound. "Where's Adam? I didn't see him in the mob."

"Probably out on the deck having a beer with Jack."

"Jack's here?" Emma kept her hands busy and her tone casual. "I'll have to say hi."

"They were talking baseball, last I heard. You know how they are."

She knew exactly. She'd known Jack Cooke for over a decade, since he and Parker's brother, Delaney, had roomed together at Yale. And Jack had spent a lot of time at the Brown Estate. He'd ultimately moved to Greenwich and opened his small, exclusive architecture firm.

He'd been a rock, she remembered, when Parker and Del's parents had been killed in a private plane crash. And he'd been a lifesaver when they'd decided to start the business by designing the remodels of the pool house and guest house to accommodate the needs of the company.

He was practically family.

Yes, she'd make sure to say hi before she left.

She turned with the glass of wine in her hand just as Sam made his way into the room. He was *so* good-looking, she thought. Tall and built, with that perpetual twinkle in his eyes. Maybe just a *tiny* bit studied, with his hair always perfectly styled, his clothes always exactly right, but—

"There she is. Hi, Vic." He passed Vicki a very nice bottle of

25

cabernet—exactly the right thing—kissed her cheek, then gave Emma a warm, warm smile. "Just who I've been looking for."

He caught Emma up in an enthusiastic kiss that barely bumped the pleasant level on her scale.

She managed to ease back an inch and get her free hand on his chest in case he got it into his head to kiss her again. She smiled up at him, added a friendly laugh. "Hi, Sam."

Jack, dark blond hair tousled from the evening breeze, leather jacket open over faded jeans, walked in from the deck. His eyebrows rose at Emma; his lips curved. "Hey, Em. Don't let me interrupt."

"Jack." She nudged Sam back another inch. "You know Sam, don't you?"

"Sure. How's it going?"

"Good." Sam shifted, draped his arm over Emma's shoulders. "You?"

"Can't complain." He took a chip, shoveled it into salsa. "How are things back on the farm?" he asked Emma.

"We're busy. Spring's all about weddings."

"Spring's all about baseball. I saw your mother the other day. She remains the most beautiful woman ever created."

Emma's casual smile warmed like sunlight. "True."

"She still refuses to leave your father for me, but hope springs. Anyway, see you later. Sam."

As Jack walked off, Sam shifted. Knowing the dance well, Emma shifted in turn—so she avoided being trapped between him and the counter. "I'd forgotten how many mutual friends Vicki, Adam, and I have. I know almost everyone here. I need to touch some bases. Oh, and there's someone I really want you to meet."

Cheerfully, she took Sam's hand. "You don't know my cousin, Addison, do you?"

"I don't think so."

"I haven't seen her in months. Let's track her down so I can introduce you."

She pulled him into the heart of the party.

JACK SCOOPED UP A HANDFUL OF NUTS AND CHATTED WITH A group of friends. And watched Emma lead the Young Executive At Play through the crowd. She looked . . . freaking amazing, he thought.

Not just the sexy, sloe-eyed, curvy, golden-skinned, masses of curling hair, soft, full-lipped amazing. That was killer enough. But you had to add in the heat and light she just seemed to emanate. She made one hell of a package.

And, he reminded himself, she was his best friend's honorary sister.

In any case, it was rare to see her when she wasn't with her regular gang of girls, some of her family, surrounded by people. Or, like now, with some guy.

When a woman looked like Emmaline Grant, there was always some guy.

Still, it never hurt to look. He was a man who appreciated lines and curves—in buildings and in women. In his estimation, Emma was pretty much architecturally perfect. So he popped nuts, pretended to listen to the conversation, and watched her slide and sway through the room.

Looked casual, he observed, the way she'd stop, exchange greetings, pause, laugh or smile. But he'd made a kind of study of her over the years. She moved with purpose.

Curiosity piqued, Jack eased away from the group, merged with another to keep her in his eyeline.

The some guy—Sam—did a lot of back stroking, shoulder draping. She did plenty of smiling at him, laughing up at him from under that thicket of lashes she owned. But oh yeah, her body language—he'd made a study of her body—wasn't signaling reception.

He heard her call out, *Addison!*, and follow up with that sizzle-in-the-blood laugh of hers before she grabbed a very fine-looking blonde in a hug.

They chattered, beaming at each other the way women did, holding each other at arm's length to take the survey before—no doubt—they told each other how great they looked.

You look fabulous. Have you lost weight? I love your hair. From his observations, that particular female ritual had some variations, but the theme remained the same.

Then Emma angled herself in a way that put the some guy and the blonde face-to-face.

He got it then, by the way she sidled back an inch or two, then waved a hand in the air before giving the some guy a pat on his arm. She wanted to ditch the some guy, and thought the blonde would distract him.

When she melted away in the direction of the kitchen, Jack lifted his beer in toast.

Well played, Emmaline, he thought. Well played.

*H*E CUT OUT EARLY. HE HAD AN EIGHT O'CLOCK BREAKFAST meeting and a day packed with site visits and inspections. Somewhere in there, or the day after, he needed to carve out some time at the drawing board to work up some ideas for the addition Mac wanted on her studio now that she and Carter were engaged and living together.

He could see how to do it, without insulting the lines and form of the building. But he wanted to get it down on paper, play with it awhile before he showed Mac anything.

He hadn't quite gotten used to the idea of Mac getting married—and to Carter. You had to like Carter, Jack thought.

He'd barely blipped on Jack's radar when he and Del and Carter had been at Yale together. But you had to like the guy.

Plus, he put a real light in Mac's eyes. That counted big.

With the radio blasting, he turned over in his head various ideas for adding on the space so Carter had a home office to do . . . whatever English professors did in home offices.

As he drove, the rain that had come and gone throughout the day came back in the form of a thin snow. April in New England, he thought.

His headlights washed over the car sitting on the shoulder of the road, and the woman standing in front of the lifted hood, her hands fisted on her hips.

He pulled over, got out, then, sliding his hands into his pockets, sauntered over to Emma. "Long time no see."

"Damn it. It just died. Stopped." She waved her arms in frustration so he took a cautious step back to avoid getting clocked with the flashlight she gripped in one hand. "And it's snowing. Do you *see* this?"

"So it is. Did you check your gas gauge?"

"I didn't run out of gas. I'm not a moron. It's the battery, or the carburetor. Or one of those hose things. Or belt things."

"Well, that narrows it down."

She huffed out a breath. "Damn it, Jack, I'm a florist, not a mechanic."

That got a laugh out of him. "Good one. Did you call for road service?"

"I'm going to, but I thought I should at least look in there in case it was something simple and obvious. Why don't they make what's in there simple and obvious for people who drive cars?"

"Why do flowers have strange Latin names nobody can pronounce? These are questions. Let me take a look." He held out a hand for the flashlight. "Jesus, Emma, you're freezing."

"I'd have worn something warmer if I'd known I'd end up

standing on the side of the road in the middle of the stupid night in a snowstorm."

"It's barely snowing." He stripped off his jacket, passed it to her.

"Thanks."

She bundled into it while he bent under the hood. "When's the last time you had this serviced?"

"I don't know. Some time."

He glanced back at her, a dry look out of smoky gray eyes. "Some time looks to have been the other side of never. Your battery cables are corroded."

"What does that mean?" She stepped up, stuck her head under the hood along with him. "Can you fix it?"

"I can . . ."

He turned his head toward her, and she turned hers toward him. All he could see were those brown velvet eyes, and for a moment, he simply lost the power of speech.

"What?" she said, and her breath whispered warm over his lips.

"What?" What the hell was he doing? He leaned back, out of the danger zone. "What . . . What I can do is give you a jump that should get you home."

"Oh. Okay. Good. That's good."

"Then you've got to get this thing in for service."

"Absolutely. First thing. Promise."

Her voice jumped a bit and reminded him it was cold. "Go ahead and get in the car, and I'll hook it up. Don't start it, don't touch anything in there, until I tell you."

He pulled his car around so it was nose-to-nose with hers. As he got his jumper cables, she got out of the car again. "I want to see what you do," she explained. "In case I ever have to do it."

"Okay. Jumper cables, batteries. You have your positive and

your negative. You don't want to get them mixed up because if you hook them up wrong you'll—"

He clamped one onto the battery, then made a strangling noise and began to shake. Instead of squealing, she laughed and smacked his arm. "Idiot. I have brothers. I know your games."

"Your brothers should've shown you how to jump-start a car."

"I think they sort of did, but I ignored them. I have a set of those in the trunk, along with other emergency stuff. But I never had to use any of it. Under yours is shinier than mine,"

she added as she frowned at his engine.

"I suspect the pit of Hell is shinier than yours."

She puffed out a breath. "Now that I've seen it, I can't argue."

"Get in, turn it over."

"Turn what over? Kidding," she said.

"Ha. If and when it starts, don't turn it off."

"Got it." In the car, she held up crossed fingers, turned the key. The engine coughed, hacked—made him wince—then rumbled to life.

She stuck her head out the window and beamed at him. "It worked!"

He had an errant thought that with that much power, her smile could have sparked a hundred dead batteries. "We'll let it juice up a few minutes, then I'll follow you home."

"You don't have to do that. It's out of your way."

"I'll follow you home so I know you didn't conk out on the way."

"Thanks, Jack. God knows how long I'd've been out here if you hadn't come along. I was cursing myself for going to that damn party when all I wanted to do tonight was zone out with a movie and go to bed early."

"So why'd you go?"

"Because I'm weak." She shrugged. "Sam really didn't want

31

to go alone, and, well, I like a party, so I figured it wouldn't hurt to meet him there and hang out for an hour."

"Uh-huh. How'd it work out with him and the blonde?"

"Sorry?"

"The blonde you palmed him off on."

"I didn't palm him off." Her gaze slid away, then rolled back to his. "Okay, I did, but only because I thought they'd like each other. Which they did. I'd've considered that good deed worth coming out tonight. Except I ended up broken down on the side of the road. It seems unfair. And mildly embarrassing since you noticed."

"On the contrary, I was impressed. That and the salsa were my favorite parts of the evening. I'm going to take the cables off. Let's see if she holds a charge. If we're good, wait until I'm in my car before you pull out."

"Okay. Jack? I owe you."

"Yeah, you do." He gave her a grin before he walked off.

When her car continued to run, he shut her hood then his own. Once he'd tossed the jumper cables back in his trunk, he got behind the wheel and flashed his lights to signal her to go.

He followed her through the lace of the light snow, and tried not to think of that moment under the hood when her breath had brushed warm over his lips.

She gave a friendly toot of her horn when she reached the private road for the Brown Estate. He eased over, stopped. He watched her taillights shimmer in the dark, then disappear around the bend that led to the guest house.

Then he sat a little while longer, in the dark, before turning the car around and heading home.

*I*N HER REARVIEW MIRROR, EMMA SAW JACK STOP AT THE MOUTH of the drive. She hesitated, wondering if she should've asked if he wanted to come down, have some coffee before he doubled back and drove home.

She probably should have—least she could do—but it was too late now. And all for the best, no question.

It wasn't wise to entertain a family friend who banged a booming ten on your spark-o-meter, alone, late at night. Especially when you still have some belly vibes going from a ridiculous moment under the hood of a car when you'd nearly humiliated yourself by moving on him.

That would never do.

She wished she could go by and talk over the whole stupid mess with Parker or Laurel or Mac—better yet, all three of them. But that, too, wouldn't do. Some things couldn't be shared even with the best friends in the world. Especially since it was clear Jack and Mac had gotten snuggly once upon a time.

She suspected that Jack got snuggly with a lot of women.

Not that she held it against him, she thought as she parked. She liked the company of men. She liked sex. Sometimes one led to the other.

Besides, how could you find the love of your life if you didn't look for him?

She turned off the car, bit her lip, then turned the key again. It made very unhappy noises, seemed undecided, then fired.

That had to be a good sign, she decided, then switched it off again. But she'd take it into the shop-as soon as she could. She'd have to ask Parker about mechanics, as Parker knew everything.

Inside the house, she got herself a bottle of water to take upstairs. Thanks to Sam and the stupid battery she wouldn't make it to bed by the righteous hour of eleven, but she could get there by midnight. Which meant she had no excuse to miss the early workout she'd planned for the morning.

No excuse, she lectured herself.

She set the water on her bedside table by a little vase of freesia and started to undress. Then realized she was still wearing Jack's jacket.

"Oh, damn it."

It smelled so good, she thought. Leather and Jack. And that wasn't a scent that was going to give her quiet dreams. She carried it across the room, laid it over the back of a chair. Now she had to get it back to him, but she'd worry about that later.

One of the girls might be going into town for something and could drop it off. It wasn't cowardly to pass the task off. It was efficient.

Cowardice had nothing to do with it. She saw Jack all the time. *All* the time. She just didn't see the point in making a special trip if someone else was already going. Surely he had another jacket. It wasn't like he needed that particular one immediately. If it was so important, why hadn't he taken it back?

It was his own fault.

And hadn't she said she'd worry about it later?

She changed into a nightshirt then went into the bathroom to begin her nightly ritual. Makeup off, skin toned and moisturized, teeth and hair brushed. The routine and her pretty bathroom usually relaxed her. She loved the happy colors, her sweet slipper tub, the shelf of pale green bottles that held whatever flowers she had handy.

Miniature daffodils now, to celebrate spring. But their cheerful faces seemed to smirk at her. Irritated, she flipped off the light.

She continued the ritual by removing the small mountain of throw pillows from the bed, setting aside the embroidered shams, fluffing up her sleep pillows. She slid under the duvet, snuggled in to enjoy the feel of smooth, soft sheets against her skin, the dreamy scent of freesia perfuming the air, and . . .

Shit! She could still smell his jacket.

Sighing, she flopped over on her back.

So what? So what if she had lusty thoughts about her best friend's brother's best friend? It wasn't a crime. Lusty thoughts were absolutely reasonable and normal. In fact, lusty thoughts were good things. Healthy things. She *liked* having lusty thoughts.

Why wouldn't a normal woman have lusty thoughts about a sexy, gorgeous man with a great body and eyes that were like smoke wrapped up in fog?

She'd be crazy not to have them.

Acting on them, now *that* would be crazy. But she was perfectly entitled to have them.

She wondered what he'd have done if she'd moved in that last inch under the hood of the car and planted one on him?

Being a man, he'd have moved in right back, she imagined. And they'd have spent a very interesting few minutes smoldering on the side of the road in the lightly falling snow. Bodies heating, hearts pounding with the snow showering over them and . . .

No, no, she was romanticizing it. Why did she always do that, always move from healthy lust to romance? That was her problem, and certainly rooted in the wonderfully romantic love story of her parents. How could she not want what they had?

Put it aside, she ordered herself. She wasn't going to find happy ever after with Jack. Stick with lust.

So they'd have gotten all hot and tangled on the side of the road. But. After that impulsive and no doubt spark-loaded kiss, they'd have been awkward and embarrassed with each other.

Then they'd have had to apologize to each other, or try to make some kind of a joke out of it. Everything would be weird and strained.

The simple fact was it was too late to act on the lusty. They were friends, the next thing to family. You didn't hit on friends and family. She was better off, tons better off, keeping her thoughts to herself and continuing to look for the real thing. For love.

The sort that lasted lifetimes.

CHAPTER THREE

$\mathscr{F}$ILLED WITH RESENTMENT AND SELF-PITY, EMMA TRUDGED UP
to the home gym at the main house. Its design reflected Parker's
efficient style and unassailable taste, both of which Emma bit-
terly detested at that moment.

CNN muttered away on the flat screen while Parker, her
phone's ear bud in place, racked up her miles on the elliptical.
Emma scowled at the Bowflex as she stripped off her sweatshirt.
She turned her back on it and the recumbent bike, on the rack
of free weights, the shelf of DVDs with their perky or earnest
instructors who might take her through a session of yoga or
pilates, torture her with the exercise ball, or intimidate her with
tai chi.

She unrolled one of the mats, sat down with the intention of
doing some warm-up stretches. And just lay down.

"Morning." Parker glanced at her as she continued to pump
along. "Late night?"

"How long have you been on that thing?"

"You want it? I'm nearly done. I'm just hitting my cool down."

"I hate this room. A torture chamber with shiny floors and pretty paint is still a torture chamber."

"You'll feel better after you do a mile or two."

"Why?" From her prone position, Emma threw up her hands. "Who says? Who decided that people all of a sudden have to do miles every damn day, or that twisting themselves into unnatural shapes is good for them? I think it's the people who sell this hideous equipment, and the ones who design all the cute little outfits like the one you're wearing."

Emma narrowed her eyes at Parker's slate colored cropped pants and perky pink and gray top. "How many of those cute little outfits do you own?"

"Thousands," Parker said dryly.

"See? And if they hadn't convinced you to do miles and twist yourself into unnatural shapes—and look good doing it—you wouldn't have spent all that money on those cute little outfits. You could've donated it to a worthy cause instead."

"But these yoga pants make my ass look great."

"They really do. But nobody's seeing your ass but me, so what's the point?"

"Personal satisfaction." Parker slowed, stopped. Hopping off, she plucked out one of the alcohol wipes to wipe down the machine. "What's wrong, Em?"

"I told you. I hate this room and all it stands for."

"So you've said before. But I know that tone. You're irritable, and you almost never are."

"I'm as irritable as anybody."

"No." Parker got her towel, mopped her face, then drank from her water bottle. "You're nearly always cheerful, optimistic, and good-natured, even when you bitch."

38

"I am? God, that must be annoying."

"Hardly ever." Moving to the Bowflex, Parker began to do some upper body exercise she made look smooth and easy. Emma knew it was neither. When she felt another pop of resentment, she sat up.

"I am irritable. I'm filled with irritable this morning. Last night—"

She broke off when Laurel came in, her hair bundled up, her trim body in a sports bra and bike shorts. "I'm switching off CNN," she announced, "because I just don't care." She snagged the remote, switched from TV to hard, pounding rock.

"Turn it down at least," Parker ordered. "Emma's about to tell us why she's full of irritable this morning."

"Em's never full of irritable." Laurel got a mat, unrolled it onto the floor. "It's annoying."

"See?" Since she was already on the floor, Emma decided she might as well stretch. "My best friends, and all these years you've let me go around annoying people."

"It probably only annoys us." Laurel started a set of crunches. "We're around you more than anyone else."

"That's true. In that case, screw you. God, *God*, do the two of you really do this every day?"

"Parker's every day, as she's obsessive. I'm a three-day-a-week girl. Four if I'm feeling frisky. This is usually an off day, but I came up with a design for the crying bride and it motored me up."

"Have you got something you can show me?" Parker demanded.

"See, obsessive." Laurel switched to roll-ups. "Later. Now I want to hear about the irritable."

"How can you do that?" Being full of irritable, Emma snarled. "It's like somebody's pulling you up with an invisible rope."

"Abs of steel, baby."

"I hate you."

"Who could blame you? I deduce irritable equals man," Laurel continued. "So I require all details."

"Actually—"

"Jeez, what is this? Ladies Day at the Brown Gym?" Mac strolled in, stripping off a hooded sweatshirt.

"I think it's Snowcones in Hell Day." Laurel paused. "What are you doing here?"

"I come here sometimes."

"You look at a picture of here sometimes and consider that a workout."

"I've turned over a new leaf. For my health."

"Bullshit," Laurel said, grinning.

"Okay, bullshit. I'm pretty sure I'm going with strapless for the wedding gown. I want amazing arms and shoulders." Turning to the mirror, Mac flexed. "I have good arms and shoulders, but that's not enough." She let out a sigh as she wiggled out of sweatpants. "And I'm becoming an obsessed, fussy bride. I hate me."

"But you'll be an obsessed fussy bride who looks fabulous in her wedding dress. Here," Parker said, "see what I'm doing."

Mac frowned. "I see it, but I don't think I'll like it."

"You just keep it steady and smooth. I'm going to cut back the resistance a bit."

"Are you intimating I'm a weenie?"

"I'm avoiding all the moaning and crying you'd do tomorrow if you started at my level. I do this three times a week."

"You do have really good arms and shoulders."

"Plus I have it on good authority my ass looks great in these pants. Okay, smooth and steady. Fifteen reps, set of three." Parker gave Mac a pat. "Now, hopefully that's the last interruption. Emma, you have the floor."

"She's already on the floor," Mac pointed out.

"Shh. Emma's irritable this morning because . . ."

"I went over to Adam and Vicki's last night—the MacMillians?—which I hadn't planned on because yesterday was a full book and today's another. I'd had a really good day, especially the last consult, and spent time writing up the contracts and notes, decided I'd make a little dinner, have a movie, an early night."

"Who called and talked you into going out with him?" Mac asked as she frowned her way through the first set.

"Sam."

"Sam's the hot computer nerd who defies that oxymoron despite—or maybe because of—the Buddy Holly glasses."

"No." Emma shook her head at Laurel. "That's Ben. Sam's the ad exec with the great smile."

"The one you decided not to date anymore," Parker added.

"Yes. And it wasn't actually a date. I said no to dinner, no to him picking me up. But . . . okay I caved on the party, and agreed to meet him there. I told him I wasn't going to sleep with him—full disclosure—two weeks ago. But I don't think he believes me. But Addison was there—third cousin, I think, my father's side. She's great, and just exactly his type. So I got to introduce them, and that was good."

"We should offer a matchmaking package," Laurel suggested, and started on leg lifts. "Even if we launched it just with the guys Emma wants to brush off we could double our business."

"Brush off has negative connotations. I redirect. Anyway Jack was there."

"Our Jack?" Parker asked.

"Yeah, which turned out to be lucky for me. I ducked out early, and halfway home, my car conks. Just cough, choke, die. And it's snowing, and it's dark, I'm *freezing*, and that stretch of road is deserted, of course."

As the leg lifts didn't look horrible, Emma shifted to mirror Laurel's movements.

"You really need to get OnStar installed," Parker told her. "I'll get you the information."

"Don't you think that's kind of creepy?" Mac huffed a little, pumping through the third set. "Having them know exactly where you are. And I think, I really think, they can hear you, even when you don't push the button. They're listening. Yes, they are."

"Because they love hearing people sing off-key with the radio. It must brighten their day. Who did you call?" Parker asked Emma.

"As it turned out, I didn't have to call anyone. Jack came along before I did. So, he takes a look, and it's the battery. He jumps it. Oh, and he lent me his jacket, which I forgot to give back. So instead of having a nice quiet evening, I'm dodging Sam's lips, trying to redirect him, standing in the freezing cold on the side of the road when all I wanted was a big salad and a romantic movie. Now I have to get my car in the shop, and make a trip to Jack's to return his jacket. And I'm completely swamped today. Just can't do it. So, irritable because . . ."

She hedged, just a little, as she rolled over to do the other leg. "I didn't sleep well worrying about getting everything done today and kicking myself for getting talked into going out in the first place."

She huffed out a breath. "And now that I said all that, it doesn't seem worth getting upset about."

"Breakdowns are always a bitch," Laurel said. "Breakdowns at night, in the snow? Serious pisser. You get a pass on the irritable."

"Jack had to point out that it was my own fault, and it's worse because, yes, it was, since I haven't had the car serviced. Ever. And that was annoying. But he did save the day, plus the jacket. Plus, he followed me home to make sure I got here. Anyway, that's all done. Now I have to hassle with having somebody check out the car and do whatever it is they do. I've got guys in

42

the family who could probably take care of most of it, but I don't want yet another lecture on how I neglect my car, blah blah. So, Parker, where should I take it?"

"I know, I know!" Mac puffed, then stopped her reps. "You should take it into that guy who towed my mother's car for me last winter. The one Del likes? Anybody who can basically tell Linda to stick it when she's on a rant gets my vote."

"Agreed," Parker said. "And he does get the Delaney Brown stamp of approval. Del's a maniac about who touches his cars. Kavanaugh's. I'll get you the number and the address."

"Malcolm Kavanaugh's the owner," Mac added. "Very hot."

"Really? Well, maybe a faulty battery's not such a bad thing. I'll try to get it in next week. Meanwhile, is anyone going into town, anywhere near Jack's office? I really have to stick here today."

"Give it back to him Saturday," Parker suggested. "He's on the list for the evening event."

"Oh. Fine." Emma looked with avid dislike at the elliptical. "Since I'm here, I might as well work up a sweat."

"How about me?" Mac demanded. "Am I cut yet?"

"The improvement's astounding. Biceps curls," Parker ordered. "I'll show you."

$\mathcal{B}$Y NINE, EMMA WAS SHOWERED, DRESSED, AND WHERE SHE wanted to be. At her work counter, surrounded by flowers.

To celebrate their parents' fiftieth anniversary, the clients wanted Emma to re-create the couple's wedding and backyard garden reception. Then kick it up a notch.

She had copies of snapshots from the wedding album pinned to a board, had added some concept sketches and diagrams, a list of flowers, receptacles, accessories. On another board she'd pinned Laurel's sketch of the elegantly simple three-tiered wedding cake

43

ringed with bright yellow daffodils and pale pink tulips. Beside it was a photograph of the cake topper the family had commissioned, replicating the couple on their wedding day, down to the lace hemming the bell of the bride's tea-length skirt.

Fifty years together, she thought as she studied the photos. All those days and nights, birthdays and Christmases. The births, the deaths, the arguments, the laughter.

It was, to her, more romantic than windswept moors and fairy castles.

She'd give them their garden. A world of gardens.

She started with daffodils, potting them in long, moss-lined troughs, mixing in tulips and hyacinths, narcissus. Here and there she added trails of periwinkle. A half a dozen times she filled a rolling cart, wheeled it back to her cooler.

She mixed gallons of flower food and water, filling tall glass cylinders. She stripped stems, cut them under running water and began arranging larkspur, stock, snapdragons, airy clouds of baby's breath, lacy asparagus fern. Soft colors and bold, she'd mass them at various heights to create the illusion of a spring garden.

Time ticked away.

She paused long enough to roll her shoulders, circle her neck, flex her fingers.

Using the foam holder she'd soaked, she circled it with lemon leaf to create a base she glossed with leaf shine.

She gathered roses for her holding bucket, stripped stems, barely bothered to curse when she nicked herself, cutting them to length to make the first of fifty reproductions of the bouquet the bride had carried a half century before.

She worked from the center out, painstakingly locking each stem in the form with adhesive. Stripping, cutting, adding—and appreciating the bride's choice of multicolored roses.

Pretty, Emma thought, happy. And when she tucked the holder in the squat glass vase, she thought: lovely.

"Only forty-nine to go."

She decided she'd start on that forty-nine after she took a break.

After carting bags of floral debris out to her composters, she scrubbed the green off her fingers and from under her nails at her work sink.

To reward herself for the morning's work, she took a Diet Coke and a plate of pasta salad out on her side patio. Her gardens couldn't compete—yet—with the one she was creating. But her happy couple had been married in southern Virginia. Give me a few weeks, she mused, pleased to see the green spears of spring bulbs, the freshening foliage of perennials.

Last night's snow was just a memory under blue skies and almost balmy temperatures.

She spotted Parker with a group of people—one of the day's potential clients doing the tour—crossing one of the terraces at the main house. Parker gestured toward the pergola, the rose arbor. The clients would have to imagine the abundance of white roses, the lushness of wisteria, but Emma knew the urns she'd planted with pansies and trailing vinca showed off very well. At the pond dotted with lily pads, the willows were just beginning to green.

She wondered if the prospective bride and groom would one day have a busy florist creating fifty bouquets to commemorate their marriage. Would they have children, grandchildren, great-grandchildren who loved them enough to want to give them that celebration?

With a small groan for muscles aching from the morning exercise and the morning's work, she propped her feet on the chair across from her, lifted her face to the sun and shut her eyes.

She smelled earth, the tang of mulch, heard a bird chittering its pleasure in the day.

45

"You've got to stop slaving away like this."

She jerked up—had she fallen asleep?—and blinked at Jack. Mind blank, she watched him pluck a curl of pasta from her plate, pop it into his mouth. "Good. Got any more?"

"What? Oh God!" Panicked, she looked at her watch, then breathed a sigh of relief. "I must've dozed off, but only for a couple minutes. I have forty-nine bouquets left to make."

His brows drew together over smoky eyes. "You're having a wedding with forty-nine brides?"

"Hmm. No." She shook her head to clear the cobwebs. "Fiftieth anniversary, and a re-creation of the bridal bouquet for every year. What are you doing here?"

"I need my jacket."

"Oh, right. Sorry I forgot to give it back to you last night."

"No problem. I had an appointment down the road." He took another twirl of pasta. "Do you have any more of this? I missed lunch."

"Yeah, sure. I owe you lunch at least. Sit down. I'll get you a plate."

"I'll take it, and I wouldn't mind a hit of caffeine. Hot or cold."

"No problem." Studying him, she pushed at hair that escaped pins. "You look a little whipped."

"Busy morning. And I've got another site to visit in about forty-five minutes. You were between the two, so . . ."

"That's handy. Be right back."

He was whipped, he thought, and stretched out his legs. Not so much from the work, or the in-your-face with an inspector that morning. Which would've handled better if he hadn't been sleep-deprived. Tossing and turning and trying to block out sex dreams of a Spanish-eyed lady would whip anyone.

So, of course, he had to be stupid and masochistic, and drop by with the excuse of the jacket.

Who knew how sexy she looked when she slept in the sunlight?

He did, now. It wasn't going to give him easier dreams.

The thing to do was get over it. He should make a date with a blonde or a redhead. Several dates with several blondes and/or redheads until he managed to put Emma back on the No Trespassing list.

Where she belonged.

She came out, his jacket over her arm, a tray in her hands.

She had, he thought, the kind of beauty that just slammed a man's throat shut. And when she smiled, the way she did now, it blew through him like a bolt of lightning.

He tried to build a No Trespassing sign in his head.

"I had some of my aunt Terry's olive bread," she told him. "It's great. I went with cold caffeine."

"That does the job. Thanks."

"No problem. And it's nice to have company on a break." She sat again. "What are you working on?"

"I'm juggling a few things." He bit into the bread. "You're right. It's great."

"Aunt Terry's secret recipe. You said you had a job near here?"

"A couple. The one I'm heading to's a never-ending. The client started out two years ago wanting a kitchen remodel, which moved into a complete reno of the master bath, which now includes a Japanese soaking tub, a sunken whirlpool, and a steam shower big enough for six friends."

She wiggled her brows over those gorgeous eyes, then took a bite of pasta. "Fancy."

"I kept waiting for her to ask if we could extend the addition a little more for the lap pool. But she turned her focus outside.

47

She decided she wants a summer kitchen by the pool. She saw one in a magazine. She can't live without it."

"How does anyone?"

He smiled and ate. "She's twenty-six. Her husband's fifty-eight, rolling in it and happy to indulge her every whim. She has a lot of whim."

"I'm sure he loves her, and if he can afford it, why not make her happy?"

Jack merely shrugged. "Fine by me. It keeps me in beer and nachos."

"You're cynical." She pointed at him with her fork before she stabbed more pasta. "You see her as the bimbo trophy wife and him as the middle-aged dumbass."

"I bet his first wife does, but I see them as clients."

"I don't think age should factor into love or marriage. It's about the two people in it, and how they feel about each other. Maybe she makes him feel young and vital, and opened something new inside him. If it was just sex, why marry her?"

"I'll just say a woman who looks like she does has great power of persuasion."

"That may be, but we've done a lot of weddings here where there's been a significant age difference."

He wagged his fork, then stabbed more pasta in a mirror of her move. "A wedding isn't a marriage."

She sat back, drummed her fingers. "Okay, you're right. But a wedding's a prelude, it's the symbolic and ritualistic beginning of the marriage, so—"

"They got married in Vegas."

He continued to eat, face bland as he watched her try not to laugh.

"Many people get married in Vegas. That doesn't mean they won't have many happy and fulfilling years together."

"By a transvestite Elvis impersonator."

"Okay, now you're making things up. But even if you're not, that kind of . . . choice shows a sense of humor and fun, which, I happen to believe, are important elements for a successful marriage."

"Good save. Great pasta." He glanced over to where Parker sat with potential clients on the main terrace. "Business seems to be clicking along."

"Five events this week on site, and a bridal shower we coordinated off site."

"Yeah, I'll be here for the one Saturday evening."

"Friend of Bride or Groom?"

"Groom. The bride's a monster."

"God, she really is." Emma leaned back and laughed. "She brought me a picture of her best friend's bouquet. Not because she wanted me to duplicate it, which she certainly did not. Hers is a completely different style, but she'd counted the roses, and told me she wanted at least one more in hers—and warned me she'd be counting them."

"She will, too. And I can pretty much guarantee no matter how good a job you do, she'll find fault."

"Yeah, we've figured that out. It's part of the job around here. You get monsters and angels and everything in between. But I don't have to think about her today. Today's a happy day."

He knew she meant it. She looked relaxed, and had a glow about her. Then again, she usually did. "Because you have fifty bouquets to make?"

"That, and knowing the bride of fifty years is going to love them. Fifty years. Can you imagine?"

"I can't imagine fifty years of anything."

"That's not true. You must imagine what you build lasting fifty years. Hopefully much longer."

"Point," he agreed. "But that's building."

"So's marriage. It's building lives. It takes work, care, maintenance. And our anniversary couple proves it can be done. And now I have to get back to them. Break's over for me."

"Me, too. I'll get this for you." He loaded up the tray, lifted it as they rose. "You're working alone today? Where are your elves?"

"They'll be here tomorrow. And there will be chaos as we start on the flowers for the weekend events. Today it's just me, about three thousand roses, and blissful quiet." She opened the door for him.

"Three *thousand*? Are you serious? Your fingers will fall off."

"I have very strong fingers. And if I need it, one of the pals will come by for a couple hours and help strip stems."

He set the tray on her kitchen counter, thinking, as he always did, that her place smelled like a meadow. "Good luck with that. Thanks for lunch."

"You're welcome." She walked him to the door where he stopped.

"What about your car?"

"Oh. Parker gave me the name of a mechanic, a place. Kavanaugh's. I'm going to call."

"He's good. Call soon. I'll see you Saturday."

He imagined her going back to her roses as he walked to his car. Of sitting, for hours, drenched in their scent, cleaning stems of thorns then . . . doing whatever it was she did, he decided, to make what women who took the plunge carried.

And he thought of how she'd looked when he'd come upon her, sitting in the sunlight, face tipped up, eyes closed, those luscious lips of hers just slightly curved as if she dreamed of something very pleasant. All that hair bundled up and slim dangles of silver at her ears.

He'd thought, briefly but actively, about just leaning down and taking that mouth with his. He could've played it light,

50

made some crack about sleeping beauty. She had a sense of humor, so maybe she'd have gotten a kick out of it.

She also had a temper, he mused. She didn't cut it loose often, but she had one.

It didn't matter either way, he reminded himself, as he'd missed that opportunity. The bevy of blondes and redheads was a better idea than scratching this increasingly annoying itch where Emma was concerned.

Friends were friends, lovers were lovers. You could make a friend out of a lover, but you were on boggy ground when you made a lover out of a friend.

He was nearly to the job site when he realized he'd left his jacket on her patio.

"Shit. *Shit.*"

Now he was like one of those idiots who deliberately left something at a woman's place so he had an excuse to go back and try to score. And that wasn't it.

Was it?

Shit. Maybe it was.

CHAPTER FOUR

At two fifteen on Saturday, Emma had her troops lined up to transform the event rooms from the cheerful Caribbean-themed daytime wedding into what she privately thought of as the Paris Explodes event.

"Everything goes." Emma rolled to the toes of her move-fast sneakers. "The bride wants all the remaining baskets, vases, centerpieces. We'll help them load up whatever hasn't already been given to guests. Beach and Tiffany, strip the garlands and swags, inside and out. Start with the portico, then move inside. Tink, you and I will start the changeover in the Grand Hall. When the portico's ready to be dressed, let me know. The bride's and groom's suites have already been changed over. New bride's due at three thirty for hair, makeup, dressing, and photos in her suite. We need the entrance, foyer, staircase complete by three twenty, and the Grand Hall completed by four. Terraces, pergola, and patios by four forty-five, Ballroom complete by five forty-five. If you need extra hands get me or Parker. Let's do this."

With Tink beside her, Emma shot off like a bullet. Tink, she knew, was reliable when she wanted to be—which was about seventy-five percent of the time. But Emma only had to show her or explain something to her once. She was a talented florist, again when she wanted to be. And was, to Emma's mind, almost spookily strong.

Tiny and toned, her wildly chopped boot-black hair liberally streaked with cotton-candy pink for spring, Tink attacked the mantel dressing like a whirlwind.

They stripped, boxed, dragged, hefted, and hauled candles of mango orange and surf white, garlands of bougainvillaea, pots of ferns and palm trees.

Tink snapped the gum she was never without and wrinkled her nose so the silver hoop in it glinted. "If you're going to want palm trees and shit, why don't you just go to the beach?"

"If they did, we wouldn't get paid to create the beach."

"Good point."

When she got the signal, Emma deserted the hall for the portico. She twined and draped and swagged miles of white tulle, acres of white roses to create a regal entryway for the bride and her guests. Colorful pots of hibiscus and orchids made way for enormous white urns filled with a forest of lilacs.

"Bride and Groom One and all guests checked out," Parker told her. She stood in her simple gray suit, her BlackBerry in one hand, her beeper hooked to her pocket, and her ear bud dangling. "My God, Emma, this looks amazing."

"Yeah, it's coming along. She balked on the lilacs—too simple a flower, according to Monster Bride, but I found a picture that convinced her." She stepped back, nodded. "Okay, yeah. Excellent."

"She's due in twenty."

54

"We'll make it."

Emma hustled inside to where Tink and Tiffany worked on the staircase. More tulle, more white roses, these twined with fairy lights, with long swags of roses dripping down every ten inches. Perfect.

"Okay, Beach, entry and gift table arrangements. We can haul over the first of the Grand Hall pieces, too."

"I can get you Carter." Parker tapped her beeper. "I drafted him to help in the Ballroom, but I can spare him."

"Handy to have Mac hooked with a strong, willing back. I'll take him."

With the gangly Carter and her fireplug Beach, Emma transported pots, vases, baskets, greenery, garland, swags, and candles.

"MB's pulling in." Parker's voice sounded through Emma's headset and made her snort. Monster Bride.

She put the finishing touches on the mantel, lush with white and silver candles, white roses, and lavender lisianthus, before making the dash to wade into the outdoor arrangements.

She set more lilacs in more urns, muscled enormous silver baskets filled with calla lilies in eggplant and snowy white, hung cones of flowers dripping with silver ribbon on the white-draped aisle chairs and guzzled water like a dying woman.

"Man, is this the best you can do?"

Rubbing the aching small of her back, Emma turned to Jack.

He stood, hands in the pockets of a gorgeous gray suit jacket, eyes shaded against the beaming sunlight by Oakleys.

"Well, she wanted simple."

He laughed, shook his head. "It looks amazing, and somehow elaborately French."

"Yes." She pointed a finger at him. "Exactly my plan. Wait!" Panic leaped in her chest like a terrier after a bone. "What are you doing here? What time is it? We can't be that far behind.

Parker would—" She broke off as she checked her watch. "Oh, thank God. You're really early."

"Yeah. Parker mentioned to Del since I was coming, maybe I could make it early and pitch in. So I'm here to pitch."

"Come with me. Tink! I need to get the bouquets. Finish up—ten minutes—then start on the Ballroom."

"On it."

"You can help me load. I'm heading over to get them now," she said into her headset. "Oh, slip a Xanax in her champagne, Parker. I can't move any faster. Ten minutes. Have Mac stall her."

Moving at a jog now, she reached the van she used for transport, then jumped behind the wheel.

"Do you do that often?" Jack asked her. "Drug the bride?"

"We never do it, but we want to with some of them. And really, we'd be doing everyone a favor. This one wants her bouquet and she wants it now because if she doesn't *love* it, there's going to be hell to pay. Laurel breezed by earlier and told me Mac told her the MB made her hairdresser cry and had a fight with her MOH. Parker smoothed it out, of course."

"MB?"

"Think about it," Emma suggested, and jumped out of the van to dash into her workshop.

He did as he followed her inside. "Mean Bitch. Monster Bitch. No, Monster Bride."

"Ding, ding, ding." She hauled open the door of her cooler. "Everything on the right goes. One rose cascade bouquet, twelve, count them twelve, attendant bouquets." She tapped one of the boxes. "Do you know what this is?"

"A bouquet. A purplish sort of thing. Pretty cool looking, actually. I've never seen anything like it."

"It's kale."

"Get out."

56

"Ornamental kale, variegated purple and green. Bride's colors are purple and silver. We've used a lot of silver accents and tones from pale orchid to deep eggplant, with lots of white and green in the arrangements."

"Son of a bitch. Cabbage bouquets. You didn't tell her what it is."

"Only after I made her fall in love with it. Okay bouquets, corsages, boutonnieres, both the pomanders—she has two flower girls, two halos of white roses and lavender, and holding vases. Check, check, double check. Let's load them up."

"Do you ever get sick of flowers?" he asked her as they carried boxed bouquets.

"Absolutely not. Do you smell that lavender? Those roses?"

"Impossible not to, under the circumstances. So, a guy's taking you out. First date or some special deal, and he brings you flowers. You're not like: Oh, flowers. Great."

"I'd think he was very thoughtful. God, every muscle in my body is begging for a glass of wine and a hot bath." She stretched her back when Jack closed the cargo doors. "Okay, let's go knock the MB's socks off. Oh wait. Your jacket. The one you lent me. It's inside."

"I'll get it later. So, did she get one more rose than her friend?"

Emma blanked for a moment, then remembered telling him about the bouquets. "Ten more. She'll bow to me before I'm done with her. Yes, Parker, yes, I'm on my way." Even as she spoke, her beeper sounded. "Now what? Can you read that? I can't get to it while I'm driving. It's hooked to my skirt, right under the jacket on your side."

He lifted the hem of the jacket, and his fingers brushed her skin just above her waist as he tilted the beeper. She thought, uh-oh, and kept her eyes straight ahead.

"It says DTMB! Mac."

57

"DTMB?" His knuckles continued to rest there, just above her waist. Very distracting. "Ah . . . Death to Monster Bride."

"Any answer? Suggestions on the method maybe?"

She managed a smile. "Not at this time. Thanks."

"Nice jacket," he said and smoothed it back into place.

She stopped in front of the house. "If you help me haul all this up, I won't tell Parker or give you grief when you sneak off to the Grand Hall for a beer before the wedding."

"That's a deal."

With her, he carried boxes into the foyer. He stopped a moment, took a survey. "You do good work. If she doesn't bow to you, she's a bigger idiot than I already think she is."

"Shh!" She stifled a laugh, rolled her eyes. "You don't know who's wandering around from the immediate family or wedding party at this stage."

"She knows I can't stand her. I told her."

"Oh, Jack." She did laugh now as she hurried up the steps. "Don't do or say anything to set her off. Consider the Wrath of Parker before you speak."

Emma balanced the box she carried and opened the door to the Bride's Suite.

"There you are. Finally! Emmaline, really, how am I supposed to take my formal portraits without my bouquet? And now my nerves are just *shot*! You know I wanted to see it early enough so you could make changes if I wanted them. Do you know what time it is? Do you?"

"I'm sorry, I didn't hear a word you said. I'm just dazzled. Whitney, you look absolutely spectacular."

That much, at least, was true. With miles of skirt, a universe of pearls and beads sparkling on the train, the bodice, and her expertly low-lighted blond hair swept up and crowned with a tiara, Monster Bride was magnificent.

58

"Thank you, but I've been a wreck worrying about the bouquet. If it's not perfect—"

"I think it's exactly what you hoped for." Carefully, Emma lifted the massive cascade of white roses from the box. She did a mental C-jump when the bride's eyes popped wide, but kept her tone professional. "I tweaked the temperature so the roses would just be partially open. And just hints of green and the silver beads to set off the blooms. I know you talked about trails of silver ribbons, but I really think that would take away from the flowers, and the shape. But I can add it in no time if you still want it."

"The silver would add a sparkle, but . . . Maybe you're right." She reached out to take the bouquet.

Nearby the mother of the bride pressed her palms together as if in prayer and lifted them to her lips.

Always a good sign.

Whitney turned, studied herself in the full-length mirror. And smiled. Emma stepped beside her to whisper in her ear. And the smile widened.

"You can count them later," Emma suggested. "Now I'll turn you over to Mac."

"Let's try between the windows over here, Whitney. The light's wonderful." Mac gave Emma a thumbs-up behind the bride's back.

"Now, ladies," Emma said, "it's your turn."

She distributed bouquets, corsages, set out the holding vases, then put the MOG in charge of the pomanders and flower girls.

She stepped out again, glanced at Jack. "Whew."

"The 'maybe you're right'? From her, that's a bow."

"Understood. I can take it from here. Go get that beer. Carter's around here somewhere. Corrupt him."

"I try, but he's a hard nut to crack."

"Boutonnieres," she said, already on the move again. "Then I need to check on the Ballroom." She looked at her watch. "We're right on schedule, so thanks. I'd be running behind if you hadn't helped me load and haul."

"I can take up the boutonnieres. It'd give me a chance to see Justin, make bad jokes about balls and chains."

"Good idea. Do that." With the few minutes of time that bought her, she opted to swing through the Grand Hall, out onto the terrace.

Satisfied after a few tweaks, she climbed up to the Ballroom where her team was well underway. Emma pushed up her sleeves and dived in.

While she worked, Parker gave periodic updates, and started the countdown in her ear.

Guests still trickling in. Most are seated or on the terrace.

Formal prewedding shots complete. Mac's on the move.

Grandparents escorted in two minutes. I'm bringing the boys down. Laurel, get ready for the pass-off.

"Roger that," Laurel said dryly. "Em, cake's assembled and ready for the table decor any time."

Boys passed off to Laurel, Parker announced a moment later as Emma finished with a stand of hydrangeas. *MOG escorted by BOG in one. MOB on deck. Escort is BOB. Queuing up attendants. Music change on my mark.*

Emma walked back to the entrance doors, shut her eyes for ten seconds, then opened them to take in the entire space. She drew a breath in, let a breath out.

Paris Explodes, she thought, but it did so in lush style. Whites, silvers, purples, touches of green to set them off spilled, spread, speared, and shimmered under a perfect April sky. She watched the groom and his party take their places in front of a pergola simply smothered in flowers.

"Guys, we rule. We *kill*. You're done. Hit the kitchen for food and drink."

Alone, she took one last circuit of the room as Parker signaled the attendants to *go!* one by one. Then she sighed, rubbed her back, the back of her neck, her hands. And went to change into her heels as Parker gave the MB her cue.

$\mathcal{J}$ACK DIDN'T KNOW HOW THEY PULLED IT OFF, EVERY TIME, ALL the time. He'd been drafted to lend a hand now and again at an event. Hauling and lifting, bartending, even bussing tables in a pinch. As payment invariably included great food, drinks, and music, he never minded.

But he still didn't know how they managed to pull it all together.

Parker consistently managed to be everywhere at once, and so subtly he suspected no one really noticed she might be prepping the best man on his toast one minute and passing out a pack of tissues to the mother of the bride the next while coordinating the service of the meal in the Grand Hall like a general coordinated troops during battle.

Mac popped up all over the place, too, and was just as cagey about it as she shot candids of the wedding party or the guests, or maneuvered the bride and groom into a quick posed photo.

Laurel streamed in and out, signaled, he supposed, through the headset they all wore, or by some sort of hand signal. Maybe mental telepathy. He wouldn't discount that one.

And Emma, of course, on the spot when a guest spilled wine on the tablecloth, or when the bored ring bearer started to poke at one of the flower girls.

He doubted anyone noticed or understood there were four women literally holding everything together, juggling all the

61

balls and passing them to each other with the grace and skill of NFL quarterbacks.

Just as he imagined no one knew the logistics and sheer timing involved in leading the guests from the Hall to the Ballroom. He lingered while Emma and her team along with Laurel swarmed on the head table to gather up the bouquets and holding vases.

"Need any help?" he asked her.

"Hmm? No, thanks, we've got it. Tink, six on either side, baskets on the end. Everything else stays in place for two hours here before undressing and loading. Beach, Tiff, snuff the candles, leave the overheads on half."

"I can get that," Tink said when Emma took the bride's bouquet.

"One bruised rose and she'll go on attack. Better she rips my throat out than yours. Let's go, first dance is starting."

While the flowers headed up the back stairs, Jack wandered to the main. He slipped into the Ballroom in the middle of the first official dance. The bride and groom chose what he considered the overused and overorchestrated "I Will Always Love You," while people stood in the flower-drenched Ballroom or sat at one of the tables strategically arranged around the dance floor.

The terrace doors stood open, inviting guests to stroll outside. He thought he'd do just that once he got a glass of wine.

When he saw Emma ducking out again, he adjusted his plan. Carrying two glasses of wine, he went down the back stairs.

She sat on the second level, and popped up like a spring when she heard his footsteps. "Oh, it's only you." She sank back down on the steps.

"Only me is bearing wine."

She sighed, circled her head on her neck. "We at Vows frown

on drinking on the job. But . . . I'll lecture myself tomorrow. Hand it over."

He sat down beside her, gave her the glass. "How's it going?"

"I should ask you. You're a guest."

"From the guest point of view, it's a smash. Everything looks great, tastes great, smells great. People are having fun and have no idea the whole business is clicking along on a timetable that would make a Swiss train conductor weep in admiration."

"Exactly what we're after." She sipped the wine, shut her eyes. "Oh God, that's good."

"How's the MB behaving?"

"She's actually not too bad. It's hard to be bitchy when everyone's telling you how beautiful you look, how happy they are for you. She actually did count the roses in her bouquet, so that made her happy. Parker's smoothed over a couple of potential crises, and Mac actually got a nod of approval over the B and G shots. If Laurel's cake and dessert table pass muster, I'd say we hit all the hot spots."

"Did she do those little crème brûlées?"

"Oh, yeah."

"You're gold. Lot of buzz on the flowers."

"Really?"

"I actually heard gasps a few times—the good kind."

She rolled her shoulders. "Then it's all worth it."

"Here."

He boosted himself up a stair, straddled her from behind, and dug his fingers into her shoulders.

"You don't have to . . . Never mind." She leaned back into his hands. "Carry on."

"You've got some concrete in here, Em."

"I've got about a sixty-hour week in there."

"And three thousand roses."

"Oh, adding the other events, we could double that. Easily."

He worked his thumbs up the back of her neck, made her groan. And as his stomach knotted in response realized he wasn't doing himself any favors. "So . . . how'd the fiftieth go?"

"It was lovely, really lovely. Four generations. Mac got some wonderful pictures. When the anniversary couple had their first dance, there wasn't a dry eye in the house. It goes down as one of my all-time favorite events."

She sighed again. "You have to stop that. Between the wine and your magic hands I'm going to end up taking a nap right here on the steps."

"Aren't you done?"

"Not even close. I have to get the tossing bouquet, help out with the cake service. Then there's the bubbles, which we hope to do outside. In an hour, we'll start breaking down the Grand Hall, boxing centerpieces and arrangements."

Her voice went a little thick, a little sleepy when he kneaded her neck. "Um . . . Loading up those, and the gifts. Loading up the outdoor arrangements. We have an afternoon event tomorrow, so we'll break down the Ballroom, too."

He tortured himself, running his hands down her biceps, back up to her shoulders. "Then you should relax while you can."

"And you should be upstairs enjoying the party."

"I like it here."

"So do I, which makes you a bad influence with your wine and staircase massages. I have to get back up, relieve Laurel on patrol." She reached back, patted his hand before she rose. "Cake cutting in thirty."

He got to his feet as she started up. "What kind of cake?"

She stopped, turned, and ended up on level with him. Her eyes, those deep velvet eyes, looked sleepy to match her voice. "She's calling it her Parisian Spring. It's this gorgeous pale lavender blue covered with white roses, sprigs of lilac, with this soft milk chocolate ribboning and—"

"I was more about what's inside."

"Oh, it's her genoise with Italian meringue buttercream. You don't want to miss it."

"It may beat out the crème brûlée." She smelled like flowers. He couldn't say which ones. She was a mysterious and lush bouquet. Her eyes were dark and soft and deep, and her mouth . . . Wouldn't it taste every bit as rich as Laurel's cake?

The hell with it.

"Okay, this is probably out of line, so apologies in advance."

He took her shoulders again, eased her to him. Those dark, soft, deep eyes widened in surprise an instant before his lips took hers.

She didn't jerk away, or laugh it off as a joke. Instead she made the same sort of sound she had when he'd rubbed her neck—just a little breathier.

Her hands clamped on his hips, and those luscious lips of hers parted.

Like her scent, her flavor was mysterious and essentially female. Dark and warm and sensual. When her hands moved up his back, he took more. Just a little more.

Then he changed angles, took more still, and pleasure hummed in her throat.

He thought of just snatching her up, carrying her off to whatever dark room he could find to finish what a moment of impulse had begun.

The beeper at her waist sounded, and both of them jolted. She made a strangled sound, then managed, "Oh. Well." In a jerky move she unclipped the beeper, stared at it. "Parker. Um. I have to go. I have to . . . go," she said, then turned and bolted up the stairs.

Alone, he lowered to the stairs again and finished off his

neglected wine in two long gulps. He decided he'd skip the rest of the reception, and take a long walk outside instead.

*E*MMA COULD ONLY BE GRATEFUL WORK KEPT HER TOO BUSY TO actually think. She helped clean up an incident involving the ring bearer and chocolate éclairs, delivered the tossing bouquet, rearranged the decor on the cake table to ease the serving, then began the stripping down of the Grand Hall.

She readied centerpieces and other arrangements for transport, loaded and supervised the loading of them for the proper recipients.

When the bubbles were blown and the last dance finished, she began the same process on the patios and terraces.

She didn't see a trace of Jack.

"Everything okay?" Laurel asked her.

"What? Yes. Sure. Everything went great. I'm just tired."

"Right there with you. At least tomorrow's event will be a breeze after today. Have you seen Jack?"

"What?" She jumped like a thief at the shrill of an alarm. "Why?"

"I lost track of him. I planned to bribe him with pastries to help with the breakdown. I guess he skipped."

"I guess. I wasn't paying attention."

Liar, liar. Why was she lying to her friend? It couldn't be a good sign.

"Parker and Mac are seeing off the stragglers," Laurel commented. "They'll do the security check. Do you want me to help you cart these to your place?"

"No, I've got it." Emma loaded the last of the leftovers she'd put back in the cooler. She'd donate the bulk to the local hospital, take the rest apart and make smaller arrangements to put around her place, and her friends'.

66

She closed the cargo doors. "See you in the morning."

She drove the van home, reversed the process and carried flowers and garlands into her cooler.

No matter how firmly she ordered her mind to stay calm and blank, it just kept opening up to one single thought.

Jack kissed her.

What did it mean?

Why should it *mean* anything?

A kiss was just that. It had just been a product of the moment. Nothing more.

She readied for bed, trying to convince herself it was nothing more.

But when a kiss blew right off the spark-o-meter, blasted through the scale, it was hard to describe it as "nothing more."

Something else was what it was, she admitted. And she didn't know what to do about it. That was frustrating because she *always* knew what to do when it came to men and kisses and sparks. She just knew.

She climbed into bed telling herself since she'd never be able to sleep, she'd just lie there in the dark until she came up with a solution.

And she dropped away in seconds, pushed off the edge by sheer exhaustion.

CHAPTER FIVE

$\mathcal{E}$MMA GOT THROUGH THE SUNDAY EVENT AND HER MONDAY consults and adjusted the arrangements for some upcoming events due to changes of bridal minds.

She canceled two dates with two perfectly nice men she now had no desire to spend evenings with. She filled those evenings by doing inventory and ordering ribbons, pins, containers, forms.

And wondering if she should call Jack and make some light, breezy comment about the kiss—or pretend it never happened.

She alternated between the top options and a third, which involved going over to his house and jumping him. So she ended up doing nothing but tying herself into knots over it.

Annoyed with herself, she arrived early for a scheduled afternoon staff meeting. She cut through Laurel's kitchen, where her friend was arranging a plate of cookies beside a small fruit and cheese platter.

"I'm out of Diet Coke," Emma announced and opened the fridge to take one. "I'm out of almost everything because I keep forgetting my car battery is dead as Disco."

"Did you call the garage?"

"That, at least, I remembered to do about ten minutes ago. When I confessed—under expert interrogation by the guy—that I've owned the car for four years, have never taken it in for a tune-up, couldn't remember exactly the last time, if ever, I've had the oil changed or some computer chip check job thing and other car business I don't remember now, he said he'd have it picked up, taken in."

Pouting a little, she popped the top and drank straight from the can. "I sort of felt as if I'd been holding my car hostage and he's releasing it. He made me feel like even more of an idiot than Jack did. I want a cookie."

"Help yourself."

Emma picked one up.

"Now I'm going to be without a car until he decides to give it back. If he does, and I'm not entirely sure he intends to."

"You've been without a car for over a week because your battery's dead."

"True, but I had the illusion of a car because it was sitting there. I guess I need to take the van and go to the grocery store, and the zillion other places I've put off going. I'm actually afraid to, as it occurred to me I've had the van for a year more than the car. It may rebel next."

Laurel tossed some pretty pastel mints on the cookie tray. "I know it's a crazy idea, but maybe once you get your car back, you can have the garage service the van."

Emma nibbled at the cookie. "The car guy tossed that idea in the hat. I need consolation. How about dinner and movie night?"

"Don't you have a date?"

"I canceled. I'm not in the mood."

Laurel blew hair out of her eyes, the better to stare in shock. "*You're* not in the mood for a date?"

"I have to get an early start tomorrow. Six hand-tied bouquets, and the bride's makes seven. That's a good six, seven hours of work. I have Tink coming in for half a day, so it cuts it back, but there's all the rest to put together for the Friday night event. And I spent most of the morning processing the flowers."

"That's never stopped you before. Are you sure you're feeling all right? You've been just a shade off."

"No, I'm fine. I'm good. I'm just not . . . in the mood for men."

"That couldn't include me." Delaney Brown walked in, lifted Emma off her feet to give her a resounding kiss. "Mmm. Sugar cookie."

Emma laughed. "Get your own."

He plucked one from the tray, grinned at Laurel. "Consider it part of my fee."

Going from experience, Laurel got out a Ziploc bag and began to fill it with cookies. "Are you in on the meeting?"

"No. I just had some legal business to go over with Parks."

Since it was there and so was he, Del went to the coffeepot.

He and Parker shared the dark brown hair, the dark blue eyes. What Laurel would have called their refined features were just a little more roughly carved on him. In the smoke gray pinstriped suit, Italian shoes, and Hermes tie, he looked every bit the successful Connecticut lawyer. The scion of the Connecticut Browns.

With the food prep complete, Laurel untied her baker's apron and hung it on a peg.

Del leaned on the counter. "I hear you kicked some ass with the Folk wedding last weekend."

"Do you know them?" Emma asked.

"Her parents are clients. I haven't had the pleasure—though from what Jack says that may be overstating—of meeting the new Mrs. Harrigan."

"You will when they file for divorce," Laurel said.

"Always the optimist."

"She's a nightmare. She sent Parker a critique list this morning. E-mailed from Paris. From her honeymoon."

"You're kidding!" Stunned, Emma gaped at Laurel. "It was perfect. Everything was perfect."

"The champagne could've been colder, the wait service faster, the sky bluer, and the grass greener."

"Well, she's just a bitch. After I gave her ten more roses. Not one, but *ten*." Emma shook her head. "It doesn't matter. Everyone who was there, and who was an actual human, knows it was perfect. She can't spoil it."

"That's my girl." Del toasted her with his coffee.

"Anyway, speaking of Jack, have you seen him? I mean, will you be seeing him?"

"Tomorrow, actually. We're heading into the city to catch the Yankees."

"Maybe you could take him his jacket. He left his jacket. Or I forgot to give it back. Anyway, I have his jacket, and he probably wants it. I can go get it. It's in my office. I can just go get it."

"I'll go by and get it on my way out."

"Good. That'd be great. Since you're seeing him anyway."

"No problem. I'd better get going." He picked up the bag, shook it lightly at Laurel. "Thanks for the cookies."

"A baker's dozen, including the one you ate, will be deducted from your fee."

He shot Laurel a grin, and sauntered out.

Laurel waited a few beats then pointed at Emma. "Jack."

"What?"

"Jack."

72

"No," Emma said slowly, laying her hand between her breasts. "Emma. Em-ma."

"Don't be funny, I can see right through you. You said 'anyway' three times in under a minute."

"No, I didn't." Maybe she had. "And so what?"

"So, what's going on with you and Jack?"

"Nothing. Absolutely nothing. Don't be ridiculous." She felt the lie burning her tongue. "You can't say anything to anyone."

"If I can't say anything it's not nothing."

"It is nothing. It's probably nothing. I'm overreacting. Damn it." Emma popped the half a cookie she had left in her mouth all at once.

"You're eating like a normal person. Something is wrong in the Emma-verse. Spill."

"Swear first. You won't say anything to Parker or Mac."

"You drive a hard bargain." Laurel swiped a fingertip diagonally across her breasts, then pointed it to the ceiling. "Sworn."

"He kissed me. Or we kissed each other. But he started it, and I don't know what would've happened next because Parker beeped me. I had to go, then he left. So, that's it."

"Wait, I lost the sense of hearing right after you said Jack kissed you."

"Cut it out. This is serious." She bit her lip. "Or it's not. Is it?"

"This isn't like you, Em. You are the goddess of handling men and romantic or sexual situations."

"I *know*. It's just this is Jack. It's not supposed to be . . ." She waved her arms in the air. "Something to handle. I'm making too much of it. It was just a moment, just the circumstances. Just a thing. Now it's done, so it's not a thing."

"Emma, you tend to romanticize men, potential relationships, but you never get flustered over them. You're flustered."

"Because it's Jack! What if you were standing around, minding

73

your own business, baking, and Jack came in and kissed you stupid. Or Del did. You'd be flustered."

"The only reason either of them come in here is to mooch baked goods. As Del just demonstrated. When did this happen? The night you broke down?"

"No. It almost did. There was a second there . . . I think because there was a second there, it just led into it happening. During the reception Saturday."

"Right, right, you said Parker beeped you. Well, how was it? How did it rank on the patented Emmaline Grant spark-o-meter?"

Emma let out a breath, pointed her thumb up, then swiped a hand through an imaginary line. "Slapped the top of the red zone before it broke the meter."

With her lips pursed, Laurel nodded. "I always suspected that about Jack. He has that red zone vibe about him. What are you going to do about it?"

"I don't know. I haven't decided. It's thrown me off. I need to get my balance back, then figure out what to do. Or not do."

"Then you have to tell me, and also let me know when the gag order is lifted."

"All right, but meanwhile, not a word." Emma picked up the cheese tray. "Let's go be businesswomen."

Vows housed its conference room in what had been the library. The books remained, framing the room and giving way in spaces for photos and mementos. The room maintained its warmth, its elegance, even as it served for business.

Parker sat at the big inlaid table, laptop and BlackBerry at the ready. As the morning client meetings and tours were complete for the day, she'd hung her suit jacket on the back of the chair. Mac sat across from her, long legs stretched out, wearing the jeans and sweater that served her for her workday.

74

When Emma set the tray on the table, Mac levered herself up to snag a cluster of grapes. "You guys are late."

"Del stopped by the kitchen. Before we start business, who's up for dinner and a movie night?"

"Me, me!" Mac shot up a hand. "Carter has a teacher thing, and that saves me from working until he gets back. I put in a full one today."

"As it happens, my calendar is clear." Laurel laid the cookie plate beside the platter.

Parker merely picked up the house phone, pressed a button. "Hey, Mrs. G, can you handle the four of us for dinner? That'd be great. Thanks." She hung up. "We'll have chicken and like it."

"Works for me." Mac bit into a grape.

"All right then, the first order of business is Whitney Folk Harrigan, aka Monster Bride. As Laurel knows, I received an e-mail from her wherein she lists several bullet points addressing what she feels we could improve."

"Bitch." Mac leaned up this time to spread some goat cheese on a rosemary cracker. "We kicked severe ass on that event."

"We should've kicked her severe ass," Laurel commented.

"Whitney feels, in no particular order of importance, that . . ." Parker opened a file to read from the e-mail she'd printed out. "The champagne was inadequately chilled, the service during dinner was slow, the gardens lacked enough color and bloom, the photographer spent more time than she deems necessary on the wedding party when the bride deserved more attention, and the offerings on the dessert table weren't as varied or as well presented as she'd hoped. She adds that she felt rushed and/or neglected by the wedding planner during some parts of the event. She hopes we'll take these criticism in the spirit with which they're offered."

"To which I respond . . ." Mac shot up a middle finger.

"Succinct." Parker nodded. "However, I responded with our

75

thanks for her comments, and our hopes that she and Justin enjoy Paris."

"Panderer," Laurel muttered.

"You bet. I could've responded with: Dear Whitney, you're full of shit. Which was my first thought. I restrained it. I have, however, upgraded her to Monster Bitch Bride."

"She must be a genuinely unhappy person. Seriously," Emma said when her friends just looked at her. "Anyone who could take a wedding day like we provided for her and pick it apart is just innately unhappy. I'd feel sorry for her if I wasn't so mad. I will feel sorry for her when I stop being mad."

"Well, mad, sorry, or fuck you, the upside is we've had four new tours booked through that event. And I expect more."

"Parks said fuck." Mac grinned and ate another grape. "She's very mad."

"I'll get over it, especially if we book four more events as a result of the stupendous job we did on Saturday. For now, I'm putting Whitney in my newly designed Closet of Doom, where everything makes her look fat, all the patterns are polka dots, and the color choices are puce or dead-flesh beige."

"That's really mean," Laurel commented. "I like it."

"Moving on," Parker continued. "Del and I met about some of the legal and financial issues of the business. The partnership agreement is coming up for renewal, which includes the percentage funneled back into Vows from the individual arms for outside events. If anyone wants to discuss changes to the agreement, including the percentages, the floor's open."

"It's working, isn't it?" Emma glanced around at her partners. "I don't think any of us really imagined we'd build what we've built when we started Vows. Not just financially, which is certainly more than I'd have made by now if I'd been able to open my own shop. But, Monster Bitch Bride aside, the reputation we've earned, together and individually. The percentage is fair, and the fact is, the cut Del takes for his part of the estate is way below what he could've asked. We're all doing what we love with people we love. And we're making a good living at it."

"I think what Em's saying is: Sign me up." Mac popped another grape. "I say ditto."

"I'm right there," Laurel added. "Is there any reason to change anything?" she asked Parker.

"Not from my perspective, but as Del advised—in his legal function—each of you should read over the agreement again, and voice any reservations, make any suggestions before we renew."

"I suggest we have Del draw up the papers, sign them, then open a bottle of Dom."

Mac pointed at Emma in agreement. "Seconded."

"And the 'ayes' have it," Laurel announced.

"I'll let him know. I've also had a discussion with our accountant."

"Better you than me," Laurel said.

"Much better." Parker smiled and sipped some water. "We've had a strong first quarter, and are on track to increase our net profit by about twelve percent over last year. I'm advised we should consider rolling a portion of the net back into the business. So, if any or all of you have a need, whim, or selfish desire for additional equipment, or ideas on what Vows could use as a whole, we can work out what we should spend our money on, and how much we should spend."

Emma shot her hand up before anyone could speak. "I've been thinking about this, especially after I looked at my books for the last quarter. We have our biggest event, to date, next spring with the Seaman wedding. The flowers alone are going to outstrip the capacity of my cooler, so we'll need to rent another for several days. I may be able to find a used one for a cost that could make it more practical, in the long term, than renting."

77

"That's good." Parker made a note. "Get some prices."

"This may be the time," Emma continued, "considering that event, and the increase we're seeing in business, to buy some of the other equipment we usually rent. The additional outdoor seating, for instance. Then, when we do an outside event, *we* rent it to the client and pocket the fee. And—"

"You really have been thinking," Mac commented.

"I really have. Since Mac's already planning to add on to her place, increasing the upstairs living area to accommodate true love, why not add on to the work space, the studio space at the same time? She needs more storage space, a real dressing room instead of the little powder room. And while I'm rolling, the mudroom off Laurel's kitchen is really redundant, as we have one off the main kitchen. If that was converted, she could have an auxiliary kitchen in there, another oven, another cooler, more storage."

"We'll just let Emma do the talking," Laurel put in.

"And Parker needs a computerized security system so she can monitor all the public areas of the house."

Parker waited a beat. "I think you've spent that net profit increase several times."

"Spending money's the fun part of earning it. You be Parker, and that'll keep us from going wild. But I really think we ought to do at least some of those things, and put the others on the list for as soon as possible down the road."

"Being Parker then, I'll say the cooler makes sense. See what you can find. Since we'd need to talk to Jack on how to work the cooler into your space, we can ask him to give us an idea how to add on to Mac's studio, and refit the mudroom."

She made more notes as she spoke. "I'd thought of the furniture buy already, and I've started researching the cost there. I'll get projections so we know where we stand on all of this, then we can decide which makes the most sense first."

Nodding, she flipped over to the next order of business.

"Now, upcoming events that will help pay for our hopes and dreams. The commitment ceremony. They got their vows and the script for the ceremony to me today. Friday evening ceremony, with, after a coin toss, Allison, now known as Bride One, arriving at three thirty, and Marlene, now Bride Two, at four. Bride One takes Bridal Suite, Bride Two Groom's Suite. As they share a MOH, she's going to float between the suites. Bride One's brother is BM, so we'll use the second floor family parlor for him, and the FOBs, as needed. BM will stand on B-One's side during the ceremony, MOH on B-Two's."

"Wait." Mac held up a finger as she keyed the details into her laptop. "Okay."

"These ladies know exactly what they want and stick to a plan, so they've been extremely easy to deal with on my end. MOB-One and siblings of B-Two aren't particularly happy with the formalization of this relationship, but are cooperating. Mac, you may have to work to get the shots the clients hope for that include them."

"No problem."

"Good. Emma, flowers?"

"They wanted unconventional, but feminine. Neither wanted to carry a bouquet, so we've gone with a headpiece for Allison and flower combs for Marlene. A halo for the MOH who'll carry four white roses. They'll exchange single white roses during the ceremony, right after the lighting of the unity candle. And each will give her mother a rose. White rose boutonnieres for the men. It should be very pretty."

Emma scrolled over to arrangements as she sipped her Diet Coke. "They wanted an airy, meadowy look for arrangements and centerpieces. I'm using a lot of baby's breath and painted daisies, Shastas and gerberas, branches of blooming cherry, wild strawberries, and so on. Minimal tulle, and garlands I'm doing like daisy chains. Bud vases for the roses during the reception.

"A lot of fairy lights and candles, Grand Hall and Ballroom, with a continuation of the natural look for arrangements. It'll be simple and very sweet, I think. If one of you can help me transport, I can do the setup solo."

"I can do that," Laurel told her. "The cake's the vanilla sponge with raspberry mousse filling, topped with Italian meringue. They wanted simple flowers there, too, echoing Emma's. I don't need to add those to the cake until around five, so I'm clear for setup. Otherwise, they want assorted cookies and pastel mints."

"We have the standard Friday night itinerary," Parker added, "excluding bouquet and garter toss. Rehearsal Thursday afternoon, so if there are any glitches, we'll deal with them then. Saturday," she began.

$\mathcal{W}$HENEVER EMMA THOUGHT OF HER PARENTS, HOW THEY MET, fell in love, it ran through her mind like a fairy tale.

Once upon a time there was a young woman from Guadalajara who traveled across the continent to the great city of New York to work in the business of her uncle, to tend the homes and children of people who needed or wanted their homes and children tended. But Lucia longed for other things, a pretty home instead of a noisy apartment, trees and flowers instead of pavement. She worked hard, and dreamed of one day having her own place, a little shop perhaps, where she would sell pretty things.

One day her uncle told her of a man he knew who lived miles away in a place called Connecticut. The man had lost his wife, and so his young son had no mother. The man had left the city for a quieter life—and, perhaps, Lucia thought—because the memories were too painful in the home he'd shared with his wife. Because he wrote books, he needed a quiet place, and because he often traveled, he needed someone he could trust with his little boy. The woman who had done these things for the three years since the sad death of his wife wished to move back to New York.

So Lucia took a great leap, and moved out of the city and into the grand house of Phillip Grant and his son, Aaron.

The man was handsome as a prince, and she saw he loved his son. But there was a sorrow in his eyes that touched her heart. The child had had so many changes in his short four years, she understood his shyness with her. She cooked their meals and tended the house, and looked after Aaron while the man wrote his book.

She fell in love with the boy, and he with her. He was not always good, but Lucia would have been sad if he had been. In the evenings, she and Phillip would often talk about Aaron, or books or ordinary things. She would miss the talks—she would miss him—when he went away for business.

There were times when she looked out the window to watch Phillip play with Aaron, and her heart yearned.

She didn't know he often did the same. For he'd fallen in love with her, as she had with him. He was afraid to tell her, lest she leave them. And she feared to tell him in case he sent her away.

But one day, in the spring, under the arching blooms of a cherry tree while the little boy they both loved played on the swing, Phillip took Lucia's hand in his. And kissed her.

When the leaves of the trees turned vivid with autumn, they were married. And lived happily ever after.

Was it any wonder, Emma thought as she pulled her van into the crowded double drive of her parents' home on Sunday evening, that she was a born romantic? How could anyone grow up with that story, with those people, and not want some of the same for herself?

Her parents had loved each other for thirty-five years, had raised four children in the sprawling old Victorian. They'd built a good life there, a solid and enduring one.

She had no intention of settling for less for herself.

She got the arrangement she'd made out of the van, and hurried across the walk for the family dinner. She was late, she thought, but she'd warned them she would be. Cradling the vase in the crook of her arm, she pushed open the door and walked into a house saturated with the color her mother couldn't live without.

And as she hurried back toward the dining room, she moved into the noise as colorful as the paints and fabrics.

The big table held her parents, her two brothers, her sister, her sisters-in-law, her brother-in-law, her nieces and nephews—and enough food to feed the small army they made.

"Mama." She went to Lucia first, kissed her cheek before setting the flowers on the buffet and rounding the table to kiss Phillip. "Papa."

"*Now* it's family dinner." Lucia's voice still held the heat and music of Mexico. "Sit before all the little piggies eat all the food."

Emma's oldest nephew made oinking noises and grinned as she took her seat beside him. She took the platter Aaron passed her. "I'm starving." She nodded, gestured a go-ahead as her brother Matthew lifted a bottle of wine. "Everybody talk so I can catch up."

"Big news first." Across the table her sister, Celia, took her husband's hand. Before she could speak, Lucia let out a happy cry.

"You're pregnant!"

Celia laughed. "So much for surprises. Rob and I are expecting number three—and the absolute final addition—in November."

Congratulations erupted, and the youngest member of the

family banged her spoon enthusiastically on her high chair as Lucia leaped up to embrace her daughter and her son-in-law. "Oh, there's no happier news than a baby. Phillip, we're having another baby."

"Careful. The last time you told me that, Emmaline came along nine months later."

With a laugh, Lucia went over to wrap her arms around his neck from behind, press her cheek to his. "Now the children do all the hard work, and we just get to play."

"Em hasn't done her part yet," Matthew pointed out and wiggled his eyebrows at her.

"She's waiting for a man as handsome as her father, and not so annoying as her brother." Lucia sent Matthew an arch look. "They don't grow on trees."

Emma smirked at her brother and cut her first sliver of roast pork. "And I'm still touring the orchards," she said sweetly.

She lingered after the others to take a walk around the gardens with her father. She'd learned about flowers and plants, had come to love them under his guidance.

"How's the book going?" she asked him.

"Crap."

She laughed. "So you always say."

"Because it's always true at this stage." He wrapped an arm around her waist as they walked. "But family dinners and digging in the dirt help me put the crap aside awhile. Then it's never quite as bad as I thought when I get back to it. And how are you, pretty girl?"

"Good. Really good. We stay busy. We had a meeting earlier in the week because profits are up, and all I could think was how lucky we are—I am—doing work we love, being able to do it with the best friends I've ever had. You and Mama always said to find what we loved, and we'd work well and happily. I did."

She turned as her mother crossed the lawn carrying a jacket.

"It's chilly, Phillip. Do you want to catch cold so I have to listen to you complain?"

"You uncovered my plan." He let his wife bundle him into the jacket.

"I saw Pam yesterday," she spoke of Carter's mother. "She's so excited about the wedding. It's lovely for me, too, having two of my favorite people fall in love. Pam was a good friend to me, always, and a champion when some were scandalized your father would marry the help."

"They didn't see how clever I was to get all the labor for free."

"The practical Yankee." Lucia snuggled up against his side. "Such a slave driver."

Look at them, Emma thought. How perfectly they fit. "Jack told me the other day you were the most beautiful woman ever created, and he's waiting to run off with you."

"Remind me to beat him up the next time I see him," Phillip said.

"He's the most charming flirt. Maybe I'll make you fight for me." Lucia tipped her face up to Phillip's.

"How about a foot rub instead?"

"We have a deal. Emmaline, when you find a man who gives you a good foot rub, look closely. Many flaws are outweighed by that single skill."

"I'll keep it in mind. Meanwhile, I should go." She opened her arms to embrace them both. "Love you."

Emma glanced back as she walked away, and watched her father take her mother's hand under the arching branches of the cherry tree with its blooms still tightly closed.

And kiss her.

No, she thought, it was no wonder she was a born romantic. No wonder she wanted that, some part of that, for her own.

84

She got in the van and thought about the kiss on the back stairs.

Maybe it was only flirtation or curiosity. Maybe it was just chemistry. But she'd be damned if she'd pretend it didn't happen. Or let him pretend.

It was time to deal with it.

CHAPTER SIX

*I*N HIS OFFICE ON THE SECOND FLOOR OF THE OLD TOWNHOUSE he'd remodeled, Jack refined a concept on his computer. He considered the addition to Mac's studio after-hours work, and since neither she nor Carter were in any particular hurry, he could fiddle, reimagine, and revise the overall structure and every fussy detail.

Now that Parker wanted a second concept to include additions on both the first and second floors, he needed to revisualize not only the details and design, but the entire flow. It was smarter, in his opinion, to do it all at once, even if it did mean scrapping his original concept.

He toyed with lines and flow, the play of light as part of the increased space that would remain studio. With refitting the current powder room and storage and increasing the square footage of both, he could widen the bath, add a shower—something he thought they'd appreciate down the road—give

Mac the client dressing area she wanted, and double her current storage space.

Carter's study on the second floor . . .

He sat back, guzzled some water, and tried to think like an English professor. What would his wants and needs be for work space? Efficiency, and a traditional bent—it being Carter. Built-ins along the wall for books. Make that two walls.

Breakfronts, he decided, shifting in his own U-shaped work space to try a quick hand sketch. Cabinets beneath for holding office supplies, student files.

Nothing slick, nothing sleek. Not Carter.

Dark wood, he thought, an Old English look. But generous windows to match the rest of the building. Angle the roof to break up the lines. A couple of skylights. Frame out this wall to form an alcove. Add interest, create a sitting area.

A place a guy could escape to when his wife was pissed at him, or when he just wanted an afternoon nap.

Put an atrium door here, and add a terrace—small scale. Maybe a guy wanted a brandy and cigar. It could happen.

He paused a moment, tuned back in to the game he had on the flat-screen to his left. While his thoughts brewed in the back of his mind, he watched the Phillies strike out the Red Sox in order.

That sucked.

He turned back to the drawing. And thought: Emma.

Cursing, he tunneled a hand through his hair. He'd been doing a damn good job of not letting her in. He was good at compartmentalizing. Work, ball game, the occasional toggle over to check other scores. Emma was in another compartment, and that one was supposed to stay shut.

He didn't want to think about her. It did no good to think about her. He'd made a mistake, obviously, but it wasn't earth-shattering. He'd kissed the girl, that's all.

88

A hell of a kiss, he thought now. Still, just one of those things, just one of those moments. A few more days to let the reverberations die down, and things could get back to normal.

She wasn't the type of woman to hold it against him.

Besides, she'd been right there with him. He scowled, guzzled more water. Yeah, damn right she had. So what was she all bent out of shape about?

They were grown-ups; they'd kissed each other. End of story.

If she was waiting for him to apologize, she could keep waiting. She'd just have to deal with it—and him. He and Del were tight, and he was friends, good friends, with the other members of the Quartet. Added to it, with the remodeling Parker was talking about, he'd be spending more time on the estate for the next several months.

He dragged his hand through his hair again. Okay, that being the case, they'd both have to deal with it.

"Hell."

He scrubbed his hands over his face, then ordered himself to push his brain back into work. Frowning, he studied the bare bones of his design. Then narrowed his eyes.

"Wait a minute, wait a minute."

If he canted the whole thing, angled it, cantilevering the study, he'd create a back patio area, partially covered. It would give them the outdoor living space they lacked, privacy, a potential little garden area or shrubbery. Emma would have ideas on that.

It would add interest to the shape and lines of the building, and increase usable space without significantly adding on to the cost of the build.

"You're a genius, Cooke."

As he began to plot it out, someone knocked on the back door.

Mind still on the drawing, he rose to walk through the main

living area of his quarters over his firm. And assuming it was Del or one of his other friends—and hoping they brought their own beer—he opened the door that led into his kitchen.

She stood in the glimmer of porch light and smelled like moonlit meadows.

"Emma."

"I want to talk to you." She breezed right by him, tossed her hair back, pivoted. "Are you alone?"

"Ah . . . yeah."

"Good. What the hell is wrong with you?"

"Give me a context."

"Don't try to be funny. I'm not in the mood for funny. You go flirty on me, jumping my car, rubbing my shoulders, eating my pasta, lending me your jacket, and then—"

"I guess I could've just waved as I passed you on the side of the road. Or let you shiver until you turned blue. And I was hungry."

"It's all of a piece." She snapped it out then strode through the kitchen into his wide hallway with her hands waving in the air. "And you conveniently left out the shoulder rubbing and the 'and then.'"

He saw no choice but to tag after her. "You looked stressed and knotted up. You were okay with it at the time."

Spinning around, she narrowed those brown velvet eyes. "And then?"

"Okay, there was an 'and then.' You were there, I was there, so 'and then.' It's not like I jumped you or you tried to fight me off. We just . . ." *Kissed* suddenly sounded too important. "Locked lips for a minute."

"Locked lips. Are you twelve? You kissed me."

"We kissed each other."

"You started it."

He smiled. "Are you twelve?"

90

She made a low hissing sound that had the back of his neck prickling. "You made the move, Jack. *You* brought me wine, *you* got all cozy on the stairs, rubbing my shoulders. *You* kissed me."

"Guilty, all counts. You kissed me right back. Then you went tearing off like I'd drawn blood."

"Parker beeped me. I was *working*. You poofed. And you've stayed poofed since."

"Poofed? I left. You ran off like the hounds of hell were on your heels, and Whitney irritates the shit out of me. So I left. And, strangely, I have a job—just like you—and I've spent the last week working. Not poofing. Jesus, I can't believe I said poofing." He had to drag in a breath. "Look, let's sit down."

"I don't want to sit down. I'm too mad to sit down. You don't just do that then walk away."

Since she pointed an accusatory finger at him, he pointed right back. "You walked away."

"That's not what I mean, and you know it. Beeper, Parker, work." She threw her hands in the air again. "I didn't *go* anywhere. I just left because the MBB decided she had to inspect the tossing bouquet before she'd deign to toss it, and insisted it had to be right then and there. She irritates the shit out of everyone, but I didn't just leave."

She gave him a little shove, palm to chest. "You did. It was rude."

"God. Are you going to scold me now? Wait, you already are. I kissed you. I confess. You have that mouth, and I wanted it—was pretty clear about that." His eyes sparked, storm clouds full of thunder and electric light. "You didn't scream for help so I took it. Hang me."

"It's not about the kiss. It is, but it isn't. It's about the why and the after that and the what."

He stared at her. "What?"

"Yes! I'm entitled to some sort of reasonable answer."

"Where, you forgot where, so I'll insert that one. Where is the reasonable question? Find it, and I'll do what I can with a reasonable answer. Thereto."

She smoldered. He hadn't known a woman could actually smolder. God, it was sexy.

"If you can't discuss this like an adult, then——"

"Screw it."

If he was going to be damned for it once, he might as well be damned for it twice. He grabbed her, jerking her forward and up to her toes. The sound she made might have been the beginning of what, or why, but before she could finish the word he plundered her mouth. He used his teeth, one quick, impatient bite, that had her lips parting in surprise or response. He wasn't in the mood to care which, not when his tongue found hers, not when the taste of her sizzled along his senses like a wire in the blood.

His hands tangled in the wild glory of her hair, tugging so her head dipped back.

Stop. She meant to say it. She meant to do it. But it was like being drenched in summer. In the heat and the wet. Every sensible thought melted away as her body leaped from temper to shock to fevered response.

When he lifted his head, said her name, she only shook her head and dragged him back.

For one wild moment his hands were everywhere, inciting, igniting, until she could barely get her breath.

"Let me——" He fumbled with the buttons of her shirt.

"Okay." She'd let him do pretty much anything.

When his hand covered her racing heart, she pulled him to the floor.

Smooth flesh, hard muscle, and a mouth mad with hunger. She arched under him, rolled over him. Yanked his T-shirt up and away to scrape her teeth over his chest. With a groan, he dragged her back up to ravish her mouth, her throat, with a frenzied desperation that matched the rush of hers.

Half mad, he flipped her onto her back, ready to rip her clothes away. Her elbow smacked the floor with a sound like a gunshot. Stars burst in front of her eyes.

"Oh! God!"

"What? Emma. Shit. Fuck. I'm sorry. Let me see."

"No. Wait." Dazed, tingling, and not a little stupefied, she managed to sit up. "Funny bone. Ha-ha. Oh, God," she said again.

"I'm sorry. I'm sorry. Here." He started to rub her forearm to help with the needles and pins he imagined were stabbing her, and struggling to steady his breathing, wheezed.

"You're laughing."

"No. No. I'm too overcome with lust and passion to draw a clear breath."

"You're laughing." She jabbed him in the chest with the index finger of her good arm.

"No. I'm fighting manfully not to." Which was, he mused, likely the first time he'd done so while sporting a massive hard-on. "Is it better? Any better?" he asked, and made the mistake of looking over, and into her eyes.

The laugh sparkled in them, like gold over brown. He lost the fight, simply collapsed and gave in to the belly laugh. "Really sorry."

"Why? When you showed such exquisite finesse."

"Yeah, that's what they all say. You're the one who headed for the floor when I've got a perfectly good couch ten feet away, and a damn fine bed up those stairs. But no, you can't control yourself long enough to let me get us to a soft surface."

"Only a wimp requires a soft surface for sex."

He shifted his gaze over with a slow, hot smile. "I ain't no wimp, sister." He sat up. "Let's try take two."

93

"Wait." She slapped a hand on his chest. "Mmm, nice pecs, by the way. But wait." Lifting her still tingling arm she pushed back her hair. "Jack, what are we doing?"

"If I have to explain it, I'm doing it wrong."

"No, really. I mean . . ." She glanced down at her open shirt, and the lacy white bra perkily peeking out. "Look at us. Look at me."

"Believe me, I was. Am. Want to keep doing that. You have this seriously crazy body. I just want to—"

"Yes, I get that. Back at you, but, Jack, we can't just . . . We got off the track here."

"Down the track, heading for home, from my viewpoint. Give me five minutes to mesh viewpoints. One. Give me one."

"It would probably take under thirty seconds. But no," she added when he grinned. "Really. We can't just do this, like this. Or at all. Maybe." Everything inside her hitched and sparked and *wanted*.

"I'm not sure. We need to think, muse, mull, maybe ponder and brood. Jack, we're friends."

"I'm feeling pretty damn friendly."

Her eyes went soft as she reached out to lay her hand on his cheek. "We're friends."

"We are."

"More, we have friends who are friends. So many connections. So as much as I'd like to say 'what the hell, let's try out that couch, then the bed and maybe take round three on the floor—'"

"Emmaline." His eyes were deep, dark smoke. "You're killing me."

"Sex isn't a kiss on the back stairs. Even a really great kiss on the back stairs. So we have to think and so on before we decide. I refuse to not be friends with you, Jack, just because right now I really want you naked. You're important."

94

He heaved a sigh. "I wish you hadn't said that. You're important. You always have been."

"Then let's take a little time and think this through." She eased back and began to button her shirt.

"You don't know how sorry I am to see you do that."

"Yes, I do. About as sorry as I am to do it. Don't get up," she said, and got to her feet, picked up the purse she'd dropped when he'd grabbed her. "If it's any consolation, I'm going to have a miserable night thinking about what would've happened if we hadn't stopped to think."

"It isn't, because I'm going to have the same."

"Well." She glanced back as she headed for the door. "You started it."

$\mathcal{I}$N THE MORNING, AFTER THE PREDICTED MISERABLE NIGHT, Emma wanted the comfort of pals and Mrs. Grady's pancakes. She bargained with herself. She could have the pals, no question, but she could only have the pancakes if she first faced the dreaded home gym.

She dragged on her gear and began the resented, caffeine-deprived trudge to the main house. On the way, she veered toward Mac's studio. She could see no good reason why her friend shouldn't suffer along with her.

Without thinking she walked right in, angled toward the kitchen. There was Mac, in cotton boxers and a tank, leaning against the counter with a wide grin and a cup of coffee. And Carter opposite her, mirroring the pose and the grin, in his tweed jacket.

She should've knocked, Emma thought instantly. She had to remember to start knocking now that Carter lived here, too.

Mac glanced her way, lifted her cup in casual greeting. "Hey."

"Sorry."

"Are you out of coffee again?"

"No, I—"

"There's plenty," Carter told her. "I made a full pot."

Emma gave him a sorrowful look. "I don't know why you have to marry her instead of me."

The tips of his ears went a little pink, but he shrugged. "Well, maybe if things don't work out . . ."

"He thinks he's cute," Mac said dryly. "And damn it, he's right." She stepped over, gave his tie a tug.

The kiss was light and sweet, to Emma's eye. The kind of morning kiss between lovers who knew there would be time, lots of time, for deeper, hotter kisses.

She envied the light and sweet outrageously.

"Go to school, Professor. Enlighten young minds."

"That's the plan." He picked up his briefcase, brushed his hand over Mac's bright hair. "See you tonight. Bye, Emma."

"Bye."

He opened the door, glanced back, and rapped his elbow on the jamb. "Damn it," he muttered, and closed the door behind him.

"He does that about every third time he . . . What's with you?" Mac demanded. "You went all blushy."

"Nothing." But she caught herself rubbing her own elbow and remembering. "Nothing. I just stopped by on my way over to the torture chamber. I plan on begging Mrs. G for pancakes after I've suffered."

"Give me two minutes to change."

While Mac dashed upstairs, Emma paced. There had to be a simple, subtle, sensible way to explain to Mac what had happened with Jack. What was happening with Jack. To ask her for dispensation from the no-sleeping-with-friends'-exes rule.

Mac and Jack were friends, so that had to be a point. And more, bigger, huge, was the fact that Mac was madly and totally in love with Carter. She was getting married, for God's sake. What kind of friend would hold another friend to the no-exes rule when she was getting married to Mr. Adorable?

It was just selfish and narrow-minded and mean.

"Let's go before I change my mind." With a hoodie flopping open over a sports bra and bike pants, Mac jogged into the kitchen. "I can feel my bis and tris beefing up. Killer arms, you are mine!"

"Why do you have to be that way?" Emma demanded.

"Way? What?"

"We've been friends since we were *babies*. I don't know why you'd be so hard-assed about this when you don't want him."

"Who? Carter? Yes, I do. You didn't have any coffee this morning, did you?"

"If I have coffee my brain wakes up enough to find reasons not to work out. And that's not the point."

"Okay. Why are you mad at me?"

"I'm not mad at you. You're the one who's mad at me."

"Then say you're sorry and all's forgiven." Mac opened the door and sailed out.

"Why should I be sorry? I stopped." Emma slammed the door behind them.

"Stopped what?"

"Stopped . . ." Groaning, she pressed her fingers to her eyes. "It's caffeine deprivation. My mind's blurring. I'm starting in the middle. Or maybe the end."

"I demand to know why I'm mad at you so I can put some effort into it. You bitch."

Emma sucked in a breath, held it. "I kissed Jack. Or he kissed me. He started it. And then he poofed, so I went over there to give him a piece of my mind, and he did it again. Then I did it again. Then we were rolling around on the floor and clothes were coming off until I rapped my elbow. Really hard. And it

97

brought me back to my senses. So I stopped and you've got no reason to be mad."

Mac, who'd been gaping at Emma since the first sentence, just kept gaping. "What? What?" She banged her palm on one ear, shook her head as if to shake out water. *"What?"*

"I'm not saying it all again. The point is I stopped, and I said I'm sorry."

"To Jack?"

"No—well, yes—but to you. I'm telling you I'm sorry."

"Why?"

"For God's sake, Mac, the *rule*."

"Okay." Mac stopped, fisted her hands on her hips and stared off into space. "No, I'm still confused. So let's try this." She made exaggerated wiping gestures with both hands. "There's the board, and it's all cleaned off. Let's start fresh. You and Jack—wow—one minute to absorb . . . Done. You and Jack shared a big sloppy."

"It wasn't sloppy. He's an excellent kisser, as you very well know."

"I do?"

"And I'm not sorry for that one. Not really, because it was completely out of the blue. All right, not completely, since I got the vibes when we were under the hood."

"Hood? What . . . Oh, the car. God, only someone who's known you forever could interpret half of what you're saying."

"But I wasn't expecting him to bring me a glass of wine while I was taking a quick break, just sitting on the back stairs, minding my own business."

"Wine, back stairs," Mac mumbled. "MBB. The wedding."

"Then he gave me a shoulder rub, so I *should've* known, but I was going. I was going back to the reception and then we were standing there and he kissed me. Then Parker beeped me, and I had to go, and I realized what I'd done. It's not really a betrayal, not really. You have Carter."

"What do *I* have to do with this?"

"But I didn't sleep with him, and that's the fine point of it."

A bird winged by, singing like a mad thing. Without sparing it a glance, Emma slapped her hands on her hips and scowled. "The kissing came as a surprise, both times. And the rolling around was just in the heat of the moment. I stopped, so I didn't—technically— break the rule, but I'm apologizing anyway."

"I'll happily accept your apology if you'll just tell me what the hell I have to do with this!"

"The ex rule."

"The . . . Oh, the *EX* rule. Still confused as to my . . . Wait. You think Jack and I were . . . You think I had sex with Jack? Jack Cooke?"

"Of course, Jack Cooke."

"I never had sex with Jack."

Emma poked her. "Yes, you did."

Mac poked her back. "No, I didn't, and I ought to know who I did or didn't have sex with, and Jack and I never did the deed. We never even got close to doing the deed. I have not rolled around on the floor removing clothes with Jack."

"But . . ." Baffled, almost weak with it, Emma dropped her arms to her side. "But when he first started coming home with Del, for vacations and holidays during college, the two of you . . ."

"Flirted. Period. Start and stop. We never hit the sheets, or the floor, or the wall, or any other surface together and in any way approaching nakedness. Clear?"

"I always thought . . ."

Mac quirked her eyebrows. "You could've asked."

"No, because, *damn* it, I wanted to flirt with him, and you already were, so I couldn't, and I thought what I thought. And then when it was obvious you were just friends again, the rule went into effect. I thought."

"You've had a thing for Jack, all this time?"

"On and off. I channeled it into other areas, or restrained it, due to the rule. But recently it's gotten more problematic, the channeling and the restraining. God." Emma slapped her hands over her face. "I'm an idiot."

"You slut." Face stern, Mac folded her arms over her chest. "You almost had sex with a man I never had sex with. What kind of friend are you?"

Emma hung her head as her lips twitched. "I said I was sorry."

"I may forgive you, but only after you tell me all—coherently and in minute detail." Grabbing Emma's arm, Mac jogged the rest of the way to the house. "Which means after coffee, which means after workout."

"We could skip the workout and go straight to coffee."

"No, I'm pumped to pump." Mac led the way through the side door of the main house and toward the stairs. When they reached the third floor, Laurel and Parker came out of the gym. "Em kissed Jack and they almost had sex."

"What?" Two voices spoke in unison.

"I can't talk about it now. I haven't had coffee. I can't talk about it until I do, and unless there are pancakes." Snarling with dislike, Emma stalked to the elliptical.

"Pancakes. I'll tell Mrs. G." Laurel dashed away.

"Jack? Jack Cooke?" Parker said.

Mac flexed her arms and headed to the Bowflex. "That's what I said."

W HEN THEY SAT IN THE BREAKFAST NOOK, AND EMMA CLUTCHED her first cup of coffee, Mac raised a hand. "Let me tell the first part, because it'll be faster and you'll still have your normal complement of brain cells at the end. So, Emma had the hots for Jack, but thought Jack and I had a thing, including sex, in

100

the way back, so sticking to the No-Ex Rule, she suffered in silence."

"I didn't suffer."

"I'm telling this part. Then during the MBB's reception, Jack did the 'oh, you're so stressed, let me rub your shoulders,' then laid a big wet one on her. Then Parker beeped her."

"That's what was wrong with you. Thanks, Mrs. G." Parker smiled at Mrs. Grady and took one of the pancakes from the platter the housekeeper set on the table.

"So last night, after waiting over a week, she went by his place to give him the what-for. One thing led to another, and they ended up rolling around on the floor naked."

"Half. It wasn't even half naked. It was maybe a quarter naked," Emma calculated. "At the most."

"This morning she apologized to me for nearly having sex with my imaginary ex."

"As well she should," Mrs. Grady put in. "No friend poaches another friend's man, even if she's kicked him to the curb."

"It just sort of happened," Emma began and hunched under Mrs. Grady's cool stare. "I said I was sorry, and I stopped before we actually . . ."

"That's because you're a good girl with an honest heart. Eat some of that fruit now. It's fresh. Sex is better when you're eating healthy."

"Yes, ma'am." Emma stabbed a little chunk of pineapple.

"I don't get why you ever thought Mac had been sleeping with Jack in the first place." Laurel dumped syrup on her pancakes. "If she had, she'd have bragged about it and talked about it until we all wanted her dead."

"No, I wouldn't."

"In the way back you would have."

Mac considered. "Yes, that's true. In the way back I would have. I've evolved."

"How hot are the hots?" Parker wanted to know.

"Extremely. He hit high prior to the back stairs. After, he set a record."

Nodding, Parker ate. "He's an exceptional kisser."

"He really is. He . . . How do you know?" When Parker just smiled, Emma's jaw dropped. "*You?* You and Jack? When? How?"

"I think it's disgusting," Mac muttered. "Yet another best pal moving on my imaginary ex."

"Two kisses, my first year at Yale, after we ran into each other at a party and he walked me back to the dorm. It was nice. Very nice. But as exceptional a kisser as he is, it was too much like kissing my brother. And as exceptional a kisser as I am, I believe he felt it was too much like kissing his sister. And that's how we left it. I gather that wasn't an issue for you and Jack."

"We're nowhere in the vicinity of brother- or sisterhood. Why didn't you ever tell us you kissed Jack?"

"I didn't realize we were supposed to report on every man we've ever kissed. But I could make a list."

Emma laughed. "I bet you could. Laurel? Any Jack incidents to report?"

"I'm feeling very annoyed and deprived that I have none. Even imaginary. It seems like he could've hit on me at least once in all this time. The bastard. How about you, Mrs. G?"

"A very nice one under the mistletoe a few Christmases back. But being the love them and leave them type, I let him off easy so as not to break his heart."

"I'd say Em plans to take him down, and take him down hard." Mac arched her eyebrows. "And that he doesn't have a prayer against the awesome power of Emmaline."

"I don't know. I need to think. It's complicated. He's a friend. Our friend. And he's Del's best friend. Del's your brother," she said to Parker, "and the next thing to a brother to the rest of us. And we're all friends, *and* business partners. Del's our lawyer, and

Jack helps out when we need him. Plus he's designing the remodeling. We have all these connections, and they're all tangled up."

"And nothing tangles up the tangles like sex," Mac put in.

"Exactly. What if we end up having this thing, then the thing goes south. Then we're awkward with each other, and that makes the rest of us awkward with the rest of us. We have a kind of balance, don't we? Sex isn't worth upsetting the balance."

"You wouldn't be doing it right then," Mrs. Grady commented, and shook her head. "Youth thinks too damn much. I'm going to start the wash."

Emma sulked over her pancakes. "She thinks I'm being an idiot, but I just don't want anyone to get hurt."

"Then set the ground rules going in. What you each expect from each other, and how you'll handle any complications."

"What kind of ground rules?"

Parker shrugged. "That's for you to decide, Em."

CHAPTER SEVEN

AT HER WORKTABLE WITH A SOOTHING NEW AGE MIX IN THE background, Emma processed a delivery. For the midweek, off-site bridal shower, she'd opted for fun and female. The gerbera daisies were just the ticket.

Visualizing the finished arrangement, she cut the lower inch of the stems under water. Fresh and pretty, she thought as she transferred the daisies to her solution of water, flower food, and preservatives.

She carried the first batch to the cooler for rehydrating. As she started on the next batch, she heard Parker call out to her.

"Back here!"

Parker came in, took a look at the flowers, foliage, buckets, tools. "McNickey bridal shower?"

"Yes. Just look at the color of these geberas. From soft to vibrant. They're going to be perfect."

"What are you doing with them?"

"For the centerpiece, a trio of topiaries in pots I'm covering with lemon leaf. I'll work in some waxflower and acacia, add some sheer ribbon. The client wants a couple others, a more elaborate arrangement for her entry table, another with candles to put in her fireplace, and something delicate, fragrant, and pretty for the powder room. I need to get them all processed before my eleven o'clock consult. It's moving along."

"Festive and female." Parker scanned the work space. "I know you've got a pretty full slate. Can you squeeze another off-site event in?"

"When?"

"Next Thursday. I know," she said as Emma slid over a cool stare. "The potential client called the main number, and since I knew you were elbow deep in a delivery I didn't transfer it. She was at the Folk-Harrigan wedding. Tells me she just couldn't get over the flowers—which is another score for us over MBB."

"You're using that to seduce me."

"Yes, I am. She'd planned to just go buy some cut flowers and do some vases, but now that she's seen your work, she's obsessed. She can't get over how beautiful they were."

"Stop it."

"How gorgeous and creative and perfect."

"Damn you, Parker."

"She can't sleep or eat or function in any normal fashion now that she's seen what can be done with flowers."

"I hate you. What kind of event, and how much is she after?"

Parker's smile managed to be both smug and sympathetic. Emma considered it a major skill.

"A baby shower, and it sounds similar to what you're doing here. Except for the fireplace arrangement. Very girly—the baby's a girl—so she's looking for a lot of pink. But told me she'd trust your judgment."

"It's cutting it close. I have to see what my wholesaler can do. And I'd have to take a look at next week."

"I already did. Your Monday's solid, but you have a block Tuesday afternoon. You start designing Wednesday for Friday's event, Thursday for Saturday's. You've got Tink coming in to help those two days, so is it realistic the two of you could add this in? It's her daughter-in-law," Parker added. "And her first grandchild."

Emma sighed. "You knew that would do it."

"Yes, I did." She patted Emma's shoulder, unrepentant. "If you need it, you can call in Tiffany or Beach."

"Tink and I can handle it." Emma carried the next batch to the cooler, then came back to finish. "I'll call the client as soon as I'm done here, make sure we understand what she's after. Then I'll make sure I can get it."

"I put her name and number on your desk."

"Of course you did. It's going to cost you."

"What's your price?"

"The garage called. My car's finished, but I can't get in to pick it up today. And tomorrow's nearly as full."

"I'll take care of it."

"Knew you would." Looking at what crowded her plate, Emma rubbed the back of her neck. "The hour you save me can go toward the expectant grandma."

"I'll get back to her, take her off her tenterhooks, and let her know you'll be in touch. And speaking of touch, have you talked to Jack?"

"No. I'm in the mulling and musing stage. If I talked to him I'd start thinking how much I'd like to jump him or be jumped by him. Which, of course, since I brought it up, I'm thinking about right now."

"Should I give you a moment of privacy?"

"Very funny. I told him we needed to stop and think, so I'm stopping and thinking." Her brow creased and she made her voice prim. "Sex isn't everything."

"Since you have more of it—and offers for more of it—than I do, I'll bow to your superior knowledge."

"That's because I'm not intimidating." She flicked Parker a glance. "I didn't mean that as an insult."

"I don't mind being intimidating. It saves time. Which," she added with a look at her watch, "I have to consider now. I'm meeting a bride in town. Mac's got a delivery to make. I'll run and catch her before she goes, have her drop me off at the garage. I should be back by four. Don't forget we have an evening consult tonight. Six thirty."

"I've got it on my appointment book."

"I'll see you then. Thanks, Emma. Really," Parker added as she hurried out again.

Alone, Emma cleaned off her work area before reaching for the Neosporin she used like other women used hand cream. With her latest nicks and scratches tended, she set up for her consult.

Satisfied with the selection of arrangements, photo albums, and magazines, she called the number Parker had left her—and made a grandmother-to-be very happy. As they spoke she took notes, made calculations on the number of baby roses, mini calla lilies. Pink for the roses, white for the callas. More calculations as she designed the larger arrangement in her head. Eggplant callas, Bianca roses, pink spray roses.

Sweet, female, but with elegant touches—if she read the client correctly. She added to her notes, jotted down the time and place for delivery, and promised the client an e-mail contract and itemization by midafternoon.

Gauging the time, she put in a hurried call to her wholesaler, then popped up to peel off her work clothes and suit up.

While she freshened her makeup, she wondered if Jack was musing and mulling.

On impulse, she dashed to her computer to send him an e-mail.

108

I'm still thinking. Are you?

She hit Send before she could change her mind.

$\mathcal{I}$N HIS OFFICE, JACK CHECKED THE CHANGES HIS ASSOCIATE had done. The new construction project continued to be tweaked as the clients waffled. They wanted stately, he thought, and they'd gotten it. They'd also wanted six fireplaces. Until they'd decided they needed nine. And an elevator.

The latest change involved enclosing the projected swimming pool for year-round use and attaching it to the house via a breezeway.

Nice job, Chip, he thought even as he made a couple of small changes. He studied the result, then the drawings submitted by the structural engineer.

Good, he decided. Very, very good. The dignity of Georgian Colonial wasn't compromised. And the client could do laps in January.

Everybody's happy.

He started to send an e-mail clearing the drawings for submission to the client, and noticed the mail from Emma.

He clicked it open, read the single line.

Was she kidding?

Every thought that didn't revolve around her—particularly a naked her—was a struggle. Everything he'd done that morning had taken twice as long as it should have *because* he was thinking.

No point in telling her that, he decided. So just how did he answer? He angled his head, and smiled as he hit Reply.

I'm thinking you should come over tonight wearing nothing but a trench coat and elbow pads.

After he clicked Send, he sat back and imagined—very well— what Emma might look like in a trench coat. And maybe really high heels, he thought. Red ones. And once he'd loosened the belt of the coat, he'd—

"Got the go to come on back."

With his mind still opening a trench coat—short, black—Jack stared at Del.

"So hey, where the hell are you?"

"Ah . . . just work. Drawings." Shit. Casually, he hoped, he brought up his screen saver. "No work for you?"

"I'm on my way to the courthouse, and you have better coffee."

Del strolled over to the setup on the counter, and helped himself. "Ready to lose?"

"Lose what?"

"It's Poker Night, pal, and I'm feeling lucky."

"Poker Night."

Eyebrows lifting, Del studied him. "What the hell are you working on? You look like you've just shifted dimensions."

"It just shows my uncanny ability to focus on the job at hand. Which I'll be doing with poker tonight. You'll have to do a lot more than feel lucky to win."

"Side bet. A hundred."

"Done."

Del toasted him, drank. "How's it going on the additions for the Quartet?"

"I've got something I like for Mac and Carter. I just want to refine it a little more."

"Good. Are you working on Emma?"

"What? Am I what?"

"Emma. The second cooler?"

"Not yet. It . . . shouldn't be complicated." Then why was it? Jack wondered. Why did he feel like he was lying to his closest friend?

"Simple works. I've got to go be a lawyer." Del set the mug

110

down, started to the door. "See you tonight. Oh, and try not to cry when you pay me the hundred. It's embarrassing."

Jack shot up a middle finger, so Del walked away laughing.

Jack waited ten full seconds, ear cocked for any sound of return before bringing up his e-mail again.

No reply, yet, from Emma.

How could he have forgotten it was Poker Night? That sort of thing was engraved on his brain. Pizza, beer, cigars, cards. Men only. A tradition, maybe even a ritual, that he and Del had established when they'd still been in college.

Poker Night was sacred.

What if she said she'd be there? That she'd be knocking on his door tonight?

He thought of Emma in a black trench coat and red high heels.

He thought of good friends, cold beer, and a hot deck of cards.

Of course, he thought, there was only one answer. If she got back to him and said she'd come by, he'd simply explain.

He'd tell Del he'd come down with a violent case of stomach flu.

No man living or dead would blame him.

*M*AC GLANCED OVER AT PARKER AS SHE DROVE TOWARD GREEN-wich. "Okay, it's just you and me. What do you really think of Emma and Jack?"

"They're both adults, single, healthy."

"Uh-huh. What do you really think of Emma and Jack?"

Parker let out a sigh that ended on a reluctant laugh. "That I never saw it coming, and I thought I was good at that kind of thing. And if it feels this weird to me, it must feel a lot weirder for them."

"Weird bad?"

"No. No. Just odd. There's the four of us, and the two of them—Jack and Del. Together it's the six of us. Well, seven with Carter, but this is all rooted in pre-Carter. We've been in and out of each other's lives and business for years. Forever for the four of us and Del, and for what, a dozen years with Jack? When you think of a man as a brother, it's an adjustment to realize not everyone in that same network feels the same. It's almost as strange as it would be if one of us really disliked him."

"That's what's hanging Em up."

"I got that."

"They get all sexy, and that's good, but then the heat backs off. Maybe it backs off for one of them before the other. That's awkward." Mac checked her mirrors before changing lanes. "Does the one who's still warmed up get their feelings hurt, or feel sort of betrayed?"

"Feelings are feelings. I don't understand why people blame other people for what they feel."

"Maybe not, but they do. And Emma is the softest of soft touches. She's a whiz at handling men—I bow in awe—but she really *feels* for them if she doesn't . . . feel for them. You know what I mean."

"Yeah." Because they approached the garage, Parked slipped back into the shoes she'd slipped off when she'd gotten in the car. "She'll end up going out with a guy a second, third, fourth time even when she figured out from the first date she wasn't interested. She doesn't want to hurt his feelings."

"Still, she dates more than the three of us put together. Pre-Carter," Mac added. "And she nearly always manages to shake a man off without denting his ego. I tell you, she's skilled."

"The trouble is, she's closer to Jack. She loves him."

"You think—"

"We *all* love him," Parker finished.

"Oh, that way. True."

"It has to be hard to break off a relationship with someone you really care about. And being Emma, she's trying to work that part of it out before they up the relationship. Hurting him isn't an option for her."

Mac considered as she waited at a light. "Sometimes I wish I was as genuinely nice as Emma. But not very often. It's too much work."

"You have your moments. Me? I'm intimidating."

Mac snorted. "Oh yeah, you scare the shit out of me, Parks." She eased through the light. "But you are pretty scary when you put the Parker Brown of the Connecticut Browns cloak on. And if you give it that little swirl, many fall dead."

"Not dead. Temporarily stunned perhaps."

"You knocked Linda cold," Mac commented, speaking of her mother.

"You handled that yourself. You stood up to her."

Mac shook her head. "I'd stood up to her before. Maybe not like this last time, not as tall and straight. But if I started it, you finished her off for me. You add in Carter, and the fact that as, God, *kind* as he is, he's not susceptible to her bullshit—then the fact she's getting pampered by her rich fiance in New York? My life's gotten a lot smoother."

"Has she contacted you since?"

"Funny you should ask. This morning, in fact, and as if we'd never had that really ugly last scene. She and Ari have decided to elope. Sort of. Those crazy kids are jetting off to Lake Como next month, and they'll be married at the villa of one of Ari's dear friends once Linda's planned all the details—which is her version of eloping, I guess."

"Oh God, if you say George Clooney, I'm going to go."

"If only. I don't think we're invited anyway. She mostly

113

called to make sure I understood she's doing a *lot* better than Vows for her wedding."

"What did you say?"

"Buona fortuna."

"You did?"

"I did. It felt good. And I actually meant it. I do wish her luck. If she's happy with this Ari, she'll leave me the hell alone. So . . ." She turned, turned again, and pulled into the lot of Kavanaugh's. "It's all good. Do you want me to wait, just in case?"

"No, you go on. I'll see you back at the house for tonight's consult."

Parker got out, adjusted her grip on her portfolio bag as she checked the time. Right on schedule.

She scanned the long building that housed what appeared to be offices attached to a large garage. She heard the *whoosh* of some sort of compressor as she approached, and saw through the open garage doors the legs, hips, and most of the torso of the mechanic who worked on a car on a lift.

She caught glimpses of shelves, which she assumed held parts and other paraphernalia, racks of tools. Tanks, hoses.

She smelled oil and sweat, not offensive to her mind. Work odors, productive scents. She approved of them, especially since she saw Emma's car sitting in the lot, very clean and very shiny.

Curious, she detoured to it. The chrome glinted in the sunlight, and through the window she noted the signs of meticulous detailing.

If, she mused, the car ran as good as it looked, she'd bring hers here instead of to the dealer for its next regular service.

She crossed the lot toward the office to settle the bill and get the key.

Inside, a woman with hair more orange than red sat on a stool at the short leg of an L-shaped counter, pecking with two fingers at the keyboard of a computer.

Her brow furrowed, her mouth twisted in a way that told Parker the computer was not her friend.

She stopped, sized Parker up over the top of a pair of bright green cheaters. "Help you?"

"Yes, thanks. I'm here to pick up Emmaline Grant's car."

"You Parker Brown?"

"Yes."

"She called, said you'd be coming to get it."

When the woman made no move, just continued to stare over the tops of her glasses, Parker smiled politely. "Would you like to see some identification?"

"No. She said what you looked like when I asked, and you look like what she said."

"Well then, if I could see the bill?"

"I'm working on it." The woman shifted on the stool, pecked at the keys again. "You can sit right down there. It won't take me long. Take less time if I could just write it out on an invoice pad, but Mal has to have it this way."

"All right."

"Vending machines through that door there if you want something to drink."

Parker thought of her client, and the distance to the bridal boutique, the traffic. "You said it wouldn't take long."

"It won't. I'm just saying . . . What does this demon from hell want from me?" The woman raked long red nails through her orange frizzy hair. "Why won't it just spit the damn thing out?"

"May I . . ." Parker leaned over the counter, scanned the screen. "I think I see the problem. Just point and click here, with the mouse." She tapped the screen. "Good. Now see where it says Print? Click that. There you go. Now click on Okay."

Parker leaned back as the printer clicked into life. "There you go."

"Click this, click that. I can never remember which click

115

comes first." But she looked over the counter and smiled for the first time. Her eyes were as bold and engaging a green as the frames of her cheaters. "Appreciate it."

"No problem."

Parker took the bill, sighed a little as she ran down the work. New battery, tune-up, timing, oil change, fan belts, tire rotation, brake pads. "I don't see the charge for the detailing."

"No charge. First-time customer. Complimentary."

"Very nice." Parker paid the bill, then tucked her copy in a pocket of her bag. She took the key. "Thank you."

"Welcome. Come back when you need to."

"I believe I will."

Outside, she walked toward Emma's car, clicking the key lock as she went.

"Hey, hey, hold it."

She stopped, turned. She recognized the legs, hips, torso she'd seen under the belly of the car in the garage. This view added chest and shoulders. The light spring breeze fluttered through dark hair—that needed a trim—disordered either from work or carelessness. She supposed it suited the strong, sharp lines of his face, and the dark stubble that indicated he hadn't picked up a razor in a day or two.

She took it all in quickly, just as she took in the hard set of his mouth and the hot green of eyes that transmitted temper.

She'd have looked down her nose if she hadn't been forced to look up when he stopped in front of her. She angled her head up, met his eyes with hers, and said in her coolest tone, "Yes?"

"You think all it takes is a key and a driver's license?"

"I beg your pardon?"

"Your battery cables were covered with corrosion, your oil was sludge. Your tires were low and your brake pads damn near shot. I bet you slather yourself with some fancy cream every day of your life."

116

"Excuse me?"

"But you can't bother to get your car serviced. Lady, this car was a disgrace. You probably spent more on those shoes than you have on maintaining it."

Her shoes? Her shoes were none of his damn business. But she kept her tone bland—insultingly bland. "I appreciate you have passion for your work, but I doubt your boss would approve of the way you speak to customers."

"I am the boss, and I'm fine with it."

"I see. Well, Mr. Kavanaugh, you have an interesting business manner. Now, if you'll excuse me."

"There's no excuse for the way you've neglected this vehicle. I've got it up and running for you, Ms. Grant, but—"

"Brown," she interrupted. "That's Ms. Brown."

He narrowed his eyes as he studied her face. "Del's sister. Should've seen it. Who's Emmaline Grant?"

"My business partner."

"Fine. Pass on what I said to her. It's a good car. It deserves better."

"Be sure I will."

She reached for the door, but he beat her to it, opened it for her. She got in, placed her bag on the seat beside her, fastened her seat belt. Then froze the air between them with a "Thank you."

He grinned, fast as a lightning strike. "You mean go to hell. Drive safe," he added and shut the door.

She turned the key, found herself mildly disappointed when the engine purred like a kitten. As she drove away, she glanced in the rearview mirror, saw him standing, hip-shot, watching her.

Rude, she thought—absurdly rude, really. But he apparently knew how to do his job.

When she parked near the bridal boutique where she intended to meet her client, Parker pulled out her BlackBerry to e-mail Emma.

Em. Car is done. Looks and runs better than it has since you bought it. You owe me more than the bill. Will discuss tonight. P

$\mathscr{A}$T HOME, EMMA USED THE TIME BETWEEN APPOINTMENTS TO write itemized contracts. She loved the choices made by her last client, a December bride. Color, color, and more color, she thought. All that hot and bold would be a pleasure to work with in winter.

She sent the contract to the client for approval, copied Parker for Vows' files. She smiled when she spotted an e-mail from Jack. Then snorted out a laugh as she read it.

"Trench coat and elbow pads. Good one. Let's see . . ."

You'll need to choose between my red lace elbow pads and the black velvet set. Or I can just surprise you. I'll try them on later with my collection of trench coats. I have a particular favorite. It's black and has a shine so it always looks . . . wet.

Unfortunately tonight won't work for me. But that gives us both more time to think.

"That ought to give you a moment or two," Emma murmured, and hit Send.

118

CHAPTER EIGHT

At six, Emma walked into the kitchen from the mud-room as Parker walked in from the hall.

"Good timing. Hi, Mrs. G."

"Grilled chicken Caesars," Mrs. Grady announced. "Use the breakfast nook. I'm not setting up the dining room when you girls are going to be coming in and out and picking."

"Yes, ma'am. I worked through lunch. I'm starved."

"Have a glass of wine with it." Mrs. Grady jerked her head toward Parker. "This one's in a mood."

"I'm not in any particular mood." But Parker took one of the glasses of wine Mrs. Grady poured. "Your bill."

Emma glanced at the bottom line, winced. "Ouch. I guess I deserve it."

"Maybe so. But *I* didn't deserve the angry lecture from the proprietor who assumed I was you."

"Uh-oh. What hospital is he in? I should send flowers."

"He survived, unscathed. Partially because I was on a schedule and didn't have time to hurt him. Your car was also detailed, expertly, inside and out—gratis to first-time customers. Which counted in his favor. Marginally."

Pausing, Parker took another sip of wine. "Mrs. G, you know everyone."

"Whether I want to or not. Sit. Eat." When they had, Mrs. Grady plopped down on one of the counter stools with her own glass of wine. "You want to know about young Malcolm Kavanaugh. Bit of a wild one. Army brat. His father died overseas when he was a boy. Ten or twelve, I think, which may account for the bit of wild. His ma had a hard time keeping him in line. She used to waitress at Artie's, the place on the avenue. He'd be her brother, Artie would, and why she moved here when she lost her husband."

Mrs. Grady took a sip of wine, and settled back a bit to tell the rest. "As you may know, Artie Frank is a complete asshole, and his wife is a prissy snob of a woman. What I heard was Artie decided to take the boy in hand, and the boy did his level best to snap that hand off at the wrist. And good for him," she added with some relish. "He went off, the boy did, to race cars or motorcycles or something like. Did some stunt work in the movies, I believe. Did well enough for himself, from what I'm told. And made sure his ma got a piece of the pie he was making."

"Well. That speaks well of him, I suppose," Parker allowed.

"Got busted up on a stunt, and got some kind of settlement out of it. He used it to buy the garage out on Route One, about three years ago. Bought his ma a little house as well. He's built up a nice business, from what I'm told, and still has a bit of the wild in him."

"I'll assume he's built up his business through his skill with engines and not through his skill with customer relations."

"Put your back up," Emma commented.

"I'll get over it, as long as he does the job well." Parker glanced over as Laurel came in. "Cutting it close."

"Coffee and cookies are set up. Some of us don't have time to sit around eating and gossiping before a consult." Laurel frowned as she combed her fingers through her hair. "Plus you're having wine."

"Parker was in a mood because—"

"I heard all about that already." Laurel poured herself a scant half glass. "I want new juice. What's the current situation with Jack?"

"I think we're having virtual sex. We're still in the early stages of foreplay, so I'm not sure where it's going."

"I've never had cyber sex. I've never liked anyone enough to have cyber sex." Laurel cocked her head as she considered. "And that sounds odd. I like a guy well enough to have actual sex, but not virtual?"

"Because it's a game." Emma got up to give Laurel the remaining half of her salad. "You might like a man enough to go to bed with him, but you might not want to play with him."

"That makes weird sense." With a nod, Laurel stabbed at the salad. "You always make weird sense when it comes to men."

"And obviously she likes Jack enough to play with him," Parker added.

"Jack's got a sense of fun, which is one of the things I've always liked about him. And found attractive." Emma's lips curved in a slow, easy smile. "We'll see how much we like playing games."

In the parlor, over coffee and Laurel's macaroons, Parker led the consult with the engaged couple and their mothers. "As I explained to Mandy and Seth, Vows will tailor our services to suit your needs. As much or as little as you want. Our goal,

121

together and individually, is to give you the perfect wedding. *Your* perfect wedding. Now, when we spoke last, you hadn't chosen a date, but had decided you wanted evening and outdoors."

Emma listened with half an ear as dates were discussed.

She wondered if Jack had gotten her e-mail yet.

The bride wanted romance. Didn't they all? Emma thought, but perked up when she said she'd be wearing her grandmother's wedding gown.

"I have a photo," Mandy announced, "but Seth isn't allowed to see. So . . ."

"Seth, would you like a beer?"

He looked over at Laurel, grinned. "I would."

"Why don't you come with me? I'll set you up. When you've finished the beer we should be ready for you again."

"Thanks." Mandy reached into a large folder when Laurel led Seth out. "I know it's probably silly—"

"Not at all." Parker held out a hand for the photo, and her polite expression turned radiant. "Oh. Oh, it's gorgeous. It's just stunning. Late thirties, early forties?"

"You're good," the mother of the bride said. "My parents were married in 1941. She was just eighteen."

"Ever since I was a little girl I talked about wearing Nana's wedding gown when I got married. It needs to be fitted, and a little repair, but Nana's taken good care of it."

"Do you have a seamstress in mind?"

"We've spoken to Esther Brightman."

As she studied the photo, Parker nodded approval. "She's a genius, and exactly who'd I recommend for this. Mandy, you're going to look absolutely amazing. And we could, if you want, build the entire wedding around this dress. Vintage glamour with class, romance with style. Tails rather than the more expected tux for the groom and groomsmen."

122

"Oh, wow. Wow. Would he go for that?" she asked her future mother-in-law.

"He'll go for anything you want, honey. Personally, I love the idea. We'd want to find vintage dresses, or the vintage style for the bridal party."

Emma studied the photo when it came to her. Fluid, she thought, Deco-inspired lines, with a sheen that said silk. She lifted her gaze to study Mandy, and decided the new bride would wear the gown as beautifully as her grandmother had. "I can replicate the bouquet," she said half to herself.

"What?" Mandy cut herself off in midsentence and swung her attention to Emma.

"The bouquet—if you wanted—I can replicate it. Look how clever she was, how smart to offset the long, fluid lines of the gown with the oversized crescent of calla lilies. Do you have the veil and headpiece?"

"Yes."

"From what I can see, she had it trimmed with lily-of-the-valley. I can do that, if it appeals to you. I just wanted to mention that before Seth comes back. Something you can think about."

"I love it! Mom?"

"My mother will be a puddle. So will I. I love it, too."

"We'll talk about it in more detail when we do our individual consult. Meanwhile, when you select the dresses for the bridesmaids, if you can get pictures then I can get copies made or you can scan them in an e-mail so I can see what kind of flowers she chose for them."

Emma handed the photo back to Mandy. "You'd better put that away."

"Mac, why don't you give Mandy an overview of the photography?"

"First, I want to duplicate the pose in your grandmother's

123

formal portrait. It's classic and gorgeous. But tonight, we should talk about what you'd like for your engagement portraits."

They moved from stage to stage, step to step, with a rhythm they'd developed over the years. As they discussed photography, cakes, food, Emma jotted down keywords that would help her create a picture of the bride, the groom, and what they envisioned.

And if her thoughts veered in Jack's direction a few times, she reminded herself she excelled at multitasking.

By the time she and her partners walked the clients to the door, she was ready to duck out and see if Jack had answered her e-mail.

"Good job," she said. "I'm going to go home and start a file for the event. So—"

"There's something else," Parker interrupted. "When I was at the boutique today, I found Mac's dress."

"You what?" Mac blinked at her. "*My* dress?"

"I know you, and what you're looking for. And since it was right there, saying I'm Mac's, I used our connections and brought it home for approval. Maybe I'm wrong, but I thought at least you'd want to try it on."

"You brought home a wedding dress for me to try on?" Eyes narrowed, Mac pointed at Parker. "Aren't you the one who's always telling brides they might try on a hundred dresses before they find the one?"

"Yes. You're not most brides. You know immediately what works and what doesn't. If it doesn't, no harm done. Why don't we go take a look? It's up in the Bride's Suite."

"Oh, we *have* to see." Thrilled with the idea, Emma grabbed Mac's hand and tugged. "Wait, we need champagne. Which Parker would have thought of already."

"Mrs. G will have it up there by now."

"Champagne and a potential wedding dress?" Mac mused.

"What are we waiting for? No hurt feelings if I don't like it," she added as they started up the stairs.

"Absolutely not. If you don't it would only tell me how vastly superior my taste is to yours." With the faintest of smirks, Parker opened the door to the Bride's Suite where Mrs. Grady poured flutes of champagne.

"Heard you coming." And she winked at Parker as Mac simply stared at the gown hanging from the hook.

"It's beautiful," Mac murmured. "It's . . ."

"Strapless, which I think will suit you," Parker continued. "And the slight A-line will flatter your build. I know you were leaning toward something completely unadorned, but I think you're wrong. The tissue organza over the silk adds romance, softens the lines. You're angular. And the back?"

Parker lifted it off the hook, turned it around.

"I love it!" Emma pushed forward. "The ruffle train, out of the organza! It's fabulous, just a little flirty. Plus the way it should drape over your butt—"

"Will actually give you one," Laurel finished. "Try it on, or I will."

"Give me a second, this is a moment. Okay, there's the moment." And Mac unhooked her pants. As she stripped down, Emma circled a finger.

"Turn your back to the mirror. You don't want to see yourself putting it on. You want the *pow* effect once you're in it."

"Dropping your clothes where you stand." Mrs. Grady shook her head as she scooped them up. "Just as you always have. Well, help her into it," she ordered, and stood back, smiled.

"Oh. I'm going to cry." Emma sniffled while Parker fastened the gown in place.

"They didn't have your size, so it's a little big."

"That's what I'm here for." Mrs. Grady picked up her pin cushion. "We'll nip and tuck a bit here and there so it shows

125

better on you. It's a shame you've always been such an ugly thing."

"Insult me, but don't stick me."

"That'll do for now." Mrs. Grady stepped around to fuss a little with the bodice, then reached up to smooth Mac's bright red hair. "We have to work with what we've got."

"Count to three, Mac, then turn and look." Emma pressed both hands to her lips. "Just look at you."

"Okay." Mac took in a breath, let it out, then turned toward the cheval glass where she'd watched so many brides study their reflections. The only thing she could say was "Oh!"

"And that says it all." Laurel blinked at tears. "It's . . . it. You're it in it."

"It's . . . I'm . . . Holy shit, I'm a bride." Mac's fingers fluttered up to her heart as she angled herself. "Oh, check out the back. It's fun, and female, and I *do* have an ass." In the glass, her gaze shifted to Parker's. "Parks."

"Am I good or am I good?"

"You're the best. This is my wedding dress. Aw, Mrs. G."

Mrs. Grady dabbed her eyes. "I'm just shedding a tear of joy that I won't have four spinsters on my hands."

"Flowers in your hair. A wide floral headband instead of a veil," Emma suggested.

"Really?" Pursing her lips, Mac studied herself, imagined. "That could work. That could work well."

"I'll show you some ideas. And you know, I think with the lines of the dress, I'd like to see a long sweep of a bouquet, probably hand tied. Maybe arm-carried." Emma angled one arm, swept her hand down to demonstrate. "Or a cascade, but with a waterfall effect. Rich, warm autumn colors, and . . . I'm getting ahead of myself."

"No. God, we're planning my wedding. I think I need that drink."

Retrieving Mac's flute, Laurel stepped to her. "It sure looks better on you than any of our old Wedding Day costumes."

"Plus, it doesn't itch."

"I'm going to make you one hell of a cake."

"Oh man, I'm watering up again."

"Turn around, all of you," Mrs. Grady ordered as she took a camera out of her pocket. "Our redhead's not the only one who can take a picture. Glasses up. There's my girls," she murmured, and captured the moment.

$\mathcal{W}$HILE THE LADIES DRANK CHAMPAGNE AND DISCUSSED WED-ding flowers, Jack popped a beer and prepared to fleece friends at Texas Hold 'Em.

And tried not to think about Emma and her latest e-mail.

"Since it's Carter's first official Poker Night, let's try not to humiliate him." Del clapped a friendly hand on Carter's shoulder. "Taking his money's one thing, embarrassing him's another."

"I'll be gentle," Jack promised.

"I could just watch."

"Now where's the fun and profit in that. For us?" Del asked.

"Ha," Carter managed.

They mingled around Del's lower level. A boy's dream space, in Jack's opinion, with its antique bar that had once served pints in Galway, its slate pool table, its flat-screen TV—an auxiliary to the even bigger one in the media room on the other side of the house. It boasted a vintage jukebox, video games, and two classic pinball machines. Leather chairs, sofas that could take a beating. And a Vegas-style poker table just waiting for action.

No wonder he and Del were friends.

"If you were a girl," Jack said to Del, "I'd marry you."

"No. You'd just have sex with me then never call me."

"You're probably right."

Since it was there, Jack snagged a slice of pizza. Skinning friends was hungry work. As he ate he considered the group. Two lawyers, the professor, the architect, the surgeon, the landscape designer—and as he watched the last player come through the door—the mechanic.

Interesting group, he thought. It fluctuated from time to time with a new addition, like Carter, or when one of them couldn't make it. The tradition of Poker Night had begun when he and Del had met in college. The faces might change off and on, but the foundation remained.

Eat, drink, tell lies, talk sports. And try to win money from your friends.

"We're all here. Want a beer, Mal?" Del asked.

"I'm breathing. How's it going?" Mal said to Jack.

"Well enough. The new blood's Carter Maguire. Carter, Malcolm Kavanaugh."

Mal nodded. "Hey."

"Nice to meet you. Kavanaugh? The mechanic?"

"Guilty."

"You towed my future mother-in-law's car."

"Yeah? Did she want me to?"

"No. Linda Barrington."

Mal narrowed his eyes. "Okay. Yeah. The BMW convertible. The 128i."

"Um. I guess."

"Nice ride. Interesting woman." Mal smirked as he lifted his beer again. "Good luck with that."

"The daughter doesn't take after the mother," Del put in.

"Lucky for you," Mal said to Carter. "I met her—the daughter. Mackensie, right? She's hot. She does the bride thing with the Cobalt I just serviced."

"Emma," Del added.

"Right. She ought to be arrested for vehicular abuse. I met

128

your sister when she picked it up," he told Del, and grinned. "She's hot, too. Even when she gives you the deep freeze."

"So . . . Emma didn't pick up her car?"

Mal glanced at Jack. "No, the other one did. *Ms. Brown*." He took a hit of his beer. "The one who says 'excuse me' and means 'fuck you.'"

"That would be Parker," Del confirmed.

"Does the car abuser look as good as the other two?"

"They all look good," Jack murmured.

"Sorry I missed her."

"Before I have to punch Mal for thinking lascivious thoughts about my sisters—biological and honorary," Del said, "let's play cards."

"Be right there." As the others wandered to the table, Jack pulled out his phone to check his e-mails.

$\mathcal{I}$T WAS NEARLY MIDNIGHT WHEN EMMA GOT HOME. ONCE they'd started talking plans and ideas for Mac's wedding, time whizzed.

She all but bounced into the house, energized by the evening, and just a little giddy on champagne.

Mac's wedding.

She could already see how utterly perfect the bride would be in her gorgeous gown, a waterfall of flowers in her arms. And she, Parker, and Laurel, triple maids of honor. Russet for her, autumn gold for Parker, pumpkin for Laurel. And oh, the flowers she'd do with that rich palette of fall.

It would be a challenge, Emma thought as she started upstairs. Parker had been right to point that out so they could begin to plan how it could and would be done. Running a wedding was one thing. Running it and being part of it was another.

129

They'd need extra help, more subs, but they'd not only do it, they'd knock it out of the park.

Cruising on the mood, she began her nightly ritual. When her bed was turned down, she nodded, smoothed the sheets. There, she'd shown a very mature restraint. An evening with friends—business and pleasure—and no neglecting of her night-time routine.

It proved she was a sensible adult.

Crossing the fingers of both hands, she dashed from her bedroom to her office to bring up her e-mail.

"There, I knew it."

She clicked open Jack's latest message.

Now you're playing dirty. Thanks.

I like surprises. I especially like unwrapping them, so I look forward to helping you out of your coat. I like to take my time with surprises, build anticipation. So I'm going to unwrap you very slowly. Inch by inch.

"Oh, she said, "my."

And when I have I'm going to want to take a good, long look. Before I touch. Inch by inch.

When, Emma?

"How about right now?"

She closed her eyes and imagined Jack slipping her out of the slick black coat she didn't even own. In a room shimmering with candlelight. Music playing, low and hot—so you felt the bass beat in the blood.

His eyes, dangerous as hellsmoke, gliding over her until heat drenched her skin. Then his hands, strong, sure, slow, following that path of heat, easing the velvet on her elbows down until . . .

"That's just silly." She straightened in her chair.

Silly, maybe, she thought, but she'd managed to stir herself up. Or he had.

Time to respond in kind.

I like to play, and I don't mind getting dirty.

Surprises are fun, and being the surprise can be even better. When I am, sometimes I like being unwrapped slowly. Fingertips patiently untying the bow, then hands carefully, very carefully, folding back that wrapping to get to what's waiting inside.

And other times I want those fingers, those hands, to just rip through the barriers. Fast and greedy, and maybe a little rough.

Soon, Jack.

Not *if* any longer, she thought.

Just when.

WITH HER THREE TOPIARIES FINISHED AND TINK DEEP INTO processing another delivery, Emma took a quick look at her notes and sketches.

"Six hand-tied bouquets including the bride's tossing bouquet for Friday's event. Six pedestal arrangements, eighteen centerpieces, white rose ball, garlands, and swags for the pergola." She muttered her way down the list. "I'll need you at least three hours tomorrow. Four would be better."

"I've got a date tonight, and I'm looking to get lucky." Fingers busy, Tink snapped her gum. "I could be here around noon."

"If you can stick till four, that ought to do it. Another four on Thursday. Five if you want it. I've got Tiffany coming in Thursday, and Beach can give me all day Friday. I can use whatever time you can give me Friday morning. We can start dressing for Friday's event at three. Saturday's another twofer. We need to start by eight for the first. That's A.M., Tink."

Tink rolled her eyes, and kept stripping thorns.

"We break down the first at three thirty, and need the second fully dressed by five thirty. Sunday, we have a big one, a single starting at four. So we'll need to start at ten or ten thirty."

"I'll try to squeeze what there is of my life in there," Tink said dolefully.

"You'll manage. I'll take what you've processed back to the cooler and get the stock we need for the arrangements." As she picked up the first container and turned, Jack walked in.

"Oh . . . Hi."

"Hi back. How's it going, Tink?"

"Emma drives the slaves."

"Yes, she is abused constantly," Emma said. "You can there-there her while I haul these back to the cooler."

God, she thought, he looked so *good* in his in the fieldwork clothes, the boots, the faded jeans, the shirt rolled up to the elbows.

She wished she could take just one quick bite.

"Why don't I give you a hand?" He hefted another tub and started back to the cooler.

"We're a little crazy this week," Emma told him. "A midweek off-site, and four events over the weekend. Sunday's wedding is a monster—in a good way." She set her tub down, gestured where Jack should place his. "Now I need to—"

He spun her around, boosted her up to her toes in one fast move. Her arms locked around his neck in a combination of instinct and answer even as his mouth laid claim to hers.

The wild, rich perfume of flowers saturated the air just as need and pleasure saturated her body. Greed and urgency swam through her blood.

Not just one bite, she thought, and not quick. She wanted gulp after gulp.

"Does that door lock from the inside?"

She tunneled her fingers through his hair to bring his mouth back to hers. "What door?"

"Emma, you're killing me. Let me just—"

"Oh, that door. No. Wait. Damn it. Just one more." She caught his face in her hands this time, let herself simply sink into the kiss, the perfume, the greed. Then eased back.

132

"We can't. Tink. And . . ." Regretfully, she blew out a breath as she glanced around. "There really isn't room in here."

"When is she leaving? I'll come back."

"I don't know, exactly, but . . . Wait."

Now he took her face, met her eyes. "Why?"

"I . . . I can't think of a good reason, but that may be because I lost many thousands of brain cells during that kiss. I can't remember if I have any evening appointments. My mind's wiped clean."

"I'm coming back at seven. I'll bring food. Unless you call me and say otherwise. Seven, here."

"Okay. All right. I'll check my book when I regain the power of cogent thought. But—"

"Seven," he repeated and kissed her again. "If we need to talk, we'll talk."

"It may have to be in short, declarative sentences and words of one or two syllables."

"We can do that." His grin shot fresh heat straight to her belly. "Do you need anything out of here?"

"Yes, but I can't remember what. Give me a second." She pushed her hands through her hair, closed her eyes. "All right, yeah. Those, those. Then you've really got to go away. I can't work if I'm thinking about you, this. Sex. Any of it."

"Tell me about it. Seven," he repeated, and helped her carry out the flowers.

"I'll, uh, get back to you on that," she told him when he set the flowers in her work area. "When I'm not so . . . busy."

"Great." The warm gray eyes lingered on her just a moment longer. "See you, Tink."

"You bet." Tink clipped another few stems while Jack left, then slid them into their holding tub. "So, when did you and Jack start doing it?"

"Doing what? Oh. Tink." Shaking her head, Emma turned

to her shelves to select the proper container for the fireplace arrangement she planned. "We're not."

"If you tell me he didn't plant a big yummy one on you back there, I'm going to call you a liar."

"I don't understand why you . . ." Stupid, Emma told herself, then reached for her flower foam. "How do you know?"

"Because your eyes were still glazed when you came back, and he looked like a guy who'd only gotten a few nibbles when he's ready for a great big bite."

"Bite. Ha-ha."

"Why aren't you doing it? He's prime."

"I'm—we're . . . You know, sex doesn't fluster me. I mean talking about sex, because if actually having sex doesn't fluster you at least a little, you're missing something. But this flusters me."

As she continued to work, Tink nodded sagely. "Moving from friends to friends with benefits has the advantage of knowing who the hell you're getting naked with."

"There's that. But it could be awkward, right? After."

"Only if one of you's an asshole about it." She gave her gum another cheerful snap. "So, my advice—don't be an asshole."

"On some odd level that's actually wise." Emma set the foam to soak. "I need to check something in my appointment book."

"Okay. I'd schedule that nookie in for tonight," Tink called after her. "You'll be the happy flower lady tomorrow."

And there's another point, Emma thought.

She saw by her book she'd left the evening open. She'd marked the date with a large X after five o'clock, her way of warning herself not to get talked into going out. Too much work lined up for a date.

But this wasn't actually a date, she decided. He'd come by, bring food, and then . . . they'd see. She didn't have to change or think about what she should wear or . . .

Who was she kidding? Of course she'd worry about what to wear. There was no way whatever was going to happen with Jack was going to happen while she was wearing her work clothes and her nails were green from stems and foliage.

Plus, she'd need fresh flowers and candles in the bedroom. And she'd be more relaxed if she could take a nice bubble bath. Choosing an outfit was a vital element in an evening like this, not just what went on top, but what was under it.

She closed the book.

When she thought it all through, a not-actual date required more work than an actual one.

She hurried back to her flowers. She had to finish her workday, give the client her best. Then she needed plenty of time before seven to make everything perfect, without making it obvious she'd gone to any trouble at all.

CHAPTER NINE

$\mathscr{S}$HE SETTLED ON A DRESS IN A BREEZY PRINT. CASUAL, EMMA
determined, simple and almost sweet with the little cropped
sweater she paired with it.

And what she wore under it was lethal.

Pleased with the results, she did a final turn in the mirror
before giving the bedroom a close inspection. Candles for soft,
romantic light, lilies and roses for romantic scents. The CD
player set on low with a quiet, romantic mix ready to play.

Pillows plumped, shades drawn.

It was, she decided, a female den of seduction. She was damn
proud of it.

Now all she needed was the man.

She walked downstairs to make sure everything was ready
on that front. Wine, glasses, candles, flowers. Music again, still
low but more upbeat than the mix waiting upstairs. She turned
it on, adjusted the volume, then circled around lighting the
candles.

They'd have some wine, she thought, and talk. Then a meal and more conversation. They'd never had problems with conversation. Even though they knew where the evening was headed—maybe because they knew—they'd be able to talk, relax, just enjoy each other's company before they—

She spun around when the door opened, giddy nerves dancing. And Laurel walked in.

"Hey, Em, can I get you to put together a couple of . . ." Laurel stopped, lifted her eyebrows as she looked around the room. "You've got a date. You have a sex date."

"What? What's wrong with you? Where do you come up with—"

"How long have I known you? This side of forever? You put out new candles. You have foreplay music on."

"I put out new candles all the time, and I happen to like this mix."

"Let me see your underwear."

Emma choked out a laugh. "No. You want me to make up a couple what?"

"That can wait. I have twenty bucks that says you have on the sexing underwear." Laurel strode over, started to tug at the bodice of Emma's dress—and got her hand slapped away.

"Cut it out."

"You took a bath in the tonight's-the-night bubbles." Laurel sniffed. "I can smell it."

"So what? I often have dates. Sometimes I have sex dates. I'm a grown woman. I can't help it if you haven't had sex in six months."

"Five months, two weeks, three days. But who's counting?" Laurel stopped again, sucked in an exaggerated breath as she pointed at Emma. "You have a sex date with Jack."

"Stop it. Will you stop it? You're freaking me out."

"When is he getting here? What's the plan?"

"Soon, and I'm still working on the plan. But it doesn't include you being here. At all. Go away now."

Ignoring the order, Laurel folded her arms. "Is it the white 'I'm a good girl but I can be bad' underwear or the black 'I'm only wearing this so you can rip it off me, big boy' underwear? I need to know."

Emma cast her eyes to the heavens. "It's the red with the black roses."

"We may need to call the paramedics. If you're functional tomorrow, can you make me up three mini arrangements? Just mixed spring types? I have a consult and little springy flowers would set the mood for what I think the client wants."

"Sure. Go home."

"I'm going, I'm going."

"You're stopping at Mac's to tell her before you go home and tell Parker."

Laurel paused at the door, flicked back the hair that fell over her cheek. "Duh. And I'm going to ask Mrs. G if she'll make frittatas for breakfast so we can fuel up while you give us all the details."

"I have a full day tomorrow."

"Me, too. Seven A.M., food and sex recap. Good luck tonight."

Resigned, Emma let out a sigh and decided she wouldn't wait for Jack to have a glass of wine. The trouble with friends, she thought as she went to the kitchen, was they knew you too well. Sex date, foreplay music, sexing underwear. No secrets among . . .

She stopped with the bottle in hand. Jack was a friend. Jack knew her very well. Wouldn't he . . . What if he . . .

"Oh, shit!"

She poured a very large glass of wine. Before she could take the first sip, she heard the knock on her door.

"Too late," she murmured. "Too late to change a thing. Time to see what happens, and deal with it."

She set the wine down, went to the door.

He'd changed, too, she noted. Khakis instead of jeans, a crisp shirt instead of a chambray. He carried a large take-out bag from her favorite Chinese restaurant, and a bottle of her preferred cabernet.

Sweet, Emma thought. And certainly another advantage of being friends.

"When you said you'd bring food you meant it." She took the bag from him. "Thanks."

"You like a little—and that's usually very little—of everything. So I got a variety." He cupped the back of her neck, leaned in to kiss her. "Hi again."

"Hi back again. I just poured myself a glass of wine. Why don't I make it two?"

"I'd say yes. How'd the work go?" he asked when he followed her to the kitchen. "You were pretty much buried in it when I was here earlier."

"We got it done. The next few days are wall-to-wall, but we'll get that done, too." She poured a second glass, offered it. "How about your summer kitchen?"

"It's going to rock. I don't know how much use the clients will get out of it, but it's going to look great. I'll need to talk to you about the work here. Your second cooler. I dropped some preliminary sketches at Parker's when I was by before, for the changes there, and Mac's plans are finished. After spending a little time in your cooler today, it's easy to see why you need another one. I like your dress."

"Thanks." Watching him, she sipped her wine. "I guess we've got other things to talk about, too."

"Where do you want to start?"

"I keep thinking it's a lot, but I realized it really comes down to two things, and they both grow out of one root. We're friends. We are friends, aren't we, Jack?"

"We're friends, Emma."

"So the first thing is I think friends should tell each other the truth. Be honest. If we realize, after tonight, that it's just not what we expected—or if either of us feel like, well, that was nice, but I'm finished—we should be able to say so. No hard feelings."

Reasonable, straightforward, and with no sticky edges or invisible strings. Perfect. "I can go with that."

"The second is staying friends." Worry wove through the words as she watched him. "That's the most important thing. Whatever happens, however it works out, we need to promise each other we'll be friends. Not just for you and me, but for everyone we're connected to. We can say it's just sex, Jack, but sex isn't a just. Or it shouldn't be. We like each other. We care about each other. I don't want anything to change that."

He brushed a hand down her hair. "Blood oath or pinky swear?" he asked and made her laugh. "I can promise you that, Emma. Because you're right. Friends." He eased over to kiss her cheeks, one, then the other, before rubbing his lips lightly over hers.

"Friends." She repeated the gesture so they stood, lips a breath apart, eyes locked. "Jack? How did we ever keep from doing this all these years?"

"Hell if I know." He touched his lips to hers again, then took her hand. "We were at the beach," he said as he led her to the stairs.

"What?"

"We'd gone to the beach for a week. All of us. A friend of Del's lent us his place—his parents' place, I guess—in the Hamptons. It was the summer before you started this place."

"Yes. I remember. We had the best time."

141

"One morning early, I couldn't sleep, so I walked down to the beach. And I saw you. For a minute—just a second or two, really—I didn't realize it was you. You were wearing this long scarf thing tied around your waist, lots of wild colors, and it blew around your legs. You had on a red bathing suit under it."

"You . . ." She literally had to catch her breath. "You remember what I was wearing?"

"Yes, I do. And I remember your hair was longer than it is now, halfway down your back. All those mad curls flying. Bare feet. All that golden skin, wild colors, mad curls. My heart just stopped. I thought: That's the most beautiful woman I've ever seen. And I wanted that woman, in a way I'd never wanted one before."

He stopped, turned a little as she simply stared at him. "Then I saw it was you. You walked off, down the beach, the surf foaming up over your bare feet, your ankles, your calves. And I wanted you. I thought I'd lost my mind."

She wouldn't be able to catch her breath much longer, she realized. Wouldn't be able to think. Wouldn't want to be able to think.

"If you'd walked down to me, looked at me the way you're looking at me now, you'd have had me."

"Worth waiting for." He kissed her long, slow, deep, then walked with her into the bedroom. "Nice," he said, noting the flowers, the candles.

"Even friends should fuss a little, I think." Because it would calm her, and set the mood, she picked up the lighter, wandered the room setting candles to flame.

"Nicer." He smiled when she switched on the music.

She turned to him, with the room between them. "I'm going to be honest with you, Jack—as promised. I have a weakness for romance, the trappings, the gestures. I also have a weakness for passion, the quick and the crazed. I'll take you either way. And tonight, you can take me, any way you want."

With those words, with Emma standing in candlelight, he was utterly seduced.

He crossed to her, and she to him so they met in the center of the room. He combed his fingers through her hair, drawing it back from her face, lowering his lips to hers slowly. Tonight, he would do all in his power to exploit all her weaknesses.

She gave, her body soft in surrender to echo the kiss. Warmth layered on warmth, longing wrapped in anticipation. When he swept her up to carry her to the bed, those dark eyes went slumberous.

"I want to touch you everywhere I've dreamed of touching you." Slowly, he slid his hand under her dress, along her thigh. "Everywhere."

He kissed her again, hints of greed now, of possession, while his fingers feathered over her skin, over the lace that barely covered her. She bowed up at his touch, offering more.

His lips trailed down her throat in whispers as he slid the sweater down her arms. Then in a fast, rough move, he flipped her over to graze his teeth over her shoulder. When he straddled her to ease down the zipper at the back of her dress, she looked over her shoulder. Her smile was full of secrets.

"Need any help?"

"I think I've got it."

"I think you do. Since I'm not in a position to do it myself, take off your shirt."

He unbuttoned it, peeled it off while she watched him. "I've always liked watching you shirtless around here in the summer. I like this even better." She rolled over again. "Undress me, Jack, and touch me. Everywhere."

She moved under him, lazy, teasing motions as he drew the

143

dress over her head, and felt the sizzle of pleasure as his gaze traveled over her.

"You're spectacular." He traced the edges of red lace, the tiny black petals. "This may take a while."

"No rush."

When he lowered his lips again, she let herself steep in the sensation of being explored.

Inch by inch, he'd said, and he was a man of his word. He touched, he tasted, he lingered until her quivers became trembles and the perfumed air thickened.

Generous curves, skin gold in candlelight, her hair spread out in lush coils of black silk. He'd thought her beautiful, always, but tonight she was a banquet willing to allow him a feast.

Every time he came back to those soft, lush lips, she gave a little more. He guided her up, slowly, slowly, felt her rise and rise, then crest and break.

Sensation drenched her, sweet and hot and lovely.

"My turn." She pushed herself up to link her arms around his neck, to fix her mouth to his.

She shifted, nudging him over and back. Now she explored, strong shoulders, hard chest, firm belly. And teased his zipper down to free him.

"I'd better—"

"I'll take care of it."

She took a condom out of her nightstand and took her time pleasuring him in the act of protection. Her hands, her lips set every muscle quivering until he gripped her hair, dragged her up. "Now."

"Now."

She slid down, bowed up. And took him into her.

The shiver ran through her, bright, silver-edged—a shimmering in the blood—as she began to move. Slowly, to draw out every drop of pleasure, with her eyes on his.

144

He gripped her hips, fighting to let her set the torturous pace. As her hands ran down her body in glorious abandon, he ached from the sight of her. Her skin glowed, like gold dust set to flame with her black velvet eyes shimmering in the flickering light. His pulse beat in wild drums while she took her fill. And fisting around him, she shuddered over the edge.

He levered up, rolled her to her back. On her gasp he pushed her knees up. "My turn."

He let control snap.

The sleepy, shimmering pleasure flashed to frenzy. She cried out from the shock of it as he drove her in fast, powerful thrusts. Lost, thrilled, she met the unreasoned demand beat for beat. The orgasm ripped through her, filled her, then hollowed her out.

She lay helpless, quivering even as he took more and reached his own.

He collapsed on her, undone. He felt her quaking beneath him, felt the hammer strikes of her heart, and still her hand came up to stroke his back in a gesture of affection that was so utterly Emma.

Jack closed his eyes a moment. He'd lost his wind, had probably lost his mind. He lay, breathing her in, absorbing the way her body, completely relaxed now, felt under his.

"Well, since we promised to be honest," he began, "I have to tell you that didn't do much for me."

Under him she laughed and pinched his ass. "Yeah, it's a shame. I guess we just don't have any chemistry."

He grinned, lifted his head. "No chemistry. That's why we blew up the lab."

"Lab, hell. We leveled the building." She sighed, long and deep as she stroked her hands down. "God, you've got a nice ass. If I may say so."

"You may, and, baby, you, too."

She smiled up at him. "Look at us."

He kissed her, softly, then again with light affection. "Are you hungry? I'm starving. How do you feel about cold Chinese?"

"I feel perfectly fine about it."

*T*HEY ATE AT HER KITCHEN COUNTER, DIGGING NOODLES, SWEET and sour pork, and Kung Pao chicken right out of the cartons.

"Why do you eat like that?" he asked.

"Like what?"

"In microscopic bites."

"Well." She worked her way through a single noodle as he topped off her wineglass. "It started as a way to needle my brothers, and became a habit. Whenever we'd get a treat, ice cream or candy, whatever, they'd just scarf theirs down. It drove them crazy that I'd have some of mine left. So I started eating even slower so I'd have *more* left and make them crazier. Anyway, I eat less and enjoy it more this way."

"I bet." Jack purposely shoveled a huge forkful of noodles into his mouth. "You know, your family's part of your appeal."

"Is it?"

"Your family's probably part of the reason you're appealing, but I meant they're all . . . great," he decided for lack of better. "They're great."

"I'm lucky. Of the four—well, six of us counting you and Del—I'm the only one with the whole shot. The Browns were amazing. You didn't know them very well, but I grew up here almost as much as at home. And they were amazing. It was devastating for all of us when they died."

"Del was wrecked. I liked them a lot. They were fun, interesting people. Involved people. Losing your parents so suddenly, both of them, out of the blue, it has to be the worst. Divorce is hard on a kid, but . . ."

"It is hard. It was tough on Mac when we were little, then it

146

happened again. And again. For Laurel I think it came out of nowhere. She was a teenager, and suddenly her parents are splitting up. She hardly ever sees them. It couldn't have been easy for you, either."

"It was rough, but it could've been a lot rougher." He shrugged and ate. It wasn't something he liked to dwell on. Why dwell on something painful that couldn't be changed? "Both my parents made a real effort not to play tug-of-war with me, and they managed to keep it civilized. Eventually, they figured out how to be friendly."

"They're both nice people, and they both love you. It makes a difference."

"We do okay." And he'd learned "okay" sometimes had to be good enough. "Plus I think we do better with the distance. My mother has her second family, my father his." His tone was a shrug, despite the fact he'd never reconciled himself to the ease with which they'd gone their separate ways, made their separate lives. "It got smoother all around when I went off to college. Smoother yet when I decided to move here."

He studied her as he drank some wine. "Your family, on the other hand, is like one of those rubber band balls you make, all twisted together into a solid core." He considered for a moment. "Are you going to tell them about this?"

She blinked. "Ah. I don't know. If they ask me, but I don't know why any of them would."

"Could be sticky."

"They like you. And they know I've had sex. They might be surprised. I mean, I'm surprised. But I don't see anyone having a problem with it."

"Good. That's good."

"The girls are fine with it."

"The girls?" Those smoky eyes widened. "You told the others we were going to sleep together?"

"We're girls, Jack," she said dryly.

"Right."

"Plus I thought, before, that you and Mac had been together."

"Whoa."

"Well, I thought you had, so I had to say something to her because of the Rule, and by the time we got that straightened out, everybody knew I was thinking about you and sex in the same sentence."

"I never slept with Mac."

"I know that now. I didn't, however, know you kissed Parker."

"That was a long time ago. And it wasn't really . . . Okay, it was, but it didn't work." He dug out more pork.

"*And* you kissed Mrs. G. You man-slut."

"Now that might've worked. I don't think we gave it enough time."

She grinned at him, poked at some chicken. "What does Del think?"

"About me kissing Mrs. Grady?"

"No. You and me. This."

"I don't know. I'm not a girl."

She paused with the glass halfway to her lips. "You haven't talked to him about it? He's your best friend."

"My best friend is going to want to kick my ass for thinking about touching you, much less doing what we just did upstairs."

"He, too, knows I've had sex."

"I'm not sure that's true. He puts that in another dimension. The other dimension Emma has sex." Jack shook his head. "You, not so much."

"If we're going to be together in bed, I'm not going to treat it like some illicit affair. He'll find out. You'd better say something to him before he does. Because if you don't, and he does, he *will* kick your ass."

"I'll figure it out. There's just one more thing, since we're on all this. Since we're together like this, I'd like to know that we're not together with anyone else like this. Is that a problem?"

She sipped her wine wondering why he'd have to ask. "Blood oath or pinky swear?" When he laughed, she took another sip. "If I'm sleeping with a man, I don't see anyone else. It's not only rude and against my principles, but it's too much trouble."

"Good. So it's you and me."

"It's you and me," she repeated.

"I have to be on-site at seven."

Here it comes, she thought. Early day tomorrow, honey. It was great. I'll call you.

"Any objection if I stay, since I'd need to get up at about five?"

Her lips curved. "No objection."

$\mathcal{J}$ACK DISCOVERED WHEN THEY FINALLY SLIPPED TOWARD SLEEP that Emma was a snuggler. The sort of woman who burrowed in and wrapped around.

He was generally a man who liked his space. Space kept a man from getting tangled up—literally and metaphorically.

But he found, under the circumstances, he didn't really mind.

She fell asleep like a stone dropped in a pond. Up and moving one minute, submerged the next. He was a drifter, with the movie reel of the day's events and the previews of the next running through his mind as his body settled down.

So he drifted, with Emma's head nestled in the curve of his shoulder, her arm flung around his waist, and her leg twined between his.

He woke, in nearly the same position, about six hours later

to the beep of his cell phone's alarm. And as he woke to the scent of her hair, she was his first conscious thought.

His attempt to ease away without waking her resulted in causing her to snuggle closer. Even as his body cheerfully responded, he tried to nudge her away.

She said, *"Hmmmm?"*

"Sorry. I've got to get going."

"Time's it?"

"Just after five."

She sighed again, then lifted her mouth to brush his lips with hers. "I've got about an hour. Too bad you don't."

He'd managed to shift her so they were front-to-front, and her hand was making slow, lazy circles over his ass.

"There are two things I'm finding really convenient at the moment."

"What?"

"Being the boss, so you don't get fired for being late. Even more, my own habit of keeping spare work clothes in the trunk. If I leave right from here, I've got most of an hour."

"Convenient. Want coffee?"

"That, too," he said, and rolled on top of her.

CHAPTER TEN

WHILE TIFFANY PROCESSED ANOTHER DELIVERY, EMMA completed the third hand-tied bouquet. She loved the combination of frilly tulips with the ranunculus and hydrangea. And though wiring the tiny crystals among the blooms abused her fingers, she knew she'd been right to suggest it. As she had with the strips of lace, the studs of pearls securing the stems.

With the steps, the details, the precision required, even with her experience each bouquet took nearly an hour to create. Wasn't she lucky, she thought, that she enjoyed every minute of it?

There wasn't a better job in the world, as far as she was concerned. And just now, as she began the painstaking assembly of the next bouquet, with Tiffany working quietly at the other end of the counter, with music and perfume winding in the air, she considered herself the luckiest woman on the planet.

She turned the flowers in her hand, adding tulips at varying heights, adjusting, interspersing the ranunculus to create the shape she wanted. She added the beads, pleased with the touch of glitter, and time clicked away.

"Do you want me to start on the centerpieces?"

"Hmm?" Emma glanced up. "Oh. Sorry, off in another world. What did you say?"

"It's really beautiful. All the textures." As she admired the work, Tiffany gulped down water. "You've got one more to go after that. I'd start it, but I'm not as good at the hand-tied. I can get the centerpieces started though. I've got the list and the design."

"Go ahead." Emma used a cable tie to secure the stems, clipped the excess plastic with her wire cutters. "Tink should be here . . . Well, she's already late, so she should be here." She exchanged cutters for clippers and began trimming the stems. "If you take the centerpieces, I'll get her started on the standing arrangements."

Emma wrapped the stems in lace, anchored the lace with pearl corsage pins. Once the bouquet was in its holding vase and in the cooler, she washed her hands—again—rubbed in Neosporin—again—then set to work on the final hand-tied.

When Tink wandered in, guzzling from a bottle of Mountain Dew, Emma merely lifted her eyebrows.

"You're late," Tink said, "blah, blah, blah. I'll stay late if you need me." And yawned. "Didn't get to bed—well, to sleep—until after three. This guy? Jake? He's Iron Man, in all good ways. Then this morning . . ." She trailed off, blowing a streak of pink out of her eyes as she angled her head. "Somebody else got lucky last night. Jack, right? Hey, Jake and Jack. Cool."

"I managed to get lucky and finish four hand-tieds. If you want to make enough to keep yourself in Mountain Dew, you'd better get started."

"No problem. Is he as good as he looks?"

"I'm not complaining, am I?"

"Who's Jack?" Tiffany wanted to know.

"You know. Jack of the excellent ass and smoky eyes." Tink stepped over to wash her hands.

"*That* Jack?" Gaping, Tiffany stopped with a hydrangea in her hand. "Wow. Where have I been?"

"It's still breaking news, so you're pretty up to date. You going back for more?" Tink asked Emma.

"Work," Emma muttered. "We're working here."

"She's going back for more," Tink concluded. "Nice bouquet," she added. "The tulips look like they come from the Planet Zorth, but in a romantic way. What am I on first?"

"The standing arrangements for the terraces. You need—"

"Hydrangeas, the tulips, ranunculus," Tink began, and rattling off the rest of the flowers and foliage, reminded Emma why she kept her on.

At five, she let Tiffany go and, leaving Tink working magic with flowers, took a break to rest her hands and clear her head. She stepped outside to stroll toward Mac's studio.

Her friend came out, a camera bag slung on her shoulder, a can of Diet Coke in her hand.

"Five thirty rehearsal," Emma called out.

"Just heading that way." Mac detoured toward Emma.

"You can tell the bride the flowers for tomorrow are amazing, if I do say so myself." When they met halfway, Emma stopped, stretched her back. "Long day, and a longer one coming."

"I heard a rumor Mrs. G's making lasagna. Big rafts of lasagna. Carter and I plan to pig out."

"I'm there. In fact, the thought of lasagna inspires me. Tink's finishing up her part. I'll give you and Parker a hand with the rehearsal, indulge, then put in an hour or two later tonight."

"There's a plan."

Emma looked down at her work clothes. "How bad am I?"

Mac took a survey while she chugged her drink. "You look

like a woman who's put in a long day. The bride will be thrilled with you."

"I say you're right. I don't want to clean up, then have to change again." She hooked her arm through Mac's free one as they started toward the house. "You know what I was thinking today? I'm the luckiest woman in the world."

"Jack was that good?"

Snorting out a laugh, Emma bumped Mac's hip with hers. "Yes, but besides that. I'm tired, my hands hurt, but I spent all day doing what I love. I got a call this afternoon after my flowers got to the off-site, the baby shower? The client just bubbled at me over the phone, just had to call me as soon as she saw the flowers to tell me how fabulous they were. Who else gets what we get, Mac?" She sighed and lifted her face to the sun. "We have such happy jobs."

"While I agree, in general, here's what I love about you. You can forget or ignore all the Monster Brides, all the Insane Mothers, Drunken Groomsmen, Bitchy Bridesmaids, and remember all the good stuff."

"It's mostly good stuff."

"It is. Despite the nightmare of an engagement shoot I did today. The happy couple had a vicious fight before I'd taken the first frame. My ears, they still ring."

"I hate when that happens."

"You? Screams, tears, storming out, storming back. Accusations, threats, ultimatums. More tears, apologies, wrecked makeup, shame, and horrible embarrassment. Screwed up my day good and proper. Plus, due to red, puffy eyes, we had to reschedule."

"Still, drama adds interest to the day. Then there's that." Emma gestured to where tomorrow's groom swept tomorrow's bride up for a spin on the walk to the house.

"Shit. They're early. Don't stop, don't stop," Mac muttered as

154

she shoved the drink at Emma and yanked her camera out of the bag.

"They're anxious to get going," Emma murmured. "And they're happy."

"Plus fairly adorable," Mac added as she managed to zoom in for a couple of candids. "And speaking of adorable, look who just pulled up."

"Oh." Spotting Jack's car, Emma instinctively brushed at her hair.

"He's seen you look a lot worse."

"Thanks very much. We both had a pretty full day, so I didn't expect . . ."

He looked so good, khakis today and a crisp pin-striped shirt, which meant client meetings and office work rather than construction sites. The easy gait, the burnished hair shining in the sun, the quick, killer smile all added up to . . . yum.

"My ass looks fat in these pants," she hissed to Mac. "I don't care because they're for work, but—"

"Your ass doesn't look fat in those. I'd tell you if it did. The red sweats with the cropped legs? Your ass looks fat in those."

"Remind me to burn them." Emma passed the drink back to Mac, then tuned up her smile as Jack crossed to them.

"Ladies."

"Man," Mac responded. "I've got to get to work. Later."

She loped off.

"Rehearsal," Emma explained.

"Are you in on that?"

"Just as backup. Are you done for the day?"

"Yeah. I had to make a stop at a client's not far from here, so I . . . Am I in the way?"

"No. No." Flustered, she pushed at her hair again. "I was just taking a break, walking over to the rehearsal in case they needed me for anything."

He slid his hands in his pockets. "We're being weird with each other."

"God. Yes. We are. Let's stop. Here." She rose to her toes, kissed him firmly. "I'm glad you came by. I've been at it since about eight, and wanted a break. Mrs. G's making lasagna. Do you want in on that?"

"Oh yeah."

"Then why don't you go charm her, have a beer, and I'll see you inside when we're finished."

"I'll do that." He caught her chin in his hand, leaned down to kiss her again. "You smell like your work. It's nice. I'll see you inside."

As they separated, her smile bloomed.

$\mathcal{E}$MMA WALKED INTO THE HOUSE TO THE GOOD, RICH SCENTS OF dinner and Mrs. Grady's big, bawdy laugh. The combination boosted her already happy mood. She heard Jack relaying what seemed to be the tail end of a work story.

"Then, when she clued in, she says, 'Oh, well. Can't you just *move* the door?'"

"She did not."

"Would I lie to you?"

"Every day and twice on Sunday. Are you moving the door?"

"We're moving the door, which will cost her about twice as much as the armoire she fell in love with. But client is king."

He took a sip from his beer, and his gaze shifted toward Emma when she walked in. "How'd it go?"

"Easy and fun, which is always a good sign for the real thing. They're trusting luck and the weather forecaster on tomorrow's predicted rain holding off until late evening, and going without the tents. So, fingers crossed on that."

As she would in her own home, Emma got out a glass for wine.

156

"They're off to the rehearsal dinner. But I think we've got the better deal here." She sniffed the air. "It smells great, Mrs. G."

"Table's set," Mrs. Grady said as she tossed a salad. "You'll eat in the dining room like the civilized."

"Parker and Mac will be right along. I haven't seen Laurel."

"She's fiddling in her own kitchen, and knows what time I'm serving."

"I'll give her a heads-up."

"All right then. Jack, make yourself useful since you're mooching, and put this salad on the table."

"Yes, ma'am. Hey, Carter."

"Hello, Jack. They're right behind me, Mrs. G."

She gave Carter a steely stare. "Did you teach anything useful today?"

"I like to think so."

"Did you wash your hands?" she demanded.

"Yes, ma'am."

"Then take that wine in and go sit down. And no picking until everyone's seated."

She served family style in the big dining room with its lofty ceiling and generous windows. Because it was Grady's Rule, cell phones were turned off, and Parker left her BlackBerry in the kitchen.

"Sunday Bride's aunt stopped by," Parker began. "She brought the chuppah, she just finished making it last night. It's a work of art. I'm keeping it upstairs. Emma, you may want to take a look at it, in case you feel you should tweak any of the arrangements. Carter, you're teaching the aunt's sister-in-law's older boy. David Cohen."

"David? He's a bright kid, who's currently using most of his creativity to cut up in class. Just last week he gave a report on *Of Mice and Men* in the style of a stand-up comic."

"How'd he do?" Mac asked him.

"I'm not sure how Steinbeck would've felt about it, but I gave him an A."

"It's such a sad book. Why do we have to read so many sad books in school?" Emma wondered.

"We're reading *The Princess Bride* in my freshman class now."

"Why didn't I have teachers like you? I like happy books, and happy endings. And look at you, with your own Buttercup."

Mac rolled her eyes. "Yeah, that's me. I'm a real Buttercup. Tomorrow's event has a nice fairy tale feel, though. All those fairy lights and candles, all white flowers."

"Tink complained she was going snowblind. But they're beautiful. A couple more hours tonight, and they're done. All the hand-tying and wiring makes this one very labor-intensive. Plus." She held up a hand sporting new nicks and scratches. "Ouch."

"You wouldn't think of a florist as a dangerous career." Jack took her hand, studied it. "But you've got the battle scars." And kissed her knuckles.

There was a long beat of silence, speculative stares.

"Stop," he ordered with a half laugh.

"You've got to expect it." Still watching them, Laurel stabbed into her salad. "We're making adjustments here. I think you should lay one on her, right here, so we can use the visual to help us adjust."

"Wait! Wait!" Mac waved a hand. "Let me get my camera."

"Pass the lasagna," Jack said.

Leaning back, Parker sipped her wine. "For all we know, the two of them are just having a joke at our expense. Pretending to be involved, then laughing at us behind our backs when we buy in to it."

"Oooh," Mac murmured. "You're good."

"I am," Parker agreed. "But really, it's not like either of them are the shy type. Certainly not too shy for one little PDA, and

158

among friends, too." She shrugged as a smile tugged at her lips. "So I'm leaning toward practical joke."

"Kiss the girl," Mrs. Grady told him, "or this bunch won't give you any peace."

"Or lasagna," Laurel decided. "Kiss!" She clapped her hands together. "Kiss!"

Mac picked up the chant. Even when she elbowed Carter he just laughed and shook his head.

Giving up, Jack turned to a laughing Emma, pulled her over and gave her a kiss that brought cheers and applause from the table.

"Looks like somebody's having a party and forgot to invite me."

The noise died away as everyone turned to the doorway, and Del. He stared at Jack, lifting a hand to stop Parker when she started to get to her feet.

"What the hell's going on?"

"We're having dinner." Laurel spoke coolly. "If you want some you'll need to get a plate."

"No, thanks," he said, just as coolly. "Parker, I've got some paperwork to go over with you. We'll take care of it another time since you're in the middle of something that's apparently none of my business."

"Del—"

"You and I." He interrupted his sister, never taking his eyes off Jack. "We'll deal later, too."

When he strode out, Parker released a long sigh. "You didn't tell him."

"I was still figuring out how to . . . No," Jack said. "No, I didn't. I need to go straighten this out," he told Emma.

"I'll go with you. I can—"

"No, better not. It may take a while, so . . . I'll call you to-morrow." He pushed back from the table. "Sorry."

159

When he left, Emma managed nearly ten seconds. "I have to at least try." She popped up, rushed after Jack.

"He looked pretty steamed," Mac said.

"Of course, he's steamed. His perfect balance has been shifted." Laurel shrugged when Parker snapped a look at her. "That's part of it. And that part's only worse because Jack didn't tell him. He's got a right to be steamed."

"I could go after them," Carter suggested. "Try to mediate."

"Mediators often get punched in the face by both parties."

He smiled humorlessly at Mac. "Wouldn't be the first time."

"No, let them hash it out." Parker sighed again. "That's what friends do."

BECAUSE EMMA'S CONCERN HELD HIM UP A GOOD TEN MINUTES, Jack didn't catch up with Del on the estate. But he knew where he'd go. Home, where he could curse, snarl, and brood in private.

He knocked, and had no doubt Del would open the door. For one thing, he had a key, and they both knew he'd use it if necessary. But more, Delaney Brown wasn't one for avoiding confrontation.

When Del yanked open the door, Jack looked him in the eye. "You swing at me, I'll swing back. We'll both get bloody, and won't resolve anything."

"Fuck you, Jack."

"Okay, fuck me. Fuck you, Del, for being an ass about—"

He took the punch to the face—because he hadn't seen it coming—and returned it. They stood there, in the doorway, mouths bleeding.

Jack swiped at his. "Do you want to beat the hell out of each other inside or out?"

160

"I want to know what the hell you were doing with your hands on Emma."

"Do you want to hear about that inside or out?"

Del merely turned, and stalked back to his great room for a beer. "How long have you been moving in on her?"

"I didn't move in on her. If anything we moved in on each other. For Christ's sake, Del, she's a grown woman, she makes her own choices. It's not like I twirled my moustache and stole her virginity."

"Watch it," Del warned, then the temper in his eyes went lethal. "You slept with her?"

"Let's back it up." Not a good start, Cooke, he thought. Not the best of springboards. "Let's just back it up."

"Yes or no, goddamn it."

"Yes, goddamn it. I slept with her, she slept with me. We slept with each other."

Something murderous flashed in Del's eyes. "I ought to beat you senseless."

"You can try. We'll both end up in the ER. And when I get out, I'm still going to sleep with her." Something equally deadly flared in Jack's. "It's none of your fucking business."

"The hell it isn't."

Because he felt he had more strikes on the wrong side of the column than Del, Jack nodded. "Okay, given the circumstances, it's your business. But it's not your right to tell either of us who to be with."

"How long?"

"It just happened. It just started turning on me, on us, I guess, the last couple of weeks."

"A couple of weeks." Del bit off the words "And you didn't say anything to me about it."

"No, I didn't, mostly to try to avoid getting punched in the face." Jack yanked open the fridge, got out a beer. "I knew you wouldn't like it, and I hadn't figured out how to explain."

"You didn't have any trouble explaining it to everyone else, apparently."

"No, I didn't, but then everyone else wasn't going to smash their bare fists into my face because I'm sleeping with a beautiful, interesting, *willing* woman."

"She's not any woman. She's Emma."

"I know that." Frustration piqued to beat down the anger. "I know who she is, and I know how you feel about her. About all of them. Which is why I kept my hands off her until . . . recently," he finished, and held the cold bottle to his throbbing jaw. "I've always had a thing for her, but I set it aside. 'Just don't go there, Jack.' Because you wouldn't like it, Del. You're my closest friend."

"You've had a thing for a lot of women."

"That's right," Jack said evenly.

"Emma isn't the type you sleep with until you catch wind of something new. She's the kind you make promises to, make plans with."

"For God's sake, Del, I'm just getting used to . . . He didn't make plans or promises—ever. Plans changed, didn't they? Promises got broken. Keeping it loose was keeping it honest.

"We were together one night. We're still figuring things out. And cut me a small break here. However many women I've been with I've never lied to them or treated them with anything but respect."

"April Westford."

"Jesus, Del, we were in grad school, and she was stalking me. She was a lunatic. She tried to break into our house. She keyed my car. She keyed *your* car."

Del paused, took a swig of beer. "All right, you've got a point with that one. Emma's different. She's different."

162

"That small break, Del? I know she's different. Do you think I don't care about her? That it's just the sex?" Unable to stand still, Jack paced from the bar to the counter and back again. It unnerved him, the depth of the caring. It was twisted up enough already without his best friend going off about promises, about Emma being different.

"I've always cared about Emma. About all of them. You know that. You damn well know that."

"Have you had sex with the rest of them, too?"

Jack took a long sip, and thought the hell with it. "I kissed your sister. Parker, since right now you're thinking of all of them as your sister. Back in college, after we ran into each other at a party."

"You hit on Parker?" It wasn't temper now but sheer shock that radiated. "Do I even know who you are?"

"I didn't hit on her. We bumped lips. It seemed like the thing to do at the time. Then since it felt like kissing *my* sister, and she had pretty much the same reaction, we had a good laugh about it, and that was that."

"Did you try out Mac next? Laurel?"

His eyes went hard and hot; his fingers itched to make another fist. "Oh yeah, I went through them all. That's what I do. I go through women like they're bags of chips then litter the streets with what's left of them. What the fuck do you take me for?"

"Right now, I don't know. You should've told me you were thinking about Emma that way."

"Oh yeah, I can see that. 'Hey, Del, I'm thinking about having sex with Emma. What do you think?'"

It wasn't temper that leaped back on Del's face, nor was it shock now. It was ice, and to Jack's mind, that was worse.

"Let's try it this way. How would you feel if you'd walked in tonight? Try that on, Jack."

"I'd be pissed. I'd feel betrayed. You want me to say I fucked it up? I fucked it up. But every way I look at it ends up like this. You think I don't know how it is for you? The position you took on when your parents died? And what they all mean to you? Every one of them. I was there with you through it, Del."

"This doesn't have anything to do with—"

"Everything does, Del." Jack paused a moment, spoke more calmly now. "I know it doesn't matter that Emma has a family. She's yours."

Some of the ice thawed. "Remember that. And remember this. If you hurt her, I'll hurt you."

"That's fair. Are we okay on this?"

"Not yet."

"Let me know when we are." Jack set down the half-finished beer.

WITH NO CHOICE, EMMA BUCKLED DOWN TO FINISH THE WORK for Friday's event. She and her full crew began early Friday morning designing and creating the flowers for the other weekend events.

Late in the afternoon, she began shifting flowers from the cooler, putting others in, loading the van so her team could start dressing the house and terraces.

Once the reception was under way, she'd come back and finish what was left on her own.

Just prior to the bride's arrival, she and Beach filled the portico urns with enormous white hydrangeas. "Gorgeous. Perfect. Go on in and help Tiffany with the foyer. I'll go work with Tink around back."

She made the dash, calculating the time, checking other pots and arrangements along the route. On the terrace, she climbed the ladder to hook the white rose ball in the center of the pergola.

"I didn't think I was going to like it." Tink hauled the standing arrangements into place. "White's so, you know, *white*. But it's really interesting, and sort of magical. Hiya, Jack. Gee, who punched you?"

"Del and I punched each other. Just something we do every so often."

"For God's sake."

If he'd expected Emma to get fluttery about his bruised jaw, he was disappointed. Annoyance in every movement, she climbed down the ladder, set her hands on her hips. "Why is it men think beating on each other fixes anything?"

"Why do women think eating chocolate does? It's the nature of the beast."

"Tink, let's finish the swags. Chocolate at least makes you feel good," Emma said as she continued to work. "A fist in the face doesn't. And did it fix things?"

"Not completely. But it's a start."

"Is he all right?" She pressed her lips together as she glanced back at Jack. "I know Parker tried to call him, but he's been in court all day."

"He hit me first." Jack took the ladder from her, moved it where she pointed, then tapped his swollen lip. "Ouch."

With a roll of her eyes, Emma gave him a very light kiss. "I don't have time to feel sorry for you right now, but I promise to make time later if you want to stay."

"I was just going to drop by, let you know things are . . . not quite, then get out of the way. I know you're slammed through the weekend."

"I am, and you can probably find something a lot better to do than hang around here."

He'd feel guilty, just a little miserable, still somewhat pissed, she thought. It called, to her mind, for friends and family.

"But . . . you could hang around here. Or with Carter, or at

165

my place. If you want. I'm going to duck out during the reception and finish up some things for tomorrow."

"Why don't we play it by ear?"

"That's fine." She stepped back, studied the pergola, then hooked an arm through Jack's. "What do you think?"

"That I didn't know there were so many white flowers in the world. It's elegant and fanciful at the same time."

"Exactly." She turned toward him, brushed her fingers through his hair and her lips at the corner of his abused mouth. "I need to go check the Grand Hall and the Ballroom."

"Maybe I'll see if Carter can come out and play."

"I'll see you later, if . . ."

"If," he agreed, then risked the pain for a more serious kiss. "Okay. I'll see you later."

She laughed, and made the dash inside.

CHAPTER ELEVEN

*A*T THE END OF THE NIGHT, WITH HER COOLER FILLED WITH
bouquets, centerpieces, arrangements for the rest of the
weekend—and the full knowledge she'd have to be up by six to
complete more—Emma made it as far as the sofa before she
dropped.

"You're actually going to do all of this again tomorrow,"
Jack said. "Twice."

"Mmm-hmm."

"And one more time on Sunday."

"Uh-huh. I need to get in a solid two hours on Sunday's, in
the morning before dressing the first event. But the team can
finish up the rest of Sunday's while I'm dealing with Saturday's.
Both Saturday's."

"I've helped out a few times, but never actually . . . It's every
weekend?"

"It slows down some in the winter." She snuggled in a little,
toed off her shoes. "April through June are the prime months,

with another big jump in September and October. But basically? Yes, every weekend."

"I took a look at your cooler when you were working. You definitely need that second one."

"I really do. When we started, none of us imagined we'd get this big. No, that's wrong. Parker did." It made her smile to think of it. "Parker always did. I just figured I'd be able to make a living wage doing what I liked." Relaxing inch by inch, she curled aching toes. "I never thought we'd get to a point where we're all juggling events and duties, clients, subs. It's amazing."

"You could use more help."

"Probably. It's the same for you, really, isn't it?" When he lifted her feet onto his lap, rubbed those cramped toes and tired arches, her eyes drifted shut. "I remember when you started your firm. It was basically you. Now you have staff, associates. If you're not working on drawings, you're on-site or meeting with clients. When it's your company, it's a whole lot different from punching time."

She opened her eyes again, met his gaze. "And every time you hire somebody—even when it's the best thing, the right thing, to do for yourself and your business—it feels like giving just a little bit of it away."

"I had myself talked in and talked out of hiring Chip a dozen times, just for that reason. The same with Janis, then Michelle. Now I've taken on a summer intern."

"That's great. God, doesn't that make us the older generation? That's hard to deal with."

"He's twenty-one. Just. I felt ancient when I interviewed him. What time do you have to start tomorrow?"

"Let me think . . . Six, I guess. Six thirty maybe."

"I should let you get some sleep." In an absent gesture, he ran a hand up and down her calf. "You're pretty tied up for the weekend. If you're up for it, we could go out Monday."

"Out? Like out there?" She waved a hand in the air. "Where there are places where people bring you food, and possibly entertainment?"

He smiled. "Dinner and a movie sound good?"

"Dinner and a movie? It sounds like whole buckets of good."

"Then I'll grab a bucket and pick you up Monday, about six thirty?"

"It works for me. Really works. I have a question." She stretched luxuriously as she sat up. "You stuck around here until after midnight, and now you're going to go home so I can get some sleep?"

"You put in a long one." He gave her calf a quick squeeze. "You must be tired."

"Not that tired," she said, and, grabbing a fistful of his shirt, pulled him down with her.

MONDAY EVENING, LAUREL WALKED HER CONSULT CLIENTS TO the door. September's bride and groom took away a container holding a variety of cake samples. But she knew they'd decided on the Italian cream cake. Just as she knew the bride was leaning toward her Royal Fantasy design, and the groom her Mosaic Splendor.

The bride would win, she had no doubt, but it was nice to have a man take a genuine interest in the details.

Plus she'd talk the bride into having her do a groom's cake in a mosaic design that complemented the wedding cake.

Everybody wins, she thought.

"Just let me know when you make up your minds, and don't worry about changing those minds. There's plenty of time." She kept the easy smile on her face, the breezy manner intact even when she watched Del coming up the walk.

169

He projected successful lawyer, she thought, in his perfectly cut suit, his perfect briefcase, his handsome shoes.

"Parker's in her office," she told him. "I think she's clear."

"Okay." He came in, shut the door. "Hey," he said when she started up the stairs. "Are you not speaking to me?"

She flicked a glance back at him. "I just did."

"Barely. I'm the one who should be pissed off here. You don't have anything to be snotty about."

"I'm being snotty?" She paused, waited for him to join her on the stairs.

"I don't expect my friends and family to lie to me, or lie by omission. And when they do—"

She poked a finger, hard, into his shoulder, then held it up. "Number one, I didn't know *you* didn't know. Neither did Parker or Mac or Carter. Or Emma, for that matter. So that's between you and Jack. Second," she continued, poking him again when he started to speak. "I agree with you."

"If you'd take a minute to . . . You agree with me?"

"Yes, I do. And in your place I'd have been hurt and pissed off. Jack should have told you he and Emma were involved."

"Well, okay. Thanks—or sorry. Whichever you prefer."

"However."

"Shit."

"However," she repeated. "You might want to ask yourself why your best friend didn't tell you. And you might want to look back at the way you handled the other night, how you came across as a tight-ass having a sulk."

"Wait a damn minute."

"That's the way I see it, just as I see—even if I don't agree— why Jack didn't tell you. You'd have gone all Delaney Brown on him."

"Just what does that mean?"

"If you don't know, telling you won't make any difference."

He grabbed her hand to stop her as she moved on. "That's such a cop-out."

"Fine. Delaney Brown disapproves. Delaney Brown knows best. Delaney Brown will manipulate and maneuver until he positions you where he wants—for your own good."

"That's cold, Laurel."

She sighed, softened. "No, it's not. Not really. Because you really do have the best interest of your friends and family at heart. You're just always so damn sure, Del, that you know what that is."

"Are you going to stand there and tell me you think what's going on with Emma and Jack is the best thing, for either of them?"

"I don't know." She lifted her hands, palms up. "I don't pretend to know. All I know is that, for the moment, they're enjoying each other."

"It doesn't even weird you out? It doesn't make you feel as if you've stepped into an alternate reality?"

She had to laugh. "Not exactly. It's a little—"

"It's like—what if I suddenly put moves on you? I just decide, hey, I'd like to have sex with Laurel."

The soft hardened; the laughter died. "You're such an idiot."

"What? *What?*" he demanded as she stormed away up the stairs. "It is an alternate reality," he muttered, and climbed the rest of the way to his sister's office.

She sat at her desk, where he'd expected to find her, talking on her headset as she worked at the computer. "That's just exactly right. I knew I could count on you. They'll need two hundred and fifty. You can deliver them to me, here, and I'll take it from there. Thank you, so much. You, too. 'Bye."

She pulled off the headset. "I just ordered two hundred and fifty rubber duckies."

"Because?"

"The client wants them swimming in the pool on her wedding day." She sat back, sipped from her bottle of water, and gave him a long, sympathetic look. "How are you doing?"

"I've been better, I've been worse. Laurel just agreed Jack was an asshole for not telling me, but apparently that's my fault because I'm Delaney Brown. Do I manipulate people?"

She studied him carefully. "Is that a trick question?"

"Damn it." He dumped his briefcase on the desk then walked to her coffee setup.

"Okay, serious question. Yes, of course you do. So do I. We're problem solvers, and good at finding solutions and answers. When we do, we do what we can to move people toward those solutions and answers."

He turned back to her, scanning her face. "Do I manipulate you, Parks?"

"Del, if you hadn't manipulated me, to some extent, regarding the estate, how you intended to set it up after Mom and Dad died, I wouldn't have just ordered two hundred and fifty rubber duckies. I wouldn't have the business. None of us would."

"That's not the kind of thing I mean."

"Would you, have you ever pushed me into doing something I didn't want to do—genuinely didn't want—and did you push because it was what you wanted? No. I'm sorry you found out about Jack and Emma the way you did. But I think the situation's a little strange for all of us. None of us saw it coming. I don't think Jack and Emma saw it coming."

"I can't get used to it." He sat, sipped his coffee. "By the time I do, it'll probably be over anyway."

"Aren't you the romantic?"

He shrugged. "Jack's never been serious about a woman. He's not a dog—exactly—but he's not the long-haul guy either. He wouldn't hurt her on purpose. He's not made like that. But . . ."

"Maybe you should have a little more faith in your two

172

friends." She sat back, swiveling side-to-side in the chair. "I think things happen between people for a reason. Otherwise I couldn't do what I do every day. Sometimes it works out, sometimes it doesn't, but there's always a reason."

"Under that you're telling me to stop being such a hardass, and just be a friend."

"Yes." She smiled at him. "That's my answer, my solution, and where I'm trying to manipulate you. How am I doing?"

"Pretty well. I guess I should stop by and see Emma."

"It would be nice."

"Let's go over these papers first." He opened his briefcase.

Twenty minutes later, he gave a quick knuckle rap on Emma's door, then pushed it open. "Em?"

He heard the music—what he thought of as her work music—harps and flutes—so walked back to her work area. She sat at the counter, arranging little pink rosebuds in a white basket.

"Em."

She jumped, swung around. "Scared me. I didn't hear you."

"Because I'm interrupting."

"Just getting a headstart on some arrangements for a baby shower this week. Del." She got up. "How mad at me are you?"

"Zero. Less than zero." He found himself ashamed she would think otherwise. "I'm at about seven out of ten with Jack, but that's an improvement."

"I should point out that when Jack's sleeping with me I'm also sleeping with him."

"Maybe we could just find a code word for that. Like you and Jack are writing a novel together, or doing lab work."

"Are you mad because we're doing lab work, or because we didn't tell you?"

"He didn't tell me. Anyway, it's mixed. I'm trying to come to terms with the lab work, and I'm pissed he didn't tell me you and he were . . ."

"Lining up the test tubes? Labeling the petri dishes?"

Frowning, he slid his hands into his pockets. "I don't like the lab work code after all. I just want you to be okay, and happy."

"I am okay. I am happy. Even though I know the two of you punched each other over it. Actually, maybe that makes me happier. It's always flattering to have guys punch each other in the face over me."

"It was an impulse of the moment."

She stepped to him, reached up so she could frame his face, and brushed her lips over his. "Try not to do it again. It involves two of my favorite faces. Let's go sit out on the back patio, drink some lemonade, and be friends."

"Okay."

WHILE THEY DID, JACK TOOK A SEAT IN MAC'S STUDIO AND unrolled the plans for the proposed addition.

"It's the same design I e-mailed you, but with more detail, and the couple of changes you wanted."

"Look, Carter! You have your own room."

He danced his fingers over Mac's bright cap of hair. "I was kind of hoping we'd still share one."

Mac laughed, leaned closer to the plans. "Just look at my dressing room. Well, client dressing room. And God, I *love* the patio space we'll get. Want a beer, Jack?"

"No, thanks. Got anything soft?"

"Sure. Diet."

"Crap. Water."

When she went into the kitchen, Jack pointed out details to Carter. "These built-ins will give you plenty of shelves for books, or whatever you want. For files, for supplies."

"What's this? A fireplace?"

"One of Mac's changes. She said every professor worth his

PhD should have a fireplace in his study. It's a small, gas log unit. It'll also provide an additional heat source for the room."

Carter glanced over as Mac came back with a bottle of water and two beers. "You got me a fireplace."

"I did. It must be love." She kissed him lightly, then bent to pick up their three-legged cat, Triad.

It must be, Jack thought when she sat and the cat curled in her lap.

While they discussed details, choices of materials, he wondered what it was like to feel that connection with and that certainty about another person.

No doubt in their minds, he mused, that this was *the* one. The one to make a home with, build a future with, maybe have kids with. Share a cat with.

How did they know? Or at least believe enough to risk it?

It was, for him, one of life's great mysteries.

"When can we start?" Mac demanded.

"I'll submit for permit tomorrow. Do you have a contractor in mind?"

"Um . . . the company we used on the initial remodel was good. Are they still available?"

"I ran it by him. I can contact him tomorrow, ask him to submit a bid."

"You're the man, Jack." Mac gave him a friendly punch in the arm. "Do you want to stay for dinner? We're making pasta. I can call and see if Emma's interested."

"Thanks, but we're going out."

"Aw."

"Stop." But he shook his head and laughed.

"I can't help it if I find it adorable that my pals are getting all cozy."

"We're going to grab some dinner and catch a flick."

"Aw."

He laughed again. "I'm getting out of here. See you on Poker Night, Carter. Prepare to lose."

"I could just hand you the money now, save time."

"Tempting, but I prefer the satisfaction of skinning you at the table. I'll get you that bid," he added as he headed for the door. "You keep that copy of the plans."

He heard Mac's "uh-oh" an instant before he spotted Del.

They stopped, about five feet apart.

"Wait!" Mac called out. "If you're going to punch each other again, I want my camera."

"I'll shut her up," Carter promised.

"Hey! Wait! I was serious," she managed before Carter dragged her back inside.

Jack jammed his hands into his pockets. "This is just fucking stupid."

"Maybe. Probably."

"Look, we punched each other, we each said our piece. We had a beer. According to the rules, that should about cover it."

"We didn't take in a sporting event."

Jack felt some of the tension in his shoulders ease. That was more like Del. "Can we do that tomorrow? I've got a date."

"What happened to bros before hos?"

A smile spread amiably over Jack's face. "Did you just call Emma a ho?"

Del's mouth opened and closed before he dragged a hand through his hair. "You see the complications here? I just called Emma a ho because I wasn't thinking of Emma as Emma, and I was being a smartass."

"Yeah, well, I know that. Otherwise I'd've had to punch you in the face again. The Yankees have a home game tomorrow night."

"You drive."

176

"Uh-uh. We get Carlos. I spring for the car service. You spring for the tip and the beer. We split the dogs."

"All right." Del considered a moment. "Would you punch me in the face over her?"

"I already did."

"That wasn't about her."

Point taken, Jack thought. "I don't know."

"That's a good answer," Del decided. "I'll see you tomorrow."

SINCE DINNER—BISTRO FARE—AND A MOVIE—ACTION FLICK— worked so well, they made a second official Monday night date. Full schedules prevented any appreciable time together between, but they managed what they termed a friendly booty call and a few teasing e-mails.

Emma wasn't sure if their current relationship led off with sex or friendship, but it felt as if both of them were trying to find a happy balance between the two.

She was nearly finished dressing for the evening when Parker came in and called up the stairs.

"Be right down. I've got the flowers you wanted in the back, in a holding vase. Though I still don't see why you have to go watch people make wedding favors."

"The MOB wants me to stop by, give it all the once-over. So I stop by, give it all the once-over. It shouldn't take that much time."

"I'd have saved you some of that time and dropped them by, but I got hung up with my last consult of the day." Emma dashed downstairs, stopped, did a runway turn. "How do I look?"

"Gorgeous. One expects no less."

Emma laughed. "The hair up works, right? Just a little messy and ready to tumble."

"It works. So does the dress. That deep red really suits you. And let me add, the workouts are paying off."

"Yeah, I hate that part because it means I have to keep it up. Wrap or sweater?" she asked, holding a choice in either hand.

"Where are you going?"

"Art opening. Local artist, modern."

"The wrap's more arty, and aren't you clever?"

"Am I?"

"Most people will be in black, so that red dress is going to pop. You could give lessons."

"If you're going to dress up, might as well get noticed, right? How about the shoes?"

Parker considered the peep-toe spikes with their sexy ankle straps. "Killers. Nobody with a Y chromosome is going to look at the paintings."

"I've only got one Y chromosome in mind."

"You look happy, Emma."

"It's hard not to, because I am. I'm involved with an interesting man who makes me laugh *and* makes me tingle, one who actually listens to what I have to say, and who knows me well enough I can be myself without any of the filters. And the same goes for him. I know he's fun, funny, smart, not afraid to work, values his friends, is obsessed with sports. And . . . well, all the things you just know when you've been around someone for a dozen years the way we have."

She led the way to her work area. "Some people might think that takes the discovery or the excitement out of things, but it doesn't. There's always something new, and there's the stability of real understanding. I can be comfortable and excited around him at the same time.

"I went with the pink tulips and the mini iris. It's cheerful, female, springy."

"Yes, it's perfect." Parker waited while Emma took them out of the vase, adjusted the sheer white ribbon.

"I could add some lisianthus if you want it fuller."

"No, it's great. Just right. Emma," Parker began as her friend coned the arrangement in clear, glossy paper, "do either of you know you're in love with him?"

"What? No. I never said . . . Of course, I love Jack. We *all* love Jack."

"We all didn't put on a red dress and sexy shoes to spend the evening with him."

"Oh, well that's just . . . I'm going out."

"It's not just that. Em, you're going out with Jack. You're sleeping with Jack. Which is what I figured was what, more or less. But I listened to you just now, I watched your face just now. And, honey, I know you. You're in love."

"Why do you have to say that?" Distress covered Emma's face. "It's just the sort of thing that's going to mess with my head, and make everything all sticky and awkward."

Brow lifted, Parker angled her head. "Since when have you thought of being in love as sticky and awkward?"

"Since Jack. I'm okay with the way things are now. I'm better than okay. I'm in an exciting relationship with an exciting man and I don't . . . I don't expect it to be anything else. Because that's not Jack. He isn't the kind who thinks about what we'll be doing five years from now. Or five weeks from now. It's . . . just now."

"You know, it's odd that you and Del, who are closer to him than anyone, both have such little confidence in him."

"It's not that. It's just that in this particular area, Jack's not looking for . . . permanent."

"What about you?"

"I'm going to enjoy the moment." She said it with a decisive nod. "I'm not going to be in love with him, because we both know what'll happen if I am. I'll start romanticizing it, and him, and us, and wishing he'd . . ."

She trailed off, pressed a hand to her belly. "Parker, I know what it's like to have someone feel that way about me, when I don't feel that way. It's just as awful for the one who's not in love as it is for the one who is."

She shook her head. "No, I'm not going there. We've only been seeing each other like this for a little while. I'm not going there."

"All right." To soothe, Parker stroked a hand over Emma's shoulder. "If you're happy, I'm happy."

"I am."

"I'd better run. Thanks for putting these together."

"Never a problem."

"I'll see you tomorrow. Follow-up consult on the Seaman wedding."

"I've got it in my book. I know they want to walk around the gardens, see them now to project what they'll want in those areas next April. I'm going to dress a couple of the urns with Nikko blue hydrangeas I've been coaxing along in the greenhouse. They're lush, and should give a good show. I've got a couple other tricks up my sleeve, too," she added as she walked to the door with Parker.

"You always do. Have a good time tonight."

"I will."

Emma closed the door, then just leaned back against it.

She could fool herself, she admitted. She could certainly fool Jack. But she could never fool Parker.

Of course she was in love with Jack. She'd probably been in love with Jack for years, and simply convinced herself it was lust. The lust had been bad enough, but love? Deadly.

She knew exactly what she wanted from love—from the down into the bones, rooted in the heart, blooming through the body love. She wanted forever.

She wanted the day after day, night after night, year after year, the home, the family, the fights, the support, the sex, the everything.

She'd always known what she wanted in a partner, in a lover, in the father of her children.

But why did it have to be Jack?

Why, when she finally felt all the things she'd waited all of her life to feel, did it have to be for a man she knew so well? Well enough to understand he was one who wanted his own space, his own direction, who considered marriage a gamble with long odds?

She knew all those things about him, and still she'd fallen.

If he knew, he'd be . . . appalled? she wondered. No, that was probably too strong. Concerned, sorry—which was worse. He'd be kind, and he'd pull the plug gently.

And that was mortifying.

There was no reason he had to know. It was only a problem if she let it be a problem.

So, no problem, she decided.

She was as skilled at handling men as she was at handling flowers. They'd go on just as they were, and if it got to a point where it caused her pain instead of pleasure, she'd be the one to pull the plug.

Then she'd get over it.

She pushed away from the door to wander into the kitchen for a glass of water. Her throat felt dry and a little raw.

She'd get over him, she assured herself. What was the point in worrying about that now when they were still together?

Or . . . she could make him fall in love with her. If she knew how to keep a man from falling for her—or nudge him into falling out if he thought he was falling in—why couldn't she make one fall in?

"Wait, I'm confusing myself."

She took a breath, took a sip.

"If I make him fall in love with me, is it real? God, this is too much to think about. I'm going out to an opening. That's it, that's all."

The knock on the door brought relief. Now she could stop thinking, stop worrying all this to pieces.

They'd go out. They'd enjoy each other. Whatever happened next, happened.

CHAPTER TWELVE

𝒮ATISFACTION, EMMA DECIDED, WENT A LONG WAY TO STAMP-ing out worry. The look in Jack's eyes when she opened the door was exactly what she'd aimed for.

"I need a moment of silence," he told her, "to offer up thanks."

She gave him a slow, sultry smile. "Then let me say you're welcome. Do you want to come in?"

Closing the distance, he trailed his fingers over her shoulder, down her arm. Those smoky eyes stayed fixed on hers. "I'm just having this thought about how I come in and we forget about the opening."

"Oh no." She nudged him back, and stepped out. Handing him the wrap, she turned her back, glanced around as he draped it over her shoulders. "You promised me strange paintings, lousy wine, and soggy canapes."

"We could go back inside." He leaned down to nuzzle her

neck. "I'll sketch some erotic drawings, we'll drink good wine, and call out for pizza."

"Choices, choices," she said as they walked to his car. "Art opening now, erotic sketches later."

"If we must." But he stopped at the car to draw her into a luxurious kiss. "I like the way you look, which is amazing."

"That was the plan." She stroked her hand over the slate gray sweater he wore under a leather jacket. "I like the way you look, Jack."

"Since we look so good I guess we'd better go be seen." When he got behind the wheel he sent her an easy smile. "How was the weekend?"

"Jammed, as advertised. And successful, since Parker talked the clients into renting the tents for Saturday. When it rained, everybody stayed dry. Even better, we scrabbled around for more candles and some of my emergency supply of flowers so we had all this soft light and fragrance while the rain pattered on the tent. It was really lovely."

"I wondered how that worked out. I was out on new construction Saturday afternoon, and we didn't. Stay dry, that is."

"I like spring rains. The way they sound, the way they smell. Not all brides feel the same, but we managed to make this one really happy. And how was Poker Night?"

He scowled at the road as his headlights cut through the dark. "I don't want to talk about it."

She laughed. "I heard Carter cleaned your clock."

"The guy hustled us with all that 'I'm not much of a card player' routine, and that open, honest face. He's a shark."

"Yes, oh yes, Carter's a real shark."

"You haven't played cards with him. Believe it."

"Sore loser."

"Damn right."

Amused, she leaned back in the seat. "So, tell me a little about this artist."

"Ah . . . yeah, I should do that." During a beat of silence, he tapped his fingers on the steering wheel. "A friend of a client. I think I mentioned that."

"You did." She'd meant the art itself, but she caught enough in his tone to zero in. "And a friend of yours?"

"Sort of. We went out a couple of times. A few times. Maybe several."

"Ah. I see." Though her interest spiked, she kept her tone casual. "She's an ex."

"Not exactly. We weren't . . . It was more we hooked up for a few weeks. More than a year ago. Closer to two, actually. It was just a thing, then it wasn't."

His uneasiness struck her as both interesting and flattering. "If you're looking at this as boggy ground, Jack, you don't need to. I've had my suspicions you've slept with other women."

"It's true. I have. And Kellye—she spells it with an 'e' on the end—is one of them. She's . . . interesting."

"And artistic."

His lips twitched, intriguing her. "You be the judge."

"So, why did the thing stop being a thing, or is that too awkward a question?"

"It got a little too intense for me. She's an intense sort, and high-maintenance."

"Required too much attention?" Emma asked, with just a hint of cool.

"*Required* is a good word for it. Anyway, it stopped being a thing."

"But you stayed friendly."

"Not so much. But I ran into her a couple months ago, and we were okay. Then she got in touch about her opening, and

185

I figured it wouldn't hurt to go. Especially since you're here to protect me."

"Do you often need protection from women?"

"All the time," he said and amused her again.

"Don't you worry." She patted his hand on the gear shift. "I'm here for you."

After he'd parked, they walked through the cool spring evening in a breeze that fluttered the ends of her wrap. The little shops she enjoyed browsing were already closed, but the bistros did brisk business. A number of diners braved the chill for a chance to eat outside with candles flickering on tables.

She smelled roses and red sauce.

"You know what I haven't done for you?" Emma began.

"I have a list, but I figured I'd work up to some of the more interesting items."

She poked him with her elbow. "Cook. I'm a good cook when I have time. I'll have to seduce you with my fajitas."

"Any time, anywhere." He stopped in front of the gallery. "Here we are. Are you sure you wouldn't rather cook?"

"Art," she said, and breezed inside.

No, not really, she thought immediately. The first thing she saw other than a number of people standing around looking intense was a large white canvas with a single, wide, blurry line of black running down the center.

"Is it a tire tread? A single tire tread on a white road, or a division of . . . something?"

"It's a black line on a white canvas. And we're going to need drinks," Jack decided.

"Mmm-hmm."

While he left her to find some, Emma wandered. She studied another canvas holding a twisted black chain with two broken links titled *Freedom*. Another boasted what seemed to be a

186

number of black dots, which on closer inspection proved to be a scattering of lower case letters.

"Fascinating, isn't it?" A man in dark-framed glasses and a black turtleneck stepped up beside her. "The emotion, the chaos."

"Uh-huh."

"The minimalist approach to intensity and confusion. It's brilliant. I could study this one for hours, and see something different each time."

"It depends on how you arrange the letters."

He beamed at her. "Exactly! I'm Jasper."

"Emma."

"Have you seen *Birth*?"

"Not firsthand."

"I believe it's her best work. It's just over there. I'd love to hear what you think."

He touched a hand to her elbow—testing, she knew—as he gestured. "Can I get you some wine?"

"Actually . . . I have some," she said when Jack joined them and offered her a glass. "Jack, this is Jasper. We were admiring *Babel*," she added when she found the title.

"A confusion of language," Jack supposed and dropped a light, possessive hand on Emma's shoulder.

"Yes, of course. If you'll excuse me."

"Busted his bubble," Jack added when Jasper slunk off. Testing the very bad wine, he studied the canvas. "It's like one of those magnet kits people buy for their refrigerator."

"Thank God. Thank God. I thought you actually saw something."

"Or somebody dropped the Scrabble tiles."

"Stop." She had to suck in a breath to stop a laugh. "Jasper finds it brilliant in its minimalist chaos."

"Well, that's Jasper for you. Why don't we just—"

187

"Jack!"

Emma turned to see a six-foot redhead, arms outflung, burst through the crowd. She wore snug black that showed miles of legs, a pencil-thin body offset by high, firm breasts that almost poured out of the scooped-neck of her top. She jangled from the clanging of a dozen silver bangles on her arm.

And nearly mowed Emma down as she threw her arms around Jack to fix her murderous red mouth to his.

The best Emma could do was grab Jack's wineglass before it upended.

"I knew you'd come." Her voice was low, and nearly a sob. "You don't know what it means to me. You can't know."

"Ah," he said.

"Most of these people, they don't *know* me. They haven't been *in* me."

Jesus. Christ. "Okay. Let's just . . ." He tried untangling himself, but her arms tightened around his neck like a garrote. "I wanted to stop by and say congratulations. Let me introduce you to . . . Kellye, you're cutting off my oxygen."

"I've *missed* you. And tonight means so much, now so much more." Dramatic tears glimmered in her eyes; her lips quivered with emotion. "I know I can get through tonight, the stress, the *demands*, now that you're here. Oh, Jack, Jack, stay close to me. Stay close."

Any closer, he thought, and he would be in her. "Kellye, this is Emmaline." Desperate now, Jack gripped Kellye's wrists to unlock them from his neck. "Emma . . ."

"It's wonderful to meet you." Cheerful, enthusiastic, Emma offered a hand. "You must—"

Kellye stumbled back as if stabbed, then whirled on Jack. "How dare you! How could you? You'd bring *her* here? Throw *her* in my face? Bastard!" She ran, shoving her way through the fascinated crowd.

188

"Okay, this was fun. Let's go." Jack grabbed Emma's hand and pulled her to the door. "Mistake. Big mistake," he said when he managed a good gulp of fresh air. "I think she punctured my tonsils with her tongue. You didn't protect me."

"I failed you. I'm so ashamed."

He narrowed his eyes as he pulled her along the sidewalk. "And you think that was funny."

"I'm a bitch, too. Cold-hearted. More shame." She had to stop, just stop and howl with laughter. "God, Jack! What were you thinking?"

"When a woman has the power to puncture a man's tonsils with her tongue, he stops thinking. She also has this trick where she . . . And I almost said that out loud." He dragged a hand through his hair as he studied her glowing face. "We've been friends too long. It's dangerous."

"In the spirit of friendship, I'm going to buy you a drink. You deserve it." She took his hand. "I didn't believe you when you said she got too intense and so on. I figured you were just being the usual no-commitment guy. But *intense* is way too quiet a word for her. Plus, her art is ridiculous. She really ought to hook up with Jasper. He'd adore her."

"Let's drive across town for that drink," he suggested. "I don't want to chance running into her again." He opened the car door for her. "You weren't the least bit embarrassed by that."

"No. I have a high embarrassment threshold. If she'd been remotely sincere, I'd have felt sorry for her. But she's as fake as her art. And probably just as odd."

He considered as he walked around to get in the driver's side. "Why do you say that? About her being fake?"

"It was all about the drama, and her in the center of it. She may feel something for you, but she feels a lot more for herself. And she saw me, before she jumped you. She knew you'd brought me with you, so she put on a show."

"Deliberately embarrassed herself? Why would anyone do that?"

"She wasn't embarrassed, she was revved." She angled her head, looking into his baffled eyes. "Men really don't see things like that, do they? It's so interesting. Jack, she was the star of her own romantic tragedy, and she fed on every moment. I bet she sells more of that nonsense she calls art tonight because of it."

When he drove in silence for the next few moments, she winced. "And all that really hammered your ego."

"Scratched it, superficially. I'm weighing that against knowing I didn't somehow give her the wrong signal so I actually deserved that entertaining little show." He shrugged. "I'll take the scratch."

"You're better off. So . . . any other ex-we-had-a-thing you want me to meet?"

"Absolutely not." He glanced at her, and the street lights sheened over the golds and bronzes in his hair." But I do want to say that, for the most part, the women I've dated have been sane."

"That speaks well of you."

$\mathcal{T}$HEY CHOSE A LITTLE BISTRO AND SHARED A PLATE OF ALFREDO.

She relaxed him, he thought, which was odd, as he'd always considered himself fairly relaxed to begin with. But spending time with her, just talking about anything that came to mind, made any problem or concern he might be dealing with in some corner of his brain vanish.

Odder still was being excited and relaxed around a woman at the same time. He couldn't remember having that combination of sensations around anyone but Emma.

"How come," he wondered, "in all the years I've known you, you've never cooked for me?"

She wound a solitary noodle on her fork. "How come in all the years I've known you, you never took me to bed?"

"Aha. So you only cook for men when you get sex."

"It's a good policy." She smiled, her eyes laughing as she nibbled away at the noodle. "I go to a lot of trouble when I cook. It ought to be worth it."

"How about tomorrow? I can make it worth it."

"I bet you can, but tomorrow won't work. No time to market. I'm very fussy about my ingredients. Wednesday's a little tight, but—"

"I have a business thing Wednesday night."

"Okay, next week's better anyway. Unlike Parker, I don't carry my schedule in my head backed up by the BlackBerry attached to my hand, but I think . . . Oh. Cinco de Mayo. It's nearly the fifth of May. Big family deal—you remember, you've come before."

"Biggest blast-out party of the year."

"A Grant family tradition. Talk about cooking. Let me check my book and all of that, and we'll figure it out."

She sat back with her wine. "It's almost May. That's the best month."

"For weddings?"

"Well, it's a big one for that, but I'm thinking in general. Azaleas, peonies, lilacs, wisteria. Everything starts budding and blooming. And I can start planting some annuals. Mrs. G will put in her little kitchen garden. Everything starts over or comes back. What's your favorite?"

"July. A weekend at the beach—sun, sand, surf. Baseball's cruising. Long days, grills smoking."

"Mmm, all good, too. All very good. The smell of the grass right after you mow it."

"I don't have grass to mow."

"City boy," she said, pointing at him.

191

"My lot in life."

As they both toyed with the pasta, she leaned in. The conversations humming around them barely registered. "Did you ever consider living in New York?"

"Considered. But I like it here. For living, and for the work. And I'm close enough to go in and catch the Yankees, the Knicks, the Giants, the Rangers."

"I've heard rumors about ballet, opera, theater there, too."

"Really?" He sent her an exaggerated look of puzzlement. "That's weird."

"You, Jack, are such a guy."

"Guilty."

"You know, I don't think I've ever asked you, why architecture?"

"My mother claims I started building duplexes when I was two. I guess it stuck. I like figuring out how to use space, or change an existing structure. How can you use it better? Are you going to live in it, work in it, play in it? What's around the space, what's the purpose? What are the best and most interesting or practical materials? Who's the client and what are they really after? Not all that different, in some way, than what you do."

"Only yours last longer."

"I have to admit I'd have a hard time seeing my work fade and die off. It doesn't bother you?"

She pinched off a knuckle-sized piece of bread. "There's something about the transience, you could say. The fact that it's only temporary that makes it more immediate, more personal. A flower blooms and you think, oh, pretty. Or you design and create a bouquet, and think, oh, stunning. I'm not sure the impact and emotion would be the same if you didn't know it was only temporary. A building needs to last; its gardens need to cycle."

"What about landscape design. Ever consider it?"

"Probably more briefly than you did New York. I like working in the garden, out in the air, the sun, seeing what I put in come back the next year, or bloom all through the spring and summer. But every time I get a delivery from my wholesaler it's like being handed a whole new box of toys."

Her face went dreamy. "And every time I hand a bride her bouquet, see her reaction, or watch wedding guests look at the arrangements, I get to think: I did that. And even if I've made the same arrangement before, it's never exactly the same. So it's new, every time."

"And new never gets boring. Before I met you, I figured florists mostly stuck flowers in vases."

"Before I met you, I figured architects mostly sat at drawing boards. Look what we learn."

"A few weeks ago, I never imagined we'd be sitting here like this." He put his hand over hers, fingers lightly skimming while his eyes looked into hers. "And that I'd know before the night was over I'd be finding out what's under that really amazing dress."

"A few weeks ago . . ." Under the table, she slid her foot slowly up his leg. "I never imagined I'd be putting on this dress for the express purpose of you getting me out of it. Which is why . . ."

She leaned closer so the candlelight danced gold in her eyes, so her lips nearly brushed his. "There's nothing under it."

He continued to stare at her, into the warmth and the wicked. Then shot up his free hand. "Check!"

$\mathcal{H}$E HAD TO CONCENTRATE ON HIS DRIVING, PARTICULARLY SINCE he attempted to break the land speed records. She drove him crazy, the way she cocked her seat back, crossed those gorgeous bare legs so that the dress slithered enticingly up her thighs.

193

She leaned forward—oh yes, deliberately, he knew—so that in the second he dared take his eyes off the road he had a delectable view of her breasts rising against that sexy red.

She fiddled with the radio, cocked her head long enough to send him a feline, female smile, then leaned back again. Recrossed her legs. The dress snuck up another half inch.

He worried he might drool.

Whatever she'd put on the radio came to him only in bass. Pumping, throbbing bass. The rest was white noise, static in the brain.

"You're risking lives here," he told her, and only made her laugh.

"I could make it more dangerous. I could tell you what I want you to do to me. How I want you to take me. I'm in the mood to be taken. To be used." She trailed a finger up and down the center of her body. "A few weeks ago, or longer than that, did you ever imagine taking me, Jack? Using me?"

"Yes. The first time was after that morning I saw you on the beach. Only, when I imagined it, it was night, and I walked down and pulled you into the water, into surf. I could taste your skin and the salt. I had your breasts in my hands, in my mouth, while the water beat over us. I took you on the wet sand while the waves crashed, until all you could say was my name."

"That's a long time ago." Her voice went thick. "A long time to imagine. I know one thing. We really need to go back to the beach."

The laugh should've eased some of the ache, but only increased it. Another first, Jack concluded: A woman who could make him laugh and burn at the same time.

He whipped the car off the road and onto the long drive of the Brown Estate.

There were lights glowing on the third floor, both wings of the main house, and the glimmer of them in Mac's studio. And there, thank God, the shine of Emma's porch light, and the lamp she'd left on low inside.

He hit the release for his seat belt even as he hit the brakes. Before she could do the same, he managed to shift toward her, grab hold of her and let his mouth ravish hers.

He molded her breasts, gave himself the pleasure of riding his hands up those legs, under that seductive red.

She closed her teeth over his tongue, a quick, erotic trap, and struggled with his fly.

He managed to yank down one shoulder of her dress before he rammed his knee into the gear shift.

"Ouch," she said on a breathless laugh. "We'll have to add knee pads to the elbow pads."

"Damn car's too small. We'd better get inside before we hurt ourselves."

Her hands gripped his jacket, yanked to bring him back for one more wild kiss. "Hurry."

They shoved out of opposite sides of the car, then bolted for each other. Another breathless laugh, a desperate moan, sounded in the silence. They stumbled, grappled, and groped as their mouths clashed.

She yanked and tugged his jacket away as they circled up the walk like a pair of mad dancers. When they reached the door she simply shoved him back against it. Her mouth warred with his, breaking only so she could drag his sweater up, nails scraping flesh before she tossed it aside.

The heels and the angle brought her mouth level with his jaw. She bit it as she whipped the belt out of his pants, and tossed that aside as well.

Jack fumbled behind him for the doorknob, and they both lurched inside. Now he pushed her back to the door, yanked her arms over her head and handcuffed her wrists with his hand. Keeping her trapped, he shoved her skirt up and found her. Just

195

her, already hot for him, already wet. And her gasp ended on a cry when he drove her hard and fast to climax.

"How much can you take?" he demanded.

Breath ragged, body still erupting, she met his eyes. "All you've got."

He drove her up again, beyond moans and cries, storming her system with his hands, with his mouth. Heat sheathed her, slicked her skin as he dragged the dress down to free her breasts, to feed on them. Everything she wanted, more than she could imagine, rough and urgent, he used and exploited her body.

Owned her, she thought. Did he know? Could he know?

Want was enough, to want like this, be wanted like this. She would make it enough. And wanting him, craving him, she braced against the door and wrapped a leg around his waist.

"Give me more."

She consumed him, in that moment before he plunged inside her, the look, the feel, the taste of her consumed him. Then with a new kind of madness, he took her against the door, battering them both while her hair tumbled out of its pins, while she said his name over and over.

Release was both brutal and glorious.

He wasn't entirely sure he was still standing, or that his heart would ever beat normally again. It continued to jackhammer in his chest, making the basic act of breathing a challenge.

"Are we still alive?" he managed.

"I . . . I don't think I could feel like this if I wasn't. But I do think my life passed before my eyes at one point."

"Was I there?"

"In every scene."

He gave himself another minute, then eased back. He was indeed still standing, he noted. And so was she—flushed and glowing, and naked but for a pair of sky-high sexy heels.

"God, Emma, you're . . . There are no words." He had to

touch again, but this time almost reverently. "We're not going to make it upstairs yet."

"Okay." When he gripped her hips, lifted, she boosted up to wrap both legs around his waist. "Can you make it as far as the couch?"

"I'm going to give it a try." He carried her there where they could fall in a tangled heap.

$\mathcal{T}$WO HOURS LATER, WHEN THEY FINALLY MADE IT UPSTAIRS, they slept in a tangled heap.

She dreamed, and in the dream they danced in the garden, in the moonlight. The air was soft with spring and scented by roses. Moon and stars silvered the flowers that bloomed everywhere. Her fingers twined with his as they glided and turned. Then he brought hers to his lips to kiss.

When she looked up, when she smiled, she saw the words in his eyes even before he spoke them.

"I love you, Emma."

In the dream her heart bloomed like the flowers.

CHAPTER THIRTEEN

*I*N PREPARATION FOR THE *S*EAMAN MEETING, *E*MMA FILLED THE entrance urns with her big pots of hydrangeas. The intense blue created such a strong statement, she thought, dramatic, romantic and eye-catching. Since the bride's colors were blue and peach she hoped the hydrangeas would fit the bill for the initial impact.

Humming, she went back to her van to unload the pots of white tulips—the bride's favorite—that would line the steps. A sweeter image than the hot blue, softer, more delicate. A nice mix, to her mind, of texture, shape, and style.

A taste, she thought, of things to come.

"Em!"

Bent over between the urns, her arms full of tulips, Emma turned her head. And Mac snapped her camera. "Looking good."

"The flowers are. I hope to look better before the consult.

Our biggest client to date requires careful grooming." She placed the pots. "All around."

In a suit as boldly green as her eyes, Mac stood, legs spread, feet planted. "Not much time left to beautify."

"Nearly done. This is the last." With her system bursting with flowers and scents, Emma took a deep breath. "God! What a gorgeous day."

"You're pretty chirpy."

"I had a really good date last night." After stepping back to examine the portico, she hooked an arm with Mac's. "It had everything. Comedy, drama, conversation, sex. I feel . . . energized."

"And look starry-eyed."

"Maybe." Briefly, she dipped her head to Mac's shoulder. "I know it's too soon, and we're not even talking about—or anywhere near—the serious L. But . . . Mac, you know how I always had this fantasy about the moonlit night, the stars—"

"Dancing in the garden." Instinctively, Mac slid an arm around Emma's waist. "Sure, since we were kids."

"I dreamed it last night, and it was Jack. I was dancing with Jack. It's the first time I ever had the dream, or imagined it where I knew who I danced with. Don't you think that means something?"

"You're in love with him."

"That's what Parker said last night before I went out, and of course, I'm all no, no, I'm not. And, of course, as usual, she's right. Am I crazy?"

"Who said love was sane? You've sort of been there before."

"Sort of been," Emma agreed. "Wanted to be, hoped to be. But now that I am, it's more than I imagined. And I imagined a lot." Emma sidestepped, pivoted, pirouetted. "It makes me happy."

"Are you going to tell him?"

"God, no. He'd freak. You know, Jack."

"Yes," Mac said carefully, "I know Jack."

"It makes me happy," Emma repeated as she laid a hand on her heart. "I can stay there for now. He has feelings for me. You know when a man has feelings for you."

"True enough."

"So I'm going to be happy and believe he'll fall in love with me."

"Emma, solid truth? I don't know how he could resist you. You're good together, that's easy to see. If you're happy, I'm happy."

But Emma knew Mac's tones, her expressions, her heart. "You're worried I'll get hurt. I can hear it in your voice. Because, well, we know Jack. Mac, you didn't want to fall in love with Carter."

"You've got me there." Mac's lips curved as she danced her fingers at the ends of Emma's hair. "I didn't, but I did, so I should stop being so cynical."

"Good. Now I've got to stop standing around and go transform into a professional. Tell Parker I'm done, will you, and I'll be back in twenty."

"Will do." And with concern showing now, Mac watched her friend rush off.

AN HOUR LATER, DRESSED IN A TRIM SUIT AND LOW HEELS, Emma took the lead in escorting the future bride, her eagle-eyed mother, and the mother's fascinated sister around the gardens.

"You can see what we'll have blooming next spring, and I realize the gardens aren't as flush as you need or want."

"They just can't wait until May or June," Kathryn Seaman muttered.

"Mom, let's not go there again."

"It is, however, prime time for tulips—which I know you favor," Emma said to Jessica. "We'll plant more this fall, white tulips, and peach tulips—you'll have a flood of them, and blue hyacinths. We'll also fill in with white containers of peach roses, delphinium, snapdragons, stock, the hydrangeas. All in your colors, popped out by the white. I plan to back this area here with a screen covered with roses."

She turned her smile on Kathryn. "I promise you, it'll be like a fantasy garden, and as full and lush and romantic as anything you could wish for your daughter's wedding."

"Well, I've seen your work so I'm going to take your word." Kathryn nodded to Mac. "The engagement photos were everything you said they'd be."

"It helps to have two gorgeous people wildly in love."

"We had so much fun, too." Jessica beamed at Mac. "Plus, I felt like a storybook princess."

"You looked like one," her mother said. "All right, let's talk about the terraces."

"If you remember from the sketches at the proposal," Emma began, and led the way.

"I've seen your work as well." Adele, the bride's aunt, scanned the terraces. "I've been to three weddings here, and all were beautifully done."

"Thank you." Parker added a polite smile to the acknowledgment.

"Actually, what you've done here, built here, has inspired me to look into plans for doing something similar. We live part of the year in Jamaica. A destination wedding spot. And a perfect place for a good, upscale, all-inclusive wedding company."

"You're serious about that?" Kathryn asked her.

"I've been looking into it, and getting more serious. My husband's going to retire," Adele told Parker. "And we plan to spend even more time in our winter home there. It would be an excellent investment, I think, and something fun."

She gave Emma a twinkling smile and a wink. "Now, if I could lure you away with the promise of unlimited tropical flowers and balmy island breezes, I'd have my first real building block."

"Tempting," Emma said in the same light tone, "but Centerpiece of Vows keeps me busy. If you move forward with your plans, I'm sure any of us will be happy to answer any questions you might have. Now, for this area . . ."

$\mathcal{A}$FTER THE MEETING ALL FOUR WOMEN COLLAPSED IN THE parlor.

"God." Laurel stretched out her legs. "That woman sure knows how to put you through your paces. I feel like we had the event instead of just talking it through. Again."

"Unless there are any objections, I'd like to black out the Friday and Sunday around the event. The size and scope of this wedding will more than make up for that lost revenue, plus the publicity and the word of mouth will bring in more." Parker toed off her shoes. "That would give us the full week to focus exclusively on this."

"Thank God." Emma heaved a long, relieved sigh. "The amount of flowers and landscaping, the type of bouquets and arrangements, centerpieces, swags, garlands, ornamental trees? I'd have to hire more designers to get it done. But with that full week on the single event, I think I can stick with the usual team. I can add someone else if need be for the actual dressing, but I'd really prefer to do as much of this as I can personally, and with the people I know."

"I'm right there with Emma," Laurel said. "The cakes, the dessert bar, the personalized chocolates, they're all on the elaborate and labor-intensive side. If I had the full week on nothing else, I'd actually get a couple hours' sleep."

"Make it three for three." Mac raised a hand. "They want full photo documentation of the rehearsal, and the rehearsal dinner, so if we had another event on Friday, I'd have to assign a photographer to that as I'd have to cover the Seamans. As it is I'm putting two more on the event itself, plus two videographers. Keeping Sunday black means we don't have to kill ourselves and our subs breaking down, and redressing."

"Which doesn't even begin to address what they expect of you," Emma said to Parker.

"So we're agreed. And," Parker added, "I'll let the MOB know we're clearing our decks for wedding week so we can give her daughter's wedding all our time, attention, and skill. She'll like that."

"She likes us," Emma pointed out. "The concept of a company founded and run by four women appeals to her."

"And her sister. Who else did the sneaky Adele try to lure to Jamaica?" Laurel asked.

All four women raised hands.

"And she didn't even realize it was rude," Parker added. "*Our* business. It's not like we're employees. We own it."

"Rude, yes, but I don't think she meant any harm." Emma shrugged. "I elect to be flattered. She considers my flowers fabulous, Laurel's cakes and pastries superb, Parker's coordinating unmatched. Added to that, Mac blew it out of the park with the engagement photos."

"I did," Mac agreed. "I really did."

"Let's all take a moment to congratulate ourselves on our brilliance and talent." Parker offered a toast with her bottle of water. "Then get back to work."

"If we're taking a moment, I'd like to thank Emma for last night's entertainment."

Emma sent Laurel a blank look. "Sorry?"

"I happened to be taking a little air on my terrace last night before settling in for the night, and noticed a car barreling down the drive. For a minute I thought, uh-oh, something happened. But no, not quite yet."

"Oh my God." Emma slapped her hands over her eyes. "Oh my God."

"When no one immediately jumped out gushing blood, or jumped out at all, I actually considered running down, prepared to do triage. But momentarily both car doors flew open. Emma out of one, Jack out of the other."

"You *watched*?"

Laurel snorted. "Duh."

"More," Mac demanded. "We must have more."

"And more you will have. They fell on each other like animals."

"Oh, we did . . . too," Emma recalled.

"Then it's the classic back against the door."

"Oh, it's been so long since I had the back against the door," Parker said with a delicate shiver for emphasis. "Too long."

"From my view, Jack's got the move down cold. Or hot, I should say. But our girl holds her own. Or was it his?"

"Jesus, Laurel!"

"She wrestled his jacket off, tosses it. Rips his sweater off, heaves it away."

"Oh boy, oh boy, oh boy!" Mac said.

"But the gold medal move was the belt. She whips that belt off—" Laurel flicked an arm through the air to demonstrate. "Then lets it fly."

"I think I need another bottle of water."

"Unfortunately, Parker, they took it inside."

"Killjoys," Mac muttered.

"The rest was left to my very . . . fluid imagination. So I

want to thank our own Emmaline for the view from my balcony seat. Sister, stand up and take a bow."

To enthusiastic applause, Emma did just that. "Now I'll leave you and Peeping Thomasina to your salacious thoughts. I'm going to work."

"Back against the door," Parker murmured. "I'm small enough to be jealous."

"If I were small enough, I'd be jealous of her having her back against anything. But it's okay, because I've declared myself in a sex moratorium."

"A sex moratorium?" Mac repeated, turning to Laurel.

"That's right. I'm in a sex moratorium so I can be in a dating moratorium, because for the last couple of months dating's just been irritating." Laurel lifted her shoulders, let them fall. "Why do something that irritates me?"

"For the sex?" Mac suggested.

Eyes slitted, Laurel shot a finger at her friend. "You're only saying that because you're getting laid regularly."

"Yes." Mac considered, nodded. "Yes, I am getting laid regularly."

"It's rude to brag to those of us who are not," Parker pointed out.

"But I'm getting laid with love." Mac drew out the final word so Laurel laughed.

"Now you're just getting sickening."

"I'm not the only one, at least on one side. Emma said you were right, Parks. She's in love with Jack."

"Of course she's in love with Jack," Laurel interrupted. "She wouldn't have slept with him otherwise."

"Um, I hate to disillusion you, Bright Eyes, but Emma's had sex with men she wasn't in love with. And," Mac added, "has gently refused to have sex with more men than the three of us combined have scored."

206

"My point exactly. What happens when the four of us go to a club, for instance? Four very hot chicks? We get some hits, naturally. But Emma? They swarm like wasps."

"I don't see—"

"I do." Parker nodded. "She doesn't have to sleep with someone just because she's attracted. She can and does pick and choose. And she's picky and choosy rather than promiscuous. If it were just lust, she could and would answer that call elsewhere, because to answer it with Jack is complicated, and risky."

"Which is the reason she waited so long to act on it," Mac pointed out. "I don't see . . . Yes, I do," she corrected. "Damn it, I hate when I don't have a chance to be right before you're right."

"Now that she's realized what I could've told her weeks ago, I wonder what she'll do."

"She had her dancing in the garden dream," Mac told them, "and it was with Jack."

"Okay that's serious. Not just in love," Laurel said, "but *in love*."

"She's okay with it. She's going to enjoy the moment."

No one spoke.

"I think," Parker said carefully, "love is never wrong. Whether it's for the moment, or it's forever."

"We all know Emma's always wanted forever," Mac pointed out.

"But you can't have forever unless you take the moment."

"And if it doesn't work?" Laurel looked at her two friends. "That's what we're here for."

*I*N HER OFFICE EMMA CAUGHT UP ON PAPERWORK WHILE SHE let a facial mask deep clean and hydrate. Just how many women were lucky enough to be able to deal with skin care *and* generate invoices at the same time? In their bare feet, with Norah Jones crooning out of the speakers?

And how many of those who might be lucky enough had also had crazed jungle sex—twice—with an amazing man the night before?

Not many, she'd wager. Not many at all.

While the mask worked its magic, she placed an order with her suppliers for flower foam, plastic ties, wire, clear and colored stones, then did a cruise through to see what might be on sale, or on special and added liquid foam and foam sheets and three dozen light bases.

That would hold her for a while, she thought, placed the order, then brought up her wholesale candle supplier to see what they had to offer.

"Knock, knock! Emmaline! Are you home?"

"Mom? Up here." She saved her shopping cart, before pushing away from the desk. She met her mother coming up the stairs. "Hi!"

"Hi, my baby. Your face is very pink."

"I . . . Oh, I forgot." Laughing, Emma tapped her fingers on her cheek. "It needs to come off. I started on candles and got caught up." She detoured to the bathroom to wash off the mask. "Playing hooky?"

"I worked this morning, and am now free as a bird so came by to see my daughter before I go home." Lucia picked up the jar of mask. "Is this good?"

"You tell me. It's the first time I've tried it." Emma finished splashing cool water on her face, then patted it dry.

Lucia pursed her lips. "You're too beautiful for me to know if it's because of the lucky genes I passed to you or from the jar.

Emma grinned. Studying her face in the mirror over the sink, she poked lightly at her cheeks, her chin. "Feels good though. That's a plus."

208

"You have a glow," Lucia added while Emma sprayed on toner, followed up with moisturizer. "But from what I hear that's not from the jar either."

"Lucky genes?"

"Lucky something. Your cousin Dana stopped in the bookstore this morning. It seems her good friend Livvy . . . You know Livvy a little."

"Yes, a little."

"Livvy was out with a new boyfriend, having dinner, and who did she spot in a quiet corner across the room sharing wine, pasta, and intimate conversation with a certain handsome architect?"

Emma fluttered her lashes. "How many guesses?"

Lucia raised and lowered her eyebrows.

"Let's go downstairs and get something to drink. Coffee, or something cold?"

"Something cold."

"Jack and I went to an art opening," Emma began as they started down. "A really terrible art opening, which is actually a good story."

"You can come back to that. Tell me about the wine and pasta."

"We had wine and pasta after we left the opening." In the kitchen, Emma got down glasses, filled them with ice.

"You're being evasive."

"Yes." With a laugh, Emma sliced a lemon. "Which is silly, since you've obviously figured out Jack and I are dating."

"Are you evading because you think I won't approve?"

"No. Maybe." Emma opened the sparkling water her mother liked, poured it over ice, added slices of lemon.

"Are you happy? I already see the answer on your face, but you can answer yes or no."

"Yes."

"Then why would I disapprove of anything that made you happy?"

"It's sort of odd, isn't it though? After all this time?"

"Some things take time, some don't." Lucia turned into the living room, sat on the sofa. "I love this little room. All the colors, the scents. I know it's a place that makes you happy."

Emma came over, sat beside her mother. "It does."

"You're happy in your work, your life, your home. And that helps a mother—even of a grown woman—sleep well at night. Now, if you're happy with a man I happen to like quite a bit, I'm happy, too. You need to bring him to dinner."

"Oh, Mom. We're just . . . dating."

"He's been to dinner before."

"Yes. Yes. Del's friend Jack has been to dinner, to some cookouts, to some parties at the house. But you're not asking me to bring Del's friend to dinner."

"Suddenly he can't eat my cooking or have a beer with your father? You understand, *nina*, I know what 'dating' means in this case?"

"Yes."

"He should come for Cinco de Mayo. All your friends should come. We'll put the pork on the grill, and not Jack."

"Okay. I'm in love with him, Mama."

"Yes, baby." Lucia drew Emma's head to her shoulder. "I know your face."

"He's not in love with me."

"Then he's not as smart as I think he is."

"He cares. You know that. He cares, and there's a really big attraction. On both sides. But he's not in love with me. Yet."

"That's my girl," Lucia said.

"Do you think it's . . . underhanded to deliberately set out to make a man fall in love with you?"

"Do you intend to lie, to pretend to be what you're not, to cheat, make promises you won't keep?"

"No. Of course not."

"Then how could it be underhanded? If I hadn't made your father fall in love with me, we wouldn't be sitting here in your pretty little room."

"You . . . Really?"

"Oh, I was so in love. Hopelessly, or so I thought. He was so handsome, so kind, so sweet and funny with his little boy. So lonely. He treated me well, with respect, with honor—and as we grew to know each other, with friendship. And I wanted him to *sweep* me away, to see me as a woman, to take me into his bed, even if it was just for a night."

Inside her chest, Emma's romantic heart simply soared. "Oh, Mama."

"What? You think you invented this? The needs, the wants? I was young and he was above me in station. The wealth, the position, these were barriers—at least I thought so. But I could dream.

"And maybe a little more than dream," Lucia added with a secret smile. "I tried to look my best, to cook meals he especially liked, to listen when he needed a friend. That's what I knew how to do. And I would make sure, when he was going out, that his tie wasn't quite straight—even when it was—so I'd have to fix it. I still do," she murmured. "I still want to. I knew there was something—I could feel it, I could see it in his eyes— something more than the bond over the little boy we both loved, something more than friendship and respect. All I could do was show him, in little ways, that I was his."

"Mama, that's so . . . You never told me all this before."

"I never needed to. Your papa, he was careful with me, so careful not to touch my hand too long, hold my gaze too long. Until that day I stood under the cherry blossoms, and I saw him

211

walking to me. I saw him coming to me, and what was in his eyes. My heart."

Lucia pressed her hand to it. "Ah! It fell, right at his feet. How could he not know? And knowing, his heart fell beside mine."

"It's what I want."

"Of course."

Emma had to blink tears away. "I don't think fixing Jack's tie is going to do it."

"The little things, Emma. The gestures, the moments. And the big. I let him see my heart. I gave it to him, even when I believed he couldn't or wouldn't take it. I gave it anyway—a gift. Even if he broke it. I was very brave. Love is very brave."

"I'm not as brave as you."

"I think you're wrong." Lucia wrapped her arm around Emma's shoulders to hug. "Very wrong. But now it's new, isn't it? New and bright and happy. Enjoy it."

"I am."

"And bring him to the party."

"All right."

"Now, I'm going home to let you get back to work. Do you have a date?"

"Not tonight. We had a long consult today—the Seaman wedding."

Lucia's eyes danced. "Ah, the *big* one."

"The big one. And I have paperwork, ordering, planning to get to tonight, and a full day tomorrow. He has a business thing tomorrow night, but he's going to try to come by after and . . ."

"I know what *and* is," Lucia said with a laugh. "Get a good night's sleep tonight then." She patted Emma's knee, rose.

"I'm so glad you came by." Standing, Emma wrapped her mother in a hard hug. "Kiss Papa for me."

"For you and for me. I think he'll take me out to dinner tonight, and we'll share wine and pasta and intimate conversation. To show we haven't lost our touch."

"As if ever."

Emma leaned on the doorjamb, waved her mother off. Then instead of going back into work, left the door open to the spring air and took a walk around the gardens.

Tight buds, fresh blossoms, tender shoots. The beginning of a new cycle, she thought. She wandered back to her greenhouses, gave herself the pleasure of puttering. Seeds she'd planted over the winter were now young plants, and doing nicely. She'd begin to harden them off in the next few days, she decided.

She circled back around, stopped to fill the bird feeders she shared with Mac. The air had already started to cool by the time she went back in. When the sun set, she thought, it would be chilly.

On impulse, she got out a pot. Then minced, chopped, poured, tossed in cubes of herbs she'd frozen the summer before. With a kettle of soup simmering, she went back up to finish her orders.

An hour later, she came down to stir, then glanced toward the window as she heard a car. Surprised, pleased, she hurried to the door to greet Jack.

"Well, hi."

"I had a meeting, and managed to wrap it up early. I left my jacket here again, so I thought I'd swing by on my way . . . You're cooking?"

"I took a walk, and it started cooling off, which put me in the mood for kitchen sink soup. There's plenty, if you're interested."

"Actually, I was . . . There's a ball game on tonight, so—"

"I have a television." She stepped in, straightened his tie, with a secret smile. "I allow it to broadcast ball games."

"Really?"

She gave his tie a little tug. "You can taste the soup. If it doesn't

213

appeal, I'll get your jacket and you can watch the ball game at home."

She strolled off, went back to stirring. When he followed, she glanced over her shoulder. "Lean over, open up."

He did just that so she held the tasting spoon to his lips.

"It's good." His eyebrows lifted in surprise. "It's damn good. How come I never knew you could make soup?"

"You never stopped by to get your jacket after you wrapped up a meeting early. Do you want to stay for dinner?"

"Yeah. Thanks."

"It needs about an hour more. Why don't you open a bottle of cab?"

"Okay." Now he leaned down, kissed her. Paused, kissed her again, softly, slowly. "I'm glad I swung by."

"Me, too."

CHAPTER FOURTEEN

$\mathcal{T}$HE MEXICAN AND AMERICAN FLAGS FLEW THEIR PROUD colors as Emma's Mexican mother and Yankee father combined cultures to celebrate Cinco de Mayo.

Every year the expansive grounds offered games, from lawn bowling and badminton to moon bounces and waterslides. Friends, relatives, and neighbors played and competed while others crowded at picnic tables, diving into platters of pork and chicken, warm tortillas, bowls of red beans or chilis, guacamole or salsa hot enough to scorch the throat.

There were gallons of lemonade, Negra Modelo, Corona, tequila, and frosty margaritas to put out the fire.

Whenever he'd managed to drop by on the fifth of May, Jack had always been amazed at the number of people the Grants managed to feed. And the choices of fajitas and burgers, black beans and rice or potato salad. Flan or apple pie.

He supposed the food was just a symbol of how completely Phillip and Lucia blended.

He sipped his beer and watched some of the guests dance to the trio of guitars and marimbas.

Beside him, Del took a pull on his own beer. "Hell of a party."

"They pull out all the stops."

"So, is it weird being here this year with the hosts' baby girl?"

Jack started to deny it as a matter of principle. But hell, it was Del. "Little bit. But so far, nobody's called for the rope."

"It's still early."

"Brown, you're a comfort to me. Is it my imagination or are there about twice as many kids as there were last year? Year before," he remembered. "I couldn't make it last year."

"Might be. I don't think they're all related. I heard Celia's pregnant again though."

"Yeah, Emma mentioned it. You're here stag?"

"Yeah." Del smiled slowly. "You never know, do you? Check out the blonde in the blue dress. Those are some nice pins she's got."

"Yeah. I always thought Laurel had great legs."

Del choked on his beer. "That's not . . . Oh," he managed when she turned, laughed, and he got a better look. "Not used to seeing her in a dress, I guess." Very deliberately he turned in the opposite direction. "Anyway, there are a bevy of sultry brunettes, cool blondes, and a sprinkle of hot redheads. Many of whom are unattached. But I guess the days of scoping the field are over for you."

"I'm dating, not blind or dead." The idea put an itch between Jack's shoulder blades.

"Where is Em?"

"She went to help somebody with something food related. We're not joined at the hip."

Del lifted an eyebrow. "Okay."

"I have friends, she has friends, and some of them happen to be mutual. We don't have to walk in step at a party."

"Right." Del took another contemplative sip of his beer. "So . . . would the guy she's currently kissing on the mouth be her friend, your friend, or a mutual?"

Jack swung around, caught the end of the kiss between Emma and some Nordic god type. She laughed, and her hands gestured expressively before she grabbed one of Thor's and pulled him over to a group of people.

"Looks like he's not one of yours," Del commented.

"Why don't you . . ." He cut off the suggestion he had in mind as Lucia stopped in front of them. "You two should be eating instead of just standing here looking handsome."

"I'm considering all options," Del told her. "There are big decisions to be made, all the way down to apple pie or flan."

"There's also strawberry shortcake and empanadas."

"You see? Not to be taken lightly."

"You should sample each, then decide. Look here!" She beamed smiles and threw out her hands as Mac and Carter walked to them. "Mackensie, you made it."

"Sorry we're so late. The shoot ran a little longer than I hoped." She kissed Lucia's cheek.

"You're here, that's what counts. And you!" Lucia threw her arms around Carter for a hug.

Carter lifted her an inch off the grass in a gesture of long-term affection.

"It's been years since you came for Cinco de Mayo."

Carter grinned. "It's bigger."

"Because there are more of us. Your mama and papa are here, with Diane's children. Sherry and Nick are here, too," she said, speaking of his younger sister. Diane and Sam should be here soon. Mac, your future mother-in-law tells me the wedding plans are going well."

"They're clicking along."

"Let me see your ring again. Ah!" She twinkled a smile at Carter after examining the diamond on Mac's hand. "Very nicely done. Come, Celia hasn't seen it yet. Carter," she called as she pulled Mac away, "get food, get drink."

Instead, Carter stood where he was. "I haven't been back for one of these in . . . it must be ten years. I'd forgotten. It's like a carnival."

"The best in the county," Del commented. "The Grants either know or are related to everybody. Including, it seems, our mechanic and poker buddy. Hey, Mal."

"Hey." In dark shades, worn jeans, and a black T-shirt, he strolled over. He carried two beers by the neck. "Want one, Maverick?" he said to Carter.

"Sure. I didn't realize you knew the Grants."

"They've been bringing their cars in for service or repair for the last six, eight months. Before you know it, you're telling Lucia your life story, eating her corn bread and wishing she'd dump her husband and run off with you to Maui."

"Ain't that the truth," Jack said.

"She said I should come by after work, backyard deal for Cinco de Mayo. I figure a cookout, maybe on the fancy side, considering, some Mexican beer, tortillas." He shook his head. "Is anybody not here?"

"I think they covered everybody."

"Sorry that took so long." Emma hurried up, a margarita in her hand. "There were circumstances."

"Yeah, I saw one of them."

After giving Jack a puzzled smile, she turned to Malcolm. "Hi, I'm Emmaline."

"You're the Cobalt."

"I . . ." Her eyes widened, then filled with contrition. "Yes. You must be Malcolm."

"Mal." He gave her a long, head-to-toe scoping out. "You know, it's a good thing you look like your mother, who I hope to marry. Otherwise I'd replay the ass-kicking I gave your partner when I thought she was you."

"And I'd deserve it. Even though I learned my lesson, and I'm being much more conscientious. You did a great job. You have serious skills. I wonder if you'd have time to service my van if I bring it in next week."

"You don't just look like her, do you?"

Emma smiled as she sipped the margarita. "You need a plate," she told him, "and a great deal of food."

"Why don't you show me where—" Mal cut himself off when he caught the warning in Jack's eyes, and the casual and proprietary stroke of his hand down Emma's hair. "Right. Maybe I'll just go graze awhile."

"I'll do the same," Carter decided.

Del's lips quirked. "Looks like I'm empty." He jiggled the beer bottle. "Em, who's the long brunette? Pink top, skinny jeans?"

"Ah . . . Paige. Paige Haviller."

"Single?"

"Yes."

"See you later."

"He should've asked me if she had any brains," Emma said as Del strolled away. "He'll be bored in thirty minutes or less."

"Depends on what they're doing for thirty minutes."

She laughed up at him. "I suppose it does." She slipped a hand into his to squeeze. "It's a good day, isn't it?"

"I can never figure out how they pull this off."

"They work for weeks, and hire a platoon to help set up the games and activities. And Parker helps coordinate. Speaking of which, I—"

"Who was the guy?"

"The guy? There are a lot of them. Give me some hints."

"The one you were kissing a little while ago."

"Bigger hint."

That crawled into his spleen. "The one who looked like the prince of Denmark."

"The prince of . . . Oh, you must mean Marshall. One of the circumstances why I was so long getting back."

"So I saw."

She cocked her head, and the faintest frown line formed between her eyebrows. "He was late getting here. With his wife and their new baby boy. After he came out to get me, I went in to fuss over the baby for a while. Problem?"

"No." Idiot. "Del was yanking my chain, and I walked into it. And the mixed metaphor. Let's rewind. Speaking of which?"

"We dated a little, a few years ago, Marshall and I. I introduced him to his wife. We did their wedding about eighteen months ago."

"Got it. Apologies."

She smiled a little. "He didn't grab my ass like a certain crazy artist grabbed yours."

"His loss."

"Why don't we mingle, be sociable?"

"Good idea."

"Oh," she said as they started to walk, "speaking of which, I had a thought. Since I have several errands in town tomorrow, if I stayed at your place tonight, I'd be in town. Parker rode in with me, as we both needed to get here early to help, but she can ride back with Laurel. It would save me from going back and forth."

"Stay at my place?"

She lifted her brows, and the eyes under them went cool. "*I* could bunk on the couch if you don't want company."

"No. I just assumed you'd need to get home after this. You usually start pretty early in the morning."

"Tomorrow I'm starting in town, not quite as early. But if it's a problem—"

"No." He stopped, turning her so they faced each other. "It's fine. It's good. But don't you need some things—for tomorrow?"

"I put some things in my car when I had the thought."

"Then we're set." He leaned down to kiss her.

"Looks like you need another beer."

Then jerked back at her father's voice.

Phillip smiled. Casually, from the looks of it, Jack thought. Unless you were the one who'd just made arrangements to sleep with his daughter.

"Negra Modelo, right?" Phillip offered one.

"Yeah, thanks. Great party, as always."

"My favorite of the year." Phillip laid an arm around Emma's shoulders. Casually, affectionately. Territorially. "We started the tradition the spring Lucia was pregnant with Matthew. Friends, family, children. Now our children are grown and making families of their own."

"You're feeling sentimental," Emma said, and tipping her face up, brushed her lips over his jaw.

"I still see you running on the lawn with your friends, trying so hard to win prizes at ring toss, or to break one of the pinatas. Like your mother, you bring the color and the life."

"Papa."

Phillip shifted his gaze, directly into Jack's. "It's a lucky man who's offered that color and life. And a wise one who values it."

"Papa," she repeated, but in a warning tone now.

"A man only gets so many treasures," he said, and tapped her on the nose with his finger. "I'm going to check the grill. I don't trust your brothers or your uncles for long. Jack," he added with a nod before he walked away.

"Sorry. He can't help it."

"It's okay. Did I sweat through my shirt?"

Laughing, she hooked an arm around Jack's waist. "No. Why don't we go show those kids how to break a pinata?"

$\mathscr{L}$ATER, THEY FLOPPED DOWN ON THE GRASS TO WATCH SOME OF the teenagers in an impromptu game of soccer. Parker joined them, slipping off her sandals, smoothing down the skirt of her sundress.

"Night soccer," Jack commented. "Not your usual."

"Do you play?" Emma asked him.

"Not my game. Give me a bat, a football, a hoop. But I like to watch."

"You like to watch anything where a ball's involved." Mac dropped down beside them, tugged Carter down with her. "Ate much too much. It just kept being there."

"Oh, that's just pitiful," Emma muttered when the ball was intercepted. "Does he think it has eyes, radar?"

"You like soccer?"

She glanced at Jack. "Girl's Varsity at the Academy. All-State."

"Seriously?"

"Cocaptains," she added, wagging her thumb between herself and Parker.

"They were vicious." Laurel knelt on the grass beside Parker. "Mac and I would go to the games, and pity the opposition. Go on." She elbowed Parker. "Go on out and kick some ass."

"Hmm. Want to?" Emma asked Parker.

"Em, it's been a decade."

Emma boosted up to her knees so she could slap her hands on her hips. "Are you saying we're too old to take those losers and weak feet? Are you saying you have lost—your—edge?"

"Oh, hell. One goal."

"Let's score."

222

Like Parker, she slipped out of her sandals.

Fascinated, Jack watched the two women in their pretty spring dresses approach the field.

There was discussion, some hoots, a few catcalls.

"What's up?" Mal sauntered over to study the two groups.

"Emma and Parker are going to kick some soccer ass," Laurel told him.

"No kidding? This ought to be interesting."

They took position on the grass in the floodlights, with Emma and Parker's team set to receive. The women glanced at each other, then Emma held up three fingers, then two. Parker laughed, shrugged.

The ball sailed through the air. Emma two-fisted it to Parker, who took it on the bounce, and dodged her way through three opponents with a blur of footwork that had the earlier catcalls turning to cheers.

She pivoted, feinted, then bulleted the ball cross-field to where Emma sprang to receive. She scored with a blurring banana kick that left the goalie openmouthed.

In unison, she and Parker shot both arms and screamed.

"They always did that," Mac told the group. "No modesty at all. Go Robins!"

"Girl's soccer team," Carter explained. "State bird."

When Parker started to leave the field, Emma grabbed her arm. Jack heard her say, "One more."

Parker shook her head; Emma persisted. Parker gripped her skirt, held it out, and whatever Emma said in response made her former cocaptain laugh.

They took defense against an opposing team who had considerably more respect now. They fought, blocking, rejecting, pushing their opponents back.

Jack's grin spread when Emma shoulder tackled an opponent. And looked gorgeous doing it, he realized—and just a little

223

fierce. A fresh wave of lust curled in his belly as she charged the player in possession. Her slide tackle—Jesus, just look at her!—had the teenager off balance with his instep pass.

On alert, Parker leaped at the next hard, high kick, skirts flying as she sprang and executed a dead-on header.

"Well, well," Mal murmured.

"Interception!" Laurel cried out when Emma trapped the ball. "Woo!"

Emma avoided her opponents' attempts to regain the ball with a quick cut back. She bicycle kicked the ball back to Parker, who shot it between the goalie's legs.

Hands up, a scream, and Parker slung an arm around Emma's shoulders.

"Done?"

"Oh, so very done." Emma sucked in a breath. "No longer seventeen, but still. Felt righteous."

"Let's leave winners." They held up joined hands, bowed to applause, then deserted the field.

"Baby," Jack said as he grabbed Emma's hand to pull her back down to the grass, "you're a killer."

"Oh yeah." And she reached out for the bottle of water Mac offered. Before she could drink, her mouth was busy with Jack's.

The kiss earned more applause.

"I'm a slave," he murmured against his lips, "to a woman who can pull off an accurate bicycle kick."

"Really?" She scraped her teeth lightly over his bottom lip. "You ought to see my instep drive."

"Anytime. Anywhere."

At the edge of the field, Mal cut across Parker's path, offered one of the two beers he held. "Want?"

"No. Thanks."

Moving around him, she pulled a bottle of water out of one of the ice tubs.

"What gym do you use, Legs?"

She opened the bottle. "My own."

"Figures. You've got some moves. Play anything else?"

She took a slow sip of water. "Piano."

As she strolled away, he watched her over a lazy pull of his beer.

𝓛ATER, LAUREL SAT ON THE GRANT'S FRONT PORCH STEPS, elbows braced behind her, eyes half closed. The quiet rolled over her, as did the smell of the grass, the front garden. The spring stars showered down.

She heard the footsteps, kept her eyes closed. And hoped whatever guest was leaving would keep moving, and let her keep her solitude.

"Are you all right?"

No such luck, she thought, and opened her eyes to look at Del. "Yeah. I'm just sitting here."

"So I see."

He sat beside her.

"I said my bye-byes. Parker's still inside—or outside—doing the Parker check to make sure nothing else has to be done. I had too much tequila to care if something else has to be done."

He gave her a closer study. "I'll drive you home."

"I gave my keys to Parker. She's driving both of us home. No rescue required, sir."

"Okay. So I heard the Robins made a comeback earlier. Sorry I missed it."

"They ruled, as ever. I guess you were otherwise occupied." She looked behind her, side to side, movements exaggerated. "Alone, Delaney? With all these pickings today? Can't believe the Robins scored and you're not gonna."

"I didn't come to score."

225

She made a *pffft* sound and gave him a shove.

His lips quirked into a reluctant smile. "Honey, you're toasted."

"Yes, I am. I'm gonna be so pissed off at me tomorrow, but right now? Feels good. Can't remember the last time I had too much tequila, or too much anything. Coulda scored."

"Sorry?"

"And I don't mean soccer." Cracking herself up, she shoved him again. "Very cute guy named . . . something made the play. But I'm in a sexual morit . . . morat . . . Wait. Sexual mor-a-tor-i-um," she said, enunciating each syllable.

Still smiling, he tucked her sunny swing of hair behind her ear. "Are you?"

"Yes, I am. I am toasted and I am in the thing I just said and don't want to have to say again." She shook back the hair he'd just smoothed, gave him a tipsy smile. "Not planning on making a play, are you?"

His smile dropped away. "No."

She *pffft*'d again, leaned back, then flicked her hand several times in dismissal. "Move along."

"I'll just sit here until Parker comes out."

"Mr. Brown, Delaney Brown, do you ever get tired of saving people?"

"I'm not saving you. I'm just sitting here."

Yeah, she thought, just sitting. On a beautiful spring night, under a shower of stars, with the scent of the first roses sweetening the air.

$\mathcal{E}$MMA PARKED HER CAR BEHIND JACK'S, RETRIEVED HER OVER-sized purse. She got out, popped the trunk, then smiled as he reached in to retrieve her overnight case.

"No comments about what the hell's in this thing?"

"Actually, I thought it would be a lot heavier."

"I restrained myself. I never asked what time you have to get started tomorrow."

"About eight. Not too early."

She linked her hand with his, added a playful swing of arms. "I'll repay your hospitality and fix breakfast. If you have anything to fix."

"I probably do." They walked up the steps to the back door of the apartment above his office.

"It makes it easy, doesn't it, to live where you work? Though I sometimes think we end up working more than we would if we had more defined lines. I love this building. It's got character."

"I fell for it," he told her as he unlocked the door.

"It suits you. The character and tradition on the outside, the clean lines and balanced flow of space inside," she added as she stepped into his kitchen.

"Speaking of clean lines and flow, I'm still trying to find words over the soccer exhibition."

"That impulse is probably going to have my quads crying tomorrow."

"I think your quads can take it. Have I told you I have a weakness for women in sports?"

She walked with him through the apartment to the bedroom. "You didn't have to. I know you have a weakness for women and a weakness for sports."

"Put them together, and I'm gone."

"And a slave to the female bicycle kick." She lifted to her toes, pecked his lips with hers. "You should've seen me in my soccer uniform."

"Do you still have it?"

She laughed, and setting her overnight on the bed, unzipped it. "As a matter of fact."

"In there?"

"Afraid not. But I do have this . . ." She pulled out something very sheer, very short, very black. "If you're interested."

"I think this is going down as a perfect day."

$\mathscr{I}$N THE MORNING, SHE FIXED FRENCH TOAST, AND DID SOMETHING crispy and mildly sweet to an apple she'd cut into slices.

"This is great. Flower artist, soccer champ, kitchen wizard."

"I am many things." She sat across from him in the alcove he used for dining. She thought the space needed flowers, something bold and bright in a copper vase. "And you're now out of eggs, and very low on milk. I'm actually doing some marketing today if you want me to pick some up, or anything else."

She saw the hitch, the hesitation before he spoke.

"No, that's okay. I need to make a run later in the week. How're the quads?"

"Fine." She ordered herself not to make an issue out of his reluctance to have her pick up a damn carton of eggs for him. "I guess the bastard elliptical is doing its job. How do you keep in shape?"

"I use the gym three or four times a week, play basketball, that sort of thing."

She sent him a slitted-eye, accusatory stare. "I bet you like it. The gym."

"Yeah, I do."

"So does Parker. I think you're both sick."

"Keeping in shape is sick?"

"No, *liking* what goes into keeping in shape is sick. I get doing it, but it should be considered a chore, a duty, a necessary evil. Like brussels sprouts."

Amusement warmed his eyes. "Brussels sprouts are evil?"

"Of course they are. Everyone knows this, even if they won't admit it. They're little green balls of evil. Just like squats are a form of torture designed by people who don't need to do squats in the first place. Bastards."

"I find your philosophy on fitness and nutrition fascinating."

"Honesty can be fascinating." She savored the last sip of her coffee. "At least when summer hits I can use the pool. That's sensible, and it's fun. Well, I should go up and shower since I slaved away over a hot stove while you had yours. I'll make it quick so I don't hold you up." She glanced back at the clock on that hot stove. "Really quick."

"Ah . . . listen, you don't have to rush. You can just lock up the back when you leave."

Pleased, she smiled. "Then I'll have another cup of coffee first."

It allowed her to linger a little, over the coffee, then over the shower. Wrapped in a towel, she slicked cream over her skin, then opened the moisturizer for her face.

As she started on her makeup, she saw Jack step in, saw in the mirror the way his gaze skimmed over the scatter of her tubes and pots on the bathroom counter. He barely missed a beat, but there was no mistaking the unease in his eyes—and no denying the hurt in her heart.

"I gotta go." The brush of his hand down her damp hair was sweet, as was the kiss. "See you later?"

"Sure."

Alone, she finished her makeup, her hair. She dressed, and she packed.

When she was done she went back into the bathroom, viciously scrubbed the sink, the counter until she was sure she'd left no trace of her or her things in his space.

"No need to panic, Jack," she mumbled. "All clear. All yours."

On the way out, she stopped and left a note on his kitchen board.

Jack—forgot I'm booked tonight. We'll catch up later. Emma

She needed a break.

She tested the back door to make sure it locked behind her, carried her case down to her car. Once she got behind the wheel, she flipped open her phone and called Parker.

"Hey, Emma, I'm on the other line with—"

"I'll be quick. Can we have a girl night tonight?"

"What's wrong?"

"Nothing. Really. I just need girl night."

"In or out?"

"In. I don't want to go out."

"I'll take care of it."

"Thanks. I'll be home in a couple of hours."

Emma closed the phone.

Friends, she thought. Girlfriends. They never let you down.

CHAPTER FIFTEEN

"I OVERREACTED."

After a full day of work, during which she'd replayed dozens of Jack details, Emma settled down.

"We'll be the judge of that." Laurel took her place in the third floor parlor, then bit into a slice of Mrs. Grady's exceptional homemade pizza.

"He didn't do anything wrong. He didn't even say anything wrong. I'm annoyed with myself."

"Okay, but you tend to be annoyed with yourself instead of anybody else. Even when the anybody else deserves it." Mac poured a glass of wine, offered the bottle to Laurel.

"Nope. Detoxifying massive quantities of tequila. It could take days."

"I don't do that." Emma scowled over her pizza. "That makes me sound like a weenie."

"You're not a weenie. You're just tolerant, and you have a sympathetic nature." Since Emma held up her glass, Mac filled it. "So when you get annoyed with somebody, you mean it."

"I'm not a pushover," Emma replied.

"Just because you're not as mean as we are, doesn't mean you're a pushover," Laurel pointed out.

"I can be mean."

"You can," Mac agreed and gave Emma a bolstering pat on the shoulder. "You have the tools, you have the skills. Mostly you don't have the heart for it."

"I—"

"Being innately nice isn't a character flaw," Parker interrupted. "I like to think we're all innately nice."

"Except for me." Laurel held up her Diet Coke.

"Yes, except for you. Why don't you just tell us what upset you, Emma?"

"It's going to sound stupid, even petty." She brooded into her wine, then down at the candy pink polish on her toes while her friends waited. "It's just that he's so protective of his space, his place. He doesn't actually say anything, but there's this invisible boundary around his area. Except he did say it before. You remember, Mac."

"Give me a hint."

"When you decided to reorganize your bedroom last winter. The closet thing. You got crazed because Carter left some of his things at your place. And Jack came over, and he agreed with you. He said all those things about what happens when you let somebody you're involved with stake territory."

"He was joking, mostly. You got mad," Mac remembered. "Walked out."

"He said that women start leaving their things all over the bathroom counter, and then they want a drawer. And before you know it, they take over. As if wanting to leave a toothbrush means you're ready to register at Tiffany."

232

"He freaked because you wanted to leave a toothbrush at his place?" Laurel demanded.

"No. Yes. Not exactly, because I never said anything about a damn toothbrush. Look, it's like this. Even if we're out somewhere and his place is closer, we come back here. Last night, I asked if I could stay at his place because I needed to be in town in the morning anyway, and he . . . he hesitated."

"Maybe his place wasn't in girl-friendly condition," Mac suggested. "He had to think if he'd left any dirty socks or Big Jugs Magazines lying around, or if he'd changed the sheets in the last decade."

"It wasn't that. His place is always neat, which may be part of the thing. He likes everything where it is. Like Parker."

"Hey."

"Well, you do," Emma said, but with a smile that held both love and apology. "It's just the nature. The thing is, you'd be okay if a guy slept over, maybe left a toothbrush. You'd just put the toothbrush in some proper space."

"Which guy? Can I have a name, an address, a photograph?"

Emma relaxed enough to laugh. "In theory. Anyway, over breakfast I mentioned I was hitting the market, and since he was out of eggs and milk, I could pick some up for him. And there it was again. That same sort of uh-oh before the no, thanks. But the killer was when he came upstairs. I was putting on my makeup and, beat me with a stick, had my stuff out on the counter. And he got this look. Annoyed and . . . wary. I told you it was going to sound stupid."

"It doesn't," Parker corrected. "It made you feel unwelcome and intrusive."

"Yes." Emma shut her eyes. "Exactly. I don't think he meant to, or that he's even fully aware, but—"

"It doesn't matter. In fact, the unconscious slight's worse."

233

"Yes!" Emma repeated, and shot Parker a grateful look. "Thank you."

"What did you do about it?" Laurel demanded.

"Do?"

"Yes, do, Em. Such as tell him to get over himself, it's a toothbrush or a tube of mascara."

"He went to work and I spent a half hour making sure I hadn't left so much as a flake of that mascara in his precious space."

"Oh yeah, that'll teach him," Laurel added. "I'd've stripped off my bra, left it hanging over his shower, left him a sarcastic love note in lipstick on the mirror. Oh, oh, and I'd have gone out and bought the economy-sized box of tampons and left them on the counter. *That* would get the point across."

"Wouldn't that be making his point?"

"No, because he has no point. You're sleeping together. Whoever's bed is in play, the other party requires some of the basics on hand. Do you get wigged out when he leaves his toothbrush or his razor at your place?"

"He doesn't. Ever."

"Oh, come on. Don't tell me he never forgets to—"

"Never."

"Well, Jesus." Laurel slumped back. "Obsessive much?"

Mac raised her hand, offered a sheepish smile. "I'm just going to say I was kind of that way. Not as—okay, obsessive. I would forget things or leave things at Carter's, and he'd do the same. But that's what started me off that day you're talking about, Em. His jacket, his shaving kit, his whatever, mixed up with my stuff. It wasn't the stuff, it was what it meant. He's here. He's really here, and it's not just sex. It's not just casual. It's real." Mac shrugged, spread her hands. "I panicked. I had this amazing man in love with me, and I was scared. Jack's probably feeling some of that."

"I haven't said anything about love."

"Maybe you should." Parker shifted to tuck up her feet. "It's easier to know how the cards should be played when they're on the table. If he doesn't know what you're feeling, Emma, how can he take those feelings into consideration?"

"I don't want him to take my feelings into consideration. I want him to feel what he feels, be what he is. If he didn't and wasn't, I wouldn't be in love with him in the first place." She sighed and took a sip of wine. "Why did I ever think being in love would be wonderful?"

"It is once you work out the kinks," Mac told her.

"Part of the problem is I already know him so well I pick up on all the little . . ." She huffed out a breath, sipped more wine. "I think I have to stop being so sensitive, and stop romanticizing everything."

"You have to feel what you feel, be what you are."

When Parker tossed her words back at her, Emma blinked. "I guess I do, don't I? And I guess I should probably have an actual conversation with Jack about this."

"I like my economy-sized box of tampons better. It requires no words." Laurel shrugged. "But if you've got to be all mature about it."

"I don't really want to, but I got tired of sulking about half-way through the day. I might as well see how a reasonable conversation works out. Next week, I think. Maybe we both need a little space."

"We should have a man-free, work-free night once a month."

"We pretty much do," Mac reminded Laurel.

"But that's because it just happens, which is good. But now that half of us are hooked up with men, we should formalize it. An estrogen revival."

"No men, no work." Emma nodded. "That sounds—"

Parker's phone beeped. She glanced at the display. "Willow Moran, first Saturday in June. Shouldn't take long. Hi, Willow!"

she said cheerfully as she rose and stepped out of the room. "No, no problem at all. That's what I'm here for."

"Well, almost no work. And more pizza for me." Laurel took a second slice.

Despite a few interruptions, Emma thought the evening had been just what she'd needed. A little space, a little time with friends. She let herself into her house feeling pleasantly tired. As she started upstairs she went through her schedule for the next few days. She'd barely have time to catch her breath, she realized. And that, too, was just what she needed.

After crossing the room, she picked up the phone she'd deliberately left behind and saw she had a voice mail from Jack. Her spirits took a quick jump. So quick, she told herself to set the phone down again. It couldn't be anything urgent or he'd have called the main house.

It could wait until morning.

And who was she kidding?

She sat on the side of the bed to listen.

Hi. Sorry I missed you. Listen, Del and I are going to work on our further corruption of Carter and drag him to a game on Sunday. I thought I might come by sometime on Saturday. Maybe I can give you a hand. I could return this morning's favor and fix you breakfast before we kidnap Carter. Give me a call when you get a chance. I'm going to work on some drawings for your place, so . . . Thinking about you.

What are you wearing?

It made her laugh. He always could make her laugh, she thought. It was a nice message. Considerate, affectionate, funny.

What else did she want?

Everything, she admitted. She wanted it all.

SHE LET IT WAIT. EMMA TOLD HERSELF SHE WAS JUST TOO BUSY for that mature conversation. May meant a full slate of weddings, bridal showers, and Mother's Day. When she wasn't neck deep in flowers, she was planning the next design.

With her schedule, it simply made more sense for Jack to come to her, when it worked for both of them. She told herself to be grateful she was involved with a man who didn't complain about her working weekends, the long hours—and who could be counted on to lend a hand if he was around.

On a stormy afternoon in May she worked alone. Blessedly. Her ears might have been ringing from the echoes of Tink's and Tiffany's chatter, but now the rolls of thunder, the whoosh of rain and wind soothed.

She finished the maid of honor's bouquet, then stood for a moment to stretch. Turning, she jumped like a rabbit when she saw Jack.

Her squeal of shock bubbled into laughter as she slammed her hand to her heart. "God! You scared me."

"Sorry. Sorry. I knocked, yelled out, but it's hard to hear over the wrath of God."

"You're soaked."

"It's probably because of the rain." He ran a hand through his hair, scattering drops. "Killed my last on-site meeting, so I took a chance and swung by. Nice," he added, nodding at the bouquet.

"It is, isn't it? I was just about to put it in the cooler and start on the bride's. Why don't you get some coffee, dry off."

"Exactly what I hoped to hear." He stepped up to kiss her, brush a hand down her back. "I brought the drawings over for you to look at. When you get a chance. Weather permitting, they'll start on Mac's place Monday morning. Early. Be prepared."

"That's exciting. Do they know?"

"I stopped in the studio first. You want coffee?"

"No, thanks."

She made the trip to the cooler and back, then settled down with the flowers, her tools, and the picture she wanted to create in her head.

She glanced up when he came back in. "I've never really watched you work, on this part. Will it bug you?"

"No. Sit down. Talk to me."

"I saw your sister today."

"Oh?"

"We ran into each other in town. Don't you need a picture or a sketch?"

"I often use both, but this one's . . ." She tapped a finger on her temple. "White spray roses, this pale viburnum for accents. Slight cascade, which will be both sweet and romantic when I coax these majolicas into full bloom."

He watched as she clipped and wired, and thunder boomed. "I thought you said it was a bouquet."

"It is."

"Why the vase?"

"I've soaked the foam, attached the holder. See this part?" She angled the vase. "I keep that anchored in the vase so I can work the flowers in, get the right shape, the right cascade."

"What do you do when you have the others working in here with you?"

"Hmm?"

"What, you're all lined up here? Assembly-line method?"

"Yes, but no. We're all sort of lined up here, but we'd all be working on whatever arrangement I assigned. It's not like I do so much, then pass the bouquet to Tink."

She worked on in the quiet punctuated by thunder and rain.

"You need an L-shaped in here." He scanned the space again, the tools, the holding tubs. "Maybe a U's better. With over and under counter bins and drawers. You were primarily solo when I initially designed this space. You've outgrown it.

Plus you need space under for a rolling bin, for your compost, another for nonbio waste. Do you ever have clients back here when you're working, or one of the others is working?"

She sucked the thumb a stray thorn pricked. "Sometimes, sure."

"Okay."

He got up, leaving Emma frowning after him.

He came back, soaked again, with a notebook she assumed he'd gotten out of his car. "Just keep working," he told her. "I just want to draw up some adjustments for what I've already done. We're going to want to move that wall."

"Move?" Her attention arrowed to him. "The wall?"

"Bump it out, open up your work and display areas. Better flow, and more efficient work space. Too much for a solo operation, but . . . Sorry." He glanced up from his drawing. "Thinking out loud. Annoying."

"No, it's fine." And a little strange, she thought, for them to be working together on a stormy afternoon.

They worked in silence for a time, though she discovered he was a mutterer with a pencil in his hand. She didn't mind it, and found it surprising that there were still things to learn about him.

When she'd finished, she lifted the bouquet out, turned it to study it from every angle. And caught him watching her. "It'll look fuller and softer when the roses open."

"You work fast."

"This sort isn't especially labor-intensive." She rose, turned to the full-length mirror. "The dress has a lot of detail, very intricate, so this simpler, softer bouquet will suit it. No ribbons, nothing trailing, just the subtle cascade. Held here, waist high, both hands. It's going to . . ."

Her eyes met his in the mirror, and she caught the faint frown in his. "Don't worry, Jack. I'm not practicing."

239

"Huh?"

"I need to put these in the cooler."

When she carried them back, placed them, he spoke from the doorway. "I was thinking that the white looked good on you—with you? Whatever it would be. But everything does. And that you never wear flowers. It's probably too clichéd for you. So maybe I made a mistake."

She stood, surrounded by scent and blossom. "A mistake?"

"Yeah. I'll be back in a minute."

She shook her head when he walked off again. She stepped out, closed the cooler. She'd need to clean off her workstation, then she should go over her notes for the next day.

"I always try out the bouquets," she said when she heard him come back, "to make sure they're comfortable to hold, that the shape and the use of color and texture work."

"Sure. I get it. I pick up a hammer at least once on every job, just to get a feel for the building. I get it, Emma."

"Okay then, I just wanted . . ." She trailed off when she turned and saw the long, slim box in his hand. "Oh."

"I had a meeting in town, and I saw this. It sort of yelled out of the display window, 'Hey, Jack, Emma needs me.' And I thought, yeah, she does. So . . ."

"You brought me a present," she said when he handed it to her.

"You said you liked getting flowers."

She opened the box. "Oh, Jack."

The bracelet burst with color, bold jeweled-toned stones, each a small, perfect rose.

"But you don't wear flowers."

Surprise and delight clear on her face, she looked up. "I will now. It's beautiful. Just beautiful." She took it out, laid it across her wrist. "I'm dazzled."

"I know the feeling. Here, the jeweler showed me how it works. The clasp slides in here, so you don't see it."

"Thank you. It's . . . Oh, look at my hands."

He took them, stained and scratched from her work, and brought them to his lips. "I do. A lot."

"I snap at you, and you give me flowers." She slid into his arms. "I'll have to snap at you more often." On a sigh, she closed her eyes. "The rain's stopped," she murmured, then leaned back. "I need to clean up a little, then go help with tonight's rehearsal. But after, we could have a drink, maybe something to eat out on the patio. If you want to stay."

"I want to stay." A sudden intensity darkened his eyes as they roamed her face. "Emma. I don't think I've told you enough that I care about you."

"I know you do." She rose up to kiss him softly. "I know."

LATER, WHEN SHE'D LEFT FOR THE MAIN HOUSE, HE ROOTED through her supplies and found what he needed to toss a quick meal together. It wasn't as if he couldn't cook when he needed to, he thought. Or that he expected her to cook for him when they stayed in.

As they did more often, he realized.

He could even put a pretty damn good meal together, the benefit of once dating a sous chef.

A little garlic and olive oil, some herbs and chopped tomatoes and they'd have some pasta. No big deal.

He'd made her breakfast before, hadn't he?

Once.

Why did he suddenly feel he was taking advantage of her, taking her for granted, the way he'd often thought others did?

241

He knew why. He knew exactly why, he admitted as he minced and chopped.

The look on her face when their eyes had met in the mirror, just that slip second of hurt before irritation had smothered it.

I'm not practicing.

He *had* been thinking of the flowers, the bracelet. But she hadn't been completely wrong in her instincts. On some level he had been . . . uneasy. Or . . . hell if he knew. But the sight of her holding the bouquet had given him a—jolt, he admitted. Just for a second.

And he'd hurt her, bruised her feelings. The last thing in the world he wanted to do was hurt her.

She'd forgiven him, or let it go, or pushed it aside. Not because of the bracelet, he thought. She wasn't the type to angle for gifts, or to sulk over a slight.

She was . . . Emma.

Maybe he had taken her for granted here and there. That would stop now that he recognized it. He'd be more careful, that was all. Just because they'd been seeing each other for . . .

The shock had him nicking his thumb. Seven weeks. No, nearly eight, which was the same thing as two months. And that was practically an entire season.

A quarter of a year.

It had been a very long time since he'd been able to measure the time in months he'd been exclusively with one woman.

In a couple of weeks they'd have been together throughout spring, and starting into summer.

And he was okay with it, he realized. More than okay with it.

There was no one else he wanted to be with.

It felt good. Whatever the hell it meant, it felt good to know she'd come back soon and they'd share a meal out on her patio.

He poured himself a glass of wine as he began to sauté garlic. "Here's to the rest of the spring," he said, lifting his glass, "and right through summer."

"*R*ED ALERT!" ATOP THE LADDER, HER HANDS FULL OF DELICATE garlands, Emma craned her neck to read the display on the beeper hooked to her pants. "Crap. Crap. Red alert. Beach, you'll need to finish the garland. Tiff, swags. Tink, ride herd."

As she scrambled down, Jack stepped forward to spot her. "Careful. It's not a national emergency."

"It is when Parker issues a red. Come with me. Sometimes an extra pair of hands, especially male, can come in handy. If it's just a girl thing, maybe you could come back, help cover chairs. Damn it. I was on schedule."

"You'll make it."

She moved like lightning, across the terrace, up the steps— that still needed to be dressed, and through the door to the corridor outside the Bride's suite.

Straight into hysteria.

The small mob of people crammed the hall, all in various states of dress. Voices pitched toward the register only dogs could hear. Tears flowed like wine.

In the midst, Parker stood like a cool island in stormy seas. But Emma recognized the fraying of desperation around the edges.

"Everyone, everyone! Everything is going to be fine. But you have to calm down, and listen. Please, Mrs. Carstairs, please sit down here. Sit down now, take a breath."

"But my baby, my baby."

Carter nudged his way forward—a brave soul—and took the weeping woman by the arm. "Here now, have a seat."

"Something has to be done. Something has to be done."

Emma recognized the mother of the bride. She wasn't crying—yet—but her face approached the color of ripe beets. Even as Emma moved in to take her, or whoever needed it most, off Parker's hands, a shrill whistle cut the air into shocked silence.

"Okay, everybody, just stop!" Laurel ordered. She wore a white bib apron smeared with what looked to be raspberry sauce.

Parker plowed into the opening. "Mr. Carstairs, why don't you sit down with your wife a moment? Groom, if you and your party would go back to your suite, Carter will give you a hand. Mrs. Princeton, Laurel's going to take you and your husband downstairs. You'll have some tea. Give me fifteen minutes. Jack, could you go with Laurel? We'll bring Mr. and Mrs. Carstairs some tea up here."

"Any of chance of scotch?" Mr. Princeton asked.

"Absolutely. Just tell Jack what you'd like. Emma, I could use you in the Bride's Suite. Fifteen minutes, everyone. Just stay calm."

"What's the story?" Emma demanded.

"Quick update. Two of the bridesmaids are severely hung over, and one was puking heroically in the bathroom moments ago. MOG had a meltdown when she went in to see her son in the Groom's Suite, which annoyed MOB—they don't get along particularly well. Words were exchanged, tempers flared, and continued to flare as the women battled their way to the Bride's Suite. The drama apparently sent the MOH, who's eight months pregnant, into labor."

"Oh my God. She's in labor? Now?"

"It's Braxtson Hicks." Parker's face was a study of sheer determination and unassailable will. "It's going to be Braxtson–Hicks. Her husband called the doctor, and the MOH convinced him to let us time the contractions for now. Mac and the bride and the rest of the party, not currently puking or moaning, are with her. She and the bride are the only ones keeping their heads. Besides Mac. So."

Parker sucked in a breath, opened the door of the Bride's Suite.

The MOH lay propped on the little sofa, pale, but apparently calm with the bride—a hairdresser's cape over her corset and garters—kneeling beside her. Across the room, Mac offered a cool compress to a bridesmaid.

"How are you doing?" Parker asked as she moved briskly toward the pregnant woman. "Do you want your husband?"

"No. Let him stay with Pete. I'm okay, really. Haven't had anything in the last ten minutes."

"Nearly twelve now," the bride told her and held up the stopwatch.

"Maggie, I'm so sorry."

"Stop saying that." The bride gave her friend a shoulder rub. "Everything's going to be fine."

"You should finish getting your hair and your makeup. You should—"

"It can wait. Everything can just wait."

"Actually, it's a good idea," Parker said in a tone that managed to be brisk, businesslike, and cheerful all at once. "If you're not comfortable here, Jeannie, we can move you to my room. It's quieter."

"No, I'm fine here, really. And I'd like to watch. I think he's gone back to sleep." She patted the mound of her belly. "Honestly. Jan's in worse shape than I am."

"I'm an idiot." The attendant with the pale green complexion closed her eyes. "Maggie, just shoot me."

"I'm going to have some tea and toast sent up. It should help. Meanwhile, Emma and Mac are here to help out. I'll be back in two minutes. Any more contractions," Parker said quietly to Emma, "beep me."

"Believe it. Come on, Maggie, let's make you gorgeous." She drew Maggie to her feet, passed her to the hairdresser. With the stopwatch in hand, Emma settled down by the expectant mother. "So, Jeannie, it's a boy?"

"Yes, our first. I've got another four weeks. I had a checkup Thursday. Everything's fine. We're fine. How's my mother?"

It took Emma a moment to remember Jeannie was the groom's sister. "She's fine. Excited and emotional, of course, but—"

"She's a wreck." Jeannie laughed. "One look at Pete in his tux and she dissolved. We heard the wails in here."

"Which, of course, set my mother off," Maggie said from the salon chair. "Then they're at each other like pit bulls. Jan's tossing it in the bathroom and Shannon's curled in a ball."

"Better now." Shannon, a little brunette currently sipping what looked like ginger ale, waved from her own chair.

"Chrissy's good, so she took the kids outside for just a bit. She should be back by now."

Judging things were under control in this area, Emma glanced at Maggie. "Looks like we've cleared the fifteen-minute mark on baby. If Shannon's up to it, she can take over the timer, and I can go find Chrissy and the kids. Bridesmaid, flower girl, ring bearer?"

"Please. Thanks so much. This is all just crazy."

"We've had crazier." She gave the stopwatch to Shannon, took one more look at Jeannie. The color was back in her cheeks. If anything, she looked serene. "Mac, you've got the fort?"

"No problem. Hey, let's take some pictures!"

"You're a cruel woman," Jan muttered.

Emma dashed out. She spotted the MOG on the terrace, sobbing into a tissue while her husband patted her shoulder and said, "Come on, Edie. For God's sake."

She detoured and headed for the main stairs. Parker was already charging back up. "Status?"

"I think we're down to yellow status. No more contractions, one hangover well on the mend, the other—hard to tell. The bride's in hair, and I'm off to round up the last attendant and the kids."

"In the kitchen having cookies and milk. If you could take the FG and RB, send the BA up. Mrs. G's putting tea and toast together. I want to check on the groom, and let the expectant daddy know everything's okay."

"On my way. The MOG's on the terrace, wildly weeping."

Parker set her jaw. "I'll deal with her."

"Good luck." Emma hurried down, swung toward the kitchen just as Jack came in from the direction of the Grand Hall.

"Please tell me there's not a woman delivering a baby upstairs."

"That crisis, it seems, has passed."

"Well, thank you, Jesus."

"POB?"

"Huh?"

"Parents of Bride?"

"Carter's got them. It seems he teaches a nephew. And the mom's repairing her makeup or something."

"Good. I've got to get the last BA, send her up and take over with the FG and RB."

His brow furrowed, then he gave up on the code. "Whatever you say."

Pausing, Emma considered him. "You're pretty good with kids, as I recall."

"I'm okay. They're just short."

"If you can take the RB—the boy, he's five—and entertain him for about fifteen minutes, it would help. You can deliver him to the Groom's Suite as soon as we get the all clear. I'll take the girl up, help get her dressed." She glanced at her beeper with

247

some trepidation when it signaled. Then blew out a breath. "Yellow and holding. Good."

"Don't these kids have parents?" he asked as he followed her toward the kitchen.

"Yes, and both are in the wedding party. They're brother and sister, twins. The BA with them is Mom. The dad's a groomsman, so you can take the RB up in ten or fifteen. Just give everything a few more minutes to smooth out. Once I get the FG settled, I need to get back out and finish dressing the outside areas. So—"

She broke off, fixed a big, happy smile on her face before she pushed into the kitchen.

In an hour, the bride and attendants were beautified, the groom and his men polished. While Mac organized the separate parties for formal photos, and Parker kept the respective mothers at a distance, Emma finished the outside decor.

"Want a job?" she asked Jack as he helped cover the last row of chairs.

"So absolutely not. I don't know how you do this every weekend."

She attached cones holding the palest of pink peonies to selected chairs. "It's never boring. Tink, I've got to run home and change. Guests are arriving."

"We're good here."

"Parker estimates we'll only be about ten minutes late, which is a miracle. There's food for all of you in the kitchen when we're done. I'm back in fifteen. Jack, go have a drink."

"I plan to."

She was back in twelve, having traded her work clothes for a quiet black suit. She pinned boutonnieres while Parker's voice sounded in her headset. "We're a go in the Bride's Suite. Cuing music. Ushers to start escort."

She listened to the countdown as she brushed lapels, joked

248

with the groom. She spotted Parker arranging the parents, and Mac getting into position for shots.

She took a moment, just one, to admire the view outside. The crisp white covers on the chairs served as a perfect backdrop for the flowers. All the greens and pinks, from the palest to the deepest, blooming against the shimmer of tulle and lace.

Then the moment was over as the groom took his place, and the mothers—one teary, the other maybe just a little tipsy on scotch—were escorted to their seats.

She turned to gather the bouquets and pass them out as Parker lined up the ladies.

"You all look so beautiful. Still holding, Jeannie?"

"He's awake, but behaving."

"Maggie, you're just stunning."

"Oh, don't." The bride waved a hand in front of her face. "I didn't think I'd get all choked up, but I'm right on the edge. I'm about to give my new mother-in-law a run for her money."

"One breath in, one breath out," Parker ordered. "Slow and easy."

"Okay. Okay. Parker, if I ever need to wage war, you're my general. Emma, the flowers are . . . Breathe in, breathe out. Daddy."

"Don't you start." He gave her hand a squeeze. "Do you want me to walk you down while I'm blubbering like a baby?"

"Here now." Parker reached under the veil, gently dabbed at Maggie's eyes. "Head up, and smile. Okay, number one, you're on."

"See you on the other side, Mags." Jan, still a bit pale but beaming, started her walk.

"And two . . . Go."

With her job done for the moment, Emma stepped back while Parker ran the show.

"Have to admit," Jack said from beside her, "I didn't think

you were going to pull this one off. Not this smooth. I'm not only impressed, I'm very nearly awestruck."

"We've had a lot worse than this."

"Uh-oh," he said when her eyes filled.

"I know. Sometimes they just hit me. I think it was the way the bride handled herself—crisis by crisis—then started to crumble at her big moment. But she's holding on. Just look at that smile. And look at him look at her." She sighed. "Sometimes they just hit me," she repeated.

"I think you've earned this." Jack held out a glass of wine.

"Oh boy, have I. Thanks."

She hooked her arm through his, tipped her head toward his shoulder. And watched the wedding.

CHAPTER SIXTEEN

$\mathscr{P}$OSTEVENT, THEY TOOK A MOMENT TO UNWIND IN THE FAMILY parlor. Appreciating every moment, Emma sipped her second glass of wine of the evening.

"No visible hitches." She rolled her shoulders, curled and uncurled her bare toes. "And that's what counts. I expect the wedding party will be telling stories of hangovers, spatting mothers, and baby alert for weeks. But that's the sort of thing that makes every wedding unique."

"I wouldn't have believed anyone could cry, almost without pause, for nearly six hours." Laurel popped a couple of aspirin, chased them down with fizzy water. "You'd think it was her son's funeral instead of his wedding."

"I'm going to have to Photoshop the hell out of the MOG's photos. And even then . . ." Mac shrugged. "I think it's a brave bride who takes on a mother-in-law who literally howled during the I do's."

Tossing back her head, Mac gave a terrifyingly accurate rendition of Mrs. Carstair's wail.

"My head," Laurel muttered. "My head."

From his perch on the arm of the sofa, Carter laughed at Mac even as he gave Laurel's shoulder a comforting pat. "I don't know about the rest of you, but that woman scared me."

"I think part of it was the upcoming grandchild. It's all just too much for her."

"Then somebody should've slipped her a Valium," Laurel said to Emma. "And I'm not really kidding. I kept waiting for her to throw herself on the wedding cake—like it was a pyre."

"Oh man, what a shot that would've been." Mac sighed. "Regrets."

"Carter, Jack." Parker lifted her bottle of water. "You were a huge help. If I'd known the MOG was a wailer, I'd have taken steps beforehand, but she was fine at rehearsal. Even bubbly."

"I bet someone slipped her drugs," Laurel said.

"What sort of steps?" Jack wondered.

"Oh, there are all sorts of tricks of the trade." Parker's smile hinted at secrets. "I may not have been able to keep her from blubbering all during the ceremony, but I'd have kept her from upsetting the bride and groom during dressing. If Pete and Maggie hadn't kept their heads, we'd have had a disaster on our hands. Keeping the overly emotional types busy, giving them little assignments usually works."

"I know that's what kept me from crying," Jack told her.

"We'll have to muddle through without the reserve troops tomorrow." Mac gave Carter a friendly kick from her chair. "They're deserting us for the Yankees."

"And speaking of tomorrow, I'm going up to fall flat so I can get up for it." Laurel rose. " 'Night, kids."

"There's our cue. Let's pack it in, Professor. God, my feet are killing me."

Carter turned his back, gestured to it. With a laugh, Mac boosted herself on. "Now this is love," she said, planting a noisy kiss on the top of his head. "Him for the offer, and me for trusting Professor Grace not to trip and drop me. See you tomorrow. Giddyup!"

"God, they're cute." Emma smiled after them. "Even Scary Linda can't dull their shine."

"She called Mac this morning," Parker told her.

"Hell."

"Told Mac she'd changed her mind, and expected Mac and Carter to be at her wedding, in Italy, next week. The usual drama and guilt trip when Mac told her it wasn't possible for her to fly to Italy on such short notice."

"Mac didn't say anything about it to me."

"She didn't want to get into it with the event. Linda, of course, called just as Mac was getting her gear packed for the morning wedding. But the point is, you're right, she can't dull the shine. Before Carter, a call like that would've sent Mac into the blue. It wasn't pleasant, but she got through it, set it aside."

"The Power of Carter defeats the Power of Linda. I owe him a big kiss."

"I'll see him tomorrow if you want to give it to me," Jack suggested.

She leaned over, gave him a prim peck.

"Kinda stingy."

"He belongs to a friend. Okay, getting up, going home."

"Eight o'clock briefing," Parker reminded her.

"Yeah, yeah." She smothered a yawn. "How do you feel about piggybacks?" she asked Jack.

"I like this way better." In a deliberately dramatic move, he swept her up.

"Wow. Me, too. 'Night, Parker."

"Good night." And just a little wistfully, Parker watched Jack Rhett Butler Emma out of the parlor.

"Great exit." Delighted, Emma pressed her lips to Jack's cheek. "You don't have to carry me all the way back."

"You think I'm going to let Carter show me up? You know nothing about true competition. It's good to see Mac look so happy," he added. "I've been around a few times when Linda did a number on her. Tough to watch."

"I know." Idly, Emma fluttered her fingers through Jack's sun-streaked hair. "She's the only person I actually and actively dislike. I used to try to find excuses for her, then I realized there just aren't any."

"She hit on me once."

Emma's head jerked up. "What? Mac's *mother* hit on you?"

"Long time ago. Actually there was another time not all that long ago. So that makes two hits. First time I was still in college, spending a couple of weeks here during the summer break. We were all going to a party, and I said I'd swing by and pick up Mac. She didn't have a car back then. So her mother came to the door, and gave me the kind of once-over you don't generally get from mothers, then sort of backed me into a corner until Mac got down. It was . . . interesting, and yeah, scary. Scary Linda. Good name."

"What were you, twenty? She should be ashamed. Arrested. Something. Now I dislike her more. I didn't think it was possible."

"I survived. But if she tries it again, I'm counting on you to protect me. And a lot better than you did with Scary Kellye."

"One of these days I'm going to tell her what I think of her. Linda, not Kellye. And if she actually shows up at Mac's wedding and tries to pull something, I might get violent."

"Can I watch?"

Emma laid her head back down on his shoulder. "I'm calling my mother tomorrow, just to tell her she's wonderful." She

254

kissed his cheek again. "And so are you. This is the first time I've ever been carried through the moonlight."

"Actually, it's overcast."

She smiled. "Not from where I'm sitting."

JACK STUDIED HIS HOLE CARDS. POKER NIGHT HAD BEEN GOOD to him, so far, but the pair of deuces didn't look promising. He checked, waited while the bet walked around the table. When it got to Doctor Rod, he tossed in twenty-five. Beside him, Mal folded. Del tossed in his chips. Landscape Frank did the same. Lawyer Henry folded.

Jack debated briefly, and coughed up the twenty-five.

Del burned the top card, then turned over the flop. Ace of clubs, ten of diamonds, four of diamonds.

Possible flush, possible straight. And he had a crap pair of deuces.

He checked.

Rod went another twenty-five.

Carter folded, Del and Frank met the bet.

Stupid, Jack thought, but he just had a feeling. Sometimes feelings were worth twenty-five.

He added his chips to the pot.

Del buried a card, turned the next up. Two of diamonds.

Now that was interesting. Still, knowing how Rod played, he checked.

Rod bet another twenty-five, with Del raising it twenty-five more.

Frank folded. Jack thought about trip deuces. But he still had a feeling.

He tossed in the fifty.

"Glad it didn't scare you off. I'm looking to score here. Need to sweeten the pot." Rod grinned. "I just got engaged."

Del glanced over. "Seriously? We're dropping like flies."

"Congratulations," Carter said.

"Thanks. Raise it back fifty more. I figured, what the hell am I waiting for? So I took the jump. Shell's all about taking a look at your sister's place. Maybe you can get me the Poker Buddy discount."

"Not a chance." Del counted out chips. "But I'll see your fifty. Seeing as it's probably the end of poker and cigars for you."

"Hell, Shell's not that way. Bet's to you, Jack."

Pocket aces, probably. Rod never bluffed, or he sucked at it so wide you saw through it like a plate glass window. Pocket aces or a couple of pretty diamonds. Still . . .

"I'll stick. Consider it an engagement present."

"Appreciate it. We're looking at next June. Shell wants the big splash. I figured, hey, we'll just fly down to some island over the winter, get some sun, get some surf, get married. But she wants the big deal."

"And so it begins," Mal said in funereal tones.

"You're having the big deal, right, Carter?"

"Mac's in the business. They do a great job. Make it really special. Personalized."

"Don't sweat it," Mal said to Rod. "You won't have any say in it anyway. Just learn to repeat 'sure, baby' whenever she asks if you like something, want something, will do something."

"A lot you know. You've never been there."

"Nearly was. I didn't say 'sure, baby' enough." Mal examined the tip of his cigar. "Fortunately."

"I'm going to like being married." Rod nudged his glasses back up his nose. "Settled in, settled down. I guess you're heading in that direction, Jack."

"What?"

"You've been tight with the hot florist for a while now. Off the market."

Del clamped his cigar in his teeth. "Are we playing poker, or should we start talking about where Rod's going to register? Three players in for the river."

Del turned over the last card, but Jack was too busy staring at Rod to notice.

"My bet. And I'm all in."

"That's interesting, Rod." Expression bland, Del puffed on his cigar. "I'll cover it. How about it, Jack? You sticking or folding?"

"What?"

"Bet's to you, brother."

"Right." Off the market? What did that *mean*? He took a slow sip of beer, ordered himself to focus. And saw the river card was the deuce of hearts.

"I'll call."

"I got myself three bullets."

"And a GSW," Del told him, flipping his cards over. "Because I've got two sparkling diamonds, just like the one you put on your sweetheart's finger. "King high flush."

"Son of a bitch. I figured you for the tens."

"Figured wrong. Jack?"

"What?"

"Jesus, Jack, show your cards or toss them in."

"Sorry." He shook himself back. "Real sorry about the GSW and the sparkles. But I've got these two little deuces, that add up to four of a kind. I believe that's my pot."

"You pulled a fourth deuce in the fucking river?" Rod shook his head. "You're one lucky bastard."

"Yeah. One lucky bastard."

*A*FTER THE GAME, WHEN JACK HAD THE WINNER'S SHARE OF everyone's fifty-dollar entry fee in his pocket, he lingered with Del on the back deck.

"Since you're having another beer, you're figuring on flopping here?"

"Thinking about it," Jack said.

"You make the coffee in the morning."

"I've got an early meeting, so the coffee's going on about six."

"Fine. I've got a divorce deposition. Man, I hate it when a friend pressures me into handling a divorce. I hate fucking divorce cases."

"What friend?"

"You don't know her. We dated off and on some back in high school. She ended up marrying this guy, moving to New Haven about five years ago. Two kids."

With a shake of his head he took a short pull of his beer. "Now they've decided they can't stand the sight of each other, and she's moved back here, staying with her parents until she figures out what the hell she wants to do. He's pissed because she wants to live back here and it complicates visitation." He tipped the bottle to the left. "She's pissed because she put her career on hold to take the Mommy Track." Then tipped it to the right. "He didn't appreciate her enough, she didn't understand the pressure he was under. The usual."

"I thought you weren't going to handle any more divorces."

"A woman whose breasts you've once fondled comes into your office asking for help, it's tough to say no."

"That's true. It doesn't happen often in my line of work, but it's true."

Del shot him a smirk over another sip of beer. "Maybe I've just fondled more breasts than you have."

"We could have a contest."

"If you can remember all the breasts you've had in your hands, you haven't had enough of them."

Jack laughed, tipped back in his chair. "We should go to Vegas."

258

"For the breasts?"

"For . . . Vegas. A couple of days at the casinos, followed by a titty bar. So, yes, breasts would be involved. Just hang out for a couple days."

"You hate Vegas."

"*Hate*'s a strong word. No, better, we could go to St. Martin or St. Bart. Something. Play the tables, scope the beach. Go deep-sea fishing."

Del's eyebrows rose. "You want to fish? To my knowledge you've never so much as held a fishing rod."

"There's always a first time."

"Itchy feet?"

"Just thinking about getting away for a few days. Summer's coming. I got locked in last winter with work, and had to cut the week at Vail down to three days. So we can make up for it."

"I could probably stretch a long weekend."

"Good. We'll do that." Satisfied, Jack took another pull on his beer. "Weird about Rod."

"What?"

"Getting engaged. It came out of the blue."

"He's been with Shelly a couple of years. Not so blue."

"He's never made any marriage noises," Jack insisted. "I didn't figure him for it. I mean, a guy like Carter, yeah. He's the type. Come home from work every night, put on the slippers."

"Slippers?"

"You know what I mean. Come home, make a little dinner, pet the three-legged cat, watch some tube, maybe bang Mac if the mood's right."

"You know I try not to think about Mac and banging in the same sentence."

"Get up the next day, do it again," Jack continued in a tone that edged toward a rant. "Add a couple of kids along the way, maybe a one-eyed dog to go with the three-legged cat. Bang less because now you've got kids running around. Deep-sea fishing and titty bars are a thing of the past because now you've got nightmare trips to the mall and daycare and a freaking minivan and college funds. And Christ!" He threw up both hands. "Christ, now you're forty and coaching Little League and you've probably got a gut because who the hell has time to go to the gym when you've got to stop by the market and pick up bread and milk. Then you blink and you're fucking fifty and falling asleep in the Barcalounger watching reruns of *Law and Order*."

Del said nothing for a minute, just continued to study Jack's face. "That's an interesting roundup of the next twenty years of Carter's life. I hope they named one of the kids after me."

"That's the way it goes, isn't it?" What was this panic, this spurt of it rising up in his chest? He didn't want to think about it. "The good part is Mac won't be coming to you to file for divorce because it'll probably work for them. And she's not the type to freak out because he's heading out to Poker Night or hit him with the 'you never take me anywhere' routine."

"And Emma is?"

"What? No. I'm not talking about Emma."

"No?"

"No." Jack took a deliberate breath, found himself mildly shocked by his own babble. "Things with Emma are fine. They're good. I'm just talking in general."

"And in general, marriage is Barcaloungers and minivans, and the end of life as we know it?"

"Could be a La-Z-Boy and a station wagon. I think they're going to make a comeback. The point is, Mac and Carter will do okay with that. So . . . good for them. Not everybody can make it work."

"Depends on the dynamic, for one thing."

"Dynamics change." His parents's had in what still seemed

to him overnight. One day a family, the next two separate people. No reason, especially, no logic. It happened all the time. It happened half the time. "That's why you're doing a deposition tomorrow." Calmer now, he shrugged. "People change, and the elements, circumstances, situation all evolve."

"Yeah, they do. And the ones who want it enough keep working at it through the evolutions."

Puzzled, and unaccountably annoyed, he scowled at Del. "Suddenly you're a fan of marriage?"

"I've never been an opponent. I come from a long line of married couples. I figure it takes a lot of guts or blind faith to go into it, and a lot of work and considerable flexibility to stay in it. Considering Mac and Carter, and their backgrounds, I'd say she's the guts, he's the blind faith, It's a good combination."

Del paused, considered his beer. "Are you in love with Emma?"

Panic spurted again. He washed it back with beer. "I said this wasn't about her. Us. Any of that."

"And that's bullshit, Jack. We're sitting here having a last beer after a night where you came out on top and I hit near the bottom. Instead of ragging me, you're talking about marriage, and deep-sea fishing. Neither of which have ever been of particular interest to you."

"We're dropping like flies. You said it yourself."

"Sure I did. And we are. Tony's coming up on three, maybe it's four years now. Frank took the plunge last year, Rod's engaged. Add in Carter. I'm not involved with anyone in particular right now, and neither's Mal as far as I know. That leaves you, and Emma. Given that, it'd be surprising if Rod's little announcement didn't get your gears turning."

"Maybe I'm starting to wonder about her expectations, that's all. She's in the marriage business."

"No, she's in the wedding business."

261

"Okay, good point. She's from a big family. A big, tight, apparently happy family. And while weddings and marriages are different things, one leads to the other. One of her best friends since childhood is getting married. You know how those four are, Del. They're like a fist. The fingers may wiggle individually, but they come out of the same hand. Just like you said you and Mal are in the field, from what I can tell so are Laurel and Parker. But Mac? That shifts things. Now one of my poker buddies is going to be talking wedding plans with them. *That* shifts things."

He gestured with his beer. "If *I'm* thinking about it, it's a sure bet she is."

"You could do something radical and have an actual conversation with her about it."

"If you have a conversation about it, it takes you a step closer."

"Or it takes you a step back. Which way do you want to head, Jack?"

"See, you're asking me." To emphasize the point, Jack shot a finger at Del. "She sure as hell will. What am I supposed to say?"

"Again, radical. How about the truth?"

"I don't know the truth." Okay, he thought, that's the source of the panic. "Why do you think I'm freaked out?"

"I guess you have to figure it out. You never answered the lead question. Are you in love with her?"

"How the hell does anybody know that? More, how do they know they're going to stay that way?"

"Guts, blind faith. You've got it or you don't. But from where I'm sitting, brother, the only person putting pressure on you is you." Crossing his ankles, Del polished off his beer. "Something to think about."

"I don't want to hurt her. I don't want to let her down."

Listen to yourself, Del thought. You're already sunk and

don't know it. "I don't want to see that happen either," he said casually. "Because I'd hate having to kick your ass."

"What you'd hate is for me to kick yours if you tried."

There followed the more comfortable interlude of insults over the last beer.

$\mathscr{B}$ECAUSE HE WANTED TO KEEP A CLOSE EYE ON MAC'S ADDITION, Jack tried to swing by the job site every day. It gave him a spectator seat to The Life of Mac and Carter.

Every morning he'd catch sight of them in the kitchen—one of them feeding the cat, the other pouring coffee. At some point, Carter would clear out with his laptop case, and Mac would get to work in the studio.

If his swing-by came in the afternoon, he might see Carter walking back from the main house—but never, he noted, when Mac was with a client. The guy must have radar, Jack concluded.

Occasionally one or both of them came out to check the progress, ask questions, offer him coffee or a cold drink, depending on the time of day he dropped by.

The rhythm fascinated him enough that he stopped Carter one morning.

"School's out, right?"

"The summer of fun has begun."

"So I notice you head over to the big house most days."

"It's a little crowded in the studio right now. And noisy." Carter glanced back toward the buzz of saws, the thwack of nail guns. "I teach teenagers, so I have a high tolerance for confusion, and still I don't know how she works with the noise. It doesn't seem to bother her."

"What the hell are you doing all day? Plotting pop quizzes for next fall?"

"The beauty of the pop quiz is that it can be repeated end-lessly through the years. I have files."

"Yeah, I bet. So?"

"Actually, I'm using one of the guest rooms as a temporary study. It's quiet, and Mrs. Grady feeds me."

"You're studying?"

Carter shifted his feet, a tell Jack recognized as mild to middling embarrassment. "I'm sort of working on a book."

"No shit?"

"It may be shit. Parts of it probably are. But I thought I'd take the summer to find out."

"That's great. How do you know when she's cleared out— the clients? Does she call over, tell you it's safe to come home?"

"She's trying to schedule clients in the morning, whenever she's doing a shoot here, and shifting most consults over to the main house while the construction's going on. I just check her book for the day, so I don't come back during a shoot, break the mood or her concentration. It's a pretty simple system."

"It seems to be working for you."

"Speaking of work, I didn't expect all this to move so fast." Carter gestured toward the studio. "Every day there's something new."

"Weather holds and the inspections pass, it'll keep moving. It's a good crew. They should— Sorry," he said when his phone rang.

"Go ahead. I'd better get started."

He pulled out his phone as Carter walked off. "Cooke. Yeah, I'm on the Brown site." As he spoke, Jack moved away from the noise. "No, we can't just . . . If that's what they want we'll need to draw up the changes and get a revised permit."

He listened, continued to walk.

His job visits also gave him a clear idea of Emma's basic routine. Clients came and went like clockwork in the beginning of the week. Midweek, she'd take deliveries. Boxes and boxes of flowers. She'd be working with them now, he thought. Early start, on her own. Tink or one of the others would probably come in later, do whatever they did.

In the middle of the day, if she could manage it, she'd take a break and sit out on her patio. If he was on-site, he'd squeeze in the time to sit out with her awhile.

How could a man resist Emma sitting in the sunlight?

And there she was now, he realized. Not on the patio, but kneeling on the ground, her hair bundled under a hat while she turned dirt with a garden spade.

"Tell them two to three weeks," he said, and she turned, tipped up the brim of her hat and smiled at him. "I'm heading out from here in a few minutes. I'll talk it over with the job boss. I'll be in the office in a couple hours. No problem."

He flipped the phone closed, scanned the flats of plants. "Don't you have enough flowers?"

"Never. I wanted to plug in some more annuals here in front. It makes a nice show from the event areas."

He crouched, kissed her. "You make a nice show. I figured you'd be working inside."

"I couldn't resist, and this won't take long. I'll put in an extra hour at the end of the day if I need to."

"Busy after the end of the day?"

She cocked her head, slanted him a killer look from under the brim of her hat. "That depends on the offer."

"How about we go into New York for dinner? Someplace where the waiters are snobs, the food's overpriced, and you look so beautiful I don't notice either."

"I'm definitely not busy at the end of the day."

"Good. I'll pick you up about seven."

"I'll be ready. And since you're here." She wrapped her arms

265

around his neck, and took his mouth in a deep, dreamy kiss. "That should hold you," she murmured.

"Pack a bag."

"What?"

"Pack what you need for overnight and we'll get a hotel suite in New York. Make a night of it."

"Really?" She did a quick dance in place. "Give me ten seconds and I'll pack right now."

"Then we're on."

"I have to be back early, but—"

"So do I." This time he kissed her, catching her face with his hands, drawing it out. "That should hold *you*. Seven," he said, and rose.

Pleased with his idea and her reaction, he drew his phone out as he walked to his truck, and got his assistant busy making reservations.

CHAPTER SEVENTEEN

"*J*TOLD HIM I COULD PACK IN TEN SECONDS. I'M SUCH A LIAR."
With the workday scrubbed off and every inch of her creamed and scented, Emma folded a shirt into her overnight case. "Obviously the coming home clothes aren't a real issue, but . . ."

She turned, held up a silky white gown for Parker's opinion. "What do you think?"

"It's gorgeous." Stepping forward, Parker brushed a finger over the delicate lace that framed the bodice. "When did you get this?"

"Last winter. I couldn't resist it, and I told myself I'd wear it just for me, whenever. Of course, I didn't. Haven't. It has this little matching robe. I love lush hotel robes, but this is romantic. I feel like I want to have something romantic to put on after dinner."

"Then it's perfect."

"I don't even know where we're going, where we're staying.

I love that. Love the feeling of being whisked away." She did a quick spin then laid the peignoir in her bag. "I want champagne and candlelight, and some ridiculously indulgent dessert. And I want him to look at me in the candlelight and tell me he loves me. I can't help it."

"Why should you?"

"Because it should be enough to be whisked away, to be with a man who'd plan a night like this. He makes me happy. That should be enough."

As Emma continued to pack, Parker stepped forward to rub her shoulders. "It's not as if you're setting limits for yourself, Emma. If you feel you have to."

"I'm not doing that. I don't think I'm doing that. I know I've had some ups and downs about this, so I'm trying to adjust my expectations. And do what I said I'd do when we started." Reaching back, she laid her hand on Parker's, squeezed. "Just enjoy and take things as they come. I've been in love with him for so long, but that's my deal. In reality we've only been together a couple of months. There's no rush."

"Emma, as long as I've known you—which is forever—you've never been afraid to say how you feel. Why are you afraid to tell Jack?"

Emma closed her case. "If he's not ready, and telling him made him feel obliged to step back, to just be friends again? I don't think I could stand it, Parker." She turned, faced her friend. "I guess I'm not ready to risk what we have. Not yet. So I'm going to enjoy our night away, and not put any added weight on it.

"God, I've got to get dressed. Okay, I'll be back by eight, eight thirty at the latest. But if for some reason we get stuck in traffic—"

"I'll call Tink, force her to get out of bed. I know how. She'll take the morning delivery and start processing."

"Good." Confident in Parker's abilities, Emma wiggled into the dress. "But I'll be back." She turned so Parker could do up the zipper.

"I love this color. Citrine. It's annoying to know it would make me sallow. It just makes you glow." She met Emma's eyes in the mirror, then wrapped her arm around her friend's waist and hugged. "Have a great time."

"Can't miss."

Twenty minutes later when she opened the door, Jack took one look and grinned. "This is an excellent idea. I should've had this idea long before. You look absolutely stunning."

"Snobby-waiter and overpriced-food worthy?"

"More than." He took her hand, kissed her wrist where the bracelet he'd given her sparkled.

Even the drive into New York struck her as perfect, whether they whizzed along or crept through a snarl of traffic. The light softening toward balmy evening, she thought, and the whole night ahead.

"I always think I'm going to get into the city more often," she told him. "To play or to shop, to check out the florists and markets. But I don't nearly as much as I'd like. So every trip in is exciting."

"You haven't even asked where we're going."

"It doesn't matter. I love the surprise, the spontaneity. So much of what I do—you, too, actually—has to run on a schedule. So this? This is like a magic minivacation. If you promise to buy me champagne, I'll have it all."

"All you want."

When he pulled up in front of the Waldorf, she lifted her eyebrows. "And the excellent ideas keep coming."

"I thought you'd like the traditional."

"You thought right."

She waited on the sidewalk while the doorman took their

bags, then reached for Jack's hand. "Thank you, in advance, for a lovely evening."

"You're welcome, in advance. I'm just going to check in, have them take the bags up. The restaurant's about three blocks from here."

"Can we walk? It's beautiful out."

"Sure. Give me five minutes."

She wandered the lobby, entertaining herself with the shop windows, the lavish flower displays, the people swarming in, swarming out, until he joined her. He skimmed a hand down her back.

"Ready?"

"Absolutely." She put her hand in his again to walk out on Park Avenue. "I had a cousin who got married at the Waldorf—before Vows, of course. Huge, ultrafancy, formal affair as many of the Grants' affairs are prone to be. I was fourteen, and very impressed. I still remember the flowers. Acres of flowers. Yellow roses the feature. Her bridesmaids were in yellow, too, and looked like sticks of butter, but oh, the flowers. They'd done this elaborate arbor of yellow roses and wisteria right there in the ballroom. It must have taken an army of florists. But it's what I remember best, so it must've been worth it."

She smiled at him. "What struck you most about a building that left that kind of impression on you?"

"There've been a few." He turned east at the corner, strolling while New York rushed around them. "But honestly? One of my strongest impressions was the first time I saw the Brown Estate."

"Really?"

"Plenty of mansions where I grew up in Newport, and some incredible architecture. But there was something—is something—about the estate that stands out. Its balance and lines, its understated grandeur, the confidence that combines dignity with touches of fanciful."

"That's it exactly," she agreed. "Fanciful dignity."

"When you walk in the main house, there's an immediate impression that people live there. Really live, and more, the people who live there love the house, and the land. All of it. It remains one of my favorite places in Greenwich."

"It's certainly one of mine."

He turned again, to open the door of the restaurant. The minute she stepped inside, Emma felt the pace, the rush drop away. Even the air seemed to hush.

"Nice job, Mr. Cooke," she said quietly.

The maitre d' inclined his elegant head. *"Bonjour, mademoiselle, monsieur."*

"Cooke," Jack said in a James Brown deadpan that had Emma biting the inside of her cheek to smother a laugh. "Jackson Cooke."

"Mr. Cooke, *bien sûr*, right this way."

He led them through elaborate flower displays and flickering candles, around the gleam of silver and glint of crystal on snowy white linen. They were seated with all expected pomp and offered a cocktail.

"The lady prefers champagne."

"Very good. I'll inform your sommelier. Enjoy your evening."

"I already am." Emma leaned toward Jack. "Very much."

"Heads turned when you walked through."

She sent him that smile—that sexy, sultry smile. "We're a very attractive couple."

"And now, every man in this place envies me."

"I'm enjoying the evening even more. Don't let me interrupt."

He glanced over at the approach of the sommelier. "Let me get back to you."

When he'd ordered a bottle that met with the wine steward's lofty approval, Jack laid his hand over Emma's. "Now, where was I?"

"Making me feel incredibly special."

"An easy job considering what I've got to work with."

"Now you're turning my head. Do go on."

He laughed, kissed her hand. "I love being with you. You're a lift to the day, Emma."

What did it say about her, she wondered, that "love being with you" made her heart jump? "Why don't you tell me about the rest of your day?"

"Well, I solved the mystery of Carter."

"There was a mystery?"

"Where does he go, what does he do?" Jack began, and told her the studio routine he'd observed. "I'm only around for short periods," he continued, "but those short periods range from morning to late afternoon, so my canny observations have taken in a variety of slices of the pie of their day."

"And what were your conclusions?"

"No conclusions, but many theories. Was he slinking off to have a torrid affair with Mrs. Grady, or indulging in a desperate and downward cycle of online gambling on his laptop?"

"He could do both."

"He could; he's an efficient sort." Jack paused to approve the label on the bottle presented to him. "The lady will taste."

As the uncorking ritual began, Jack leaned closer to Emma. "And there, our beloved Mackensie, unaware, trusting, slaving away. Could the seemingly innocent and affable Carter Maguire have these shameful secrets? I had to know."

"You put on a disguise and followed him to the house?"

"Considered and rejected." He waited while the sommelier poured a taste of the champagne into Emma's flute. She sipped, paused, then sent the man a smile that melted the dignified ice. "It's wonderful. Thank you."

"A pleasure, *mademoiselle*." He poured the rest expertly. "I hope you'll enjoy every sip. "*Monsieur*." He replaced the bottle in its bucket, bowed away.

"All right, how did you solve the mystery of Carter?"

"Give me a minute, I lost my train with the spillover dazzle. Oh yeah, my method was ingenious. I asked him."

"Diabolical."

"He's writing a book. Which, you already knew," Jack concluded.

"I see them every day, or nearly. Mac told me, but your method was a lot more fun. He's been writing it on and off for years, when he can squeeze in the time. Mac gave him a nudge to work on it this summer instead of teaching summer classes. I think he's good."

"You've read it?"

"Not what he's working on, but he's had some short stories and essays published."

"He has? He's never mentioned it. Another mystery of Carter."

"I don't think you ever learn everything about anyone, no matter how long you know them, or how well. There's always another pocket somewhere."

"I guess we're proof of that."

Her eyes smiled and warmed as she took another sip of champagne. "I guess we are."

"THE WAITERS AREN'T SNOOTY ENOUGH. YOU'VE CHARMED THEM so they want to please you."

Emma took a scant spoonful of the chocolate souffle she'd asked to share. "I believe they achieved the perfect level of

273

snoot." She slipped the soufflé between her lips. Her quiet moan spoke volumes. "This is every bit as good as Laurel's, and hers is the best I've ever tasted."

"*Tasted* is the operative word. Why don't you actually eat it?"

"I'm savoring." She scooped up another smidgen. "We did have five courses." She sighed over her coffee. "I feel like I've had a little trip to Paris."

He traced his finger over the back of her hand. She never wore rings, he thought. Because of her work, and because she didn't want to draw attention to her hands.

Odd he felt they were one of the most compelling aspects of her.

"Have you been?"

"To Paris?" She savored another stingy bite of soufflé. "Once when I was too young to remember, but there's a picture of Mama pushing me in my stroller down the Champs-Élysées. I went again when I was thirteen, with Parker and her parents, Laurel and Mac and Del. At the last minute Linda said Mac couldn't go, over some slight or infraction. It was awful. But Parker's mom went over and fixed it. She'd never say how. We had the best time. A few days in Paris then two amazing weeks in Provence."

She allowed herself another spoonful. "Have you?"

"A couple times. Del and I did the backpack through Europe thing the summer of our junior year in college. That was an experience."

"Oh, I remember. All the postcards and pictures, the funny e-mails from cyber cafes. We were going to do it, the four of us. But when the Browns died . . . It was too much, and so many things to deal with. And Parker channeled everything into putting together a business model for Vows. We just never got around to it."

She sat back. "I really can't eat another bite."

274

He signaled for the check. "Show me one of your pockets."

"My pockets?"

"One of those things I don't know about you."

"Oh." Laughing, she sipped her coffee. "Hmm, let's see. I know. You may not be aware that I was the Fairfield County Spelling Bee Champion."

"Get out. Really?"

"Yes, I was. In fact, I went all the way to the state competition, where I was this close . . ." She held up her thumb and finger, a fraction apart. "*This* close to winning, when I was eliminated."

"What was the word?"

"Autocephalous."

His eyes slitted. "Is that a real word?"

"From the Greek, meaning being independent of external authority, particularly patriarchal." She spelled it out. "Except under pressure, I spelled it with an *e* for the second *a*, and that was that. I remain, however, a killer at Scrabble."

"I'm better at math," he told her.

She leaned forward. "Now, let me see one of yours."

"It's pretty good." He tucked his credit card in the leather folder discreetly placed at his elbow. "Nearly up there with spelling bee champion."

"I'll be the judge."

"I was Curly in my high school's production of *Oklahoma!*"

"Seriously?" She pointed at him. "I've heard you sing. You're good. But I didn't know you had any interest in acting."

"None. I was interested in Zoe Malloy, who was up for the part of Laurey. Crazy about her. So I put it all out there for "Surrey with the Fringe on Top," and got the part."

"Did you get Zoe?"

"I did. For a few shining weeks. Then, unlike Curly and Laurey, we parted. And that was the end of my acting career."

275

"I bet you made a great cowboy."

He sent her a quick, teasing grin. "Well, Zoe certainly thought so."

With the bill addressed, he rose, held out a hand for hers.

"Let's walk the long way around." She laced her fingers with his. "I bet it's a beautiful night."

It was. Warm and sparkling so even the traffic jamming the streets glittered and gleamed. They strolled, winding their way around the blocks and back to the grand front entrance of the hotel.

People swept in and out, in business suits, in jeans, in evening clothes. "Always busy," she said. "Like a movie where no one ever says 'cut.'"

"Do you want a drink before we go up?"

"Mmm, no." She tipped her head toward his shoulder as they walked to the elevators. "I've got everything I want."

In the elevator she turned into his arms, tipped her face up to his. Her pulse rate climbed as the car did, up and up, level by level.

When he opened the door, she stepped into candlelight. On the white-draped table a silver bucket held a bottle of champagne. A single red rose speared from a slim vase while around the room tea lights flickered in clear glass. Music drifted, whisper soft.

"Oh, Jack."

"How did this get here?"

Laughing, she took his face in her hands. "You've just bumped this up from great date to dream date. This is amazing. How did you manage it?"

"I arranged for the maitred' to alert the hotel when they brought the check. Planning isn't just your business."

"Well, I like your plan." She kissed him, lingered for another. "A lot."

"I had a feeling. Should I open the bottle?"

"Absolutely." She wandered to the window. "Look at the view. Everything's still so bright and busy, and here we are."

The bottle opened with a sophisticated *pop!* When he'd poured the glasses and joined her, she tapped hers to his. "To excellent planning."

"Tell me something else." He touched her hair, just a skim of the fingers. "Something new."

"Another pocket?"

"I've discovered the spelling bee champ, the ace soccer player. These are interesting facets."

"I think we've covered all my hidden skills." She reached out, trailed a fingertip down his tie. "I wonder if you can handle the dark side."

"Try me."

"Sometimes when I'm alone at night, after a long day . . . especially if I'm feeling unsettled. Or on edge—" She broke off, lifted her glass for a sip. "I'm not sure if I should confess this one."

"You're among friends."

"True. Still, not many men really understand some of a woman's needs. And some just can't deal with the fact that there are certain needs they can't meet."

He took a long drink. "Okay, I don't know whether to be scared or fascinated."

"I once asked a man I was seeing to join me one evening for this particular activity. He wasn't ready for it. I've never asked another."

"Does it involve tools? I'm good with tools."

She shook her head and strolled over to top off her glass, then held up the bottle in invitation.

"What I do is . . ." She poured bubbling wine into his glass. "First, I'll take a big glass of wine up to my bedroom, then I'll light candles. I'll put on something soft and comfortable, some-thing that makes me feel relaxed. Feel . . . female. Then I get into bed with all the pillows arranged just so, because I'm about to take a journey just for myself. And when I'm ready . . . When I'm just sinking in . . . I watch my DVD of *Truly, Madly, Deeply*."

"You watch porn?"

"It's not porn." Laughing, she gave his arm a quick slap. "It's an amazing love story. Juliet Stevenson is devastated when the man she loves, Alan Rickman, dies. She's overwhelmed with grief. Oh, it's painful to watch." Eyes radiating emotion, she laid a hand just under her throat. "I cry buckets. Then he comes back as a ghost. He loves her so much. It rips your heart out, and it makes you laugh."

"Rips out your heart and makes you laugh?"

"Yes. Men never get that. I'm not going to tell you the whole thing, just that it's wrenching and charming and sad and affirm-ing. It's unspeakably romantic."

"And that's what you do, secretly, in your bed at night, when you're alone."

"It is. Hundreds of times. I've had to replace the DVD twice."

Obviously baffled, he studied her as he drank champagne. "A dead guy's romantic?"

"Hello? Alan Rickman. And yes, in this case, it's wonder-fully romantic. After I watch it—and finish crying—I sleep like a baby."

"What about *Die Hard*? He's in *Die Hard*. Now that's a movie you can watch a hundred times. Maybe we should do a double feature some time. If you can handle that."

"Yippee-ki-yay."

He grinned at her. "Pick a night next week, and you're on. But there has to be popcorn. You can't watch *Die Hard* without popcorn."

"Fair enough. Then we'll see what you're made of." She brushed her lips to his. "I'm going to change. It won't take me long. Maybe you should bring the champagne into the bedroom."

"Maybe I should."

In the bedroom he took off his jacket and tie, and thought about her. Thought about the surprises and facets and layers of her.

It was odd, really, to think you knew someone inside and out, and discover there was more to learn. And the more you learned the more you wanted to know.

On impulse, he took the rose from the vase and laid it on a pillow.

When she stepped out into the candlelight, he lost his breath. Black hair tumbling over white silk, smooth skin gold against white lace. And those eyes, he thought, deep and dark, looking into his.

"You said something about dream date," he managed.

"I wanted to do my part."

The silk flowed over her curves as she walked to him, and as she lifted her arms to wind them around his neck in a way that was so essentially Emma, her scent shimmered in the air like the candlelight.

"Did I thank you for dinner?"

"You did."

"Well . . ." She scraped her teeth over his bottom lip—lightly, lightly—before the kiss. "Thanks again. And the champagne? Did I thank you for that?"

"As I recall."

"Just in case." On a sigh her mouth met his. "And the candlelight, the rose, the long walk, the view." Her body moved against his, leading him into a slow, circling dance.

"You're welcome."

He drew her in, closer still, so her body pressed to his. Time spun out as they circled, as mouth clung to mouth, as heart beat to heart.

She drew in his scent, his flavor. So familiar and still so new. Her fingers trailed up into hair bronzed and gilded by the sun, then curled, tugged to bring him just a little closer.

They slid down together onto smooth white sheets, and into the perfume of a single red rose. More sighs now, more dreamy movements. A caress, a tender touch, shimmered over her skin. She stroked his face, opened—body and heart—as she found, with him, passion wrapped in the shimmer of romance.

Here was all she wanted, had ever wished for. The sweetness and the heat. And as she gave, more and more, she filled until she was dizzy with love.

His flesh to her flesh, so warm, brought her a quiet joy even as pulses spiked. His lips pressed to her heart as it beat for him.

Did he know it? Couldn't he feel it?

And when he took her up, slowly up, his name—just his name—bloomed in that heart.

She clouded his mind like a silver mist, sparkled in his blood like champagne. Every languorous move, every whisper, every touch seduced, entranced.

When she broke for him, rising up like a wave, she breathed his name. And she smiled.

Something inside him stumbled.

"You're so beautiful," he murmured. "Impossibly beautiful."

"I feel beautiful when you look at me."

He skimmed his fingers over her breast, watched her eyes glow with fresh pleasure. He lowered his mouth, a gentle taste with teeth and tongue, and felt her body quiver with fresh need.

"I want you." Her breath caught as she arched under him. "You're what I want, Jack."

She surrounded him, taking him in, moving with him in slow, savoring beats. Surrounded, he lost himself in her.

𝒮ATED, HE RESTED HIS CHEEK ON HER BREAST, LET HIS MIND drift.

"No chance of playing hooky tomorrow and staying right here?"

"Mmm." Her fingers threaded through his hair. "Not this time. But what a nice thought."

"The way things stand we'll have to get up at dawn."

"I find I often do better on no sleep than with a few stingy hours."

He lifted his head, smiled at her. "That's funny. I was thinking the same thing."

"It would be a shame to waste the rest of that champagne, and those lovely chocolate-covered strawberries."

"Criminal. Stay right here. Don't move. I'll get them."

She stretched, sighed. "I'm not going anywhere."

CHAPTER EIGHTEEN

$\mathcal{F}$IVE MINUTES AFTER EMMA GOT HOME, MAC CAME THROUGH the door.

"I waited until he left," Mac called out as she climbed the stairs. "That's herculean restraint." She scowled when she walked into Emma's bedroom. "You're unpacking. Putting everything away. I hate this level of efficiency. Why can't at least one of us be a slob like me?"

"You're not a slob. You're just a bit relaxed with your personal space."

"Hey, I like that. Relaxed with my personal space. Okay, enough about me. Tell me all. I left my own lover to his lonely bowl of corn flakes."

With last night's dress in her hands, Emma spun a happy circle. "It was fabulous. Every minute."

"Deets, deets, deets."

"An elegant French restaurant, champagne, a suite at the Waldorf."

"God, that's all so you. Snazzy date-wise. Casual date-wise, maybe moonlight picnic at the beach, red wine, candles tucked into little shells."

Emma closed her empty suitcase. "Why aren't I dating you?"

"We'd make a lovely couple, it's true." Draping an arm over Emma's shoulder, Mac turned to the mirror and studied— Emma in her trim jeans and soft shirt, and herself in the cotton pants and T-shirt she'd slept in. "Stunning, really. Well, we can keep it in reserve if things don't work out otherwise."

"Always good to have a backup. Oh, God, Mac, it was the most perfect night." She turned, squeezed Mac into a hug before doing another spin. "We didn't sleep. At all. It's amazing, really, that we have so much to talk about, to find out about each other still. We talked all through dinner, then took a long walk. And he'd had them bring up champagne and light candles, put on music."

"Wow."

"We drank more champagne and we talked, and we made love. It was so romantic." On a humming sound, she closed her eyes, hugged herself. "Then we talked and drank more champagne, and we made love again. We had breakfast by candlelight and—"

"Made love again."

"We did. We drove home through horrible traffic with the top down, and the traffic didn't matter. Nothing did. Nothing could." She gave herself another hug. "Mac? I'm a happy person most of the time."

"Yeah, it can be annoying."

"I know, but too bad. Anyway, I'm a happy person, but I never knew I could be this happy. I didn't know I could feel like this. Like I just want to jump and dance and spin and sing. Like Julie Andrews on a mountaintop."

"Okay, but don't do that because that's seriously annoying."

"I know, so I'm only doing it on the inside. All the times I imagined what it would be like to be crazy in love, I never knew."

She dropped down on the bed, grinned up at the ceiling. "Do you feel this way all the time? With Carter?"

Mac flopped down beside her. "I never thought I'd be in love. Not really. I never imagined it the way you always did, or looked for it. In some ways it snuck up on me, and in others it fell on me like a ton of bricks. It's still a shock to the system to realize I have this inside me—not the spinning and singing part, because even inside it would annoy me. But I've got the jumping and dancing going on. And somebody has it inside for *me*. Talk about shocking."

Emma reached out to take Mac's hand. "I don't know if Jack has it back for me, not the way I do for him. But I know he cares. I know he feels. And I have so much, Mac. I have to believe all this love I have will . . . take root, I guess. I thought I loved him before, but now I think that was a kind of infatuation mixed up inside lust. Because this is different."

"Can you tell him?"

"I would've said no, even a couple of days ago. Don't want to ruin anything, don't want to tip the scales. Actually did say no when Parker and I talked about it. But now I think I can. I think I should. I just have to figure out how and when."

"It scared me, when Carter told me he loved me. Don't be upset if it scares him a little, at least at first."

"I don't think you tell someone you love them because you expect something. I think you tell them because you have something to give."

"You unpack as soon as you get home from a trip. You have a happy nature. And you're wise about love. I'm surprised the three of us haven't ganged up and beaten hell out of you regularly."

"You can't. You love me."

Mac turned so they faced each other. "We do. I'm pulling for you, Em. We all are."

"Then how can I go wrong?"

𝒯HE KNOCK INTERRUPTED EMMA HALFWAY THROUGH PRO-cessing the morning delivery. Grumbling only a little, she left the flowers holding. She winced when she saw Kathryn Seaman and her sister through the glass. Wet and messy weren't ways to impress important clients.

Trapped, she fixed an easy smile on her face and opened the door. "Mrs. Seaman, Mrs. Lattimer, how nice to see you."

"I apologize for dropping in on you this way, but Jessica and her girls decided on the bridesmaids' dresses. I wanted to bring you the swatch of the material."

"That's perfect. Please come in. Can I get you something to drink? Maybe some sun tea? It's a warm day."

"I'd love some," Adele said immediately. "If it's no bother."

"Not at all. Why don't you sit down, be comfortable? I'll just be a minute."

Tea, Emma thought as she hurried into the kitchen. Lemon slices, the good glasses. Crap, crap. A little plate of cookies. Thank God for Laurel's emergency tin. She scrambled everything onto a tray, shoved at her hair.

She pulled her emergency lip gloss out of a kitchen drawer, glided some on, then pinched her cheeks.

As that was the best she could manage under the circumstances, she took two deep breaths to make sure she looked un-rushed. She strolled back in to find both women wandering her greeting area.

"Kate told me what a pretty setup you had here. She was right."

"Thank you."

"And your private rooms are upstairs?"

"Yes. It's not only convenient, but very comfortable."

"I noticed your partner—Mackensie—is expanding her studio."

"Yes." Emma poured the tea, then continued to stand as neither woman seemed inclined to sit. "Mac's getting married this December, and they'll need more room in their private space, so they're expanding the studio space as well."

"Isn't that exciting?" Sipping tea, Adele continued to wander, fluffing at flowers, studying photos. "Planning a wedding for one of your own."

"It really is. We've all been friends since we were children."

"I noticed the photo here. Is that you, and two of your partners?"

"Yes, Laurel and Parker. We loved playing Wedding Day," Emma told her as she smiled at the photo. "I was the bride that day, and Mac, in a glimpse of the future, official photographer. She'll tell you it was that moment—the blue butterfly moment—when she knew she wanted to be a photographer."

"It's charming." Kathryn turned to Emma. "We've interrupted your work, and are taking up entirely too much of your time."

"It's always lovely to have an unexpected break."

"I hope you mean that," Adele put in, "because I'm dying to see where you work. Are you arranging today? Making bouquets?"

"Ah . . . actually I'm processing a morning delivery, which is why I'm a little messy."

"I'm shameless, and I'm going to ask if I can see where you work."

"Oh. Of course." She shot a look at Kathryn. "Don't panic."

"I've seen where you work."

"Yes, but not while I was working," Emma pointed out as she led the way. "Processing is . . . Well, as you can see." She gestured to her work counter.

"Just look at the flowers!" Flushed with excitement, Adele moved forward. "Oh, and smell the peonies."

"The bride's favorite," Emma told her. "We'll be using this wonderful rich red for her bouquet, contrasted with the bold pinks down to the palest blush. It'll be hand-tied with wine-colored ribbon and candy pink studs. The attendants will carry smaller versions, in the pinks."

"And you keep them in these buckets?"

"In a solution that hydrates and feeds. It's an important step to keep them fresh, and to help them last after the event. I'll keep them in the cooler until we're ready to start designing."

"How do you—"

"Adele." Kathryn clucked her tongue. "You're interrogating again."

"All right, all right. I'm full of questions, I know. But I'm very serious about launching a wedding planning company in Jamaica." Nodding, Adele scanned the area again. "It seems you have a perfect arrangement here, so there's little hope in luring you away."

"But I'm happy to answer questions. Still, for an overview of a business model, Parker's your girl."

"We're going to get out of your way." Kathryn reached in her bag. "The swatch."

"Oh, what a beautiful color. Like a spring leaf through a drop of dew. Perfect for a fairy-tale wedding." She turned to her display and chose a white silk tulip. "See how the white just gleams against this watery green?"

"Yes. Yes, I do. As soon as the final designs are approved, we'll send you the sketches. Thank you, Emma, for the time."

"We're all here to make certain Jessica has the perfect day."

"You see." Adele poked her sister's arm. "That's exactly the sort of attitude I want to offer. In fact, I think The Perfect Day would be a wonderful name for the business."

"I like it," Emma told her.

"If you change your mind, you've got my card," she reminded Emma. "I'll promise you ten percent over what you make annually now."

"I'M TRYING NOT TO BE ANNOYED SHE'D TRY TO STEAL YOU. Again." Parker slipped off her shoes after the second of two full consults.

"How much did she offer you to move to Jamaica?" Emma asked.

"Carte blanche, which I told her was a rudimentary mistake. No one's worth a blank check, especially when you're designing a business model."

"She's rolling in it," Laurel pointed out. "And yes, I know that doesn't matter on a practical, business level. But she's used to rolling in it."

"She has a good concept. An exclusive and inclusive wedding company in a popular destination wedding site. And she's smart to try to hook people with solid experience. But she's got to create a budget, and stick."

"Then why aren't we doing it?" Mac wanted to know. "I don't mean let's all pack up and move to Jamaica or Aruba, or wherever, but a branch of Vows in some exotic locale? We'd kill."

"I'll kill *you*." Laurel formed a gun with her thumb and finger, and went bang. "Haven't we got enough work?"

"I've thought about it."

Laurel gaped at Parker. "Let me reload."

"Just a loose outline, for the future."

289

"When they perfect human cloning."

"A franchise rather than a branch," Parker explained. "With very specific requirements. But I haven't worked out all the details or kinks. If and when I do, we'll all talk it through. And we'll all have to agree. But for now, yes, we do have enough work. Except for the third week in August. We're blank."

"I saw that. I meant to ask you about it," Emma continued as she stretched out some kinks in the small of her back. "I figured I'd forgotten to plug something in."

"No, we don't have an event that week because I blacked it out. I can change that if nobody's interested in taking a week at the beach."

There was a moment of stunned silence, then three women leaped up to do a happy dance. Laurel snatched Parker's hand and pulled her up to join them.

"I take it you're interested."

"Can we pack now? Can we? Can we?" Mac demanded.

"Sunscreen, a bikini, and a blender for margaritas. What else do you need?" Laurel swung Parker around. "Vacation!"

"Where?" Emma asked. "What beach?"

"Who cares?" Laurel flopped down on the couch again. "It's the beach. It's a week without fondant or sugar paste. I wipe a tear from my cheek."

"The Hamptons. Del bought a house."

"Del bought a house in the Hamptons?" Mac lifted her fists in the air. "Go, Del."

"Actually, Brown LLC bought it. That's what some of the paperwork he's been bringing over was about. A property came up. It's a good investment. I didn't say anything, in case it fell through. But it's a done deal now. So, we'll all pack ourselves off to the beach for a week the end of August."

"All?" Laurel echoed.

290

"The four of us, Carter, Del, Jack, of course. It's six bed-rooms, eight baths. Plenty of room for everyone."

"Does Jack know?" Emma wondered.

"He knows Del was looking at the property, but not about August. We both felt there wasn't a point in talking about tak-ing the week if we didn't go through with it. Now we have."

"I have to go tell Carter. Yay!" Mac gave Parker a smacking kiss before she rushed out.

"This is so great. I'm going to go put it on my calendar, with lots of little hearts and shiny suns. Moonlight walks on the beach." Emma hugged Parker. "It's nearly as perfect as dancing in a moonlit garden. I'm going to call Jack."

When they were alone, Parker looked at Laurel. "Is anything wrong?"

"What? No. God, what could be wrong. Beach, a week. I think I'm in shock. We need new beach clothes."

"Damn right."

Laurel pushed up. "Let's go shopping."

WHEN INSPIRATION STRUCK, EMMA RAN WITH IT. IT TOOK SOME juggling and a client flexible enough to bump up a consult by an hour, but she managed to clear her Monday afternoon.

She planned to surprise Jack with a twist on their usual Monday night date.

On the way out she stopped by the main house and tracked down Parker in the office.

Parker paced, her headset in place, and rolled her eyes when Emma came in.

"I'm sure Kevin's mother didn't mean to be critical or insult-ing. You're absolutely right, it is your wedding, your day, your choice. You're entitled to . . . Yes, he is very sweet, Dawn, and extremely well behaved. I know . . . I know."

Parker closed her eyes, mimed strangling herself for Emma's benefit.

"Ah, why don't you let me take care of this for you? It would take the stress off you and Kevin. And sometimes an outside party is better able to explain and . . . I'm sure she doesn't. Yes, of course. I'd be angry, too. But—But . . . Dawn!" Her tone sharpened just a fraction, enough, Emma knew, to shut down whatever rant the bride might be on. "You have to remember, above anything else, any detail, any complication or disagreement, the day and everything about it is for you and Kevin. And you have to remember, I'm here to see that you and Kevin have the day you want."

This time Parker shot her gaze to the ceiling. "Why don't you and Kevin go out and have a nice dinner tonight, just the two of you? I can make a reservation for you wherever . . . I love that restaurant." Parker scribbled down a name on a pad. "Say seven? I'll take care of that for you right now. And I'll speak to his mother this evening. By tomorrow, everything will be fine. Don't worry about a thing. I'll talk to you soon. Yes, Dawn, that's what I'm here for. Good. Great. Mmm-hmm. Bye."

She held up a finger. "One more minute." Once she'd contacted the bride's choice of restaurant, wrangled a reservation, she pulled off the headset.

Parker took a breath, let out a short but enthusiastic scream, then nodded. "Better. Much better."

"Dawn's having a problem with her soon-to-be mother-in-law?"

"Yes. Oddly, the MOG doesn't understand or approve of the bride's choice of ring bearer."

"It's really not her—"

"Which is Beans, the bride's Boston bull terrier."

"Oh, I'd forgotten about that one." Emma's brow creased. "Wait. Did I know about that one?"

"Probably not, as she only told me a couple of days ago. The MOG thinks it's silly, undignified, and embarrassing. And said so in very clear terms. The bride's decided her future mother-in-law is a dog hater."

"Is he wearing a tux?"

Parker's lips twitched "At this point, just a bow tie. She wants the dog, she gets the dog. So I'll ask the MOG to have a drink with me—as such matters are best done in person and with alcohol—and smooth this over."

"Good luck with that. I'm heading into town. I'm going to surprise Jack, cook him dinner, so I won't be back until morning. But I'm also going to see if you and Laurel left any sexy summer clothes anywhere in Greenwich."

"There may be a halter top left. Possibly one pair of sandals."

"I'll find them. I'm going to the market, and by the nursery. Is there anything you need? I can drop it back by in the morning."

"Are you going by the bookstore?"

"I'm going to town; what would my mother say if I didn't drop in?"

"Right. She's got a book I ordered."

"I'll get it for you. If you think of anything else, just call my cell."

"Have fun." As Emma left, Parker looked at her BlackBerry. Sighed. And picked it up to call Kevin's mother.

DELIGHTED TO HAVE A FEW HOURS OUT AND ABOUT, EMMA stopped at the nursery first. She gave herself permission to just wander and enjoy before settling down to the business of selection.

She loved the smells—the earth, the plants, the green—so much she had to order herself not to just buy some of everything.

But she promised herself she'd take another swing through in the morning and pick up a few more plants for the estate.

For now, she debated on pots while envisioning Jack's back porch entrance. She found two slim urns in a rusted bronze color she decided would be perfect flanking his kitchen door.

"Nina?" She signaled to the manager. "I'm going to take these two."

"They're great, aren't they?"

"They are. Can you have them loaded in my car? It's right out front. And the potting soil? I'm just going to pick out the plants."

"Take your time."

She found exactly what she wanted, sticking with deep reds and purples with a few sparks of gold to set them off.

"Gorgeous," Nina commented when Emma pushed her cart through toward the cashier. "Strong colors, great textures. And that heliotrope smells wonderful. Is this for a wedding?"

"No, actually they're a gift for a friend."

"Lucky friend. Everything's loaded."

"Thanks."

In town, she wandered the shops, treated herself to new sandals, a breezy skirt, and thinking of the long-ago summer, a boldly printed scarf to use as a beach wrap.

She swung into the bookstore, waved to the clerk ringing up a sale at the counter.

"Hi, Emma! Your mom's in the back."

"Thanks."

She found her mother opening a recent delivery of books. The minute she saw Emma, Lucia set the shipment aside. "Now this is the best kind of surprise."

"I've been out spending money." Emma leaned over the box to kiss Lucia's cheek.

"My favorite activity. Almost. Did you buy something that

made you so happy, or . . ." She tapped a finger on Emma's bracelet. "Are you just happy?"

"Both. I'm going to cook dinner for Jack, so I still have to go to the market. But I found the cutest sandals, which—of course—I had to wear out."

Emma did a pivot, a turn, showing them off.

"They *are* cute."

"And . . ." Emma flicked her index fingers at her new gold dangles to make them sway.

"Ah, pretty."

"Plus a wonderful summer skirt just covered with red poppies. A couple of tops, a scarf, and . . . so on."

"That's my girl. I saw Jack this morning. I thought he said you were going to the movies tonight."

"Change of plans. I'm going to make him your flank steak. Mrs. G had one in the freezer so I begged it from her and it's been marinating all night. It's out in the car in a cooler. I thought I'd do those roasted fingerling potatoes with rosemary, maybe asparagus, a nice chunk of bread with dipping oil. What do you think?"

"Very manly."

"Good, that was the idea. I couldn't bring myself to hit Laurel up for a dessert. She's swamped. I thought maybe just ice cream and berries."

"A manly and thoughtful meal. Is this an occasion?"

"Partly to thank him for the incredible night in New York, and the rest . . . I'm going to tell him, Mama. I'm going to tell him how I feel about him, that I love him. It seems almost wrong to have all this"—she pressed a hand to her heart—"and not tell him."

"Love is brave," Lucia reminded her. "I know when he says your name, he looks happy. I'm glad you told me. Now I can think good thoughts for you, for both of you, tonight."

"I'll take them. Oh, and you have a book for Parker. I told her I'd pick it up for her."

"I'll get it for you." Lucia wrapped an arm around Emma's waist as she walked her out of the storeroom. "You'll call me tomorrow? I want to know how your dinner went."

"I'll call you, first thing."

"Emma?"

Emma looked over, smiled at the pretty brunette she desperately tried to place. "Hi."

"It is you! Oh, hi, Emma!"

Emma found herself gripped in an enthusiastic hug and rocked side-to-side. Baffled, she gave the girl a friendly squeeze in return as she shot questioning looks at her mother.

"Rachel, you're home from college." Lucia beamed as she gave her daughter hints. "It seems like last week Emma was heading out to babysit for you."

"I know. I can hardly—"

"Rachel? Rachel Monning?" Emma pulled her back, stared into bright blue eyes. "Oh my God. *Look* at you. I didn't recognize you. You're grown-up and gorgeous. When did you stop being twelve?"

"A while ago. It's just been so long, between this and that and college. Oh, Emma, you look awesome. You always did. I can't believe I ran into you this way. I was actually going to call you."

"You're in college now? Home for the summer?"

"Yes. One more year. I'm working at Estervil, in public relations. It's my day off because I needed a book. A wedding planning book. I'm engaged!"

She held out her hand to show off the sparkle of her diamond.

"Engaged?" Emma pushed through the moment of speech-

296

less shock. "But you were playing with your Barbies ten minutes ago."

"I think it's closer to ten years." Rachel's face lit up with her laugh. "You have to meet Drew. He's amazing. Of course you'll meet him. We're going to get married next summer, after I graduate, and I really want to have you do the flowers, and, well, everything. My mother says Vows is *the* place. Can you believe it? I'm getting married, and you'll make my bouquet. You used to make those Kleenex bouquets for me, and now, it'll be real."

She felt the jab straight in the belly, hated herself for it, but felt it. "I'm so happy for you. When did this happen?"

"Two weeks, three days and . . ." Rachel checked her watch. "Sixteen hours ago. Oh, I wish I had more time, but I have to get the book and run or I'll be late." She hugged Emma again. "I'll call and we'll talk flowers and cakes and, oh God, everything. Bye! Bye, Mrs. Grant. I'll see you soon."

"Rachel Monning's getting married."

"Yes." Lucia patted Emma's shoulder. "She is."

"I used to babysit for her. I used to French braid her hair and let her stay up past her bedtime. Now I'm going to do her wedding flowers. Good God, Mama."

"There there," Lucia said and didn't bother to mask a chuckle. "Aren't you about to spend the evening with a wonderful man?"

"Yes. Right. I get it. Everyone takes different directions. But . . . Good God."

She managed to put babysitting and weddings aside to finish her shopping. She'd barely stepped out of the market before being hailed again.

"Buenos tardes, bonita!"

"Rico." Instead of a hug she had both cheeks affectionately kissed. "How are you?"

"Better for seeing you."

"Why aren't you flying somewhere fabulous?"

"Just back from a run to Italy. The owner took his family to Tuscany for a little R and R."

"Ah, the hard life of the private pilot. And how's Brenna?"

"We broke up a couple of months ago."

"Oh, I'm sorry. I hadn't heard."

"The way it goes." He shrugged. "Let me carry those for you." He took her grocery bags, peeked in as he walked her to her car. "Looks like good eating, and a lot better than the Hungry Man dinner I have on tap."

"Oh, poor thing." She laughed at him then unlocked the passenger side door. "Just in here. I'm already pretty loaded in the back."

"So I see," he said as he glanced at the plants and bags in the back seat. "It looks like you've got a busy evening planned, but if you want to change your mind, I'll take you to dinner." He trailed a flirtatious finger down her arm. "Or better yet, give you that flying lesson we used to talk about."

"Thanks, Rico, but I'm seeing someone."

"It ought to be me. Feel free to change your mind about that, too—any time—and give me a call."

"If I do you'll be the first." She brushed her lips over his cheek before rounding the hood to her door. "Do you remember Jill Burke?"

"Ah . . . little blonde, big laugh."

"Yes. She's single again, too."

"Is that so?"

"You should call her. I bet she'd love a flying lesson."

His grin flashed adding a sparkle to his eyes and reminding her why she'd enjoyed spending time with him. She got in, and sent him a wave as she drove away.

Considering the planters, plants, groceries, Emma parked in the back of Jack's building and as close to the steps as she could manage. She angled her head as she studied the little kitchen deck, then nodded. The planters would do very well there, very well indeed.

Eager to get started, she walked around to the front of the building to use the main entrance. The beveled glass in the door and the tall front windows brought in pretty light, adding a sense of style and comfort to the reception area. He'd been right to keep it cozy rather than sleek, she thought. It projected calm and quiet dignity, while she knew in the individual offices and planning rooms, chaos often reigned.

"Hi, Michelle."

"Emma." The woman working on a computer at a ruthlessly organized desk stopped to shift her chair. "How are you?"

"I'm great. How are you feeling?"

"Twenty-nine weeks and counting." Michelle patted her baby belly. "We're perfect. I *love* your sandals."

"Me, too. I just bought them."

"They're great. Monday night date, right?"

"Exactly."

"You're a little early, aren't you?"

"New plan. Is Jack busy? I haven't actually told him the new plan."

"He's not back yet. Running late, glitch on a site. Not very happy with the subs or the new county inspector, or, well, anything just at the moment."

"Oh." Emma winced. "Well, my new plan is either very good or very bad under those circumstances."

"Can you share?"

"Sure. I thought I'd cook dinner, surprise him with that and some planters for his little deck. Dinner and a movie at home, instead of going out."

"If you want my opinion, it's inspired. I think he'd be thrilled to have a home-cooked meal after the day he's put in. You can

299

call and check, but he may be in around three with the building inspector."

"Why don't we just let that play out? The problem is, Michelle, I don't have a key."

There was a beat, just a quick bump of surprise. "Oh, well, that's no problem." Michelle opened a drawer of her desk to fish out a spare set.

"Are you sure it's okay?" And how mortifying is it, Emma thought, to have to ask?

"I can't think of why it wouldn't be. You and Jack have been friends for years, and now you're . . ."

"Yes, we are," Emma said, deliberately bright. "Second problem? The two planters I bought weigh about fifty pounds each."

"Chip's in the back. I'll send him out."

"Thanks, Michelle," Emma said as she took the keys. "You're a lifesaver."

She closed her hand around the keys as she started around to the back again. No point, she told herself, in feeling embarrassed. No point in feeling slighted that the man she'd been sleeping with for nearly three months—and had known for more than a decade—hadn't bothered to give her a key.

It wasn't symbolic, for God's sake. He wasn't locking her out. He was just . . .

It didn't matter. She would forge ahead with her plans for the evening. Give him flowers, cook him dinner, and tell him she loved him.

And, damn it, she was going to ask for a key.

300

$\mathscr{S}$HE SPENT A HAPPY HOUR PUTTING AWAY GROCERIES, ARRANGING the sunflowers she'd brought from her stock for his kitchen counter, then prepping the planters.

She'd been right, she thought, about how perfect they'd be flanking the door. Deep, bold spots of color, she decided as she tucked red salvia behind purple heliotrope. The combination of plants she'd chosen would give him color and bloom all season, and be even showier when the lobelia spilled and the sweet allysium foamed over the lip.

A nice welcome home, she thought, every time he walked up the stairs. And, she thought with a little smile, a living reminder of the woman who'd laid out that welcome.

Sitting back on her heels, she studied the result. "Gorgeous, if I do say so myself."

After stacking the empty pots and cell packs, she shifted to duplicate the arrangement in the second urn.

She wondered if he had a watering can, then decided probably not. She should've thought of that, but they'd make do until he got one. Happy to have her hands in dirt, she hummed along with the radio she'd switched on. His front entrance planters needed more zip, she mused as she worked. She'd try to pick up a few more things in the next week or so.

When she'd finished, she swept up the spilled dirt, then carried the plastic trays and pots, her gardening tools down to her car. Brushing off her hands she looked up to admire the work.

Flowers, she'd always thought, were an essential element of home. Now he had them. And, she'd always believed, flowers planted with love bloomed more beautifully. If true, these would be spectacular right up to the first hard frost.

When she checked the time, she dashed back up the stairs. She needed to wash up and start on dinner, especially since she'd decided to add an appetizer to the menu.

$\mathscr{D}$IRTY, SWEATY, AND STILL PISSED OFF DUE TO THE DISAPPEARING plumber and a rookie building inspector with an attitude, Jack turned toward the rear of his offices.

He wanted a shower, a beer, maybe a handful of aspirin. If the general contractor wasn't going to fire the asshole plumber—who also happened to be his brother-in-law—then *he* could explain the delay to the client. And *he* could take on the building inspector who decided to throw his weight around because a doorway was a damn seven-eighths of an inch off.

Okay, maybe the aspirin, the shower, then the drink.

Maybe that would smooth out a day that had begun with a call at six A.M. from a client with a tape measure who'd gone ballistic because the framing for his service bar came in at five feet eight inches instead of six feet.

Not that he blamed the client. He'd felt ballistic himself. Six feet on the plans meant six feet on the job, not whatever the sub decided would do.

And, Jack thought as he tried to roll the worst of the tension out of his shoulders, the day had just gone downhill from there. If he was going to put in a twelve-hour day, at least he wanted to finish up feeling he'd accomplished something instead of just riding around the goddamn county putting out fires.

He made the last turn, telling himself to be grateful he was home, where, since the office was now closed, nobody—please God—was going to ask him to fix anything, negotiate anything, or argue about anything.

When he spotted Emma's car he struggled to think past the headache. Had he mixed things up? Had they planned to meet in town, go from there?

No, no, dinner, maybe a movie—which he'd intended to switch to carry-out, possibly a DVD, and that *after* he'd had a chance to cool off and settle down. Except he'd forgotten to call her about that as he'd been hip-deep in crises and complaints.

But if she was in town somewhere, he could just . . .

His mind switched gears as he noticed his back door open to the screen, and the pots of flowers beside it. He sat where he was a moment, then tossed his sunglasses on the dash. When he stepped out of the truck, he heard the music pouring through the screen door.

Where the hell did the plants come from? he wondered as fresh irritation banged against an already full-blown headache. And why the hell was his door open?

He wanted air-conditioning, a cool shower, and five damn minutes to shake off the worst of the day. Now he had flowers he'd have to remember to water, music blasting, and somebody who'd require attention and conversation in his house.

He trudged up the steps, scowled at the plants, pushed through the screen door.

And there she was, singing along with the radio—which was blasting through his aching head, cooking something on his stove when he'd set his system on take-out pizza, and his spare keys sat on the counter beside a vase of enormous sunflowers they made his eyes throb.

She shook the frying pan with one hand, reached for a glass of wine with the other—then saw him.

"Oh!" She laughed when her hand jerked on the handle of the pan. "I didn't hear you."

"Not surprising, as you're entertaining the neighborhood with . . . Jesus, is that ABBA?"

"What? Oh, the music. It is loud." She gave the pan another shake before adjusting the heat under it. With an easy side step, she picked up the remote, lowered the volume on the stereo. "Cooking music. I thought I'd surprise you with a ready-made meal. These scallops just need another minute. The sauce is already done, so you can have a little something right away. How about a glass of wine?"

"No. Thanks." He reached over her head into the cabinet for a bottle of aspirin.

"Hard day." In sympathy, she rubbed a hand down his arm as he fought open the bottle. "Michelle told me. Why don't you sit down for a minute, get your bearings?"

"I'm filthy. I need a shower."

"Well, you're right about that." She rose on her toes to brush a light kiss on his lips. "I'll get you some ice water."

"I can get it." He moved past her to the refrigerator. "Michelle gave you the key?"

"She said you were stuck out on a job, and having a bad day. I had the food out in the car, so . . ." She shook the pan again, turned off the flame. "I've got a flank steak marinating. Red meat ought to help your headache. You can just clean up and relax. Or I can hold dinner awhile if you want to stretch out until you feel better."

"What is all this, Emma?" Even at the lower volume, the music scraped against his nerves. He grabbed the remote, turned it off. "Did you haul those pots up here?"

"Chip did the heavy work. I had the best time picking out the urns, the plants." She sprinkled the scallops with a mixture of cilantro, garlic, and lime, poured on the sauce she'd prepared. "They really pop against the house, don't they? I wanted to do something to thank you for New York, and when inspiration hit, I juggled a few things and hit the road."

She set the empty bowl in the sink, turned. Her smile faded. "And I miscalculated, didn't I?"

"It's been a lousy day, that's all."

"Which I've added to, clearly."

"Yes. No." He pressed his fingers to the drill trying to bore through his temple. "It's been a bad day. I just need to smooth out some. You should've called if you wanted to . . . do this."

Without thinking, out of sheer habit, he picked up the spare keys and shoved them in his pocket.

He might as well have slapped her.

"Don't worry, Jack, I didn't hang anything of mine in a closet, put anything in a drawer. My toothbrush is still in my bag."

"What the hell are you talking about?"

"My trespassing only went as far as the kitchen, and it won't happen again. I didn't run out and make a copy of your precious keys, and I hope you won't give Michelle any grief for giving them to me."

"Give me a small break, Emma."

"Give *you* a break? Do you have any idea how humiliating it was to have to tell her I didn't have a key? To know we've been sleeping together since April and I can't be trusted."

305

"It has nothing to do with trust. I just never—"

"Bullshit, Jack. Just bullshit. Every time I stay here—which is very rare because it's *your* space, I have to make sure I don't leave so much as a stray hairpin behind because, dear God, what's next? An actual hair brush? A shirt? Before you know it I'll actually feel welcome here."

"You are welcome here. Don't be ridiculous. I don't want to fight with you."

"Too bad, because I want to fight with you. You're irritated because I'm here, because I invaded your space, made myself at home. And that tells me I'm wasting my time, I'm wasting my feelings, because I deserve better than that."

"Look, Emma, all this just caught me at a bad time."

"It's not the time, Jack, not just the time. It's always. You don't let me in here because that's too close to a commitment for you."

"Jesus, Emma, I am committed. There's no one else. There hasn't been anyone else since I touched you."

"It's not about someone else. It's about you and me. It's about wanting me, but only on your terms, on your—your blueprint," she said waving her hands in the air. "As long as we stick to that, no problem. But that's not going to work for me anymore. It's not going to work when I can't pick up a quart of milk for you or leave a damn lipstick on your bathroom counter. Or give you some damn plants without pissing you off."

"Milk? What milk? Jesus Christ, I don't know what you're talking about."

"It's not going to work when cooking you a fucking meal is like a criminal act." She snatched up the plate of scallops, tossed it into the sink with a crash of stoneware.

"Okay, that's enough."

"No, it isn't enough." She whirled, shoved him back with both hands as tears of anger and heartbreak clouded her eyes, thickened her voice. "And I'm not going to settle for what isn't

306

enough. I'm in love with you, and I want you to love me. I want a life with you. Marriage and babies and a *future*. So this? This isn't enough, not nearly. It turns out you were right, Jack. Absolutely right. Give them an inch, they'll take a mile."

"What? How? Wait."

"But don't worry, no need to run for the hills. I'm responsible for my own feelings, my own needs, my own choices. And I'm done here. I'm done with this."

"Hold it." He wondered his head didn't explode. Maybe it already had. "Wait a damn minute so I can think."

"Time's up, thinking's over. Don't touch me now," she warned when he started toward her. "Don't even think about putting a hand on me. You had your chance. I'd have given you everything I had. If you'd needed more, I'd have found it, and given you that. It's the way I love. It's the only way I know how. But I can't give where it's not wanted and valued. Where I'm not."

"Be pissed off." He snapped it out. "Break dishes. But don't stand there and tell me I don't want you, don't value you."

"Not the way I want or need. And trying not to want, Jack? Trying not to love you the only way I know how to love? It's breaking my heart." She grabbed her bag. "Stay away from me."

He slapped a hand on the screen door to stop her. "I want you to sit down. You're not the only one with things to say."

"I don't care what you want. I'm done caring. I said stay away from me."

She looked up at him then. It wasn't temper or heat in her eyes. Those he would've ignored until they'd burned this out. But he had no power against her pain.

"Emma. Please."

She only shook her head, and, pushing past him, ran to her car.

★ ★ ★

$\mathcal{S}$HE DIDN'T KNOW HOW SHE MANAGED TO DAM THE TEARS. SHE only knew she couldn't see through them and she had to get home. She needed home. Her hands wanted to shake so she gripped the wheel tighter. Every breath hurt. How was that possible? How could the simple act of drawing breath burn? She heard herself moan, and pressed her lips together to hold back the next. It sounded like a wounded animal.

She wouldn't let herself feel that. Not now. Not yet.

Ignoring the cheerful ringtones of her phone, she kept her eyes focused on the road.

The dam collapsed; the tears broke through when she turned into the drive. She swiped at them, a fast, impatient hand until she'd navigated along the curve, parked.

Now the trembling came, so that she shook as she stumbled from the car, up the walk. She made it inside, safe, home, before the first sob took her.

"Emma?" Parker's voice carried down the stairs. "What are you doing back so early? I thought you were—"

Through the flood of tears, Emma saw Parker rush down the stairs. "Parker."

Then there were arms around her, strong and tight. "Oh, Emma. Oh, baby. Come on now, come with me."

"What's all this commotion? What's . . . Is she hurt?" Like Parker, Mrs. Grady hurried forward.

"Not that way. I'm going to take her upstairs. Can you call Mac?"

"I'll see to it. There now, lamb." Mrs. Grady stroked a hand down Emma's hair. "You're home now. We'll take care of everything. Go on with Parker."

"I can't stop. I can't make it stop."

"You don't have to stop." With an arm around Emma's waist, Parker led her upstairs. "Cry all you want, as long as you need. We'll go up to the parlor. To our place."

As they started up to the third floor, Laurel bolted down. Saying nothing, she simply wrapped an arm around Emma from the other side.

"How could I be so stupid?"

"You weren't," Parker murmured. "You aren't."

"I'll get her some water," Laurel said, and Parker nodded as she led Emma to the couch.

"It hurts, so much. So much. How can anyone stand it?"

"I don't know."

When they sat, Emma curled up, laid her head in Parker's lap.

"I had to get home. I just had to get home."

"You're home now." Laurel sat on the floor, pushed tissues into Emma's hand.

Burying her face in them, Emma sobbed out the pain and grief throbbing in her chest, twisting in her belly. Raw sobs scorched her throat until there were none left. Still, tears spilled down her cheeks.

"It feels like some horrible illness." She squeezed her eyes shut for a moment. "Like I may never be well again."

"Drink a little water. It'll help." Parker eased her up. "And these aspirin."

"It's like a terrible flu." Emma sipped water, took a breath, then swallowed the aspirin Parker handed her. "The kind where even when it's over, you're weak and sick and helpless."

"There's tea and soup." Like Laurel, Mac sat on the floor. "Mrs. G brought it up."

"Not yet. Thanks. Not yet."

"This wasn't just a fight," Laurel said.

"No. Not just a fight." Exhausted, she rested her head on Parker's shoulder. "Is it worse, do you think, since it's my own fault?"

"Don't you dare blame yourself." Laurel squeezed Emma's leg. "Don't you dare."

"I'm not letting him off the hook, believe me. But I got myself into it. And tonight, especially tonight, I worked myself up to wanting—expecting," she corrected, "things that weren't going to happen. I know him, and still I jumped off the cliff."

"Can you tell us what happened?" Mac asked her.

"Yeah."

"Take a little tea first." Laurel held out the cup.

After one sip, Emma blew out a breath. "There's whiskey in here."

"Mrs. G said to drink it. It'll help."

"Tastes like medicine. And I guess it is." Emma took another sip. "I crossed his lines, I guess you could say. I don't find those lines acceptable. So we're done. We have to be done because I can't feel this way."

"What are the lines?" Parker asked.

"He doesn't make room." Emma shook her head. "I wanted to do something for him. Part of it was certainly for me, but I wanted to do something special. So I went by the nursery," she began.

When she finished the tea, the ache throbbed behind a thin cushion. "I had this moment, when I had to tell Michelle I didn't have a key. Part of me stepped back, said: Stop."

"What the hell for?" Laurel demanded.

"And that's what the rest of me said. We were together, a couple. And under that, good friends. What could be wrong with going into his place to surprise him with dinner? But I knew. That other part of me knew. Maybe it was a test. I don't know. I don't care. And maybe it was worse—the buildup, the crash—because I'd run into Rachel Monning at the bookstore. Do you remember her, Parker? I babysat her."

"Yes, vaguely."

"She's getting married."

"You *babysat* for her?" Laurel held up her hands. "They're letting twelve-year-olds get married?"

"She's in college. Graduating next year, followed by her wedding. Which she wants here, by the way. And when I got over the genuine shock, all I could think was, I want that. I want what this girl I *babysat* has. Damn it, I want what I see on her face. All that joy, that confidence, that eagerness to start a life with the man I love. Why shouldn't I want that? Why aren't I entitled to that? Wanting marriage is as legitimate as not wanting it."

"Preaching to the choir," Mac reminded her.

"Well, I do want it. I want the promise and the work and the children and all of it. All of it. I know I want the fairy tale, too. Dancing in the moonlit garden, but that's just . . . Well, it's like a bouquet or a beautiful cake. It's a symbol. I want what it symbolizes. He doesn't." She leaned back, closed her eyes a moment. "Neither of us are wrong. We just don't want the same thing."

"Did he say that? That he doesn't want what you want?"

"He was angry to find me in his house," she said to Parker. "Not even angry. Worse. Annoyed. I'd been presumptuous."

"Oh, for God's sake," Mac muttered.

"Well, I had presumed. I presumed he'd be pleased to see me, to have me willing to fuss over him a bit after he'd had a long, hard day. I had my copy of *Truly, Madly, Deeply* with me. We joked about doing a double feature so he could see why I loved it, and we'd pair it up with *Die Hard*."

"Alan Rickman." Laurel nodded.

"Exactly. I had sunflowers, and the planters—God they're really beautiful—and I'd nearly finished making the appetizer when he came in. I just bubbled along for a while. Let me get you some wine, why don't you relax? God! What a moron. Then it got through, loud and clear. He . . . picked up the spare keys, and put them in his pocket."

311

"That's cold," Laurel said with quiet fury. "That's fucking cold."

"His keys," Emma stated. "His right. So I told him what I thought, what I felt, and that I was finished trying *not* to want and *not* to feel. I told him I was in love with him. And all he could really say to that is to give him a minute to think."

"There's your moron."

Emma nearly managed a smile at Mac's disgusted tone. "I got the 'caught him off guard, wasn't expecting.' Even the 'caught me at a bad time.'"

"Oh my God."

"That was before I told him I was in love with him, but it doesn't matter. So I ended it, and I walked out. It hurts. I think it's going to hurt a really long time."

"He called," Mac told her.

"I don't want to talk to him."

"Figured that. He wanted to make sure you were here, that you got home. I'm not taking his side, believe me, but he sounded pretty shaken up."

"I don't care. I don't want to care. If I forgive him now, if I go back—settle for what he can give me—I'll lose myself. I have to get over him first." She curled up again. "I just need to get over him. I don't want to see him or talk to him until I do. Or at least until I feel stronger."

"Then you won't. I'm going to reschedule your consults for tomorrow."

"Oh, Parker—"

"You need a day off."

"To wallow?"

"Yes. Now you need a long, hot bath, and we're going to heat up that soup. Then after your second cry—there will be another."

"Yeah." Emma sighed. "There will."

312

"After that, we're going to tuck you into bed. You're going to sleep until you wake up."

"I'm still going to be in love with him when I wake up."

"Yes," Parker agreed.

"And it's still going to hurt."

"Yes."

"But I'll be a little bit stronger."

"You will."

"I'll fix the bath. I have a formula." Mac rose, then leaned over and kissed Emma's cheek. "We're all here."

"I'll take care of the soup, and I'll ask Mrs. Grady to make a batch of her fabulous french fries. I know it's a cliché." Laurel gave Emma's leg another squeeze. "But it's a cliché for a reason."

"Thanks." She closed her eyes, reached for Parker's hand when they were alone. "I knew you'd be here."

"Always."

"Oh, God. Parker. Oh, God, here comes the second one now."

"It's okay," Parker soothed, and rubbed Emma's back as she wept. "It's okay."

WHILE EMMA WEPT, JACK KNOCKED ON DEL'S DOOR. HE HAD TO do something or he'd drive over to Emma's. If she hadn't made it clear he wasn't wanted—and she had—Mac had made it double.

Del pulled open the door. "What's up? Jesus, Jack, you look like shit."

"It goes with how I feel."

Del's brow creased. "Oh man, if you're coming over here to cry in your beer over a fight with Emma—"

"It wasn't a fight. Not . . . just a fight."

Del took a harder look, stepped back. "Let's have a beer."

Jack shut the door behind him, then noticed Del's jacket and tie. "You're going out?"

"I was heading that way in a while. Get the beer. I have to make a call."

"I should say it's no big deal, it can wait. But I'm not going to."

"Get the beer. I'll be out in a minute."

Jack got two beers and went out on the back deck. But instead of sitting he walked to the rail and stared out at the dark. He tried to remember if he'd ever felt this bad before. He decided other than waking up in the hospital with a concussion, a broken arm, and a couple of cracked ribs after a car wreck, the answer was no.

And even then, the seriously bad had been only physical.

No, he thought, he remembered feeling like this before, nearly exactly like this. Sick and baffled and confused. When his parents had sat him down, so civilized, to tell him they were getting a divorce.

You're not to blame, they'd told him. We still love you, and always will. But . . .

In that moment his world had turned upside down. So why was this worse somehow? Why was it worse to realize that Emma could and would walk away from him? Could and would, he thought, because he'd made her feel *less* when he should have done everything in his power to make her feel *more*.

He heard the door open. "Thanks," he said as Del came out. "Really."

"I should say it's no big deal, but I'm not going to."

Jack managed a weak laugh. "God, Del, I fucked up. I fucked it up and I'm not even sure exactly how. But what I know is I hurt her. I really hurt her, so you're welcome to kick my ass as promised. But you'll have to wait until I'm finished doing it."

"I can wait."

"She said she's in love with me."

314

Del took a pull on his beer. "You're not an idiot, Jack. Are you going to stand there and tell me you didn't know?"

"Not completely, or altogether. It's all just happened, and . . . No, I'm not an idiot and I know we were heading toward something. That. But then there's this leap, and I'm flat-footed. Can't keep up, can't figure out how to deal with it, or what to say, and she's so hurt, so hurt and pissed off she won't give me a chance. She hardly ever gets mad. You know how she is. She hardly ever blows, and when she does, you don't have a prayer."

"Why did she blow?"

He went back for the beer, but still didn't sit. "I had a pisser of a day, Del. I'm talking the kind of day that makes hell look like Disney World. I'm filthy and pissed off and have a motherfucker of a stress headache. I pull up, and she's there. In the house."

"I didn't know you gave her a key. Major step for you, Cooke."

"I didn't. I hadn't. She got it from Michelle."

"Uh-oh. Infiltrated the front lines, did she?"

Jack stopped, stared. "Is that how I am? Come on."

"It's exactly how you are, with women."

"And that makes me, what, a monster, a psycho?"

Del hitched a hip onto the deck rail. "No, a little phobic, maybe. So?"

"So, I'm filthy and my mood matches it, and she's there. She's made these pots for the deck. What are you laughing at?"

"Just imagining your shock and dismay."

"Well, Jesus, she's cooking, and there's flowers, and the music's blasting, and my head's screaming. God, if I could rewind it, I would. I would. I'd never hurt her."

"I know."

"She's hurt and pissed because . . . I'm being a prick. No question, but instead of having a fight, maybe yelling at each other for a while, clearing the air, it turns." Because the head-ache wanted to bully its way back, Jack rubbed the cold bottle over his temple. "It turns and dives south. It's how I don't trust her, and she's not welcome in my house. How she's not going to settle. She's in love with me, and she wants . . ."

"What does she want?"

"What do you think? Marriage, kids, the whole ball. I'm trying to keep up, trying to keep my head from just blasting off my shoulders and *think*, but she won't give me time. She won't let me deal with what she just said. She's done with me, with us. I broke her heart. She cried. She's crying."

Her face flashed back into his mind until he was sick with regret. "I just want her to sit down, to wait a minute, and sit down. Just until I can get my breath, until I can think. She won't. She told me to stay away from her. I'd rather she'd shot me than look at me the way she did when she told me to stay away from her."

"Is that it?" Del asked after a moment.

"That's not enough?"

"I asked you once before, and you didn't answer. I'll ask you again. Yes or no this time. Are you in love with her?"

"Okay." He took a long drink of beer. "Yes. I guess it took an ass-kicking to shake it out of me, but yes. I'm in love with her. But—"

"Do you want to fix it?"

"I just said I was in love with her. Why wouldn't I want to fix it?"

"You want to know how?"

"Goddamn it, Del." He drank again. "Yes, since you're so fucking smart. How do I fix it?"

"Crawl."

Jack blew out a breath. "I can do that."

CHAPTER TWENTY

$\mathscr{H}$E STARTED CRAWLING IN THE MORNING. HE HAD THE SPEECH he'd edited, revised and expanded most of the night in his head. The trick, as far as he could tell, would be getting her to listen to him.

She'd listen, he told himself as he turned into the Brown Estate. She was Emma. No one was more kind, more open-hearted, than Emma—and wasn't that only one of the dozens of reasons he loved her?

He'd been an idiot, but she'd forgive him. She had to forgive him because . . . she was Emma.

Still his stomach clutched when he saw her car parked at the main house. She hadn't gone home.

He wouldn't just be facing her, he thought with genuine, back-sweating fear, but all of them. The four of them, with Mrs. Grady for backup.

They'd roast his balls.

He deserved it, no question. But, dear God, did it have to be the four of them? Fucking A.

"Strap it on, Cooke," he muttered, and got out of the truck.

As he walked to the door he wondered if the condemned walking the last mile experienced this same feeling of doom and dull terror.

"Get a grip, get a freaking grip. They can't kill you."

Maim possibly, verbally assault most definitely. But they couldn't kill him.

He started to open the door out of habit, then realized as a persona non grata he wasn't entitled. He rang the bell.

He thought he could get around Mrs. G. She liked him—really liked him. He could throw himself on her mercy, then . . .

Parker answered. No one, he thought, absolutely no one got around Parker Brown.

"Uh," he said.

"Hello, Jack."

"I want—need—to see Emma. To apologize for . . . everything. If I could talk to her for a few minutes and—"

"No."

Such a small word, he thought, so coolly delivered. "Parker, I just want to—"

"No, Jack. She's sleeping."

"I can come back, or wait, or—"

"No."

"Is that all you're going to say to me? Just no?"

"No," she said again without any hint of irony or humor. "It's not all we're going to say."

Mac and Laurel stepped up behind her. As battle plans went, he had to admit it was superior. No choice but surrender.

"Whatever you're going to say, I deserve. You want me to say I was wrong. I was wrong. That I was an idiot? I was. That—"

318

"I was thinking more along the lines of selfish prick," Laurel commented.

"That, too. Maybe there were reasons, maybe there were circumstances, but they don't matter. Certainly not to you."

"They really don't." Mac eased forward a step. "Not when you hurt the best person we know."

"I can't fix it, I can't make up for it if you don't let me talk to her."

"She doesn't want to talk to you. She doesn't want to see you," Parker said. "Not now. I can't say I'm sorry you're hurting, too. I can see you are, but I can't say I'm sorry for it. Not now. Now, this is about Emma, not about you. She needs time, and she needs you to leave her alone. So that's what you're going to do."

"For how long?"

"As long as it takes."

"Parker, if you'd just listen—"

"No."

As he stared at her, Carter started down the hall from the kitchen. Carter shot him one brief, sympathetic look, then turned around and walked back again.

So much for male solidarity.

"You can't just close the door."

"I can, and I will. But I'll give you something first, because I love you, Jack."

"Oh God, Parker." Why not just roast his balls? he thought. It couldn't be more painful.

"I love you. You're not just *like* a brother to me, you *are* a brother to me. To us. So, I'll give you something. I'll forgive you eventually."

"I'm not on board with that," Laurel told him. "I have reservations."

"I'll forgive you," Parker continued, "and we'll be friends again. But more importantly, Emma will forgive you. She'll

319

find a way. Until she does, until she's ready, you're going to leave her alone. You're not going to call her, or contact her, or try to see her. We're not going to tell her you came here this morning, unless she asks. We won't lie to her."

"You can't come here, Jack." The slightest hint of sympathy eked into Mac's voice. "If there's any problem or question with the work on the studio, we'll handle it by phone. But you can't come here until Emma's okay with it."

"How are you supposed to know when that is?" he demanded. "Is she just going to say, 'Hey, I'm okay if Jack comes around'?"

"We'll know," Laurel said simply.

"If you care about her, you'll give her all the time she needs. I need your word."

He dragged a hand through his hair as Parker waited. "All right. You, all of you, know her better than anyone. You say this is what she needs, okay, it's what she needs. You've got my word I'll leave her alone until . . . until."

"And, Jack," Parker added, "you'll take that time for yourself, too. Time to think about what you really want, really need. I want your word on one more thing."

"Want me to sign in blood?"

"A promise will do. When she's ready, I'll call you. I'll do that for you—and for her—but only if you promise to come here and talk to me before you go to her."

"All right. I promise. Can you just get in touch once in a while, let me know how she is? What she's—"

"No. Good-bye, Jack." Parker closed the door, quietly, in his face.

On the other side of the door, Mac heaved out a breath. "It's not being disloyal to say I have to feel a little bit sorry for him. I know what it's like to be a complete jerk about this kind of thing. Having someone love you and being an ass."

Laurel nodded. "Yeah, you do. Take a minute to feel a little bit sorry for him." She waited, glanced at her watch. "Done?"

"Yeah, pretty much."

"I guess I'll take a minute, too, because the guy looked rough." Laurel glanced toward the steps. "But she's had it rougher. We should go check on her."

"I will. I think we need to stick to routine as much as we can," Parker added. "She'll only feel worse if things get too backed up, if it affects the business. So for now, we work—and if we do get backed up or hit snags, let's try to keep her out of it until she's steadier."

"If we need an extra hand with anything, we can ask Carter. My guy is the best."

"Do you ever get tired of bragging about that?" Laurel asked Mac.

Mac considered. "Really don't." She slung an arm around Laurel's shoulders. "I guess that's why I feel a little bit for Jack, and a whole lot for Emma. Love can really screw you up before you figure out how to live with it. And once you do? You wonder how the hell you ever lived without it. I think I need to go give Carter a real kick-in-the-ass kiss. I'll check back in this afternoon," Mac added as she started toward the kitchen. "Call if she needs me sooner."

"'Love can really screw you up before you figure out how to live with it.'" Laurel pursed her lips. "You know, we could put that on the web page."

"It has a ring."

"She's right about Carter. He's the best. But that man is not coming in my kitchen when I'm working. I don't want to have to hurt him, Parker. Let me know if Em needs another shoulder, or you need a soldier on the front line of the bride wars."

With a nod, Parker started up the steps.

321

★ ★ ★

𝒰PSTAIRS, EMMA ORDERED HERSELF TO GET OUT OF BED, TO stop lying there feeling sorry for herself. Instead, she hugged a pillow close and stared at the ceiling.

Her friends had drawn the curtains over the windows so the room would stay dark and quiet. They'd tucked her in like an invalid, with extra pillows, a vase of freesia on the nightstand. They'd sat with her until she'd slept.

She should be ashamed, she told herself. Ashamed of being so needy, so weak. But she could only be grateful they'd been there, they'd understood what she'd needed.

But now it was another day. She needed to move on, needed to deal with reality. Broken hearts healed. Maybe the cracks were always there, like thin scars, but they healed. People lived and worked, laughed and ate, walked and talked with those cracks.

For many, even the scars healed and they loved again.

But how many of those people had the one who'd broken their heart so entrenched in their life that they had to see him over and over again? For how many was that person like a thread that was so woven into the tapestry of their every day that to pull it out meant everything else unraveled?

She didn't have the option of shutting Jack outside the structure of her life. Of not seeing him again, or only seeing him at specified times.

That was why office romances were so fraught with pitfalls, she decided. When they went bad, you had to face the pain every day. Nine to five, five days a week. Or you quit, you transferred, moved to another city. You escaped so you could heal and go on.

Not an option for her because . . .

Jamaica. Adele's offer.

322

Not just another office, another city, but another country. A completely fresh start. She could continue to do the work she loved, but be a new person. No complicated relationships, no interwoven ties. No Jack to face whenever he dropped by the house, or whenever they happened to be in the market at the same time. Invited to the same party.

No looks of sympathy from the scores of people who'd know she had those cracks on her heart.

She could do good work. All those tropical flowers. A perpetual spring and summer. A little house on the beach, maybe, where she could listen to the waves every night.

Alone.

She shifted when she heard the door ease open.

"I'm awake."

"Coffee." Parker crossed to the bed, offered the cup and saucer. "I brought it just in case."

"Thanks. Thanks, Parker."

"How about some breakfast?" Moving briskly now, Parker walked over to open the drapes, let in the light.

"Just not hungry."

"Okay." Parker sat on the side of the bed, brushed the hair back from Emma's cheek. "Did you sleep?"

"I did, actually. I guess it was an escape route, and I took it. I feel sort of musty and dull now. And stupid. I'm not suffering from some fatal disease. I don't have broken bones or internal bleeding. No one died, for God's sake. And I can't even talk myself into getting out of bed."

"It's been less than a day."

"You're going to tell me to give myself time. It'll get better."

"It will. Some people say divorce can be like death. I think that's true. And I think something like this, when the love is so big, so deep, it's the same." Parker's eyes, warm and blue, radiated sympathy. "There has to be grief."

323

"Why can't I just be mad? Why can't I just be pissed off? The son of a bitch, the bastard, whatever. Can't I skip off the grief part and just hate him? We can all go out, get drunk, and trash him?"

"Not you, Emma. If I thought you could do it, if I thought it would help, we'd blow off the day, get drunk, and start the trashing right now."

"You would." Finding a smile, finally, Emma sat back against the pillows and studied her friend's face. "You know what I was lying here in my ocean of self-pity thinking right before you can in?"

"What?"

"That I should take Adele's offer. I could go to Jamaica, relocate, help her launch her business. I'd be good at it. I know how to set it up, handle the reins. Or at least find the right people to handle the various reins. It would be a fresh start for me, and I could make it work. I could make it shine."

"You could." Rising, Parker walked to the window again, adjusted the curtains. "It's a big decision to make, especially when you're in emotional upheaval."

"I've been asking myself how, for God's sake, how can I deal with seeing Jack all the time? Here, in town, at events. He's invited to one of our events every month or so. We all know so many of the same people, our lives are so interlinked. Even when I get to the point I can think about him, about us, without . . ."

She had to pause, dig for control. "Without wanting to cry, how can I handle all of that? I knew it could be this way, I knew it going in, but . . ."

"But." Parker nodded, turned back.

"So I was lying here imagining taking the offer, starting fresh, building something new. The beach, the weather, a new challenge to focus on. I considered it for about five minutes. No, probably

324

closer to three. This is home, this is family, this is you, this is us. This is me. So I'll have to figure out how to deal with it."

"I can be really pissed off at him for bringing you to the point you'd have considered that for even three minutes."

"But if I'd decided it was best for me, you'd have let me go."

"I'd have tried to talk you out of it. I'd have done spread sheets, bullet points, graphs, charts, and many, many lists. With a DVD."

Tears spilled over again. "I love you so much, Parker."

Parker sat again, wrapped her arms around Emma and held tight.

"I'm going to get up, take a shower, get dressed. I'm going to start figuring out how to deal with it."

"Okay."

SHE GOT THROUGH THE DAY, AND THE NEXT. SHE BUILT AR-rangements, created bouquets, met with clients. She cried, and when her mother came by to be with her, she cried some more. But she dried the tears, and got through the day.

She dealt with crises, managed to handle her teams' spoken and unspoken sympathy when they dressed an event. She watched brides carrying her flowers walk to the men they loved.

She lived and worked, laughed and ate, walked and talked.

Even though there was a void inside her nothing seemed to fill, she forgave him.

She came into the midweek briefing a few minutes late. "Sorry. I wanted to wait for the delivery for Friday night's event. I've got Tiffany processing, but I wanted to check the callas. We'll be using a lot of Green Goddess and I wanted to check the tone with the orchids before she started."

She went to the sideboard, chose a Diet Pepsi. "What did I miss?"

"Nothing yet. Actually, you can start," Parker told her. "Since Friday's our biggest event this week, and the flowers just arrived. Any problems?"

"With the flowers, no. Everything came in, and looks good. The bride wanted ultracontemporary, with a touch of funk. Green calla lilies, the cymbidiums—which are very cool in a yellow-green shade—with some white Eucharist lilies to pop the colors, in a hand-tied bouquet. Her ten, yes ten, attendants will carry three hand-tied Green Goddess callas. Small bouquet of Eucharist lilies, and a hair clip of orchids for the flower girl. Rather than corsages or tussy-mussies, the MOB and MOG will each carry a single orchid. Vases for all will be on the tables at dinner and reception."

Emma scrolled down on her laptop. "We have the Green Goddess again for the entrance urns, with horsetail bamboo, the orchids, trails of hanging amaranthus and . . ."

She tipped the top of the computer down. "I need to step out of business mode for a few minutes. First just to say I love you, and I don't know what I'd have done without all of you the past week or so. You must've gotten sick of me moping and whining at first—"

"I did." Laurel rose her hand, waved it, and made Emma laugh. "Actually, your moping is substandard and your whining needs considerable work. I hope you'll do better in the future."

"I can only strive. Meanwhile, I'm done. I'm okay. I have to assume, since Jack hasn't dropped by, hasn't tried to call me, or e-mail or send up a smoke signal, you warned him off."

"Yes," Parker confirmed, "we did."

"Thanks for that, too. I needed the time and distance to work the whole thing out and, well, level off. Since I haven't seen a sign of Del either, I'm going to assume you asked him to steer clear for a while."

"It seemed better all around," Mac said.

"You're probably right. But the fact is we're all friends. We're family. We've got to get back to being those things. So if you've worked out an all-clear signal, you can send it. Jack and I can clear the air, if it needs to be cleared, and we can all get back to normal."

"If you're sure you're ready."

She nodded at Parker. "Yes, I'm sure. So, moving to the foyer," she began.

J ACK SLID INTO A BOOTH AT COFFEE TALK. "THANKS FOR MEET-ing me, Carter."

"I feel like a spy. Like a double agent." Carter considered his green tea. "I kind of like it."

"So, how's she doing? What's she doing? What's going on? Anything, Carter, just anything. It's been ten days. I can't talk to her, see her, text her, e-mail her. How long am I supposed to . . ." He trailed off, frowned. "Is that me?"

"Yeah, that's you."

"Jesus Christ, I can't stand to be around myself." He glanced up at the waitress. "Morphine. A double."

"Ha-ha," she said.

"Try the tea," Carter suggested.

"I'm not quite that bad. Yet. Coffee, regular. How is she, Carter?"

"She's okay. There's a lot of work right now. June is . . . It's insane, actually. She's putting in a lot of hours. They all are. And she spends a lot of time at home. One of them usually goes over, at least for a while, in the evenings. Her mother came over, and I know that was pretty emotional. Mac told me. That's the double-agent part. Emma doesn't talk about any of this with me. I'm not the enemy, exactly, but . . ."

"I get it. I haven't gone by the bookstore either because I don't think Lucia wants to see me. I feel like I should be wearing a sign."

Caught between annoyance and misery, Jack slumped back in his seat. "Del can't go over there either. Parker decree. God, it's not like I cheated on her or smacked her around or . . . And yes, I'm trying to justify. How can I tell her I'm sorry if I can't talk to her?"

"You can practice what you're going to say when you can say it."

"I've been doing a lot of that. Is it like this for you, Carter?"

"Actually, I'm allowed to talk to Mac."

"I meant—"

"I know. Yes, it's like that. She's the light. Before, you can fumble around in the dark, or manage in the dim. You don't even know it's dim because that's the way it's always been. But then, she's the light. Everything changes."

"If the light shuts off, or worse, if you're stupid enough to shut it off yourself, it's a hell of a lot darker than it was before."

Carter shifted forward. "I think, to get the light back, you have to give her a reason. What you say is one part, but what you do, that's the big one. I think."

Jack nodded, then pulled out his phone when it signaled. "It's Parker. Okay. Okay. Yeah?" he said when he answered. "Is she— What? Sorry. Okay. Thanks. Parker— Okay. I'll be there."

He closed the phone. "They opened the door. I have to go, Carter. There are things I need to—"

"Go ahead. I'll get this."

"Thanks. God, I feel a little sick. You could wish me a whole shitload of luck."

"A whole shitload of luck, Jack."

"I think I'll need it." He shoved out, strode quickly to the door.

Jack arrived at the main house at exactly the time Parker

specified. He didn't want to piss her off. Twilight fell softly, sweet with the perfume of flowers. His palms were sweaty.

For the second time in more years than he could count, he rang the bell.

She answered. The gray suit, and the smooth roll of hair at the nape of her neck told him she hadn't changed from work mode. One look at her—so neat, so fresh, so lovely, made him realize how much he'd missed her.

"Hello, Parker."

"Come in, Jack."

"I wondered if I'd ever hear you say that again."

"She's ready to talk to you, so I'm ready to let you talk to her."

"Are you and I never going to be friends again?"

She looked at him, then cupped his face, kissed him lightly. "You look terrible. That goes in your favor."

"Before I talk to Emma, I want to tell you, it would've killed me to lose you. You, Laurel, Mac. It would've killed me."

This time she put her arms around him, let him hold on. "Family forgives." She gave him a squeeze before stepping back. "What choice do we have? I'm going to give you two options, Jack, and you'll pick when you go to Emma. The first. If you don't love her—"

"Parker, I—"

"No, you don't tell me. If you don't love her, if you can't give her what she needs and wants—not just for her, but for yourself— make it a clean break. She's already forgiven you, and she'll accept it. Don't promise her what you can't give or don't want. She'd never get over that, and you'll never be happy. Second option. If you love her, if you can give her what she needs and wants, not just for her, but for yourself, I can tell you what to do, what will make the difference."

"Then tell me."

$\mathscr{S}$HE WORKED LATE AND ALONE, AS SHE DID MOST NIGHTS NOW. That would have to stop soon, Emma thought. She missed people, conversations, movement. She was nearly ready to step outside the safety zone again. Clear the air, she decided, say what she had to say, then get back to being Emma.

She missed Emma, too, she realized.

She took the finished work to the cooler, then came back to clean her station.

The knock stopped her. She knew before she walked out it would be Jack. No one was more efficient than Parker.

He held an armload of bold red dahlias—and her heart twisted.

"Hello, Jack."

"Emma." He let out a breath. "Emma," he said again. "I realize it's shallow. Bringing flowers to clear the way, but—"

"They're beautiful. Thank you. Come on in."

"There's so much I want to say."

"I need to put these in water." She turned, went into the kitchen for a vase, a jug of the food she kept mixed, her snips. "I understand there are things you want to say, but there are things I need to say first."

"All right."

She began to clip the stems under water. "First, I want to apologize."

"Don't." Temper licked around the edges of his tone. "Don't do that."

"I'm going to apologize for the way I acted, for what I said. First, because when I got over myself I realized you were exhausted, upset, not feeling well, and I had—very deliberately—crossed a line."

"I don't want a damn apology."

330

"You're getting one, so deal with it. I was angry because you didn't give me what I wanted." She arranged the flowers, stem by stem. "I should've respected your boundaries; I didn't. You were unkind, so that's on you, but I pushed. That's on me. But the biggest issue here is we promised each other we'd stay friends, and I didn't keep that promise. I broke my word, and I'm sorry."

She looked at him now. "I'm so sorry for that, Jack."

"Fine. Are you done?"

"Not quite. I'm still your friend. I just needed some time to get back to that. It's important to me that we're still friends."

"Emma." He started to lay his hand on hers on the counter, but she slid it away, fussed with the flowers.

"These really are beautiful. Where'd you get them?"

"Your wholesaler. I called and begged, and told them they were for you."

She smiled, but kept her hand out of reach. "There. How can we not be friends when you'd think to do something like that? I don't want any hard feelings between us. We still care about each other. We'll just put the rest behind us."

"That's what you want?"

"Yes, it's what I want."

"Okay then. I guess we get to talk about what I want now. Let's take a walk. I want some air to start with."

"Sure." Proud of herself, she put away her snips, her jug.

The minute they stepped outside, she put her hands in her pockets. She could do this, she thought. She was doing it, and doing it well. But she couldn't if he touched her. She wasn't ready for that, not yet.

"That night," he began, "I was exhausted and pissed off, and all the rest. But you weren't wrong in the things you said. I didn't realize it, about myself. Not really. That I put those shields up or restrictions on. I've thought about that since, about

331

why. The best I can figure is how when my parents split, and I'd stay with my father, there'd be stuff—from other women. In the bathroom, or around. It bothered me. They were split, but . . ."

"They were your parents. Of course it bothered you."

"I never got over the divorce."

"Oh, Jack."

"Another cliché, but there it is. I was a kid, and oblivious, then suddenly . . . They loved each other once, were happy. Then they didn't and they weren't."

"It's never that easy, that cut and dried."

"That's logic and reason. It's not what I felt. It's come home to me recently that they were able to behave civilly, able to make good, happy lives separately without waging war or making me a casualty. And I took that and turned it on its head. Don't make promises, don't build a future because feelings can change and they can end."

"They can. You're not wrong, but—"

"But," he interrupted. "Let me say it. Let me say it to you. But if you can't trust yourself and your own feelings, and you can't take a chance on that, what's the damn point? It's a leap, and I figure if you take that leap, if you say this is it, you have to mean it. You'd better be sure because it's not just you. It's not just for now. You have to believe to make the leap."

"You're right. I understand better now why things . . . Well, why."

"Maybe we both do. I'm sorry I made you feel unwelcome. Sorry you now feel you crossed a line by trying to do something for me. Something I should've appreciated. Do appreciate," he corrected. "I've been watering the planters."

"That's good."

"You were . . . God, I've missed you so much. I can't think of all the things I've worked out to say, practiced saying. I can't think because I'm looking at you, Emma. You were right. I

332

didn't value you enough. Give me another chance. Please, give me another chance."

"Jack, we can't go back and—"

"Not back, forward." He took her arm then, shifted so they were face-to-face. "Forward. Emma, have some pity. Give me another chance. I don't want anyone but you. I need your . . . light," he said remembering Carter's word. "I need your heart and your laugh. Your body, your brain. Don't shut me out, Emma."

"Starting from here, when we both want—both need—different things . . . It wouldn't be right for either of us. I can't do it."

When her eyes filled, he drew her in.

"Let me do it. Let me take the leap. Emma, because with you, I believe. With you, it's not just now. It's tomorrow and whatever comes with it. I love you. I love you."

When the first tear spilled, he moved with her. "I love you. I'm so in love with you that I didn't see it. I couldn't see it because it's everything. You're everything. Stay with me, Emma, be with me."

"I am with you. I want . . . What are you doing?"

"I'm dancing with you." He brought the hand he held to his lips. "In the garden, in the moonlight."

Her heart shuddered, swelled. And all the cracks filled. "Jack."

"And I'm telling you I love you. I'm asking you to make a life with me." He kissed her while they circled, swayed. "I'm asking you to give me what I need, what I want even though it took me too much time to figure it out. I'm asking you to marry me."

"Marry you?"

"Marry me." The leap was so easy, the landing smooth and right. "Live with me. Wake up with me, plant flowers for me that you'll probably have to remind me to water. We'll make plans, and change them as we go. We'll make a future. I'll give you everything I've got, and if you need more, I'll find it and give it to you."

She heard her own words come back to her in the perfumed air, under the moonlight while the man she loved turned her in a waltz.

"I think you just did. You just gave me a dream."

"Say yes."

"You're sure?"

"How well do you know me?"

Smiling, she blinked away tears. "Pretty well."

"Would I ask you to marry me if I wasn't sure?"

"No. No, you wouldn't. How well do you know me, Jack?"

"Pretty well."

She brought her lips to his, lingered through the joy. "Then you know my answer."

$\mathcal{O}$N THE THIRD FLOOR TERRACE, THE THREE WOMAN STOOD watching, their arms around each other's waists. Behind them, Mrs. Grady sighed.

When Mac sniffled, Parker reached in her pocket for a pack of tissues. She handed one to Mac, to Laurel, to Mrs. Grady, then took one for herself.

"It's beautiful," Mac managed. "They're beautiful. Look at the light, the silver cast to the light, and the shadows of the flowers, the gleam of them, and the silhouette Emma and Jack make."

"You're thinking in pictures." Laurel wiped her eyes. "That's serious romance there."

"Not just pictures. Moments. That's Emma's moment. Her blue butterfly. We probably shouldn't be watching. If they see us, it'll spoil it."

"They can't see anything but each other." Parker took Mac's hand, then Laurel's, and smiled when she felt Mrs. Grady's rest on her shoulder.

The moment was just as it should be.

So they watched as Emma danced in the soft June night, in the moonlight, in the garden, with the man she loved.

Keep reading for a special preview of
the next book
in the Bride Quartet
by Nora Roberts

SAVOUR THE MOMENT

Out Now
from Piatkus

PROLOGUE

As the clock ticked down on her senior year in high
school, Laurel McBane learned one indisputable fact.

Prom was hell.

For weeks all anyone wanted to talk about was who might
ask who, who did ask who—and who asked some other who,
thereby inciting misery and hysteria.

Girls, to her mind, suffered an agony of suspense and an embarrassing passivity during prom season. The halls, classrooms,
and quad throbbed with emotion running the gamut from giddy
euphoria—because some guy asked them to some over-hyped
dance—to bitter tears—because some guy didn't.

The entire cycle revolved around "some guy," a condition
she believed both stupid and demoralizing.

And after that, the hysteria continued, even escalated, with
the hunt for a dress, for shoes; the intense debate about updos
versus down-dos. Limos, after parties, hotel suites—the yes, no,
maybe of sex.

She would have skipped the whole thing if her friends, especially Parker Right-of-Passage Brown, hadn't ganged up on her.

Now her savings account—all those hard-earned dollars and cents from countless hours waiting tables—reeled in shock at the withdrawals for a dress she'd probably never wear again, for the shoes, the bag, and all the rest.

She could lay all that on her friends' heads, too. She'd gotten caught up shopping with Parker, Emmaline, and Mackensie, and spent more than she should have.

The idea, gently broached by Emma, of asking her parents to spring for the dress wasn't an option, not to Laurel's mind. A point of pride, maybe, but money in the McBane household had become a very sore subject since her father's dicey investments fiasco and the little matter of the IRS audit.

No way she'd ask either of them. She earned her own money, and had for several years now.

She told herself it didn't matter. She didn't have close to enough saved for the tuition for the Culinary Institute, or for the living expenses in New York, despite the hours she'd put in after school and on weekends at the restaurant. The cost of looking great for one night didn't change that one way or the other and—and what the hell, she did look great.

She fixed on her earrings while across the room—Parker's bedroom—Parker and Emma experimented with ways to prom-up the hair Mac had impulsively hacked off to resemble what Laurel thought of as Julius Caesar takes the Rubicon. They tried various pins, sparkle dust, and jeweled clips in what was left of Mac's flame-red hair while the three of them talked nonstop, and Aerosmith rocked out of the CD player.

She liked listening to them like this, when she was a little bit apart. Maybe especially now, when she *felt* a little bit apart. They'd been friends all their lives, and now, rite of passage or not, things were changing. In the fall Parker and Emma would head off to college. Mac would be working and squeezing in a few courses on photography.

And with the dream of the Culinary Institute poofed due to finances and her most recent parents' marital implosion, she'd settle for community college part-time. Business courses, she supposed. She'd have to be practical. Realistic.

And she wasn't going to think about it now. She might as well enjoy the moment, and this ritual Parker, in her Parker way, had arranged.

Parker and Emma might be going to Prom at the Academy while she and Mac went to theirs at the public high school, but they had this time together, getting dressed and made-up. Downstairs Parker's and Emma's parents hung out, and there'd be dozens of pictures, and "oh, look at our girls!", hugs, and probably some shiny eyes.

Mac's mother was too self-involved to care about her daughter's senior prom, which, Linda being Linda, could only be a good thing. And her own parents? Well, they were too steeped in their own lives, their own problems, for it to matter where she was or what she did tonight.

She was used to it. Had even come to prefer it.

"Just the fairy dust sparkles," Mac decided, tipping her head from side to side to judge. "It's kind of Tinkerbelly. In a cool way."

"I think you're right." Parker, her straight-as-rain brown hair a glossy waterfall down her back, nodded. "It's waif with an edge. What do you think, Em?"

"I think we need to play up the eyes more, go dramatic." Emma's eyes, a deep, dreamy brown, narrowed in thought. "I can do this."

"Have at it." Mac shrugged. "But don't take forever, okay? I still have to set up for our group shot."

"We're on schedule." Parker checked her watch. "We've still go thirty minutes before . . ." She turned, caught sight of Laurel. "Hey. You look awesome!"

"Oh, you really do!" Emma clapped her hands together. "I *knew* that was the dress. "The shimmery pink makes your eyes even bluer."

"I guess."

"Need one more thing." Parker hurried to her dresser, opened a drawer on her jewelry box. "This hair clip."

Laurel, a slim girl in shimmery pink, her sun-shot hair done—at Emma's insistence—in long, loose sausage curls, shrugged. "Whatever."

Parker held it against Laurel's hair at different angles. "Cheer up," she ordered. "You're going to have fun."

God, get over yourself, Laurel! "I know. Sorry. It'd be more fun if the four of us were going to the same dance, especially since we all look seriously awesome."

"Yeah, it would." Parker decided to draw some of the curls from the sides to clip them in the back. "But we'll meet up after and party. When we're done we'll come back here and tell each other everything. Here, take a look."

She turned Laurel to the mirror, and the girls studied themselves and each other.

"I do look great," Laurel said and made Parker laugh.

After the most perfunctory of knocks, the door opened. Mrs. Grady, the Browns' longtime housekeeper, put her hands on her hips to take a survey.

"You'll do," she said, "which you should after all this fuss. Finish up with it and get yourselves downstairs for pictures. You." She pointed a finger at Laurel. "I need a word with you, young lady."

"What did I do?" Laurel demanded, looking from friend to

friend as Mrs. Grady strode away. "I didn't do anything." But since Mrs. G's word was law, Laurel rushed after her.

In the family sitting room, Mrs. G turned, arms folded. Lecture mode, Laurel thought as her heart tripped. And she cast her mind back looking for an infraction that might have earned her one from the woman who'd been more of a mother to her than her own through her teenage years.

"So," Mrs. Grady began as Laurel hurried in, "I guess you think you're all grown up now."

"I—"

"Well, you're not. But you're getting there. The four of you've been running around here since you were in diapers. Some of that's going to change, with all of you going your own ways. At least for a time. Birds tell me your way's to New York and that fancy baking school."

Her heart took another trip, then suffered the pinprick of a deflated dream. "No, I'm, ah, keeping my job at the restaurant and I'm going to try to take some courses at the—"

"No, you're not." Again, Mrs. G. pointed a finger. "Now, a girl your age in New York City best be smart and best be careful. And from what I'm told, if you want to make it at that school you have to work hard. It's more than making pretty frostings and cookies."

"It's one of the best, but—"

"Then you'll be one of the best." Mrs. G. reached into her pocket. She pulled out a check to Laurel. "That'll cover the first semester, the tuition, a decent place to live, and enough food to keep body and soul together. You make good use of it, girl, or you'll answer to me. If you do what I expect you're capable of, we'll talk about the next term when the time comes."

Stunned, Laurel stared at the check in her hand. "You can't—I can't—"

"I can and you will. That's that."

"But—"

"Didn't I just say that's that? If you let me down, there'll be hell to pay, I promise you. Parker and Emma are going off to college, and Mackensie's dead set on working full time with her photography. You've got a different path, so you'll take it. It's what you want, isn't it?"

"More than anything." Tears stung her eyes, burned her throat. "Mrs. G., I don't know what to say. I'll pay you back. I'll—"

"Damn right, you will. You'll pay me back by making something of yourself. It's up to you now."

Laurel threw her arms around Mrs. Grady, clung. "You won't be sorry. I'll make you proud."

"I believe you will. There now. Go finish getting ready."

Laurel held on another moment. "I'll never forget this," she whispered. "Never. Thank you. Thank you, thank you!"

She rushed for the door, anxious to share the news with her friends, then turned, young, radiant. "I can't wait to start."

CHAPTER ONE

ALONE, WITH NORAH JONES WHISPERING THROUGH THE IPOD, Laurel transformed a panel of fondant into a swatch of elegant, edible lace. She didn't hear the music, used it more to fill the air than as entertainment, while she painstakingly pieced the completed panel onto the second tier of four.

She stepped back to eye the results, to circle, to search for flaws. Vows' clients expected perfect, and that's exactly what she intended to deliver. Satisfied, she nodded, and picked up a bottle of water to sip while she stretched her back.

"Two down, two to go."

She glanced toward the board, where she'd pinned various samples of antique lace and the final sketched design for the cake Friday evening's bride had approved.

She had three more designs to complete—two for Saturday, one for Sunday—but that was nothing new. June at Vows, the wedding and event business she ran with her friends, was prime time.

In a handful of years, they'd turned an idea into a thriving enterprise. Sometimes just a little too thriving, she mused, which was why she was making fondant lace at nearly one in the morning.

It was a very good thing, she decided. She loved the work.

They all had their passions. Emma had the flowers, Mac the photography, Parker the details. And she had the cakes. And the pastries, she thought, and the chocolates. But the cakes stood as the crowning touch.

She got back to it, began to roll out the next panel. Following habit, she'd clipped her sunny blond hair up and back out of her way. Cornstarch dusted the baker's apron she wore over cotton pants and T-shirt, and the slide-on kitchen shoes kept her feet as comfortable as possible after hours of standing. Her hands, strong from years of kneading, rolling, lifting, were capable and quick. As she began the next pattern, her sharp-featured, angular face set in serious lines.

Perfection wasn't simply a goal when it came to her art. For Icing at Vows it was a necessity. The wedding cake was more than baking and piping, sugar paste and filling. Just as the wedding photos Mac took were more than pictures, and the arrangements and bouquets Emma created more than flowers. The details and schedules and wishes Parker put together were, in the end, bigger than the sum of their parts.

Together, the elements became a once-in-a-lifetime event, and the celebration of the journey two people chose to make together.

Romantic, certainly, and Laurel believed in romance. In theory, anyway. More, she believed in symbols and celebrations. And in a really fabulous cake.

Her expression softened into pleasure as she completed the third tier, and her deep blue eyes warmed as she glanced over to see Parker hovering in the doorway.

"Why aren't you in bed?"

"Details." Parker circled a finger over her own head. "Couldn't settle. How long have you been at this tonight?"

"A while. I need to finish it so it can set overnight. Plus I have the two Saturday cakes to assemble and decorate tomorrow."

"Want company?"

They knew each other well enough that if Laurel said no, it was understood and there'd be no offense. And often, when deep in work, *no* was the answer.

"Sure."

"I love the design." Parker, as Laurel had, circled the cake. "The delicacy of the white on white, the interest of the different heights of each tier—and the intricacy of each. They really do look like different panels of lace. Old-fashioned, vintage. That's our bride's theme. You've nailed it with this."

"We're going to do pale blue ribbon around the pedestal," Laurel said as she started on the next panel. "And Emma's going to scatter white rose petals at the base. It's going to be a winner."

"The bride's been good to work with."

Comfortable in her pajamas, her long brown hair loose rather than its work mode of sleek tail or smooth chignon, Parker put on the kettle for tea. One of the perks of running the business out of her home, and of having Laurel living there—with Emma and Parker right on the estate as well—was these late-night visits.

"She knows her mind," Laurel commented, choosing a tool to scallop the edges of the panel. "But she's open to suggestion, and so far hasn't been insane. If she makes it through the next twenty-four that way, she'll definitely earn Vows' coveted Good Bride status."

"They looked happy and relaxed tonight at rehearsal, and that's a good sign."

"Mmm-hmm." Laurel continued the pattern with precisely placed eyelets and dots. "So, again, why aren't you in bed?"

Parker sighed as she heated a little teapot. "I think I was having a moment. I was unwinding with a glass of wine out on my terrace. I could see Mac's place, and Emma's. The lights were on in both houses, and I could smell the gardens. It was so quiet, so pretty. The lights went off—Emma's first, and a little while after, Mac's. I thought about how we're planning Mac's wedding, and that Emma just got engaged. And about all the times we played Wedding Day, the four of us, when we were kids. Now it's real. I sat there in the quiet, and the dark, and found myself wishing my parents could be here to see it. To see what we've done here, and who we are now. I got stuck"—she paused to measure out tea—"between being sad they're gone and being happy because I know they'd be proud of me. Of us."

"I think about them a lot. We all do." Laurel continued to work. "Because they were such an essential part of our lives, and because there are so many memories of them here. So I know what you mean by being stuck."

"They'd get a kick out of Mac and Carter, out of Emma and Jack, wouldn't they?"

"Yeah, they would. And what we've done here, Parker? It rocks. They'd get a kick out of that, too."

"I'm lucky you were up working." Parker poured hot water into the pot. "You've settled me down."

"Here to serve. I'll tell you who else is lucky, and that's Friday's Bride. Because, this cake?" She blew stray hair out of her eyes as she nodded smugly. "It kicks major ass. And when I do the crown, angels will weep with joy."

Parker set the pot aside to steep. "Really, Laurel, you need to take more pride in your work."

Laurel grinned. "Screw the tea. I'm nearly done here. Pour me a glass of wine."

348

★ ★ ★

*I*N THE MORNING, AFTER A SOLID six HOURS OF SLEEP, LAUREL got in a quick session at the gym before dressing for the workday. She'd be chained to her kitchen for the bulk of it, but before that routine began, there was the summit meeting that prefaced every event.

Laurel dashed downstairs from her third-floor wing to the main level of the sprawling house, and back to the family kitchen, where Mrs. Grady put a fruit platter together.

"Morning, Mrs. G."

Mrs. Grady arched her eyebrows. "You look feisty."

"Feel feisty. Feel righteous." Laurel fisted both hands, flexed her muscles. "Want coffee. Much."

"Parker's taken the coffee up already. You can take this fruit, and the pastries. Eat some of that fruit. A day shouldn't start with a danish."

"Yes, ma'am. Anyone else here yet?"

"Not yet, but I saw Jack's truck leave a bit ago, and I expect Carter will be along giving me the puppy eyes in hopes of a decent breakfast."

"I'll get out of the way." Laurel grabbed the platters, balancing them with the expertise of the waitress she'd been once upon a time.

She carried them up to the library, which now served as Vows' conference room. Parker sat at the big table, with the coffee service on the breakfront. Her BlackBerry, as always, remained within easy reach. The sleek ponytail left her face unframed, and the crisp white shirt transmitted business mode as she sipped coffee and studied data on her laptop with midnight blue eyes Laurel knew missed nothing.

"Provisions," Laurel announced. She set the trays down, then tucked her chin-length swing of hair behind her ears before she

349

obeyed Mrs. Grady and fixed herself a little bowl of berries. "Missed you in the gym this morning. What time did you get up?"

"Six, which was a good thing, since Saturday afternoon's bride called just after seven. Her father tripped over the cat and may have broken his nose."

"uh-oh."

"She's worried about him, but nearly equally worried about how he's going to look for the wedding, and in the photographs. I'm going to call the makeup artist to see what she thinks can be done."

"Sorry about the FOB's bad luck, but if that's the biggest problem this weekend, we're in good shape."

Parker shot out a finger. "Don't jinx it."

Mac strolled in, long and lean in jeans and a black T-shirt. "Hello, pals of mine."

Laurel squinted at her friend's easy smile and slumberous green eyes. "You had morning sex."

"I had stupendous morning sex, thank you." Mac poured herself coffee, grabbed a muffin. "And you?"

"Bitch."

With a laugh, Mac dropped down in her chair, stretched out her legs. "I'll take my morning exercise over your treadmill and Bowflex."

"Mean, nasty bitch," Laurel said and popped a raspberry.

"I love summer when the love of my life doesn't have to get up and out early to enlighten young minds." She opened her own laptop. "Now I'm primed, in all possible ways, for business."

"Saturday afternoon's FOB may have broken his nose," Parker told her.

"Bummer." Mac's brow creased. "I can do a lot with Photoshop if they want me to, but it's kind of a cheat. What is, is. And it makes an amusing memory, in my opinion."

350

"We'll see what the bride's opinion is once he gets back from the doctor." Parker glanced over as Emma rushed in.

"I'm not late. There's twenty seconds left." Black curls bouncing, she scooted to the coffee station. "I fell back to sleep. After."

"Oh, I hate you, too," Laurel muttered. "We need a new rule. No bragging about sex at business meetings when half of us aren't getting any."

"Seconded," Parker said immediately.

"Aww." Laughing, Emma scooped some fruit into a bowl.

"Saturday afternoon's FOB may have a broken nose."

"Aww," Emma repeated, with genuine concern at Mac's announcement.

"We'll deal with it when we have more details, but however it turns out, it really falls to Mac and me. I'll keep you updated," Parker said to Mac. "Tonight's event. All out-of-town attendants, relatives, and guests have arrived. The bride, the MOB, and the attendants are due here at three for hair and makeup. The MOG has her own salon date and is due by four, with the FOG. FOB will arrive with his daughter. We'll keep him happy and occupied until it's time for the formal shots that include him. Mac?"

"The bride's dress is a beaut. Vintage romance. I'll be playing that up."

As Mac outlined her plans and timetable, Laurel rose for a second cup of coffee. She made notes here and there, continued to do so when Emma took over. As the bulk of Laurel's job was complete, she'd fill in when and where she was needed.

It was a routine they'd perfected since Vows had gone from concept to reality.

"Laurel," Parker said.

"The cake's finished and it's a wowzer. It's heavy, so I'll need help from the subs transferring it to reception, but the design

351

doesn't require any on-site assembly. I'll need you to do the ribbon and white rose petals, Emma, once it's transferred, but that's it until it's time to serve. They opted against a groom's cake, and went for a selection of mini-pastries and heart-shaped chocolates. They're done, too, and we'll serve them on white china lined with lace doilies to mirror the design of the cake. The cake table linen is pale blue, eyelet lace. Cake knife and server, provided by the B&G. They were her grandmother's, so we'll keep our eye on them.

"I'm going to be working on Saturday's cakes most of today, but should be freed up by four if anyone needs me. During the last set, the subs will put leftover cake in the takeaway boxes and tie them with blue ribbon we've had engraved with the B&G's names and the date. Same goes if there are any leftover chocolates or pastries. Mac, I'd like a picture of the cake for my files. I haven't done this design before."

"Check."

"And Emma, I need the flowers for Saturday night's cake. Can you drop them to me when you come to dress today's event?"

"No problem."

"On the personal front?" Mac lifted a hand for attention. "No one's mentioned that my mother's latest wedding is tomorrow, in Italy. Which is, thankfully, many, many miles away from our happy home here in Greenwich, Connecticut. I got a call from her just after five this morning, as Linda doesn't get the concept of time zones and, well, let's face it, doesn't give a shit anyway."

"Why didn't you just let it ring?" Laurel demanded even as Emma reached over to rub Mac's leg in sympathy.

"Because she'd just keep calling back, and I'm trying to deal with her. On my terms, for a change." Mac raked her fingers through the bold red of her gamine cap of hair. "There were, as expected, tears and recriminations, as she's decided she wants me

352

there. As opposed to a week ago when she didn't. Since I have no intention of hopping on a plane, particularly when I have an event tonight, two tomorrow and another on Sunday, to see her get married for the fourth time, she's not speaking to me."

"If only it would last."

"Laurel," Parker murmured.

"I mean it. You got to give her a piece of your mind," she reminded Parker. "I didn't. I can only let it fester."

"Which I appreciate," Mac said. "Sincerely. But as you can see, I'm not in a funk, I'm not swimming in guilt or even marginally pissed off. I think there's an advantage to finding a guy who's sensible, loving, and just really solid. An advantage over and above really terrific morning sex. Each one of you has been on my side when I've had to deal with Linda, you've tried to help me through her demands and basic insanity. I guess Carter just helped tip the scales, and now I can deal with it. I wanted to tell you."

"I'd have morning sex with him myself, just for that."

"Hands off, McBane. But I appreciate the sentiment. So." She rose. "I want to get some work done before I need to focus on today's event. I'll swing by and get some shots of the cake."

"Hang on, I'll go with you." Emma pushed up. "I'll be back with the team shortly and I'll drop the flowers off for you, Laurel."

When they'd gone, Laurel sat another moment. "She really meant it."

"Yes, she really did."

"And she's right." Laurel took a last moment to sit back and relax with her coffee. "Carter's the one who turned the key in the lock. I wonder what it's like to have a man who can do that, who can help that way without pushing. Who can love you that way. I guess when it comes down to it, I envy her that even more than the sex."

Shrugging, Laurel rose. "I'd better get to work."

* * *

$\mathcal{L}$AUREL DIDN'T HAVE TIME TO THINK ABOUT MEN OVER THE next couple of days. She didn't have the time, or the energy, to think about love and romance. She might have been neck-deep in weddings, but that was business—and the business of weddings demanded focus and precision.

Her Antique Lace cake, which had taken her nearly three days to create, had its moment in the spotlight before being disassembled and devoured. Saturday afternoon featured her whimsical Pastel Petals with its hundreds of embossed, gum-paste rose petals, and Saturday evening her Rose Garden, where tiers of bold red roses layered with tiers of vanilla-bean cake and silky buttercream frosting.

For Sunday afternoon's smaller, more casual event, the bride had chosen Summer Berries. Laurel had done the baking, the filling, the assembly, and the basketweave frosting. Now, even as the bride and groom exchanged vows on the terrace outside, Laurel completed the project by arranging the fresh fruit and mint leaves on the tiers.

Behind her, the subs completed table decorations for the wedding brunch. She wore a baker's apron over a suit nearly the same color as the raspberries she selected.

Stepping back, she studied the lines and balance, then chose a bunch of champagne grapes to drape over a tier.

"Looks tasty."

Her eyebrows drew together as she grouped stemmed cherries. Interruptions while she worked were common, but that didn't mean she had to like them. Added to it, she hadn't expected Parker's brother to drop by during an event.

Then again, she reminded herself, he came and went as he pleased.

But when she spotted his hand reaching for one of her containers, she slapped it away smartly.

"Hands off."

"Like you're going to miss a couple blackberries."

"I don't know where your hands have been." She set a trio of mint leaves, and didn't bother, yet, to spare him a glance. "What do you want? We're working."

"Me, too. More or less. Lawyer capacity. I had some paperwork to drop off."

He handled all their legal dealings, both individually and as a business. She knew, very well, that he put in long hours on their behalf, and often on his own time. But if she didn't jab at him, she'd break longstanding tradition.

"And timed it so you could mooch from catering."

"There ought to be some perks. Brunch deal?"

She gave in and turned. His choice of jeans and a T-shirt didn't make him less of an Ivy League lawyer, not to her mind. Delaney Brown of the Connecticut Browns, she thought. Tall, appealingly rangy, his dense brown hair just a smidge longer than lawyerly fashion might dictate.

Did he do that on purpose? She imagined so, as he was a man who always had a plan. He shared those deep, midnight blue eyes with Parker, but though Laurel had known him all her life, she could rarely read what was behind them.

He was, in her opinion, too handsome for his own good, too smooth for anyone else's. He was also unflinchingly loyal, quietly generous, and annoyingly overprotective.

He smiled at her now, quick and easy, with a disarming flash of humor she imagined served as a lethal weapon in court. Or the bedroom.

"Cold poached salmon, mini chicken florentine, grilled summer vegetables, potato pancakes, a variety of quiches, caviar with

full accompaniment, assorted pastries and breads along with a fruit and cheese display, followed by the poppyseed cake with orange marmalade filling and Grand Mariner buttercream frosting, topped with fresh fruit."

"Sign me up."

"I expect you can sweet-talk the caterers," she said. She rolled her shoulders, circled her head on her neck as she chose the next berries.

"Something hurt?"

"The basketweave's a killer on the neck and shoulders."

His hands lifted, then retreated to his pockets. "Are Jack and Carter around?"

"Somewhere. I haven't seen them today."

"Maybe I'll go hunt them down."

"Mmm-hmm."

But he wandered across the room to the windows and looked down at the flower-decked terrace, the white slippered chairs, the pretty bride turned toward the smiling groom.

"They're doing the ring thing," Del called out.

"So Parker just told me." Laurel tapped her headset. "I'm set. Emma, the cake's ready for you."

She balanced the top layer with an offset stem loaded with blackberries. "Five-minute warning," she announced, and began loading her bin with the remaining fruit. "Let's get the champagne poured, the Bloody Marys and Mimosas mixed. Light the candles, please." She started to lift the bin, but Del beat her to it.

"I'll carry it."

She shrugged, and moved over to hit the switch for the background music that would play until the orchestra took over.

They started down the backstairs, passing uniformed waitstaff on their way up with hors d'oeuvres for the brief cocktail

mixer designed to keep guests happy while Mac took the formals of the bride and groom, the wedding party, and family.

She swung into her kitchen, where the caterers ran full steam. Used to the chaos, Laurel slid through, got a small bowl and scooped out fruit. She passed it to Del.

"Thanks."

"Just stay out of the way . . . Yes, they're ready," she said to Parker through the headset. "Yeah, in thirty. In place." She glanced over at the caterers. "On schedule. Oh, Del's here. Uh-huh."

He watched her, leaning on the counter and eating berries as she stripped off her apron. "Okay, heading out now."

Del pushed off the counter to follow her as she headed through the mudroom that would soon be transformed into her extra cooler and storage area. She pulled the clip out of her hair, tossed it aside, and shook her hair into place as she stepped outside.

"Where are we going?"

"I'm going to help escort guests inside. You're going away, somewhere."

"I like it here."

It was her turn to smile. "Parker said to get rid of you until it's time to clean up. Go find your little friends, Del, and if you're good boys you'll be fed later."

"Fine, but if I get roped into cleanup, I want some of that cake."

They separated, him strolling toward the remodeled pool house that served as Mac's studio and home, her striding toward the terrace where the bride and groom exchanged their first married kiss.

Laurel glanced back once, just once. She'd known him all her life—that was fate, she supposed. But it was her own fault, and her own problem, that she'd been in love with him nearly as long.

She allowed herself one sigh before fixing a bright, professional smile on her face to lend a hand herding the celebrants into Reception.